# Unbelievable fac
# page t
# Yo

Follow rise of the terrifying nemesis called *'Boots'* as he develops an increas thirst for sexually motivated attacks. Able to hide, concealing his crin safe within the ranks of the British Army. Seemingly the attacks take pl t the behest of demonic nightmare figures, which haunt Boots' dreams.

After particular terribly vicious assault, the woman who he leaves for dead a disused grain warehouse on the banks of the River Tyne, is incredib ound when the ghost of a previous victim guides the girl's savour. T young woman's uncle, who by a strange twist of fate, heads a vastly althy Chinese criminal organisation, is intent on revenge. To do so the riad king unleashes assassins from Hong Kong to track down and kill h attacker. At the same time the girl's father convinces his oldest and most trusted friend, Lieutenant Colonel (retired) Simon Boeck to, reluctant use his extensive special forces skills as well as unbelievable psychic p vers to help locate the culprit.

All the hile acting police Sergeant Sue Parish, an attractive, ambitious detective om the Newcastle police Serious Crimes Squad, starts to piece clues toget er as she too closes in on the rapist. Increasingly the police and Simon Boeck's endeavours overlap. When the assassins fail, in bloody fashion, Simon is finally propelled on deadly pursuit. As Sergeant Parish and Simon converge on Boots, Simon's psychic warriors warn him of a far more dead y, truly evil adversary lurking, stalking him and ultimately his family.

The ter ying climax pits the police against Simon, against the bowels of hell in a race to get to Boots first. One to bring him to justice, the others intent on *fa al* revenge.

The final spine tingling twist reveals the end to be, in effect, just the beginning...

# Editor's Explanatory Notes

I was, out of the blue, at the beginning of the new millennium asked to arrange the incredible memoirs belonging to a Lieutenant Colonel (Retired) Simon Boeck, this being the first package. In doing so, I've tried to stick to his own words as closely as possible. He wants you to know his story as, in Simon's lifetime, he has done some amazingly dangerous things, had truly fantastic adventures and at times faced terrifying supernatural foes.

You will see that I've added some factual explanatory footnotes and a number of endnotes. There are also two detailed appendixes, which aim to give you some insight pertaining to Simon's background and outlook on all things psychic/supernatural. In addition, as best I can, translated some of the Geordie (North East) and Jock (Scottish) dialect Simon used. Other than that I have only gone through, correcting spelling and grammar which, for the most part, was minor.

Throughout, Simon is adamant about protecting the real identity of individuals mentioned in these memoirs. To ensure this, with the exception of three individuals, he has changed their names. Simon assures me all three have given their written consent to be identified, which ones I don't know. Those Simon did change he used subtle puzzles of their correct names. If anyone recognises their name, themselves, living or dead (other than the three mentioned above) or anywhere mentioned this is purely a coincidence. Enjoy the journey...

ND Scott

# *Simon Boeck*

Born in 1951 in Northern England, one of two sons of hard working parents, 2nd generation immigrants. After attending a local primary school, his father just about managed to afford for Simon to go through a well-known, quality 'country' public school.

After school, Simon obtained his 1st Degree from one of the better red brick universities, followed by a short period of work in the tough part of Cumbria. Disillusioned, he joined up and served for a number of months as a soldier (Private Class 3), in order 'to see what it's like from the bottom up', before attending Officer training at The Royal Military Academy Sandhurst.

Commissioned in 1975, he served all around the world, doing tours in: Central America, Cyprus, Europe, the Middle East, Northern Ireland, The South Atlantic as well as mainland UK.

Simon has also undertaken a number of assignments working undercover for MI6 and 14 Intelligence Company. In America, recruited by P20G, Boeck worked within the highly secret Intelligence Support Activity, known simply as 'The Activity'.

Extensive travel, in and out of uniform: Africa, Asia, throughout The Americas', China and Japan amongst others.

Honours and Awards: South Atlantic Medal – MiD, General Service Medal (clasps, NI – MiD, Cyprus), 1st Gulf War (clasp), UN Medal (Bosnia & Kosova), 2nd Gulf War – Silver Star (USA), Tribal Award American Indian Nation & Legion of Merit (USA), Amaja sacred stone & pair RM Williams Boots from a grateful nation (Australia), Letter of thanks – HRH.

Simon Boeck is:

> A marksman 1st class, Judo Black Belt, Wo Sho practitioner and both Shaman healer and Reiki Master.
>
> An excellent outdoor pursuit enthusiast, trained in ice climbing, diving and free fall parachuting.
>
> Psychic since childhood. He loves the UK TV programme Black Adder and can't stand chewing gum! He prefers Bollinger above Tattinger champagne and supports Leicester Tigers Rugby Union Football Club and tirelessly follows Sunderland FC.

Simon is happily married with grown up children. He and his wife, live both in the United Kingdom and abroad.

Editors closing note. I have never, knowingly, met Simon face to face.

# ABOUT THE AUTHOR

ND Scott is in his 40's, an ex British army Officer with, including military operations, experience all over the world. Some special intelligence training. Recipient of a commendation for bravery. Published work includes an account of his travels in remote Peru. Possesses 3 degrees, including MSc in HRM, majoring in Psychology. Highly experienced psychic, expert psychometrist and practicing Master Reiki Healer.

**For more information visit www.ndscott.com**



Note for Librarians: A cataloguing record for this book is available from Library and Archives Canada at www.collectionscanada.ca/amicus/index-e.html
ISBN 1-4120-9518-2

*Printed in Victoria, BC, Canada. Printed on paper with minimum 30% recycled fibre. Trafford's print shop runs on "green energy" from solar, wind and other environmentally-friendly power sources.*

TRAFFORD PUBLISHING

*Offices in Canada, USA, Ireland and UK*

**Book sales for North America and international:**
Trafford Publishing, 6E–2333 Government St.,
Victoria, BC V8T 4P4 CANADA
phone 250 383 6864 (toll-free 1 888 232 4444)
fax 250 383 6804; email to orders@trafford.com
**Book sales in Europe:**
Trafford Publishing (UK) Limited, 9 Park End Street, 2nd Floor
Oxford, UK OX1 1HH UNITED KINGDOM
phone +44 (0)1865 722 113 (local rate 0845 230 9601)
facsimile +44 (0)1865 722 868; info.uk@trafford.com
**Order online at:**
trafford.com/06-1273

10 9 8 7 6 5 4 3

*Special thanks go to the following for their advice as well as being Subject Matter Experts*

HA Evans (UK) – Psychic

Dr SN Evetts (UK) – Technical

Capt AN Other (SAS) – Military & Intelligence

DI S Parish (UK) – Police

Lt Col M Smith (US Army) – Motivation & Military

N Smith (California, USA) – Japanese

Team of test readers – you are the best.

Without your enthusiasm and advice I'm not sure you'd be reading this.

So thanks to:

Eva – Osnabrück, Germany

Fat Ed – The Toon, God's own North East

Jacki – Stocksbridge, UK

Mark – Eastleigh, UK

Sue – Wodonga, Australia.

Finally the finest as well as the most beautiful – Debbie.

*In memory of Choura Pratchek*
*1927 – 2003*

**A percentage of the profits, from this book, will go to Cancer research.**

# ND SCOTT

# MOVES
# WITH
# SPIRITS

# CHAPTER 1

# *Wasted Force*

1946–1971...

In true abandonment style, at three days old, William Finnigan found himself on the steps of the local police station with a note only giving his Christian name and date of birth. He'd then spent all his young life growing up moving from one foster home to the next, adoption never a realistic option. Just after the war no one wanted in their respectable middle class home, a brown half caste kid with curly ginger hair.

Both life and school came naturally to Finnigan as the combination of brains and brawn saw that he kept one step ahead of the police and all but the biggest bullies. For the majority of senior school, dedication and application to his studies impressed various foster parents. Always doing his homework on time, invariably getting top or near top marks, Bill's determination, coupled by natural ability ensured he shined scholastically. So much so that not only did he get a place at grammar school, but at sixteen, gained nine O levels.[1]

The young Glaswegian however needed more, much more. His aspirations were to make something of his life. Above all Bill wanted to leave Scotland and see something of the world.

Realising at a very young age, sixteen to be precise, that if he was ever going to amount to anything Bill would have to get the hell out of Paisley. Growing up in the early sixties, some ten miles West of Glasgow was alright, yet anyone living in Glenburn on its outskirts, did so either on the edge of their seats or frequently in gaol.

Lieutenant Colonel Mathew Monash was, by anyone's visual reckoning, not an inconsiderable chap. Standing at only five foot seven he weighed in at a well fed fourteen stone. Slightly dishevelled in attire, short business like cropped hair having receded well behind his ears. In twenty-seven years the Colonel had seen active service in any number of dangerous places. As a junior officer, towards the end of the 2nd World War, he'd twice received 'Mentioned in Dispatches'. No one could say he hadn't served his country with distinction. Now in the twilight of a hectic, otherwise fairly ordinary career he had taken to recruiting. He revelled in being able to *suss out* the potential. In short, being able to sort out quality from swaths of adolescent weeds. Glasgow certainly ensured there was more than enough gardening to keep the colonel busy.

Although the recruiting office mainly recruited soldiers he was also always on the lookout for potential Officers. It was the Officer side, Mathew told his even more portly wife any number of times, which was critical. Those fighting subsequent wars may not realise it but his decisions now, were shaping the future army's success. The young men he allowed to progress to The Regular Commissions Board down at Westbury had to be, in his eyes, good enough to serve as Officers in his own regiment, The Gordon Highlanders. Never lowering his standards had resulted in every single potential cadet he'd sent to Sandhurst being successfully commissioned. One protege ending up being honoured with the Sword of Honour for best cadet.

In his opinion, Colonel Monash was neither biased nor did he hold any unacceptable prejudices. Of course these did not include: long haired hippies, junkies or queers. In addition, any young man who came through the doors with earrings was immediately sent packing. All of these *afflictions*, in the Colonel's eyes, being totally unacceptable. He knew what would and what wouldn't make a good Officer or soldier.

That particular Tuesday, Colonel Monash was sipping his morning tea, reading obituaries. Funny how, when you reached fifty, you tended to recognise more and more of the photo's he thought as he scrutinised The Times. The head of Glasgow's recruiting was enjoying reading about a First World War flying ace. The chap, who had skilfully managed to evade countless enemy bullets, had dropped down dead whilst holidaying on the Moselle. Strange irony to it Colonel Monash thought to himself. The knock on his door was his recruiting sergeant, an equally portly, slightly less follicly challenged, Korean War veteran. Putting down the paper and breakfast tea, he beckoned him enter through the open door, "yes sergeant McCrann what is it?"

"*Well sur, I've got a lad oot here who seems I ken just mita be offisu material. I'm just nay sure.*"

"Well then, I would like to be sure, so best you show him in, there's a good chap."

With mutual combatant respect unseen yet present, the sergeant stepped briskly back out of the office.

A minute later the good colonel wasn't sure either. He was puzzled almost perplexed, not just by Mr Finnigan's looks. In front of him stood a six foot plus lad with tight, short, ginger curly hair on top of a brown nervously smiling face. Yet more critically, even after two years in the job on Queen's Street central Glasgow, understanding the boy through his incredibly broad Glaswegian was proving very difficult.

After an hour, punctuated by countless 'pardons' and 'what did you says'? Colonel Monash was impressed. The young man was evidently bright, the recruiting form he'd completed proved that, yet there was something else about the lanky, strange looking chap. Having given the lad a cup of tea whilst, asking him to look over some brochures, the senior recruiter studied the potential trainee. He was very polite, understandably nervous, yet there was a steely glint to his youthful eye.

Ten minutes later the Colonel finished explaining about Officer training and the fact that he was sure he could do well. Finally getting to the real question. He'd have to finish school as surely the lad wanted to go to Sandhurst, didn't he?

"Nae tar sar. I've had well inufoffa studyin I just wan a join up, ya ken?"

Colonel Mathew thought he kennded what the boy was saying, "now listen, I feel you are potential Officer material so I strongly recommend you go back to school and get your A levels?"

"Sar, can I nay gan and start trainin tabe a solja pleez?"

The combination of the lads determination and his terrible accent finally getting the better of the Colonel. Having filled out the necessary paperwork and with clear instructions that he would have to get his foster parents involved he sent the boy on his way.

As one walked to the central station and the other sipped fresh tea, both felt they had achieved something. Bill Finnigan was going to be in the army and Colonel Monash had potentially signed up another recruit, albeit destined to the wrong training.

Back in his office Colonel Monash put the tea down and studied the notes he'd made whilst interviewing the boy. Reading out aloud, 'intelligent, street wise, with heaps of common sense'. Placing his pen down the Colonel was however sure that, that kind of common sense had very little to do with school and far more to do with years fine-tuning skills living just on the right side of the law, back in Glenburn. Finally he wrote on the back page of the application, under 'Summary', 'This candidate will go far. Highly suitable for accelerated training.'

Having come out top on all the subsequent entry tests Finnigan had been dispatched twelve weeks later to Junior Leaders.[2]

Arriving by train the new recruits were transported by antiquated white army coaches to the bland, uninviting, windswept vast barracks. Upon leaving the coach recruit Finnigan was screamed at by a nasty looking midget of a man who Finnigan would later learn was his own squad Junior Non Commissioned Officer. In effect the near dwarf was to be his mother, father, brother, friend and hated enemy all rolled into one. The first day they all bounced from clothing store to barbers, via a medical and rapid dental check. The next morning was equally chaotic. Having tried to dress in his uniform as best he could, 'Finnigan' attempted to march onto the vast parade ground.

Along with seemingly hundreds of other equally startled young men, Finnigan tried not to fidget as the Commanding Officer strolled purposefully onto the parade ground to address the new recruits.

" Many of you will fall by the wayside," announced the tall slim man with only one arm, his other having been taken care of by the Japanese during the war.

Somehow he seemed to be staring straight at Finnigan. He went on, "however with determination, pride and insistence to succeed, those that pass out in twelve months time are destined to become the future Regimental Sergeant Majors' of the Army."

Later as they crudely marched off the square, Bill was certain of two things. He would return to the parade square in twelve months and more importantly, he had found his true home.

Over the next few days not only was his new family tough on Trainee Finnigan it was also impressed. Tall, fast and unlike the majority of the others smart, *street smart*! Seemingly Finnigan only had one obvious flaw, that being his clear addiction to small cigars. A habit ignited whilst hanging around with 'low life' down by the river, near Paisley Station. How the hell he retained such fitness a mystery to his vertically challenged instructor.

Initially the training was simple enough to Bill. Tough aggressive men shouted, blasted orders at him. Each day he'd get up before dawn, run, jump and crawl. Only then would he be allowed to dash flat out to the showers, Bill always sprinting to ensure his was hot. This was followed by breakfast, which consisted of greasy bacon, a single sausage, piles of beans, hot thick tea and as much bread as he could shovel into his face in five minutes.

Bill loved it. The food, the exercise and unlike most of the other potential junior leaders the academic work. Where others struggled Bill flourished. Maths, science, English even military history all seemed like new adventures to match those outside the classroom.

In week five Bill's company, some seventy odd recruits were instructed that it was their turn to go through milling.[3]

Changed into issue shorts, PT vests rounded off by whitewash clean training pumps, Bill entered the gym.

The enormous hall was dominated by a four foot raised boxing ring. Some of the other combatants looked anywhere from nervous to utterly terrified. After a few hectic haymaker brawls it came to Bills turn.

"Finnigan you're next," came the bark as some poor individual was carted off to the medical centre to receive stitches to a nasty gash to their eyebrow.

The lithe PTI Warrant Officer* standing in the middle had had no difficulty in finding a match for him, if only in height. The other recruit was easily two and a half stone heavier.

Bill pulled himself up into the ring. Standing in his corner, his 'second', a seasoned corporal instructor, told him that there were rarely any rules when it came to milling, safe from *dogooders* eyes two miles behind the gates of the camp. The only rules as far as the corporal knew were that 'participants' couldn't bite, or kick to the face. Bill stared eyes wide open, this was obviously going to be unlike any boxing he had seen. The bell clanged and Bill moved with purpose toward the centre, gloves raised in what he assumed were the correct position. The gorilla opposite crashed forward head butting him on the bridge of the nose.

Blood spurted everywhere as Bill sank to his knees, for the one and only time in his military career, "one, two, three…." pronounced the referee.

Shaking blood all over, Bill was up at the rush. The referee stopped him, checked his face, wiped it then said, "get on with it Finnigan. You've just started and there's still three rounds to go".

Standing back the umpire boomed, "box on."

Bill just managed, somehow, to survive the remainder of the round. Back in his corner the corporal mopped a throbbing, purple nose, "listen you prat, I warned you about the *rules* – there aren't any. Now go and knock his fucking block off." The second then slapped Bill hard across the face.

Bill almost punched out at him.

"Yes that's it," the corporal grinned as he pointed, "now take it out on him over there."

The bell sounded before Bill moved forward, this time with controlled rage. The brute threw a vicious right, which Bill easily blocked with a strong forearm. Ducking under, darting forward, turning, with all his might, he punched to the kidneys. 'Goso the gorilla' moaned but turned menacingly ready to pummel him. Giving his opponent no chance, sinking to his haunches Bill punched him as hard as he could in the balls. The

* Physical Training Instructor.

lad went down like a sack of spuds, moaning, in serious pain this time.

"One, two, three, four, five, six, seven, e.i.g.h.t, time in slow motion, nine."

The PTI raised Bill's arm, 'the winner by a knock out." The gathered masses of Entry Number 46, some one hundred and fifty raw recruits, roared in awe and approval.

"Reckon you learned that back in the Gorbals son," said his cornerman, as Bill stooped back out under the ropes.

"*Eye Staff, ya ken one ama foster fatha taught me a lota dortie tricks.*"

Following the showing in the ring most of his fellow recruits treated Bill with considerable caution.

The weeks turned to months, Bill preferring to go adventure training near Betws-y-Coed, Gwynedd in north Wales for four weeks instead of taking mid course leave. His last foster parents were already busy looking after the next troubled kid.

As months passed by his abilities didn't go unnoticed. When Bill rose to every challenge, coming top in every test from maths to military history, cross country running and weapon handling, he was the obvious choice for recruit sergeant major for the remaining four months.

---

After what seemed like a lifetime, the long sought after day of the final passing out parade arrived.

Bill's platoon, now with practiced precision, marched onto the parade ground, much to the delight of parents, girlfriends and honoured local guests and dignitaries. Twenty minutes later Bill and his fellow graduates stood rock still, the band now silent, listening intensely as the Commanding Officer gave his rousing final address. He commended them for their achievement, finally summing up by saying the army would be in good hands when the junior leaders stood in front of him reached the Field Army.

When it came to the presentation of the awards, no one thought an injustice had occurred when Bill turned to the right and smartly marched forward to collect the best shot trophy. Two minutes later he returned to collect The Slim prize for academic work. Every new soldier present that day wasn't at all surprised when Bill also received the best recruit prize.

"Well done Private Finnigan, your family must be very proud."

Bill hadn't corrected the CO but thanked him for the book token and the large impressive trophy which a lance corporal relieved him of moments later, before marching back to take up his place with his fellow junior leaders.

When they marched off the parade ground Private Finnigan was the only Soldier Class 3 not to have a mother crying, father gulping back with pride or sister waving. Later, back in the soldier's mess hall, over sandwiches washed down by tea and beer, Bill stood to one side watching happy families congratulating their offspring. Neither lonely nor sad, Bill had the only family he would ever need all around him. Propping up the bar content to light a small cigar, a rather expensive one which he'd bought at central station the day he left Glasgow. Blowing the smoke in a ring, actually he rather enjoyed not having family fussing all round him. Later that afternoon, as he left the cookhouse, Bill had no idea that the training had only just begun.

Arriving at his regiment, The Scots, ten days later, Bill's platoon sergeant had been impressed how smart Pte Finnigan looked. Within a fortnight his sergeant was further impressed how diligently Pte Finnigan committed to and performed each and every task. As an *old school* tough war veteran, the Senior Non Commissioned Officer knew quality when presented with it. The big jock who had arrived from junior leaders was a future star. Over the next few months Bill excelled at everything he attempted and invariably succeeded at. He was never late, past all his mandatory tests first time and (unlike any number of his fellow privates) never got into any kind of bother. The nearest being after about two months his accommodation block *barrack room lawyer** attempted to tell the new private how it was going to be in 'his' accommodation block. After the altercation which ensued, two teeth missing, the other man understood exactly where Pte Finnegan fitted in, in *the scheme of things*, simply above him!

Bill just loved every aspect of his life. The girls in the local town fancied the tough rugged lad from Glasgow. Every Thursday he would split his pay, with equal measures going into beer and anything he fancied, the rest saved as one of his foster parents, years earlier, having insisted Bill open a post office savings account.

Sport especially boxing, after his initial experiences milling, Bill proved to be a, so to speak, dab hand at. Not brilliant he was however easily good enough to win the Divisional championships.

All in all Pte Finnigan was turning out to be a model soldier.

Promotion to Lance Corporal came after only two years, a record for the battalion. Eighteen months later when he gained promotion to full corporal, again, coming top of his cadre at the age of twenty one, even the CO sat up and took notice. Seeking answers about the promising Junior Non Commissioned Officer, one evening in the Officers' Mess he'd questioned Corporal Finnigan's *green* Home Counties born Sandhurst second lieutenant.

"Well sir, he's really bright, dedicated, bloody fit, willing to help others in his section and above all honest."

The CO now thoroughly intrigued. An honest Glaswegian?

"How tough?" he enquired, thoughtfully sipping his Gordon's & Tonic.

"Very sir, almost always first on his basic fitness test and on the long endurance runs as well as the new obstacle course comes first and never fails to rush back to encourage the others." With a smile the junior officer finished with, "his section is clearly the best in the platoon if not the whole regiment. If it wasn't for the infernal cigars he insists on smoking and the fact that I can hardly understand his Glasweigan he'd be the model Junior NCO."

The CO didn't like subalterns who were unable to understand *his jocks,* "learn to understand!" Continuing in a now frosty tone, "weapon handling?"

With an inbuilt caution developed by a concentrated respect for the war veteran sat next to him, Second Lieutenant Moore answered, "bloody impressive sir, he's already a marksman 1st class."

* Normally an older private, invariably with a chip on their shoulder. They perceive themselves to be: all informed, know it alls'.

The next morning after Platoon Parade, Mister Moore had insisted his Platoon Sergeant start to teach him how to communicate with even the worst of *his boys*. The new subaltern didn't appreciate his sergeant's grin. Not caring that he was, in reality, the second youngest *boy* in the whole platoon.

At eleven, after morning tea, the same day, Cpl Finnigan sat slightly nervously as the CO offered him a cup of coffee. Over his half rim glasses the CO studied, clearly the best JNCO in his whole battalion. He wouldn't want to loose such a good operator but knew there were others who would be very interested in a man of corporal Finnigan's quality and obvious ability.

"Corporal Finnigan have you ever considered doing something a little different in the army?"

Shifting uneasily in his seat, Bill hated not being in control.

*"Not sure I ken your meaning sar?"*

Several months later, now Number 27, Corporal Finnigan stood outside Hereford train station conscious that there were a number of similarly nervous young men stood around, none of whom were exactly sure what to do next.

Two minutes later, he and they knew exactly what to do. Screamed at, Bill and the other thirty six soldiers were bundled into anonymous white service buses.

It had only taken five minutes to get to Stirling Lines, the home of the Special Air Service Regiment.

On the very first day, after a pointless physical and a rude awakening to the fact that he was no longer the fittest soldier in the universe, Number 27 settled into a new and as far as he was concerned, brilliant adventure.

Anyone who thought the selection was going to be anything like the beat up training they'd been put through back in their own regiments, was in for a rude shock.

Bill wasn't, he revelled in the ever-tougher challenges and tests which were put before his selection cadre. He didn't care whether it was explosives, parachuting, combat medical training or even the language training. The latter certainly stretching his instructors who tried and only just managed to teach him basic French and Spanish.

The combat medical training was partly conducted in the A&E department of a local hospital. After three weeks Bill was certain there was little in the way of injuries he hadn't seen or been taught how to control, treat or repair. It was however the more physical aspect of the training he particularly relished as well as excelled at. Something many of his fellow troopers hated with a vengeance. He felt, was, almost at home, tabbing* for all he was worth through frozen Welsh Hills. The only time he had come remotely close to quitting had been when he'd been sent back from the top of one of the highest peaks to fetch a Mars Bar wrapper dropped some two thousand feet down the rugged scree slope. Five hours later Bill just managed, in a total white out, to struggle through the four foot drifts reaching the check point with only minutes to spare. Flopping down in a heap in the blizzard, one thing was certain he'd never forget the lesson. SAS troopers moved through terrain, any terrain, without leaving any discernible marks. Their lives depended upon remaining invisible.

* Army slang for forced fast march, usually carrying heavy kit.

His other area of definite expertise was without doubt unarmed combat. As the instructor had told him, when it came to one on one combat there was no point pussy footing around. If you needed to *silence* someone in combat there was only one way and that was with *maximum violence.* This took a little getting used to but Bill and the twenty five remaining potential troopers were fast realising that the Regiment they aspired to, was involved in real war fighting, nothing like the way it was portrayed in Hollywood films. When they went into action, anyone classified *enemy* were to be, if required, killed quickly and preferably silently.

Throughout everything Bill shined. As a result his instructors pushed him even harder. Where others faltered and some went by the wayside, Corporal Finnigan drove on with a determination fostered by years toughing it out in the grotty flats back in Glenburn.

Time went by with Bill rarely knowing what the date was. Having coped, just, with The Jungle Phase based in Borneo and British Honduras. This was the ultimate challenge, renowned to be the definitive leveller for all potential troopers. It achieved its aim, severely testing Bill.

As the course drew to a climax the remaining cadre went through the final test exercise. Again with typical resilience, Bill focused on his goal. Apart from a bent nose given him by a formidably solid paratrooper, who had delighted in punching Bill, his hands tied, whilst being temporarily captured. Again, another simple lesson, never get captured, especially during the hunter phase with a whole regiment of infantry after ten tired men. It was with a great deal of satisfaction that he, along with only eight others, stood on another passing out parade. Now wearing the famous sandy beret, Bill proudly marched forward to collect The Best Trooper award, being the first to be given the regiments blue stable belt.

Immediately given a two year secondment/posting from his original regiment to 22 SAS, Sergeant Finnigan spent his life seemingly constantly on operations or if not, on frighteningly real exercises. *Train hard fight easy* being so true to every aspect of their business. During this time he saw active service in a couple of small African countries, a number of 'contacts' in a Central American jungle and of course South Omagh,

The commencement of The Troubles in Northern Ireland had given the SAS the perfect medium through which to put their training around the globe to good use. Some more mature members being able to recount events from Korea and even a couple from the war in Africa. Not that the wet green hills of Northern Ireland bore much resemblance to the dry frozen windswept mountains of Asia or the deserts of northern Africa.

Bill was like a pig in shit. He loved the weather, the hills, the towns even the people who on the most part were polite, if not terrified, when a brick[*] of heavily armed camouflaged men came silently into view. Often with the look out positioned they would sit up against a wall and chew the fat with the local farm worker. Intelligence, no matter how trivial, was never irrelevant. The little snippets of information always added to the collective G2 Intelligence knowledge.[4]

After a particularly bloody Operation against *Paddy* where one of his team had been slightly injured (pride taking more of the scar than the bullet to the arm). The enemies'

* Army term to describe a four man team. The SAS favour working as 'bricks' or multiple of bricks.

casualty figure standing at one dead and two seriously injured, currently under strict guard in Mulgrave Military hospital.

Having been debriefed back in camp, Bill flew from Aldersrove to the mainland and made his way back to Hereford, Sergeant Finnigan had been ordered to take some leave. "Go home", his Squadron Commander barked. As far as Bill was concerned he was.

Reluctantly he decided to visit Scotland to look up an old pal from his original regiment. After a great five days drinking and chatting up the local talent, Bill set off south, home on his motorbike. On the A1, well into England, the back wheel of his Triumph Tigercub seized. The next thing Bill knew about anything was a blur of the ambulance and a smiling bearded, concerned face looking down on him.

*"Divant worry mate ya in canny hands noo, we'll have ya outa this thing in nee time."*

Once again Bill lapsed into unconsciousness.

---

Not that he knew it, the next day Bill woke in Male Ward Number 3. Legs perched up, encased in plaster. Wow his chest hurt and his head throbbed like fuck. Instinctively surveying the situation he looked round. Obviously in hospital, the beds and uniformed nurses gave that away. Add the hospital smell and Bill was sure. Which hospital he had no idea, his mind and memory still fairly scrambled.

Bill noticed the bed to his left lay empty, the tight hospital corners plainly visible. The bed on the right was however occupied. The chap in it, lay very still, slowly the man, who Bill recognised as being quite a bit older, swivelled only his head toward Bill. The mans grin exposing a few large gold crowns, "I was wondering when you'd wake up, names' Sasha."

His mind still numb, through an extremely dry mouth, "*ey, Bill Finnigan's me name, wur the hell ama?*"

"Dryburn Hospital, Mens Ward," replied Sasha.

Bill's fuzzy memory kicked in as he recalled the ambulance paramedic. The dull ache both in his chest and eyes intense. Instinctively closing them, sleep took him.

What he assumed, by the lightness creeping through the nets covering the few windows, that it was sometime in the early morning. The fact was, the new patient had slept a further sixteen hours from his initial introduction to Sasha.

Blinking, wincing through a sore dry mouth, hell Bill needed a piss. Closing his eyes he felt then recognised the catheter inserted into his dick. How bloody embarrassing. His medical training furnishing his mind. He must have been in a bad way to have required one of those things inserted.

An overweight, sturdy male nurse, noticed Bill struggling to adjust his pillow, waddled over. "Hello, good morning Mr Finnigan and how are we feeling today?"

"Three things," snapped Bill, his training automatically kicking in. Then forcibly regaining his composure he continued, *"sorry, it's just I'm starvin, me heed and chest hurt like buggery and I'd reet like to get this thing oota me di.... well ya ken what I meen."*

"All in good time, all in good time Mr Finnigan, The nurse recognising confusion merged with male embarrassment asked, "Bill isn't it?"

Ignoring the question, Bill thought shit, what about the regiment?

Seeing his patient's obvious concern the nurse set about reassuring Bill, "don't worry we've got your ID card," nodding over to the drawers next to his cubicle, "and the police have assured us that they've notified the Army."

Smiling in an attempt to build some form of patient nurse relationship, "they know your alive, not AWOL."

With that the nurse chuckled, fat wobbling, before rippling back to his desk.

Six hours later, fed and free from the 'knob pipe', Bill felt almost human. To alleviate the boredom he'd struck up conversation with his fellow patient. He liked Sasha who was both interesting as well as very funny. Clearly the man was also a mine of information about god damn everything. Never in his twenty odd years had Bill met anyone with so much knowledge. Sasha had already mesmerised Bill with tales of the Minoan civilisation (never being quite sure how they had got onto the subject). Sasha also knew a hell of a lot about military stuff, having served in the Intelligence Corps during the war.

Underlying their friendly conversation, Bill's medical training exposing the fact that his new friend was clearly seriously injured. They had had a good laugh, Bill's somewhat stifled by broken ribs, about how Sasha had somehow managed to ride his push bike into the River Wear, resulting in a broken lumbar vertebrae. His near bed companion explained how, just next to a tumbling stream, on the opposite bank to the Count's House, he'd plunged twenty feet into the four foot shallows.* The remainder of Bill's day was taken up with x-rays, blood tests and a lot of questions. Quickly he learnt from various worried looking medical staff that his left leg was broken above the knee, as was the right ankle and badly at that. In addition he had three broken and two cracked ribs. To cap it off a sore relocated shoulder (the paramedic having just popped it back in whilst racing to the hospital). Adding insult to injury Bill had a hell of a lot of cuts, bumps and a few beautiful purple wheels where he had bounced along the A1 road. All in all Bill recognised he was in a pretty bad way, but broken bones would always heal. He knew with time and care he would be fixed by the dedicated staff. He rationalised this by the fact that just about every limb he had, had something wrong with it so care was of the utmost, especially the ribs which although unseen caused probably the worst pain. Breathing, sneezing even farting hurt like hell.

Lying in bed after just passable food, Christ he'd die of starvation on the stuff they fed him. Looking over, Sasha smiled and then proceeded to explain that he had arrived the same day but was being treated with great care as the crushed vertebrae could render him paralysed if they moved him suddenly. Bill saw through Sasha's self-reassuring smile, he knew this type of injury was considerably worse. Bill'd even overheard the young doctor explaining to Sasha that he would be lucky if he was out of a wheel chair in less than eighteen months. In amongst their chatting of everything under the sun, Sasha's conversations had a re-occurring theme which was sport. Sasha loved everything from rugby to running. Clearly a sport mad chap, hell, thought Bill, he was in for a tough ride.

The following morning Sasha's son, an ordinary looking, average height, late teen-

---

* In Durham City take the south path from Prebends Bridge (away from Durham School Boat House). After a few minutes you will come across the tiny beck. The single room building, known as The Counts House, stands on the far bank. In reality it lies someway off from the original house occupied by Count Borulawski, destroyed by the great floods of 1771.

ager arrived, anxiety written across his face. He had in tow, another man who appeared about forty five who Bill assumed was Sasha's brother.

Leaning over the lad kissed his father on both cheeks, "dad, see I've brought Mr Rumbar as you asked me to."

Almost ignoring his son's embrace and opening statement, Sasha addressed Mr Rumbar, "am I glad to see you Dennis."

Bill silently observed as the conversation unfolded.

"Now look Sasha," chipped in Dennis, " I know you think I'm some kind of miracle worker but your son here has explained what the doctors have said and I ain't some Phillipino witch doctor who can magically remove broken bones."

Dennis continued, "understand, I never normally do house calls, let alone hospitals. If your son hadn't been so insistent I wouldn't be here at all."

Sasha tried to interrupt. Dennis raised a silencing hand, "OK, well now that I'm here lets get on with it."

Turning to Sasha's son, "if you could tell the nurse that your dad wants to go to the loo and say I'll give him a hand".

Obediently Sasha's son went across and told the nurse what was requested. The portly staff nurse more than happy to have someone else do 'the honours' so to speak. At ten thirty in the morning, holding grown men's *tackle*, no matter how professional he was, wasn't that appealing.

As the lad drew the privacy curtain round, in the adjoining bed Bill, now thoroughly intrigued, watched on.

Ten minutes later, the curtain swished back. Opening his eyes Bill could have sworn Sasha, seemingly now sound asleep, somehow looked a damn sight better. His new friend almost looked like he had some kind of glow about him?

Bill watched enthralled as Sasha's son and the other bloke moved away on the far side of the bed, talking quietly. The youth then returned to his father's bed, kissing him again on both cheeks. With a quick smile directed towards Bill the two men wandered towards the door, stopping to briefly chat to the incredibly naive looking doctor. The lad had shaken hands with the young houseman, strangely holding onto the docs' forearm with his left hand for a few seconds. Goodbyes said, the visitors withdrew towards the swing doors at the far end to the small twelve bed ward.

Out of idle curiosity mixed with hospital boredom, Bill watched. The doctor, motionless, considered the swing doors as they slapped together in ever decreasing arcs. Seemingly in some kind of staring trance, he eventually physically shook his head as if perplexed by something the two visitors had said. With what appeared to be a heavy sigh he looked up and over towards Bill, a thin smile flickering across his face. Picking up a clipboard, he moved rather too slowly towards Bill's bed. Looking directly into his eyes, Bill saw the doctors own eyes were bloodshot, drawn and tired. It had obviously been a long day for the bloke.

The tall gangly, young doctor perched on the corner of Bill's bed. His bedside manner skills still requiring considerable refinement. In almost a whisper he said, "Mr Finnigan, I need to talk to you about your treatment."

In the next ten minutes Bill's life changed forever.

During the x-rays they had noticed some 'shadows'. Later, thinking back, Bill had thought it strange that they'd needed to do another two x-rays of his chest.

Looking into Bills now vacant, sightless eyes the doctor continued, "we have a number of treatments which must start immediately."

Bill jolted back to reality, eyes focussing on the man. The words almost visible as they left the doctors mouth, Bill felt sick.

The physician went on, "you are obviously a very fit man and I assume as a soldier, tough. Together we can fight this."

Bill stared as the words washed over him. Years of training having to cope with the unexpected took control, he felt strangely calm although his heart beat fast, ready to react. His brain raced. There was obviously some mistake surely. No, not possible, the doctor had made a terrible error. He was only twenty-five and fit as hell. How could he have lung cancer?

Young Doctor Winter didn't make errors.

Hours later, still in a denial trance, Bill toyed with his lumpy Smash potato, gazing into space. Sasha who had been snoozing, lying motionless as instructed, opened his eyes and gingerly looked over on his young pal, "hey Bill what's up? You look like you've just seen a ghost."

If Bill had had a mirror, Sasha's comment would have been accurate.

Sasha had listened in disbelief when Bill, with tears in his eyes for the first time since using CS gas on the Falls Road[5], had explained that the doctor was 100% certain it was cancer. He had two small tumours in his left lung and one, slightly larger, in the right. They were also extremely concerned about the small lump on Bill's lower back. Bill had thought nothing of the bump, which he had noticed and disqualified as, just another hazard of service in the special forces.

Seemingly overnight, as is often the case when people are diagnosed with the dreadful disease, Bill seemed to visibly age.

Sasha on the other hand, over the following few days recovered at an extraordinary rate.

After about a week, Sasha told Bill that the doctors were no longer worried about paralysis, rather that the traumatic damage would take at least twelve months to heal. The cycling nut wouldn't be able to ride again for at least another two or three months after that. Even then, only for a mile or so at first.

A few days later, having eaten what looked remarkably like a squashed hedgehog, followed by stewed prunes for lunch, Sasha let Bill into his secret. The bloke Bill had taken as his brother wasn't a relative at all and was, in actual fact, sixty-nine years old. Bill's mouth physically opened in disbelief, he'd looked so much younger and bloody fit. Dennis Rumbar wasn't technically a medical practitioner but was unlike any doctor Bill knew. On that first visit Dennis had worked his 'magic' behind the curtains.

To the complete utter amazement of all the doctors in the hospital Sasha walked slowly to the toilet after only twelve days. As a result, he became something of a patient celebrity. Not one person in Dryburn General had known someone with such injuries, recover as quickly as Sasha had.

All the subsequent *gawpers*, who came to see the miracle patient, had only glanced across at the *middle aged man*, still encased in plaster, in the next bed.

Where Sasha's doctors had seemingly made a mistake, Bill's were frighteningly accurate in their diagnosis. It was a tumour on the spine.

Exactly two weeks, regardless of the plaster and the issue of his ribs, the tumour was removed.

As the days passed, Bill's condition deteriorated as Sasha's improved. Throughout, their mutual support, moulded a strong friendship. Bill also got to know his son well. The skinny lad was a good laugh, always so positive yet with caring eyes. Their friendship flourishing even more than that between the two patients.

Sasha joked that his son was visiting Bill not his own father. Frequently, apart from the customary French salutation on arrival and when he left, he'd hardly speak to Sasha.

His father didn't mind, they were pretty much the same age and clearly had a lot in common not least a thirst for adventure and life in general.

After one particularly harrowing day of treatment, after the lights were out and Sasha snored quietly in the next bed, Bill lay in the darkness wishing that if only he could swap bodies with his ward friend's son. The lad was smaller and lighter than he but was obviously very bright, fit and seemingly afraid of nothing, yes it would be a worthwhile exchange. As he drifted towards painful sleep Bill knew he was on his own, body swaps were a thing of science fiction films.

Waking during the silent hours Bill considered his newest friend. The lad seemed so gentle yet there was something else about him which Bill couldn't pin point. He had a sort of power, almost the same steely glint he had seen in his fellow SAS men, and what was it about his handshake? Every visit he would shake Bill's hand, holding his forearm the way he'd seen him do with the doctor. It was after they'd let go that he could feel heat in his own hand. It was remarkable how warm it became, strangely always giving him a renewed energy.

Thirty six days later the inevitable moment arrived, months early than forecast, Sasha was almost trumpeted as he walked from the ward. The previous evening the two men had talked long into the night, Sasha promising to continue to visit no matter how difficult it was. Over the next weeks, without missing a single day, he kept his promise.

One afternoon they'd laughed, as Sasha described how nurses clearly didn't believe that he walked to the hospital each and every day. Sasha telling the staff it was good for his rehabilitation. Bill knew Sasha was telling the remarkable truth.

Bill was also delighted as Sasha's son continued to visit, if not every day at least two or three times a week. With the visits grew a deep respect.

When the doctors told Bill a month later that he would be going to a *country hospital* where he 'could get better rest and care.' Bill could only see this as a nail in *his* coffin. The consultant explained that if he wanted, he could go pretty much anywhere in the country, so long as his family understood and were prepared to take on a very sick person.

Bill's 'family' had visited in the guise of the Quartermaster from Hereford, The CO had written. The only other member of his family to actually visit was Captain Moore, his old platoon commander. The young officer said he'd wanted to '*look in on him.*'

Bill knew that the young man had in actual fact flown on the air trooper from Germany and driven up from RAF Lynham, 'he'd go far that one'.

Later when Bill explained to Sasha's son that they were going to move him fifty miles away, the lad was devistated, dismayed, "how the hell am I going to visit you way out there?" he almost demanded.

After a sad visit Sasha's boy had gone home despondent. There was no way he could travel that far to visit Bill. Shit, life could be such a bastard.

The following morning, Bill nodded as he saw Sasha arrive. This time accompanied by a now familiar face. Sasha and or his son had, for the last eight weeks, been bringing along Mr Rumbar. Bill had been completely 'gobsmaked' by the power in Dennis' hands. It was not like the chiropractor Bill visited when he'd jarred his back leaping from the rear plate of a Herc'* at seven hundred feet and one hundred and fifty miles an hour. God the regiment *had* made them do crazy stuff *back then.* He sighed, tensing up at the implication of his thoughts.

Dennis was altogether very very different as he gently moved, pushed and prodded. Twisted and sometimes did nothing more than gently place his hot mits across the base of Bill's scull. What the hell, it worked, even after the strongest chemotherapy, ½ hour of 'hands on' as he referred to it, he felt the mind numbing dullness and ache leave his chest and the sick feeling in his throat vanish. The only discernible physical evidence was that the staff had been amazed that not one strand of his thick red hair had fallen out.

"Hello Dennis, good to see you again." Shaking his head with a hint of cruel sarcasm Bill went on, "pity you don't have a cure for the big C in those paws of yours."

It had been a bad night.

With understanding both the visitors brushed aside the words.

"Bill, I have discussed it with the family, and Dennis has agreed to continue to see you at our house. Listen I, or rather we, want you to come home with me. I'm not prepared to let you go to that crappy place surrounded by dieing souls, Sorry I..." Sasha grimaced with realisation of what he had just said.

Understanding Sasha's 'faux-pas', *"forget it,"* replied Bill. "*Whatyu mean gan hairm with you, du ken that theyve told me tha great andtha gory truth. I'm gan ta start ta deteriorate reet fast noo. Especially as theyva all but stopped me ceema*".

Pausing, his breath already noticeably shorter, before continuing, *"theyva said, ut best Ive got nay more than four munths."* With a final effort he finished all but flopping the last few words out, *"since tha discovered thee bastard inma liva aswel."*

Bill leant back onto his pillow exhausted after such a verbal and physical effort.

"Listen Bill," it was Dennis this time, "if you want my advice you jump at the offer, it's the only one you'll get. Also, I'll be able to visit more often as I'd like to help you fight this. Together we can make one hell of a stand.'

"Fuchin' *last* stand," Bill coughed out.

Yes it must have been a really shitty night for the cancer patient.

Politely ignoring his outburst, Dennis went on, " Sasha here and his family under-

---

* Hercules: Royal Air force transport plane. The Armies personnel and kit workhorse.

stand the difficulties, but hell they want to do this for you."

For only the second time since he could remember, tears flooded into Bill's eyes. He couldn't understand why someone who was a complete stranger a few months earlier, was now prepared to take on caring for him knowing that it was a one way trip. It would almost certainly be pretty horrid along the way with a painful conclusion for all concerned.

"I really dinna ken what ta say, What we ya Mam think, from what yu sey she is reet canny, somut special? And anywey I'd be a sorta bide in."*

Sasha had expected this response, "Lilli understands. Oh I think it will be the other way round. How will you cope with her! Actually, never mind Mum, how the hell are you going to cope with any of us. Especially with the boy being around most of the time."

Slightly confused, mainly due to the pain relieving drugs, Bill wasn't sure what to think, "*whataboot tha doctor, tha army for that matta*!"

"My son has sorted all that out", replied Sasha. "He's spoken with your Medical Officer back in Hereford. Your MO seems far too busy flying round the world patching bullet holes to start to consider long term care for a SNCO† with cancer."

With a man on either side of his bed Bill glanced from one to another. Sasha continuing, "they've agreed, if you do. Even Doctor Winter thinks its a fantastic idea. He said you can return for treatment whenever required. You know we're only ten minutes in the car?"

Two days later Bill had walked (his broken bones mended now) slowly through the garden gate towards a seemingly normal, large double fronted terraced house. The connection with normal stopped there.

As he neared the end of the twenty foot path one half of the double doors opened and standing in front of him was a small, round, white haired lady in her seventies.

"Bonjour Bill, welcome." Lilli's watery sea grey eyes sparkling.

The lady of the house retreated allowing Bill to follow. Walking from the winter sunshine into the gloom made him blink. This wasn't a home, it was a bloody medieval museum. The walls were completely covered in 'stuff'. Elephant leaders spike's from India, a rather impressive twelve point set of antlers, guns and swords, numerous paintings covering every possible remaining space.

Bill had settled into his new home quickly. Sasha's son came home from university most weekends and they would wander, increasingly slowly around the local park. They discussed anything and everything. Dennis's visits became an increasing necessity. Bill started to take the self-prescribed painkillers during the Easter weekend.

On one of their walks, Sasha's son, apparently in a melancholy mood, had asked him if he believed in heaven, ghosts and where did he think he would go when it came to *the time*?

They always spoke completely frankly, something Bill really appreciated, unlike the home social workers who had danced around the whole subject only to leave Bill pissed off with them, life, the crappy hand he had been dealt and those fucking cigars!

* Bide in – Scottish slang to describe someone who moves in with their partner out of wedlock.
† Senior Non Commissioned Officer – Sergeant and Staff Sergeant ranks.

"*Nay sure. Whataboot yee*?" replied Bill.

"Well about heaven, I believe everyone goes somewhere, not sure, but for me it's different for everyone. I also think there is a hell. Ghosts, well that's a long story. I've seen my fair share."

"*Ey watyamean real ghosts, your kidding*?" wheezed a perplexed Bill.

Sasha's son knew this was the normal response, "no, honest I've always been able to see them, it's not really a big deal for me."

It was to Bill, as here was this sane, obviously bright lad, telling him matters of fact like that he regularly saw ghosts.

His friend went on, "OK I know you think I'm mad but to me it's perfectly normal. My mum always said she was psychic and I guess it passed to me."

Bill pondered, his new adopted family rarely talked about Sasha's 'ex'. From what he could ascertain the women had moved out some years ago and now lived miles away.

"There's plenty of other stuff", continued the lad, " I don't really bother too much with it. Anyway I'm too busy shagging girls, playing rugby and looking after a SAS trooper."

They laughed, Bill clutching his heavy chest.

Over the next few weeks Bill would learn all about the *'other stuff'*, that Sasha's son had referred to.

Bill really enjoyed, slowly moving round the great house. God it was like the TARDIS from Dr Who[6]. Each room contained an Aladin's Cave of treasures. He was particularly impressed by the attic with its wonderful collection of beautifully coloured Japanese portrait prints. Sasha had explained they were like 19th century film billboards. Each one heralding some famous Japanese actor or celebrity.

He also realised where Sasha gained his knowledge of weapons from as he had Russian flintlocks, Kris from Java and even a turn of the century whaler's spear. Lilli was also fascinating. She had travelled extensively and could speak even more languages than Sasha, who spoke fluent French, Russian and a little Spanish. Long into the night when Bill could not sleep due to the pain, she would tell him wonderful stories about Paris after the 1st World War. Laughing so much, her white hair fell over her smile, having embarrassed Bill with the detail she went into about some of the clients 'exploits', clearly witnessed from Lilli's balcony, when she had lived above a brothel. She'd made him ache with laughing as they had studied her Norman Lindsey print, Merchandise.[7] The famous Australian artist had produced any number of works depicting nubile women often naked in very risky posses. They both agreed the naked girl perched in the left-hand basket had such a terribly wicked smirk.

The old lady had described how she and her, long dead, husband had fought the Germans from 'within', during the second war. Bill could sense there was still, after all these years, no love lost between the two.

She really was, the whole family were, incredible.

Towards the end, Bill knew his weeks and days were numbered. He hadn't bothered with a will as there wasn't anything to leave. The Tigercub bike had been a right off, but had though insisted Sasha let him pay his savings and the armies 'disability pension' into the family account. Why the Army didn't call it what it was, dieing pay, he didn't know.

Sasha' son was on long summer holidays when the inevitable finally came. It was a balmy, still evening. A few days earlier they had set up a bed in the back parlour so that Bill could look out over the garden as well as the beautiful art deco paintings adorning the walls. Bill was propped up as Sasha's son grasped his hand. God he had such warm, powerful hands and Bill had believed Dennis when he'd said, "that boy has the power and will learn to use it." They both knew the energy coursing up his arm was probably the only thing keeping him conscious.

"*Ya ken I'd nair hae believed*," croaked Bill, "*I'd dee like this. I'd far better u Colombian drug bullet orua paddy bomb. I'm ready noo." With a feeble grin his voice quiet and light,*

"*I'll nar reet soon enuf whether your ideas aboot tha afta life are reet. Eye its a bugga, I had a canny amoont ofa fighting I wanted ta dee, I bloody loved tha SAS.*"

His voice trialed off as he looked through waxy eyes, not for the last time, at his dear friend. Watching the tears dropping onto the sheets Bill knew it was sure a lot for a young bloke to go through, seeing a big tough man disintegrate and slowly wither in the space of ten months.

Bill felt the pulse of energy surge up his wrist. His friends grasp seemed to lighten before closing his eyes, Bill smiled and was gone.

The funeral took place a week later. Some of Bill's army pals attended along with the CO of The Scots. The CO of 22 SAS sent a reading and gave his regrets but couldn't leave the undisclosed country as things being a bit *dodgy*.

Sasha's son stood in stony silence as the honour party fired the final salvo. The Scots CO then read out his fellow CO's moving words about a brave tough soldier who would be missed by one and all. The Colonel had then moved across and handed Sasha's son the flag which had been draped over the coffin.

The young man looked so very sad thought the CO. Sasha's son stood for a long time when everyone had moved off back towards the cars, tears merging with the drizzle as they streamed down his young face. Through his grief, speaking as he looked to the appropriately dark clouds above, "you take care my friend, I'll not mourn for you as you'd not want that, so you enjoy all those fights up there."

With that Sasha's son, Simon Boeck turned to walk towards his father, grandmother Lilli and the patiently waiting hearse.

The words drifting on light drizzle, "yee looked afta me in life, so I'll protect yee from death."

Simon's grief turned to a smile, his hearing perfect.

## CHAPTER 2

# *In Debt of Life*

NEWCASTLE, JUST OFF STOWELL STREET
APRIL, 1977

Danny Chang always enjoyed going to 'Bow-Hows', not least because he actually owned over eighty percent of the club.

Sat in the Jaguar next to his beautiful young wife, they watched as the humanity of the last few football supporters meandering their way home. The car turned up past the Central Station, along Pink Lane.* Then having zigzagged across Westgate Road before cruising along Stowell Street. As it drew up outside the main entrance, the front passenger jumped out opening the door for Danny's wife. "Thanks Tony," Lin said. As Danny followed his wife out of the car Tony asked, "sir, if you don't mind, I'll go with the driver to the parking lot and join you in a few minutes?"

Danny looked up, "no problem, I'm sure to be safe in my own club."

"See you upstairs in a moment then, sir," replied Mr Chang's bodyguard.

Just on the entrance step stood a barn door of a bouncer, large enough to be almost blocking the light from within, "good evening, Mr Chang and how are you and Mrs Chang?"

"Fine thanks, where's Barry?" asked Danny, "I thought he always took a stint on the door first up? Especially as Newcastle got stuffed by the Makams† earlier tonight".

"Please don't spoil the night before its even started," pleaded the fanatical Magpie‡ supporter and number two bouncer.

As the young couple entered towards pulsating music, "Barry's gone upstairs for a coffee I'm sure he'll come and say hello reet soon," replied the second bouncer to Mr Chang's disappearing back.

Back then, Bow-Hows was a very modern night club. Danny knew he had taken something of a risk, ploughing so much capital into the place. A large dance floor in the centre, with the upper two floors surrounding in a impressive circle. The whole internal area encased in sound proof glass. A bar on every floor, plus a high quality restaurant on the raised, third floor. It certainly was an impressive structure with the all up safety capacity in the region of five hundred.

A small group of female punters could already be seen dancing to the pounding disco music of Sister Sledge, their shouted communications inaudible.

Lin and Danny climbed the stairs rather than take the central glass lift, Lin having described it as like riding in a glass coffin.

---

* Pink Lane–named after the colour of 19th Centure postitute's petticoats.

† A Makam is the generic term to describe a supporter of Sunderland Football Club.

‡ A Magpie is a supporter of Newcastle United Football Club.

As they did Danny noticed a group of young men at the bar on the ground floor, taking advantage of free entry and the end of half price happy hour. The drinkers were watching girls, in various states of dress, gyrate to Supernature*.

Upstairs there were perhaps six guests taking advantage of the excellent lamb special on offer. Apart from that, Danny could only see a few punters on the third floor. This was his favourite as, if he fancied they could go down to dance, retire to *his* table, ones senses safe to recover behind the three inch glass, or possibly indulge at the restaurant.

He was just showing Lin to the table when an enormous man pushed past her. "Excuse me, please be careful," Danny said, by way of appealing to his *gentlemanly* nature.

Fish was a man but wasn't gentle, "fuck off chink."

Lin looked at Danny, her eyes alarmed. The man spoke again, "listen ya twat just get oot of me face."

Danny watched as another man moved and also stood blocking his path. Equally as large and just as ugly both in appearance and stance.

The second man spoke, "Fish, ya hear what this fucka just said and him a slimy little chink with his slanty eyed bitch in tow."

Enough was enough.

Danny attempted to shove the one called 'Fish', only to receive a well-aimed left jab to the side of his head. At five foot five and just under ten stone, Danny spun and fell to the floor.

"Watch the little fucka spin like a doll," piped in Fish's buddy, Tommo.

---

Three and a half hours earlier Fish and Tommo left the Magpie's Pub having downed four pints of 'broon' ale.

Tonight as part of the 'Toon Army'†, they were going to watch Newcastle absolutely destroy Sunderland especially as they were near the bottom of the league. All that mattered was defeating the enemy, in one of the most passionate of local Derby's in the country.

The game had started well, McDermott scoring in the tenth minute. After that everything had *gone tits up.*‡

Sunderland scored just before half time. Then, as the game restarted, *that fucka* Moncure scored twice.

Disgusted, the two men left thirty minutes before the final whistle.

It was Tommo who had suggested checking out the new 'posh' joint, so they took a taxi home, changed and caught the number 31 down from the Benwell Estate. After fish and chips, they arrived at Bow How's at ten and had promptly taken up the last minutes of the 'happy hour', having taunted the bar girl that she surely didn't have her watch right. With two pints each they had decided to check out the top floor. They might even get lucky and pull a rich bitch.

* *Supernature* was a popular funk/disco tune. Actually Simon has made a slight error here as the tune was not out in 1977.

† Toon Army is a generic description for the collective that supports Newcastle United.

‡ Army slang– "everything had gone horribly wrong!"

Fish snarled down at Danny, "look fuckwit stay doon."

Danny leapt up, the taste of blood strong in his now swelling mouth.

Tommo had by then taken more than a passing interest in Lin, grabbing her wrist he started to squeeze her tits. Chink or no chink they felt good.

Danny, seeing this, now incensed made a lunge, only to be sent backwards by Fish's Scotswood Boys Boxing Club trained right uppercut.

Fish turned to his friend, "Tommo let's get her oota heer, it mighta be fun te mess aroond with one of these."

"You," the word oozing, imposing authority followed by a simple command, "let her go."

Neither Tommo nor Fish had noticed the slim young man appear next to them.

"Like fuck I will – so fuck you", snorted Fish.

"I won't tell you again."

At this, Tommo slapped Lin who fell to the floor, both men turning menacingly.

Standing over the youth, Fish said, "look dick head, ye leave us with the chinks and run along now. If not, I'll mayk sure ya have a face tee remember."

"I won't and you will go", replied the strangely calm young man.

Tommo came forward, threw his, not so well trained, left.

With the youth facing more towards Fish, Tommo was absolutely certain that in a millisecond he would have dropped the stupid interfering git.

Remembering nothing except, that in the last instant, his fist became an open hand, searing pain running up Tommo's forearm.

He fell, well flipped, to the ground swearing his head off.

Fish, watching this as if in slow motion, leapt forward.

Tommo screamed in agony, as the man gave the Goose Neck an extra twist for good measure.* Dropping like a panther to his haunches, spinning, kicking Fish's feet from under him.

The youth rose slowly, almost gracefully and said, "now listen, I don't want a fight. Just get up, leave these people alone and go."

Shaking the pain out of his wrist Tommo snapped, "leek fuck I will!"

Both men now mad. Who the hell did he think he was – chink lover!

"Youa fucked marra."

Violence flooding their simple minds as they moved forward.

Like most things in their lives, Fish and Tommo's certainty that they would show this youth, was in fact a long way from reality. The only real certainty was that they would loose the fight but fortunately not their lives.

They came forward like a pair of angry bears, each man doing so at a slightly different angle.

Approximately one and a half seconds later, Tommo's nose was very broken and Fish on his knees clutched his throat, having felt the Adams Apple actually pop back out. Even through six pints, the pain was unbelievable.

* A Goose Neck is a unarmed combat technique which, although simple to perform, is incredibly painful.

Barry Pact had been enjoying his coffee, not least because he knew that at three thirty the next morning he'd be in bed with the tasty little blonde smiling at him across the bar.

Barry'd been the head bouncer at Bow-Hows since it had opened four months earlier, having actually been 'poached' at considerable cost, from Virgo's located forty miles down the road at Hartlepool.

The undisputed top bouncer to inhabit the whole of the North of England. Few knew that the reason Barry was, had a lot to do with the fact he had a 1st in Psychology from Nottingham University. Certainly it had even more to do with the fact that Barry had been two times the British Universities Karate Champion.

Barry never heard a thing, predominantly due to the three inch glass, two dividing glass safety doors and the thirty odd feet between him and Danny's table. It was the bar girl's changing facial expression which immediately alerted him that something was up.

As he looked, the head bouncer took in a number of things.

Mr Chang lay sprawling on the floor next to his prostrate wife.

Secondly, that the owners minder was hurtling up the stairs, alert to the danger. By the speed of the man he'd be there in a matter of moments. Barry knew that the three men standing over Danny would be no match for Tony as he could easily deal with all of them, otherwise why had he got the job *looking after* Mr and Mrs Chang in the first place.

Barry set off briskly walking round, watching events unfold.

The youth spun one man with incredible speed into a goose neck hold on his hand. Seemingly at the same time drop to the floor spinning, lifting the big bloke off his feet.

The smaller man stood facing the other two. A second later they were up and rushing at him.

The speed of the man's palm, driving up into Tommo's nose was, even at thirty feet, bone crunchingly painful. The other big bloke managed to punch with a massive fist certain, Barry thought, to connect with the other chaps jaw. Instead, the youth had somehow anticipated the blow, swaying away like a cat, swung back and delivered a, sometimes deadly, punch to the throat.

Barry was impressed. This kid had obviously learnt his fighting in the streets as well as the ring. As he neared the final glass partition Barry saw the chap helping Lin up onto a chair, his boss gathering himself up.

Mr Chang's bodyguard saw the fight erupt. In doing so Tony saw his own life flash before his eyes. If Lin, niece to the great Mr Bo was injured, God himself would not be able to protect him.

The minder knew he must get to these assassins otherwise he'd certainly be in serious pain himself.

Leaping up the two flights of stairs in a matter of seconds, Tony burst through the doors at a sprint. He saw the third, much smaller thug draw Lin up at the same time pick up a broken glass, smashed in the fight.

'God, no, he was going to glass her'.

Tony's hand fired from his jacket, the blade glistened as it leapt out. As the assassin had his back to Tony, in two more strides and the man's kidneys would be all over the carpet.

Drawing the knife back to strike, he was stopped in his tracks by a frighteningly powerful grip to his shoulder. At the same time a numbing pain in his elbow where he was held in a vice like clamp.

"Yul nay harm him pal."

Tony turned to strike his unseen attacker. As he swivelled his head round, he could smell disgusting smokers breath.

Perplexed, where had the Jock gone? Never mind, Tony's elbow was now free, so refocussing he turned intent on murder, the blade ready to strike.

"Stop Tony", Danny yelled, "it's these bastards who attacked us," pointing at the two sprawling men. He then nodded towards the gently swaying youth, "not him, he saved us."

At that moment two of the regular bouncers came running in from the stairs, eager to enter the melee. Barry arriving at the same time.

Lin started to cry, having never witnessed the brutality of a fight first hand. Danny was also shaking but not just from the two punches. He'd never seen a man move so fast. It was as if the lad knew where the blows were coming from. His actions appeared as if they were being guided by something unseen? He'd moved like a dragon, swaying and gliding, only to strike with near deadly precision.

Danny had been aware that Tony was right behind him, knife out, only to stop at the very moment of attack?

Danny helped his wife up, their hands shaking.

The two bouncers were now half marching, half dragging Fish and Tommo out. They'd be thrown in a taxi and sent to The General Hospital – one way, charge to pay.

Barry had seen the big bloke right behind Tony. How come they had let someone in wearing jeans and boots, in the first place? He'd watched him come from nowhere grabbing hold of the bodyguard. Moments later Barry pushed through the final separating door. In doing so he glanced down at Mrs Chang, noticing a tiny trickle of blood on her lips.

When he had looked up, the bloke in jeans had vanished?

"How can I thank you – you saved my life," Danny said to his saviour.

The stranger replying, "I wouldn't go as far as that, maybe a few broken bones, I reckon your men here," looking round at the assembled muscle, "would have intervened if I wasn't just passing. Anyway I'm not sorry. I can't stand racist language and it's certainly totally unacceptable to strike a women."

Danny still shaking realised his manners.

Shrinking his eyes as he smiled up at the young man, "Danny, my name is Danny Chang and this is my wife Lin." As Danny spoke, for the first time, he actually looked the man full in the face. In that moment he saw the most amazing green eyes Danny'd ever seen.

"Simon, Simon Boeck, pleased to meet you Lin, Danny."

Danny never forgot that night in 1977, or his friend Simon Boeck.

# CHAPTER 3

## *Spectre's Potion*

1970–1997...

Squadron Leader Wellington was oblivious, immune to the army jokes relating to his surname, not caring having flown Herc's for sixteen years, spending many a tour on *alternative* operations with the special forces. Few civilians realised they are an incredible transport plane, which in the right hands, could land on a football pitch.

Sqn Ldr and Mrs Wellington had two children, Lisa and Robert.

Robert Steven Wellington who was born on the last day in November 1970, had a most privileged upbringing, well as best his father's airforce pay could afford.

Mr and Mrs Wellington despaired over their son. Unlike his sister, Robert was blatantly idle, deceitful and anything but the son of a serving RAF Officer. In a vain attempt to salvage the boy, at the tender age of eight, Robert was dispatched to a very austere boarding school in the Welsh hills.

Throughout his school years, all that was achieved by the way of an education was for young Robert to learn how he could get away with violence on the rugby pitch and a love for the outdoors. With only five O levels, Wellington junior was never going to follow his sister, the prodigal younger child, from Harrogote Ladies College to read medicine at Queens in Belfast.

'Boots', as those he thought of as friends called him, could see he was perfect for the forces.

As a result Mr Wellington had tried everything he knew to get him into Cranwell.

'It wasn't his academic qualifications', his friend on the airforce commissioning board told him, 'he just isn't a team player. You know he almost had a fight with one of the other candidates over a leaderless task'.

Mr Wellington hadn't, but sighed as that was his son all over. He wasn't going to even entertain the thought of The Senior Service, The Navy having far too much style than to accept his son.

He'd failed The Regular Commission Board for The Royal Military Academy, Sandhurst on any number of points with a '*do not re-apply*' letter arriving four days later.

Not giving a flying fuck, Boots hated the pricks anyway. Stuck up faceless wonders, especially the army lot. He did however concede to his father, in the local pub the following weekend, that the Army, as a soldier, might entice him from a life on the dole. Boots 'senior' seized the glimmer of employment, throttling it with both hands.

Eight weeks later, having actually done quite well on the aptitude test, there had never been anything wrong with his brains, trainee Wellington stepped off the train at Glencourse Recruit Training Centre, Scotland.

Having been back squadded for biting a fellow recruit in a brawl, finally, after eighteen weeks, Boots 'passed out' with his parents more relieved than proud, looking on.

As he marched past, Boots noticed his sisters' absence. That bitch of a sister, obviously far too lazy to bother to make the trip across the Irish Sea.

In reality, Lisa Wellington was sitting and passing her 1st year anatomy, near top of her class.

Boots had chosen The Welsh Borderers, his simple logic being that he knew Wales well and they were a major rugby playing unit. Which at, six foot three inches and muscular, meant he immediately became a natural for the regimental team.

The Regiment was populated mostly by young men, who had never been given the chances Sqn Ldr Wellington had lovingly bestowed upon his wayward son.

Flourishing in the mud and rough regime of a Country regiment, compared to the majority, Boots was pretty bright, most of his peers not even having woodwork O level. He'd made Lance Corporal after four years, not bad going for a twenty three-year-old.

The jump to full corporal however proved much more of a challenge for the young JNCO. Promotion required leading a team and that involved motivation, trust and team work. Most of which, Boot's had in limited supply. In desperation, due to manning shortages, his Company Commander had made LCpl Wellington up to Acting Corporal, with pay.

"Listen corporal Wellington you've two years to pass the promotion cadre otherwise you go back to lance jack," the plumb mouthed *major* said at Boots' interview.

'Fuck you' was Boots only thought as he left the office.

Thirty minutes later, Boots told his close knit group of friends, known as 'The Tribe', that he'd shout the first round of beers. With that they dashed off to the NAAFI to celebrate.*

A few in the regiment knew it had a problem with the Tribe. They were all tough vulgar and uncouth, most playing on the COs beloved 'rugger team'. As a result they were pretty much immune to the Provost Sergeant's discipline and more worryingly, the Adjutant's authority.

Boots had always had nightmares. Initially centred on not being picked up from boarding school. In the dreams he'd stay on, alone, in the draughty old manor house to be terrorised by goblins. His dreams peppered, embellished by ideas fostered by the batty old history teacher who was forever reading the pupils strange Celtic fairly tales. Most of the boys preferring them to the more mundane stuff contained in Lesson 5, 18th Century Reform Acts.

The nightmares worsened in his senior years. The goblins were now larger and demonic and chased him, some even sat on his bed goading Boots to bully some poor little first year. Sweating, regardless of the cold, he'd often wake shouting.

The other boys in the draughty dormitory would grunt for him to be quiet, turn over wrapping themselves like cocoons in their thin blankets. Anything to try to keep warm in the freezing Welsh air.

* Navy Army and Air Force Institution–Forces club.

Boot's would often lie awake, sweat cold, fearing the beasts would return to his sleeping realm.

During recruit training he'd been so tired, *they* seemed to leave him alone. However, after infantry training, once Boots reached his regiment, stationed at Aldershot, they'd returned with vengeance. He knew he couldn't tell the MO for fear the doctor would dispatch him to 'the trick cyclist'.*

Boots always drank more than he should. This did however provide him with the mind-numbing route out of their whispering taunts which plagued him during the dark hours.

---

In town, Boots had even taken an extra job as a bouncer. This was with the reluctant agreement of his Adjutant, who Boot's knew was under the heal of the CO, who'd told a perplexed adjutant, 'it will allow the boys to keep out of mischief'.

The adjutant later thought the actual reality would be at the far end of the dichotomy.

The Ram where Boots and two other members of the Tribe *worked* provided an excellent cover for them to beat the crap out of anyone they didn't like.

They had the power and abused it. The owner of The Ram knew this yet put it down as an occupational hazard of running probably one of the busiest, roughest, yet profitable pubs in the county. He always turned a blind eye, agreeing that *they,* the punters, had started the fight and anyway what were the bounces for if not to keep the *unruly sort* out. Deep down the manager knew he had most of *them* on the pay roll.

---

Since puberty, Boots had seen women mostly as an object to masturbate over in magazines. If lucky enough and he 'pulled a bird' he'd have such rough sex with them that even the most desperate didn't return for a second thrashing.

It was during a particularly detailed terrifying nightmare, one of the now ever present shadows had suggested he try drugs. Boots had been indoctrinated that they were bad, the Army having actually managed to teach him something. This was different, he wouldn't take them as he'd use them to get women.

It took only a few nights of unsubtle questions to find the local pusher.

Speaking as if he were describing a seemingly harmless low alcohol drink, "yer mate, what ya want? Dope, acid, I can even get the hard stuff."

"What I want," snorted Boots, "is tranquillises, you know to knock me out?"

"Hell that's easy, what for? You planning on drugging your way to Sergeant?" Boots glared down at the open sore of a thing stood in front of him. "Listen friend," continued the pusher, trying to calm the tension, "mate, whatever you want I can get. D'you know some of the good tranquillisers mixed with poppers can turn the girls horny as hell, yet they don't remember who has fucked them the next day."

"Yer get me some of them," Boots licked his lips at the prospect...

Thus started Boots campaign, his *mission* as he referred to it, in his darkest moments trapped in sleep, with the ever present voices and shapes.

* Army slang to describe a clinical psychologist.

He'd perch at the pub door, ready to swoop, watching the gathered masses of squaddies swilling drink, mixing with the low life females, who frequented the place. The local female soldiers, mostly dykes,* would be in, often intimidating the younger male soldiers. He certainly wasn't interested in them.

The Manager, in an attempt to raise the standards, knowing it would increase the takings, had resorted to bussing girls in from London on the promise of meeting big, handsome *gentlemen.*

Many a innocent'ish cockney girl found themselves, not in love with a tall man in uniform but in the clinic getting treated for all manner of sexually transmitted disease, predominantly clamidea.[8]

This influx suited Boots *campaign* perfectly. Faceless girls, away from home looking for a good time. The last coach driver was under orders, if they weren't back on the bus back to London by 0430hrs they were to leave. In an attempt to avoid having to clean the spew from the bus the next morning, the last driver often left early.

This meant that all Boots had to do was chat them up. As he looked smart in his dark suit and tie, this was far from impossible.

Once he'd drugged his victim, he'd leave, saying that he had pulled a really drunk bird. The other Tribe members would grin and cover for him. He'd then take them down by the canal and then.......

By the summer of 97, he'd been on six *missions.* The last two times he'd been unable to *get it up,* so in frustration near desperation, Boots stripped them and cum over their naked bodies.

That would teach his sister, he'd thought to himself.

Throughout these missions Boots heard the voices laughing at/with him. They told him that these sluts, as that is what they were, would be so disgusted with themselves when they woke up the next day, they'd never make any sort of complaint. Anyway who would they complain to, they couldn't remember anything?

In July Boots decided to go alone to a 20's holiday in Benidorm, Spain, not telling the Company clerk where he was going, preferring to give his parents address in East Anglia.

The first day it was too hot for Boots so didn't get involved in any of the childish games which the match making club used to break the ice. Later he propped up the bar looking to single out a couple of girls. Preferably two together as he knew that if he drugged both, the one who woke up slumped outside the bar would go back to her room equally as embarrassed as the girl he dragged off to the bushes, dotted along the beach.

On the second night he noticed two girls from Liverpool, both barely eighteen, who had obviously drunk too much sangria during the day. Both were red from the sun and wine, neither that pretty. As far as Boots could tell they were obviously standing about weighing up *the talent.* Boots frowned, the slags would learn he had power over them.

Sauntering over, striking up a brief conversation. Almost surprised as the two girls

* Lesbians. *Editor's note*–lesbianism was very common amongst female soldiers in the 70s and 80s , not so now.

seemed sort of interested in the big muscly builder from London. A few minutes later Boots easily slipped the liquid in their respective drinks. Quickly the concoction of drink, sun, lack of food and the powerful tranquilliser took its effect. Beyond laughing, the two girls sat mumbling in their chairs, no one taking the slightest interest as the drinking games were in full swing on the main stage.

As if sat on his shoulder, voices buzzing all around, having selected his target Boots easily lifted the girl under her slender shoulders and skimpy top. Laughing and talking at the girl he led her off. Her friend was now slumped down on the wooden table. Prey, as two young Spanish youths eyed up the easy carrion.

No one had taken the blindest notice as Boots half dragged her along the beach until they came to a massive development block, crudely jutting out towards the golden sand. Boots realising no one was around, bodily picked the scouse bitch up, taking her into the concrete mess.

Not bothering to go inside Boots undressed the deserving slapper. The voices were very clear, '*take her, use her, get rid of her*'. He shook his head, he didn't want to kill her. Earlier he'd managed to get hold of some poppers. Taking one from his pocket, Boots snorted hard. This combined with her naked body in the semi dark, aroused him.

The girl moaned incomprehensibly which further hardened him as he dropped his trousers, knelt and thrust into her.

She was a slut, easy, so sitting back his dick dry, he slapped her with all his force across the face. Again she groaned as the pain somehow drilled through the concoction of drink and drugs. Further aroused, his erection firm, he punched her full in the face. This time she shouted out. He quickly covered her face, knelt down and finishing what he had started.

Standing over her pulling up his trousers, Boots looked down, consumed by a feeling of enormous power over the used goods, before kicking her hard in the ribs.

He controlled her as the voices were now clear in his head, he should finish her. Boots bent down and held his massive hand over her mouth and nose. Lamely struggling as if the lack of oxygen somehow revived her slightly. The girl's eyes came into focus only to see the grinning spectre staring back at her.

The *slag* continued to struggle but Boots' overwhelming strength and the drugs and drink took over as she lapsed into unconsciousness. Boots removed his hand, rubbed her below and smeared the grit, sand and semen all over her face.

His mission complete, so with a final sneer he walked off to get thoroughly drunk, content that he had carried out his and their mission successfully.

For the next two days Boots decided to stay clear of the water fights and drinking games going on in the main club area. On the fourth night he'd had terrible nightmares about his old school and faceless demons cutting and pulling his hair. Even though the temperature was twenty five degrees at three in the morning, he woke in a terrible freezing sweat.

With only one night left of his seven day 'package' Boots decided that he must go on another mission. He was smart, in as much as he dressed like all the other twenty something's, so easily mingling with the crowds crammed around the disco and pool area where lots of girls had been pushed in. Young men leaping in their rescue, only to rip off their tops and feel them up. How crude thought Boots as he looked on.

Almost by chance, whilst trying to physically dust off invisible shadows from his shoulder, Boots saw her. Tall, plain but not unattractive. Checking about, realising she was at that point, on her own. So like the trained vulture he had become, he moved in, "hi names *Grant*, fancy a drink?"

"Hello I'm Lotte. My girlfriend hasn't turned up yet, but yes thank you that would be kind".

Fuck a boxhead* thought Boots. As if somehow the fact that she was German heightened the missions intensity.

She was obviously waiting for someone and didn't seem that interested in him. Boots had, however, easily slipped the potion into her diet coke, before handing it over.

Within minutes, she was reeling around terribly. It was as if she had never in her life been drunk. Boots grinned as he put an arm round, kissing her neck, tasting the perfume on his lips. No one was taking the blindest bit of notice. Just two more pissed kids soon to be shagging on the beach. Physically gabbing her arm round his neck, holding on with his free hand, they, she stumbled out of the mayhem.

Boots followed his route from the second night. As it was fairly early on, the night strollers paid them no attention. Moving along, he alone made the pretence at conversation, laughing as the girl wobbled next to him.

This time he physically dragged her by the hands across the site and behind a mound of unused builders sand. Dropping her against the pile before roughly ripping the cloths from her body. He spat into her face, rubbing it in.

She'd learn that he, Boots, was all-powerful over her. She was slightly more conscious than the first girl. Almost seemingly focussed on his face she lay paralysed unable to move.

He hoped, no Boots knew it was in fear of *his* power. He groped her breasts so roughly she actually half moaned, half screamed. In doing so she started to wave her arms in a pathetic attempt to struggle. To stop her Boots punched the tart hard in the mouth. Blood oozed out as the woman's focus and strength seemed to desert her.

"Good bitch, now we can get down to business."

Standing over Boots was panting from restraining her. Dropping his jeans and Y fronts sneering, he decided she was not worth the effort.

Thirty seconds later he'd ejaculated over her breasts, face and hair. Crudely grunting, he knelt down and tore at her hair. She would be satisfied. His hand, seemingly guided, resting on her throat. He pushed. This time she genuinely struggled, eyes staring wildly as if she had some how come round. Now with some strength, lashing out.

Boots grip tightened closing his face with hers. He could smell the cum mixed with expensive perfume. With a terrifying laugh, he grinned down at the dying woman. In the gloom he could see the shadows move around him, he needed a drink. With brute force he waited until she had stopped any movement. Eyes wide, strangely still fixed on his.

He didn't care if she was gone as the bitch deserved it.

That night the nightmares returned, this time with shadows splintered by her fixed glare.

The next day Boots flew back to Luton.

---

* Boxhead is British Army slang for a German person.

Doctor Lotte Jenk's body was found the same morning by the first of the construction workers. Her lover, Heidi identified the body that afternoon. Six days later, Heidi had taken Lotte's body back to Osnabrück, Germany to be buried by a distraught Dr Jenk, her father.

## CHAPTER 4

# *Shadows of Evil*

ARMY CAMP JUST OUTSIDE ALDERSHOT
0815 HRS MONDAY, SUMMER 1997

Forty miles west of London, acting Corporal Wellington was on Monday morning parade.

Boots watched with distain as the rodney* pranced about walking amongst the stationary soldiers. Christ, the junior officer even called them *his platoon.*

The rodney paused just in front of Boots. "Morning Corporal Wellington and how are the men today?"

Boots thought he really was a prick. Who the hell did he think he was staring at him, giving him the once over. He'd better not make any comment about his section or sure as hell he'd find some way to screw up his pathetic life.

"Sir, Section Two on parade, two soldiers, Alders and Pepperday away on course, one man, Flinders attending the MRS†," snapped Boots.

The young platoon commander continued past Boots, "very good, lets have a look at *the chaps* then."

Half an hour later Boots was drinking NATO coffee.‡

"He's a dickhead that new rodney. I'd love him to get lost in The Ram one night. I'd give him something to write home to his *mummy* about." The Corporals laughed *with* Boots, some nervously.

Boots dislike for authority, especially junior officers, was well known amongst the Tribe. Even though he normally obeyed orders, he did so reluctantly. Often Boots'd accompany them with a muffled insulting repost.

The seven men looked up to the Platoon Sergeant as he entered the corporal's smoky coffee room.

"I need someone to go up to Workop training camp with a 'works party', for a few days. Miller who was meant to go's, sick." The Sergeant was experienced and commanded *his men* with a very firm, yet fair hand.

Boots arm went up.

"Err alright then Boots, not like you to volunteer though."

The others laughed *at* Boots.

Boots eyes narrowed, he'd remember their snipes, if they ever had too much to drink in The Ram.

Boots replied, "just fancy getting out of this shite hole. Get a few days fresh air *sarge*."

"*Sergeant*," there was no love lost between the two.

---

* Army slang to describe a Commissioned Officer (normally junior in rank).

† Medical Reception Station.

‡ NATO coffee is Army slang for white coffee with two sugars.

"Sergeant," Boots replied not looking up at his superior.

All the paperwork had been done in LCpl Millers' name. Boots didn't care as he'd travel up with the works party and, once the kit was stowed away for the forthcoming Battle Camp, have the rest of the week messing around in Newcastle. Best of all they were not due back until Monday. Bugger it thought Boots, they'd head back Sunday morning so as not to miss Happy Hour in The Ram.

The works party consisted of only six. Boots new them all, yet as the senior JNCO he'd call the shots. After giving them a scrappy brief, they loaded up with everything aboard and set off early Tuesday morning. Boots settled into the passenger seat and slept until they stopped at Scotch Corner five hours later.

Workop, a further hour and a half, was/is pretty much in the middle of nowhere. If it wasn't for the hourly bus to Newcastle, *itabe a shite hole*, thought Boots, as the convoy of two lorries and one landrover rumbled into the camp, just after four in the afternoon.

Boots who had been to Workop many times, wondered into the camp office, got the keys before putting the two 4 toner lorries in the secure compound. Boots knew no one would nick any of their goochy kit* from in there. After that, they went off to find their transit accommodation. Boots grinned, not often did he get to stay in a single room in a training camp. Good old Miller, he certainly 'had his shit squared away'†.

The first night he'd gone to the pokey NAAFI for a few beers with some of the lads from the Black Watch who were using the live firing ranges that week.

Boots stayed well past closing time, having befriended the old slapper who ran the place. She'd allowed Boots and a few of the other corporals to stay back for a few extra pints. Boots just managed to get to bed by midnight.

Sweat soaked the pillow as Boots reached out for the wooden table lamp attached to his narrow bed, the safety of light flooding his small room. Even though he had been pretty tanked up when he had flopped into bed, it hadn't stopped the nightmares from closing in on his subconscious.

The red eyed spectre's moving from the shadows. Sticky clammy beasts, miniture deformed wolves, which clawed at his shoulder, all the time whispering terrible things.

In the dream he was back in Spain, staring as the demon's, eyes red with glee, ripping, slashing *her* face and body terribly.

One terrifying goblin type, had turned and glared at Boots, blood dripping from his horrid teeth. In its claw it held a fabulously jewelled knife, taunting Boots to lick the blood from the woman's flesh.

The creatures seemingly in a frenzy slashed open the girls stomach, only to start eating her insides.

Waking shaking violently Boots thought, wished he had a bottle of whisky. Wondering how he could get hold of one he lay motionless until the morning light overtook his lamps.

It had taken longer than expected to get all the defence stores squared away, as detailed

* Army slang for highly attractive, flash, often easily stolen items of kit.

† Army slang for 'very organised'.

in Cpl Miller's comprehensive administrative instruction.

"Fucking idiot," said Boots, as he realised that they wouldn't be finished until lunchtime Friday.

That afternoon Boots finally managing to catch some sleep, whilst the guys worked away unloading the stores.

Later that night he made sure, as, when they had gone into Carlisle to get some stuff for the weekend, he'd bought a bottle of cheap whisky.

Later in bed, even through a haze of four pints and half a bottle of cheap whisky, *the things* still managed to invade his drunken mind.

Again, they wanted him to eat some deformed mutilated girls body. He should cut her heart out to feast on. This time, shaking as much from the booze as the thought of their suggestions, Boots woke blinking as his small, sixty-watt, bulb burst light throughout the room.

Boots froze. In the corner of his room, behind his clothes strewn chair, he could just see a terribly deformed claw.

He wanted to shout out, get the hell away. He tried, yet felt fixed, glued under the grey issue blankets.

As if in slow motion, the dark shadow came from behind, the terrible red eyes focussed, seemingly drilling into his very mind.

"*Hello Boots we're here to be your friend. Your eyes and ears.*"

Gulping back in terror, Hell, for that was where Boots felt he had woken to, there were three of the terrible things and one of them had spoken to him.

Please wake up, Boots pleaded with himself. In desperation he bit his tongue hard, the salty blood draining into his incredibly dry mouth.

Keeping their terrible eyes on him, the creatures jumped against the walls.

Boots transfixed, could not stop looking at them. Were they going to attack him, eat his flesh?

"*We fear no one. Neither should you,*" one of them cackled. It came from a deformed wolf like creature, perched above the curtains.

"*We enjoy watching you and have come to help you on your* missions."

How the fuck did they know about his *missions?*

"*We will be there, watching and guiding you in the future.*"

One of them seemed to mutate in front of Boots eyes. As if by some demonic metamorphism it turned into a massive dog.

Boots blinked in utter disbelief. Could it somehow know his thoughts?

Again it spoke,

"*We fear naught. Unless you allow us to watch, fear us.*"

Boots bit his tongue as hard as he could. It didn't work.

The demonic gargoyle, come goblin, leaped with startling speed onto his bed and drew its jaggered claw across Boots' chest. It was so close he could smell the foul saliva dripping onto the blankets. Boots felt real pain as he saw the gash open near his tattoo of a leopard, two inches above his left nipple.

Just as suddenly the creatures moved away, becoming nightmare shadows. As they did Boots could clearly hear as if in a far distant valley, their howls as they faded through the walls.

---

Boots woke with blood on his pillow where his now very sore and slightly swollen tongue had bled. He got up and pissed in the sink in the corner of his room, leaving the tap running, he'd washed, shaved, dressed and hurried to the cookhouse.

A few of The Black Watch were still around, tidying up. Seeing Boots one of them spoke, "Fuckin' hell, look at Taffy. Hey, Boots isn't it? I hope you were alone last night otherwise the girl you had in there with you must have been rough."

They all laughed, Boots oblivious didn't reciprocate as his mind was now a melting pot of confusion.

*They* had been in his room. *They* were real. All those years, it hadn't been nightmares but real creatures, terrorising him.

Boots just about managed somehow to pull himself together by the time the lads had had their coffee break.

"Corporal Boots," one of the lads asked, "what ya going to do tonight boyo? Were going into Carlisle as it's miles closer than Newcastle and at a push we could even walk back, that's if we spend all our dosh."

Boots blinked, focussing, "err, I think I'll just get my head down. I had a really heavy night last night with the jocks."

"Your call corp' but if you change yu mind we'll be easy to find. It's not that big a place."

---

"Everything squared away?" asked Major Bride, the silver haired Camp Commandant.

Major Bride who was in his late forties wore out of date insignia of The ROYAL SIGNALS on his material rank shoulder epaulettes. Nearly average in height, a full head of silver cropped hair his only distinguishing feature. Boots liked 'this kind' of officer; they'd met a number of times when Boots had been on previous battle camps. Major Bride had once explained that he had opted to get off the promotion conveyer belt. Shortly before his death, at sixty three, the majors father had said, 'you only get one go at life, why keep slogging your guts out for the 'promise' of promotion and a bigger pension'.

Boots looked up and replied, "yes sir, we'll be back for the training camp in five weeks."

"Yes I know, corporal Wellington. Boots isn't it?" replied the Camp Commandant.
"Yes sir, but please, no fucking jokes about the name."

"Don't worry *Boots*. I can't be doing with all this formal shit any more so, if no ones around, it's Tom, please call me Tom."

"OK Tom , Sir." They both laughed.

Tom continued, "may see you later? We often keep the NAAFI open late when we don't have troops on camp. Your party and a few jocks are all that's in just now. You're welcome to join us so long as you can stand the sight of the manageress fat ankles."

Again, they both laughed. As they did suddenly Boots felt so much better.

Maybe he wouldn't go into Newcastle. He'd just stay here and get pissed with Tom?

After eating *tea* in the cookhouse, Boots hardly touching anything, he cautiously returned to his room. Opened the door, the late sun cascaded in through his semi drawn curtains. The only apparent disgusting insult to his sensors being smelly sweaty kit which he had left festering in the corner of the room.

In the disinfectant smelling washroom down the corridor Boots took a long bath, drinking the rest of his whisky.

Smelling now acceptable, he dressed in his civis.

Intent on going to the NAAFI, he'd got half way there when Boots suddenly thought sod it, he'd go into town. As he changed direction Boots hoped he might get lucky? Going back to the room grabbed his jacket and a few of the small phials from their hiding place. Maybe tonight might need a little bit of a push.

Going past the accommodation block, Boots snuck back round the cookhouse, towards the beat up old obstacle course. Behind the disused twenty-five meter range there was a spot where you could climb the fence and gain access to the little side road, which in turn led to the main road and the bus stop. This was easily ten minutes faster than going through the front gate.

What the hell, he jumped up grabbing the top of the plain wire. Over in a matter of seconds, *Tom* wouldn't' be too friendly if he knew Cpl Wellington had just breached security.

The bus arrived almost immediately. No one took any notice of him as he settled back watching the cow's, tails swishing flies, in the field opposite.

"*How mayt, yarat centrul staysion noo.*"

Boots startled, blinked having slept the whole way. It had been the best sleep he'd had since they'd gone north. Boots looking at the bus driver standing at the front of the bus, "sorry mate, too much booze last night."

"*Booze or nee booze ifya divunt want to gan ta Durum yad berra gerof.*"

Boots, for once, obeyed without question.

Strolling along, wow he'd forgotten how big and busy the place was. It certainly was the party capital of the north. Walking aimlessly about, he ending up going down past The Theatre Royal as patrons streamed in to watch Grease The Musical. *Ponces* thought Boots and walked on down the hill.

Recognising the garish sign hanging outside *The Star in India Restaurant*, Boots knew it was a pretty good curry house which he'd been into on a previous visit to the city months ago.

He sat alone, studying the menu. The only trade being, financially acceptable tempo, early evening, home delivery. Ten minutes after ordering the waiter brought Beef Madras, plain rice and a few complementary poppadums. Boots washed this down by three pints of Tiger Beer. He felt a lot better, so much so, he was actually looking forward to chatting up one of the local slappers in the hope of a quick fuck.

After paying, he emerged into the long shadows of the early evening sunshine.

The Quay Side was/is notorious with hundreds already wandering from pub to pub. Bulky bouncers standing at every entrance, occasionally frisking people.

Boots stopped, 'shit'.

He felt the Stanley knife in his jacket pocket. They had been using it the day before on the packing boxes. He'd taken it back to his room. When the CQMS* found out it was missing he'd right it off, stolen. Boot's had used it to get some irritating gum off his shoes.

* Company Quarter Master Sergeant–in charge of stores for a Company of soldiers.

Then, not thinking, slipped it into his jacket pocket.

Not to worry, easily he shoved it inside his pants, under his crotch. Anyone watching would have thought he was rearranging his 'tackle'. Even back at The Ram they didn't frisk men that closely. Anyway once hidden, it was warm and he could hardly feel it. Boots smiled.

He went into a couple of the bars. All sorts of sailing paraphernalia adorning the walls and ceiling. After a snakebite he moved onto Calsberg Special Brew, practice ensuring Boots remained pretty sober. A couple of pints later, he entered The Atlantic Pub. A massive trendy pub, far bigger than The Ram.

One of the bounces actually frisked him saying, "divint moan its managemunt rule. Ay yer a reet in ya coem marra."

Boots stood at the bar grinning, amused as he watched the girls, some half naked and seemingly covered in fake tan. Their make up giving them the appearance of walking oranges. The lights flashed, noise thumping and reverberating all around offended at least two of Boots' senses. Immune, Boots was too busy selecting his next victim.

Someone bumped into his shoulder. Ready to give the clumsy idiot a mouth full Boots swung round.

No one was within four feet?

It was only then he noticed them. Obviously in their early 20's, three very pretty girls standing close by. They were laughing about something, one of them gesticulated her hands, as if winding up a propeller blade.

Boots *glided* over to the pillar which they were propped up next to.

The tall one was saying, "listen Susie, I'm telling you, they were flying all over, almost bashing into my face."

They all laughed again. The small dark haired one then chipped in, "stop waving your arms around, you look like a demented windmill."

They all burst out giggling.

Boots was now right next to them although they were paying him absolute no notice as he was partially hidden by the pillar. All round the three foot pillar were disregarded drinks, smouldering ashtrays strewn everywhere.

The one called Susie said she was going to the loo, putting her drink down so close to Boots' pint, she almost touched his hand.

Boots recognised his chance.

Yes there were three of them but he might be able to get stuff into each of their drinks and then take his pick. His eyes widened in anticipation.

No one noticed as he leant forward, seemingly, reaching for an overflowing ashtray.

Susie returned picking up her drink, noticed Boots, "hi."

Boots, big and fit looking, was not completely unattractive, "hi to you too."

The girl laughed, "my nae' Susie." tilting her head towards the other two, "this is Penny and the windmill's Fay." The girls all laughed, Boots joining in.

"*R*oots is my name."

Again giggles, "what really, ya kiddin us?" It was the one called Fay.

"No really." Boots replied.

As he spoke Boots smiled realising he'd given himself an excellent alibi, not that he'd need one. Continuing, he made it up as he went along, describing how he had come to get such a weird nickname. They were all listening through the pounding music, seemingly interested in him.

Five more minutes later Boots offered to buy the girls a drink.

Looking at their near empty drinks Fay said that they were in a round but did he fancy a drink on them?

""Yer that'll be great, thanks," replied Boots.

"I *feeel* a little drunk *oredy*, "Susie slurred.

"OK you stay here and Penny and I'll get them. A pint of larger is it?"

"Fosters, please."

The two girls sauntered towards the bar.

Focusing in on the pray, "hey Susie what do you do for a living?"

Susie, now under the influence of the powerful drug, rolled her eyes and said that she was training to be a *cheecher*.

As she spoke Sue looked round to where the other two had gone to the bar. Slipping, Susie mumbled that she was going to the loo as she felt sick.

"No problem, I'll tell your friends." Boots mission was now falling into place.

Having lied about his job, he'd put on his best Scottish accent, honed from drinking with the jocks back in the NAAFI. They had believed Roots and why shouldn't they as he explained that he was a plumber from the coast.

After a while and some loud chatter he'd gone over and bought three drinks. Susie had had enough, the other two said.

Ten minutes later, they were *all* his for the picking.

It was dark inside the place, most punters hardly able to get a good look at each other, especially with the strobe lighting flashing through the smoke machine.

No one took any notice of three obviously drunk girls, slurring their words. If it wasn't for the table cirling round the pillar they would hardly be able to stand.

Boots went round, sort of gathering them together, to have a good look at them.

"So *ladies*, which one of you wants me to fuck your brains out?"

The girls, now only vaguely conscious, stared at the lights, their eyes hazing over.

Boots felt the power he always felt when on a mission. He was the commander now, not that fucking Rodney back at camp and as for that dick head of a sergeant of his. Finally Boots was in charge.

As he'd hardly drank anything for nearly an hour, he certainly felt sober, ready for action.

In the smoke and flashing lights, in turn, he fondled their breasts, deciding which to choose. He put the arm of one of them round his neck, then almost picked up another who was much smaller and lighter. Discarding the one called Fay, her head slumped down on the table.

Punters were now streaming in, so the bouncers had their hands full as drunk yobs and loud groups of girls, nosily complained about having to wait to get in.

Boots had moved past, totally unnoticed. Even if the CCT had been working that night, it would not have picked them up, moving amongst the shadows.

Outside, Boots now fully alert, the sea air coming up the river from Tynemouth.

In a small alleyway, just along from the pub, he propped them against the back of a large van, their heads lolling like rag dolls. He could, in the dusk, clearly see them now.

Boots made his mind up. Right, she would do.

In doing so he just let the other girl slump, unconscious to the pavement. Dishevelled drunk women not being that uncommon on a Friday night. The police picked Susie up four hours later, when someone had taken pity on a girl sprawled in the gutter.

The *target,* he had selected, was light as a feather so Boots moved her easily along the road, sticking to the darker side, next to the buildings. Being so small, the girls had been particularly affected by the drugs. Her eyes glazed over as she walked like a zombie doll.

Now enjoying the shadows, Boots moved on. Behind him the wind caught some crisp packets lifting them, rustling, against a fence. Boots turned, seeing nothing, looked down at the girl, then ahead again.

In the periphery of his vision he saw the eyes, lurking in the shadows. Red, fixed not on him, but the girl.

The power of the mission gave Boots courage, "see I am on a mission. I have one." The pair of red eyes narrowed. As the eyes withdrew into the darkness of an alley, Boots moved on, now with renewed confidence, down along the road.

Few, if any, people were this far along the banks of the river. Those that were, were mostly walking their dogs. They paid no attention to some drunks stumbling home early. Anyway the man looked big, so no one even tried to make eye contact, let alone walk on the shadowy side of the road.

Boots no longer knew exactly where he was. He was moving into *enemy* territory. Quietly, he turned up a seemingly deserted road. In the distance a car draw away possibly with a whore, making probably her first round, *of business,* for the night.

A little further up the steep road, Boots propped the girl up against the fence as he panted hard. Although she was light they'd gone over a mile.

Even after ten, it wasn't that dark, the lights from the one remaining working warehouse beaming in. Distant forklifts like metallic bees buzzed about nosily. He could even hear the odd command being barked out.

He took the girl through into some wasteland. Boots stumbled, picking the girl up he bodily dragged her over some old piles of rubbish.

Through an entrance.

Boots thought that, before the lights came on in the evening, it would be pretty gloomy inside. Yet with the street and the arc lights from the warehouse he could see easily. He negotiated around some broken chairs and entered a separate room. The girl moaned. Petite as she was, the drugs only rarely lasted much more than a few hours before she'd start to come round or fall fast asleep for hours.

Loosing his sweaty grip he dropped her, the girl's head banging and jarring against an old table before she sprawled down onto the floor on her side, breathing erratically.

Boots bent down over her and grabbed her jet black hair. Pulling it back he licked the blood from her temple. She tasted sweet and salty at the same time.

He started to undress her. Fuck it, it was taking too long. Reaching inside his pants, past his stiffening dick, Boots pulled out the Stanley Knife. First he ripped her blouse apart before cutting open the bra, exposing young firm breasts. Slicing through the belt holding her sensible skirt on. Boots dragged her pants down around her one remaining shoe. Sweating now he drooled down at her small black bush of pubes. Grinning he toyed with the Stanley knife as it glistened in the cascading light falling through the broken windows, across the empty cool warehouse.

Voices were in his head, he could see the red eyes watching him from the gloom of the emptiness. The demonic growl clear in his ears as it penetrated the very walls of the seedy, squalid room.

Looking up Boots saw the creature from the previous night as it slowly came from the shadows, growling quietly. As if mutating each time it appeared, this time almost walking on hind legs.

*"You work well. She is soft and will cut easily."*

Boots shivered in the cool damp room.

*"Take her, take her now. Use her. Then we can taste her."*

Boots although terrified, was electrified. He was still in *command.* Rolling her over he spread her legs. Similar to his previous *mission*, dropping his trousers and pants, his erection hard before kneeling between her legs, dripping.The creature pacing back and forth, like a caged animal, crazy eyes fixed. Boots felt *strange* at being watched. He'd never been good at going to public toilets when someone else stood next to him.

His erection softened.

*"I see you want us to have her."*

The creature moved close to the girls limp, open hand. Reaching down *it* picked up the discarded blade. As it did, Boots seemingly, regaining excitement, started to masturbate. He watched transfixed as the creature slowly, deliberately cut into the girls temple, blood flowing down her cheeks. It lent forward, sniffing the scent and blood.

Just as it looked round, Boots came over the girl's stomach and breasts.

*"Good, now we can feast."* The creature then in a fit or energy, slashed the girl's breasts with its claw. Boots watched as the pink flesh was replaced by deep, dark red.

The creature leaning forward, licked the blood with its revolting pitted tongue.

Then it bent its head back and howled. A terrible, low howl that reverberated round the whole building.

Boots looked down, the girl was covered in blood, slashed all over her head. Her breasts were in a mess, the pools of blood slowly growing. Between her legs the creature had slashed wildly. The girl's pubes and groin now a matted mess of hair, blood and cum.

---

The creatures gone, Boots, as if coming out of a trance, blinked. He looked down at the Stanley knife in his hand, covered in blood. He dropped it. She was dead. He had finally completed the mission. They would surely leave him to rest in peace now?

He stood up, staring down at the filth. Glass, paper, crumpled cigarette packets, blood and the girls mutilated body. Head shaking, he, no they had killed her. With this Boots bent down picking up the knife, withdrew the blade and put it into his pocket. Stepping back, he turned, walking briskly out of the building. Still in the shadows he recce'd the road. The place was deserted.

Retracing his route quickly, along the way, getting rid of the knife. Up a side street, he found a deserted foul smelling public toilet where he quickly washed his hands in the filthy sink, noticing that, amazingly he hardly had any blood on his clothes. Anyway you couldn't see any due to their dark colour. Boots smiled, camouflage.

He walked back through the hectic Quay Side, up the same road. Having bought a kebab he waited for the bus. Climbing aboard it was packed, full of drunken youths, desperate to get the eleven thirty bus back to the numerous villages on route to Carlisle.

On returning to the camp Boots once again disobeyed standing orders, climbing the fence. Back in his room he changed, being very careful to put all his outer clothes in a double black bin liner. He'd bin' them at a service station on the way back to Aldershot. After a quick shower he'd swaggered over to the NAAFI.

A short while later he joked with Tom that, yes, the manageress did indeed have disgustingly fat ankles.

A good deal later the manageress switched off the last remaining light as the two men walked, swaying out into the cool, almost dawn, air.

"Cheerio Tom me old mucka, thanks for a champion night."

Boots was very drunk. He'd had seven pints and five double whiskies. He'd been in the NAAFI for over three hours. "Neet," said an equally intoxicated Camp Commandant.

Boots head hit the pillow just as the early morning chorus commenced.

---

The following night, a day early, the recce' party just managed to get to The Ram before closing time. Not that Boots really felt like drinking as his head was still pounding from the previous nights booze, the subsequent dehydration plus an almost complete lack of sleep.

The next day, still smelling of drink, Boots stood on first parade, a smirk nestling on his smug face. The fucking muppet of a Rupert*, coming along the line, wasn't so great. He'd never been on a successful mission.

* Rupert is another sightly derogative name given to junior Commissioned Officers'.

## CHAPTER 5

# *Scented Saviour*

DISUSED WAREHOUSE AREA NEXT TO THE TYNE RIVER
SUMMER 1997, 4PM SUNDAY

Two hours after lunch, Olly Jones finished the Sunday papers having decided it was time to take Bounce for his walk. Olly always enjoyed their walks, late on Sunday afternoons. Firstly, there were no pissed youths staggering around. Even the worst of whom had managed to navigate, from whence they had come and it was also too early for the next session of drinkers. Finally, it was far too early for girls on the game or any of the other low life you'd expect to find down by the river after dark.

He didn't put Bounce on the lead as the dog had never in his life crossed a road without checking with its master. Even next doors cat hadn't managed to get Bounce to bolt, feline crazed, across the road.

Master and pet walked down the side street, across the high bridge overlooking the park. From there, he descended the steep hill which took them down amongst the derelict grain warehouses. Like giant monoliths standing in rows, impressive, sometimes five or six storeys tall, some with winches resembling crows hooked beaks, still exposed. Amazingly, one or two of the warehouses were still operating. In bygone years they'd all been full of all manner of goods. Cotton from the Midlands, lead ore from the Dales and all sorts of other commodities to be exported round the, once, greatest empire in the world.

Olly always thought it such a shame that they'd now been allowed to go to rack and ruin. He, like many, thought that one day some very wealthy business consortium would come along and restore them to their former glory creating penthouse apartments inhabited by wealthy yuppies, bringing investors vast profits in the process.

A few of the buildings had been partially demolished, forming urban wastelands between the remaining buildings. Most were fenced off. All that the fences now seemed to protect were brambles, shrubs and juvenile trees which had, over the years, sprung up. The natural flora and fauna camouflaging years of accumulated rubbish left by once floundering businesses. Obviously: winos, druggies, the odd desperate whore and possibly kids used them for; drinking, mainlining, earning a living and generally messing around. In his youth he'd have made great dens in them. Did kids still make dens mused Olly?

He wandered on, Bounce walking dutifully a few feet ahead.

At fifty four, Olly thought himself pretty fit. He'd recovered from a massive heart attack and subsequent multiple bypass which had put paid to the autumn of his career as a police sergeant. He didn't actually care. His wife still worked the cosmetic counter in Fennicks Department Store. He had his pension, there was the book collecting and of course, walking Bounce.

Bounce who was now in the prime of his life, had been a working police dog for four years, Sergeant Jones being his handler. The day the dog had badly broken its leg, the Northumbrian constabulary had retired him. Olly's wife had begged with him to break the tradition and bring Bounce home to become the family pet.

She'd pleaded, saying, " he's only five and is such a good dog, anyway he'll be there when your out. I can't imagine many burglars taking on a long haired German Shepherd trained to bite to the bone."

Olly had finally given in, only to collapse six months later, whilst running after some drugged up shithead for not paying his Metro underground fare. His emergency heart surgery taking place the following day.

Bounce ran ahead, darting off into somewhere. "Bounce HEEL, come here, stop barking you daft dog."

Olly couldn't see Bounce. Where had the dog got to? He'd obviously gone into one of the wastelands just up ahead. Pursuing his dog Olly shoved open the rusty old gate come fence.

"Bounce come here."

Why in amongst all this debris could he smell perfume? "Bugger, Bounce, stop bloody barking your head off and HEEL!"

For some inexplicable reason Olly felt a soft warm wind draw across his face as if a gentle hand were stroking his cheek. He was going bloody daft as his wife often said after he'd had too many lagers. She was forever nagging him that the drink was sure to finally kill him!

Olly would have to put the damn dog on the lead, maybe he should never have brought the stupid thing home in the first place?

Reluctantly he pushed through the bushes stumbling over a pile of rubble. 'Shit, you stupid dog, get here." Olly was bleeding where he had broken the fall by shoving his hand on the sharp edge of steel poking out of a slab of concrete.

There it was again, perfume? His wife had brought enough damn free samples home over the years for him to recognise it as Chanel No5.

As he was beginning to stand, inspecting his now bleeding hand, Olly again felt a strange wind, almost a breath across his neck.

A moment later, Olly was certain that someone was touching him just behind his ear. He spun round, only to stare straight at a bush.

Hang on.

In that moment, thirty four years of police training brought the hairs on the back of his neck prickling up.

Out of the corner of his eye he'd just noticed a ladies shoe.

Just about anyone else would have disregarded it as some drunks or a prostitutes lost in the throes of the oldest profession.

Crouching down being careful not to touch. The pretty blue shoe had evidently fallen down between the slabs of concrete. He'd have missed it, had he not snapped his head round a moment ago. It was almost brand new and probably very expensive and had definitely only been there a day or so.

Why would a new, expensive shoe be discarded in amongst all this crap and rubbish?

Bounce barked. This time it had an echo kind of hollow sound to it.

Bugger the damn mutt had gone inside. "Fucking animal." Olly said aloud.

Treading with caution the retired sergeant clambered over a pile of stinking, rotten office cushions. Looking up, concealed behind a large clump of bushes, he could see the entrance to one of the warehouses. Bounce was sat just inside a large sliding door. Seeing its master, Bounce immediately stopped barking and 'sat' looking up, not at Ole though?

Obviously all those nights in the back of the van combined with chasing and subsequently being kicked by football thugs had flipped the stupid dogs mind.

Bounce had never disobeyed a command when in sight of his master.

Olly turned to go, commanding Bounce as he did. Bounce started to bark again. Now thoroughly annoyed, Olly clambered over the rubble, chairs, desks and general debris from the once profitable warehouse. As he entered the warehouse, the dark smell of piss, rubbish and general damp decay an offence to his senses. It was also fairly gloomy compared to the bright late afternoon sunshine outside.

He stepped towards Bounce who, as if being commanded by a new master, smartly turned and trotted away.

Bounce was definitely going to get the front end of his shoe up his arse, thought Olly.

Reluctantly he followed, further into the gloom.

Olly blinked hard, gulping with purpose as he stepped over what looked like a torn, well worn, sticky, porn magazine. Obviously some boys had been reading wank mags in here.

Bounce had once again stopped at what looked like the entrance to the shop floor manager's office.

The glass crunched beneath Olly's shoes as he crossed the twenty odd meters.

Bounce was seated and looking up at some god damn invisible Crufts handler.... Chanel No 5 wafted up Olly's nose.

As it did he began to get the creeps. Vastly experienced he'd witnessed all manner of strange things in his time on The Force but this was getting to him. The thoughts bringing both elbows in to his side in a little shudder.

"Look you stupid dog, when I say Hee........

Staggering back, slipping on the glass and some rusty office drawers, Olly fell, landing in, what his wife later refused to describe, lest to say it was probably human and sticky.

Stumbling to his feet, Olly moved forward. This time with Bounce walking right next to his left thigh. In the door frame, he glanced through the remaining shards of glass, praying to God he'd been wrong.

Perfume instantly replaced by filth. The flies buzzed around in a swarm.

In front of him behind the now disused desk was a person lying on their back. He carefully went to the front of the desk that was slewed round, sprawled against the interior wall.

A woman.

Sod crime scene protocol, he wasn't on the force any more, Olly rushed forward and knelt next to the body.

Her clothes had been almost totally cut off, a pretty dress lay over to the side, her knickers were down around one ankle. Her bra had been cut in the centre. The cups resembling dried up ponds partially filled with congealed blood. This Olly took in as he felt for a pulse. At the same time, he reached for his mobile which his wife had insisted he carry at all times, in case he had a turn, whatever the fuck that meant.

"Which service please?" the calm, clear operator enquired. "Urr, police and ambulance, she's covered in blood."

"Calm down sir."

Olly regained his training. This time in a very clear, deliberate, but not calm voice, "my name is Olly Jones, retired Sergeant Jones, my mobile is 60567229. He repeated it slowly; six, zero, five, six, seven, two, two nine. I am in a warehouse halfway down Front Lane, on the right going towards the river. I've found a woman, I think she's dead, she's been attacked. You need to get here real quick."

"I understand, very clear, thank you Sergeant Jones, the emergency services will be with you in a matter of minutes. Please stay with her."

Staring at the woman, Olly recognised that some sort of jagged blade had slashed her breasts. Her head cut down to the bone. Dried blood completely covering her face.

Eyes transfixed in utter disbelief, it was only then that Olly realised the girl was Chinese.

Who knew *what* had done this to the poor girl.

As he looked down at the girl's groin, sick rising in his throat. It was a complete mess, she had been slashed almost open.

When he saw the maggots, Olly turned and spewed his lamb, three veg and most of the two glasses of average red wine, all over the debris strewn floor.

Wiping his mouth with his sleeve, he forced himself to look back.

Bounce was licking the girl's face.

That was it, the dog would have to go. "For Christ sake Bounce, get the hell away."

At last, the dog did as it was told. Strangely sitting back and looking, clearly a few feet to Olly's left?

Olly turned to see what had got the dogs attention. As he turned back ....her matted eyes twitched.

Blinking in the gloom, Olly frantically checked her pulse again. Very light, but there, yes, he could feel the faintest of beats.

He tried to brush away the maggots, giving up, partly due to their size but mainly because he felt so terribly uneasy touching the girls naked, pubic area. Licking his hand he wiped his cheek. Bending over, placing his cheek as near as he dare to where her face used to be.

Shit, she was breathing. Shallow and light, but breathing.

At the same moment he heard the siren come to a wailing halt on the road somewhere outside. Almost involuntarily, "don't worry love the paramedics will be here in a second, you just lie still." Olly immediately realised the absurdity of his words.

Dashing out, glass everywhere, shouting as loud as he could.

A young Police Constable came crashing over the rubble, "we got a call about a body."

Olly didn't recognise the young constable. "There's a girl in there, over in the old office." The PC went forward, into the semi gloom. Olly pointed where the PC was looking, "yes over there." Olly continued, out of breath, "listen, she's nearly dead, where the hell's the paramedics?

The constable ignoring him moved purposefully forward, noticing the large German Shepherd sat obediently, near the office door.

As they crunched forward, the PC explained that the paramedics were just behind him. His colleague was helping them get their stuff.

Olly knew the drill, he moved past the PC and stood by the office door entrance. The constable went straight past him into the room only to stop in his tracks.

He turned and stared at Olly, innocence forever removed.

The two paramedics came rushing in. Each carrying large reflective holdalls, bursting with equipment. Olly and the PC stood back, the PC pointing. Bounce now resting his chin on his foreleg watched, sadness in his eyes.

It had taken them thirty five minutes before they were able to finally move her. By then six other police officers were swarming around, busy photographing and cordoning off the whole crime scene.

Olly had gone back outside to the road and was now seated in an opened police car, waiting. They'd given him some tea. It was warm and sweet, the usual for shock. A young female PC offered him some more from the Stanley thermos flask. Declining he still felt sick.

Having made an initial statement, he was waiting for his wife to come and fetch him. That poor girl, he prayed she was an orphan, God could be so fucking cruel.

He recognised their red Golf VW pull up outside the now cordoned off road. Olly watched as his wife got out. She appeared drawn, yet relieved that it was not her husband who had been injured.

Alone now, Olly slowly, with lethargy borne from the haunting memory of the poor girl, stood up ready to move over to his now waving wife.

Bounce gave a little yelp. Turning to look down at the animal that was now definitely on the lead, he watched as Bounce tailed his wag. Recognising the scent of perfume Olly froze, someone or something had just kissed him on the cheek.

## CHAPTER 6

# *Pain of Reality*

### NEWCASTLE GENERAL HOSPITAL, 1997
### THE NEXT DAY 7:45 AM MONDAY

Lin's chest ached so, her eyes bloodshot, red from crying. Danny's face was sunken and ashen, his eyes crimson also. The cold disinfectant mixed with the pretty but cheap pot pouri on the little table in front of their chairs gave the room an unpleasant, unnatural sickly chemical smell.

It couldn't be true, their beautiful Penny wasn't the girl the consultant, sat just across from them, was talking about. It was obviously a mistake as both parents minds wrestled with the incomprehensiveness of it all.

No way could it be their daughter who he was describing. Yet the warm tears cascading down toward Danny's mouth assured him that this was reality and it was their daughter who Mr Winter, the consultant, was talking about. As if returning from a dream, the haze broken by Lin's sobbing. "Please tell us it's not true, not our little Penny," pleaded Danny.

It had been a horrific six hours since he'd answered the phone in the early hours on the morning.

The consultant continued, "Mr and Mrs Chang, I'm so sorry but we must look toward the positive. Your daughter is breathing, albeit with the aid of a ventilator." Pausing, he thought it better not to recap her terrible genital injuries, "the cuts to her scalp are away from her face. I promise we're doing everything possible for your daughter."

Danny's mind again slipping from reality. His Penny was such a good girl: bright, respectful, beautiful and definitely a daddies little girl.... His mind drifted further back. The infant on his knee was laughing, "Daddy, bounce me faster, faster."

A distant phone rang as Danny smelt the horrid hospital smell. Wham, the bland blue walls once again closed in on him.

The phone was answered.

God why Penny? She'd only recently graduated from York with a very credible 2:1 degree in Chemistry. They'd been so very proud of her. His daughter had been so very excited about the new phase of her life she was entering.

This was clearly all gone now.

"I would recommend you go home and try to get some rest," Mr Winter's voice was like a North Sea blast of cold air snapping Danny back to the present.

Looking up at the consultant, replying without thinking, "ow, yes I suppose so."

Lin, who had stopped crying, was staring blankly as if in some distant hypnotic trance. Tears drying, streaked and merged with the mascara forming tramlines down her high cheekbones, "I'll stay here just in case, you go home and ..."

Danny's reply was almost a command, "no you go Lin. Get her some things. I'd have no idea where to look in her room." He realised this was not what Lin needed right now so finished with, "sorry darling."

Mr Winter noted the tension, "why don't you both go. We are not going to be able to do anything until she shows signs of coming out of the coma, She's lost such a lot of blood and I believe the shock of the attack has probably played a role. I assure you we're doing everything we can but I must remind you her condition although stable remains grave."

Both Danny and Lin's expression, one of disbelief. Neither wanting to allow the horror of it all to invade their numb brains. After a full minute both reluctantly acknowledged that the consultant was probably right.

Anyway he had all their numbers and it only took fifteen minutes from Jesmond to the hospital. Two minutes later they walked back to the car in silence, both parents engulfed in sadness.

Tony, who had been waiting at a respectful distance down the corridor, went ahead past the reception desk and out into the warm fresh air. Instinctively, he looked around walking a few paces ahead checking past them every few seconds without actually looking at either of his charges.

Seeing them approach the driver jumped out, opening the door for Lin, who flopped down sobbing weakly. Tony remained silent, having more sense than to ask how Penny was. Anyway one of the nurses had given him a quick update less than twenty minutes earlier.

He knew things were bad.

As he closed the door Tony remembered his bosses frantic call to the hospital as they had sped through red lights in the earlier hours of the morning.

Tony's brain raced. God no, Penny couldn't die.

Who would do such a thing? *They* could not have found them? Anyway why would *they* target Mr Chang's daughter?

Suddenly, somehow terribly, it all sort of made sense. To get to Mr Chang's uncle, what better way than to kill the daughter of the one he loved most.

The Jag moved off out of the hospital car park, down past the ten-pin bowling alley and into the afternoon traffic, despair permeating the whole interior.

# CHAPTER 7

## *Morning Fix*

DURHAM, 1997,
THE SAME DAY, MONDAY MORNING

The climb up the steep rocky bank in Haughall Woods was not new to Simon. For the first few years it had been a tedious exercise, imposed upon every boy by their school PE teacher.

Now it was pure pleasure.

Admittedly, that had been over thirty years earlier when he had been a skinny fifteen year old. At only five foot ten he'd filled out. That said he probably had less fat on him now, than when he'd left school.

As the bank steepened considerably up the final hundred feet of the climb, Simon lent into the hill and drove, running on his toes. His heart pounding and so it should after thirty minutes of running at, just over, six-minute mile pace.

Cresting the hill panting fiercely, he knew that this was the time to drive on. Many a race, way back when he finally discovered the joys of running cross country, had been won on this crest. Opposition teams often tried to take a short restbite. When they had, Durham's runners had gained an unbeatable hundred and fifty foot advantage. With only a mile or so to go, only the best county standard runners managing to claw back the, normally unassailable, lead.

Simon swung left, along the short road, past the University Botanical Department's greenhouses. At that time in the morning the first few gardeners having arrived, were discussing their wives, football and how many pints they'd drunk,  during the Sunday session in the main bar of The Coalpits, the night before. Not of course, necessarily, in that order.

Sun burnt through the mist, which lay predominantly in the valley five hundred feet below. Simon gained pace again, running in his heavy, cumbersome, yet pacy style. Way back his running coach had said, 'with legs like those, he'd be better sticking to rugby'. He shouldn't 'beat himself up' in an attempt to compete at the level he aspired and, much to his coaches amazement, succeeded at.

Dropping down now, from the single tarmac road, back into Haughall Woods he hugged the contours of the hill. Ahead of him Simon could hear the familiar *pinking* of blackbirds alerting everyone that danger was less than a hundred feet away. This natures call, on more than one occasion, alerted Simon to imminent danger of an altogether more lethal, human kind.

As if being pursued by some ghostly apparition, his pace increased. Going fast down the hill, Simon thought he heard someone cough behind him. Turning to see who it was, only to catch a toe on an exposed root, stumbled and went headlong, sprawling dangerously downhill.

Just about everyone his age would have either, snapped their wrist breaking the fall or worse still had gone 'arse over tit' landing in a heap of rocks, brambles and nettles with cuts all over their prostrate bodies.

Not Simon, in true *ukemi* style,* as if in slow motion, with the agility of a cat, Simon curled his head under, pushed hard with his trailing leg, wrapping his left arm forward round his neck.

His momentum pushing his free arm into the hard dirt track first, however the spurt of power sent him seemingly head over heals in a heap.

Not so.

Wrapping his body into a ball and bending one leg up under, he in effect did an air-borne, childs 'rolly pollie'. The similarity ending there.

Simon was well over forty and going at a near sprint, down a stony track. As if guided by some magical force, pushing with his folded leg, he sprang straight back up at the run, his right arm drawn back in an unconscious, bolt action, fist.

Anyone watching would have demanded he do it again, such was the ballet like poetry of the motion.

Simon wiped the dirt and dust from his sweaty brow, smiled and relaxed the fist. He had learnt a lot from Judo and Section 9.†

Continuing running, now with a little patch of nettle stings on his forearm, he took the last steep five foot of the decline like a Grand National steeplechaser.

Sheep jumped, startled, bolting, flocking together as they tried to evade the intruder to their early morning feed. Simon pressed on.

The last mile towards Shincliffe was uphill, a longer steadier climb, which after the previous forty minutes, would have slowed most twenty year olds down.

He surged on trying to close the gap on a mountain bike cyclist, wheezing and panting some hundred feet up ahead.

As Simon rounded the Seven Stars Pub off the main road he could clearly read the small Shimano logo on the cyclist back. His mind and body now forced to its limit as he sprinted the last hundred and fifty feet, coming to a very non biomechanical juddering halt, lungs bursting.

Leaning over for a second with his hands on his knees before jogging back down the lane for a further minute, before turning back towards home, Summer View Cottage.

Simon stopped by the gate, bent over the gutter and promptly snorted, in turn, through each nostril. Very unsophisticated, but very effective.

His wife Lynda would definitely not approve.

---

* In Judo, Ukemi means the art of falling. Simon in effect doing an elaborate airborne Zenpo Kaiten–forward roll.

† For detail on Simon's involvement with Section 9, see Appendix A.

# CHAPTER 8

# *Hacienda Grande*

Having finished my early morning run I knew something was up yet couldn't explain how I knew. Like a lot of things in my life something's were just plainly unexplainable. I was however as usual certain it had nothing to do with coincidence.

It was quiet when I went though the front door, Lynda having dressed had already left for her part-time job.

After a shower I went back downstairs to our large, sunny living room where I did a number of Chi Gong moves, including my favourite, Peeping Monkey,[9] before settling down with the bay windows open, comfortable in my meditation chair.

Breathing slower, my tongue resting on the roof of my mouth, just behind the top front teeth, exactly how the Tibetan monk had taught me years earlier. Breathing slower and slower, my heart beat now down to less than forty five beats per minute. Not bad after a hard run.

It was now that my mind came into it's own.

Levels of consciousness are in reality only alternate states of mind. When someone dreams they leave this level of conscious thought only to enter another. Meditation, some believe, is yet another level of consciousness. The reality is these are only two of any number of layers of awareness. Actually the deeper an individual reaches the further they can venture. Highly trained individuals can move to other realms, even different dimensions. Such journeys are not easy and require specially gifted people with extraordinary skills, honed by years of training. Simon inherited his gift, clearly possessing ability which, combined with diligent practice over many years, had afforded him access to the amazing levels he now roamed.

Drifting off.

I sat on the banks of my river watching the swallows swoop down, sometimes taking snatches of water. Trout, the mirror image, trying to catch elusive flies as they drifted tantalisingly close to the surface.

Turning, I saw *Pied Wagtail* as he bobbed tail feathers, "hello Simon. Where are we going to today?"

Here nothing was quite like reality, although this was/is very real, "up to the Hacienda Grande," my reply.

Wagtail fluttered ahead as we climbed a beautiful grassy bank. At the top stood a truly magnificent almost stately home, sturdy practical fencing surrounded it. On the raised front porch, lying a number of wonderfully comfy cane chairs with, strangely, a large old school trunk standing in front, acting as a low table.

Opening the beautiful wrought iron gate I wondered over to the steps. Wagtail had flown ahead and now perched on the railings, "enter, learn great wisdom and give to those who would receive."

I thanked him.

Opening the beautiful grand door, I stepped inside.

Sitting just past the main entrance was my old headmaster, one of the wisest men I'd ever known, "Simon be seated, let us talk for a while. I feel sadness and danger approaching."

"Health and happiness to you. Hello, Doctor Laurance," I replied.

He was an impressive sight. Not tall, the doctor was stocky, a man oozing authority. He stood, hands drawn behind under his black masters' cloak. Strange how he insisted on wearing his mortarboard, tassels cascading down to one side.

We sat on the large bench off to one side of the grand hallway.

"How should I approach such challenges?" I enquired.

The headmaster replied, "bring around you those that would protect you. Draw close your healing spirits. I see a new, powerful spirit come close. Welcome them, they have knowledge which you need. They can heal to an incredible level but are, as yet, clouded in their sight."

I wasn't certain what he meant so said, "I already have Dr Klieman and Bobby, why do I need more help? You know there are always others."

The doctor continued, "they draw near because you are the solution to their pain as they can manipulate but not protect. With revenge, peace they will find. Presently crestfallen and no longer able to heal the living. *She* will however once again, soon treat the sick."

My old headmaster frowned before continuing, "Simon you will need your friends to protect you. The one your after is surrounded by foul spirits who would do you harm. They are the ones you should fear. You know, in your darkest moments, there's another who seeks you."

I did.

"Thanks Doctor Laurence, your words are wise and I'm forever in your debt. Go peacefully. Watch over pupils and those who would impart knowledge."

"Move on Simon, smile and give love," the headmaster nodded before wandering over, starting to climb the main, sweeping staircase.

Turning, I followed him, Dr Laurance's gown billowing before me. He proceeded up the stairs. I didn't continue, turning instead to the right, moving towards The Knowledge Room. Opening the door, three very famous faces calmly looked up.

The tall elegant lady stood and spoke, "Simon, we greet you with warmth from our hearts. It isn't us you seek as The Commander requests your presence."

"Grant knowledge and learning wherever you feel inclined."

Smiling I closed the door and moved back over to the stairs. Dr Laurance had gone, looking up above me, as if perpetually about to commence decent, stood The Commander.

"Simon we'd talk a while on the stairs?" His voice clear, authoritative.

"Yes commander I'm coming."

Walking up the stairs, the tall impressive figure of a Cossack General stood looking down his hooked nose at me, "I would speak with you of campaigning."

He always spoke in a slightly old fashioned military style. Language barriers didn't exist here. Distance, time, space were all there but here, and when required there, challenges not barriers.

"Colonel Boeck, you should know that enemies draw from the gloom towards your light. Their intent is harm." He continued, "your warriors see these things so move closer. Note their power will be seen by a shadow from your past."

Thoughtfully I enquired, "how will I know who the shadow is and what should I do?"

The Commander touched the hilt of the beautiful Damascus blade thrust in his belt and replied, "you must do them harm in your realm, Colonel. Destruction of the one who sits on the devils shoulder."

I knew better than to push further. I'd know when the time came, "general, thank you, may you fight with courage and guide honourable soldiers."

With that I descended the carpeted stairs, reaching the bottom, smiling across at the open door of The Treatment Room. Smiling back were a First World War, non qualified, doctor. Standing next to Dr Klieman was a vet, Bobby, both laughing. Their warmth and energy flowing toward me.

You may think all this impossible but here everything was as real as the sun rising.

Space, distance and what you know of normality are often very different to those that seek and find.

Without another word I walked back out of the grand doors. Moving again across, descending the grassy slope.

Sitting down from where I had commenced my journey. The swallows still diving down close to the water. Wagtail, bobbing next to me, "Simon, I trust you enjoyed your walk? Gained wisdom from your friends and guides. You have sought knowledge and strength within. Now move with purpose."

---

Breathing deeply Simon heard a thrush warble outside the double windows. Opening his eyes, the phone rang.

"Simon it's Danny. I desperately need your help."

"I know," Simon's simple reply.

# CHAPTER 9

## *Life favour*

Simon parked his car in the drive, having only taken forty minutes to drive to the Chang residence. The 'gate man' letting him in having imminently recognised *The Green Eyed Dragon.**

Moments later Simon could easily tell his friend was a complete mess, torn between disbelief, sickening pain and rage, their daughter lying on the brink of death. Lin had taken tablets having fainted through nervous exhaustion and mental anguish.

"Danny this is so terrible. I want to help Penny. To do so, I will need private time with her. You must trust me."

After a tiny pause for consideration Danny replied, "they have her in intensive care. The main doctor said that there wasn't any point going private. She was already receiving the finest care possible. He seemed so genuinely concerned, I believe him."

Simon blinked hard and slow, before asking, "his name wouldn't be Winter by any chance?"

Jolted from his grief Danny not for the first nor last time, wondered how the hell he did it, "yes, tall skinny bloke, in his fifties."

Simon smiled, "yes, we know each other," continuing, " I will need your permission for doctor Winter to tell me everything about Penny's injuries, no matter how personal or detailed."

Danny, now incredibly tired replied, "of course anything, please Simon I've never asked anything of you apart from your friendship but now I'm begging you, save my little girl."

The weight of expectancy was not unknown to *The Green Eyed Dragon.*

Before and since, people had looked to Simon as a holy saviour capable of miracles. He wasn't, only on a very few occasions had he performed what people referred to as *miracles.* To Simon, he was only doing what came so very natural to him. He had extraordinary powers and invariably used them for good.

This was different, even by Danny's non scientific diagnosis, Penny was gravely ill and there seemed little he could do to save her from becoming a possible resident at the Hacienda Grande.

Turning to Danny, Simon calmly gave his request, "I'll go to her now so please call mister Winter," Simon using the consultants correct title, " tell him to expect a friend, who needs a favour."

Simon then left, careful not to speed as he hurried off toward the hospital.

Danny spoke briefly to a seemingly unsurprised Dr Winter, when he'd mentioned Simon's name, relaying what he had been told.

As Danny put the receiver down, his thoughts turned to his darling Penny and those

* Simon was given this Chinese name some five years earlier.

terrible injuries. He just wanted her back.

From pain came rage.

Whoever had done this had unknowingly brought the might of every ounce of Danny's vast wealth and enormous underworld connections to bare. He'd convince Simon that, he would have his revenge.

Focussing on this thought only for a moment Danny sighed deeply, wearily, before going upstairs to check on Lin.

Simon entered the head consultants, small but efficient office, "Mike I wish it was under better circumstances."

The greeting familiar with those incredibly warm hands and unusual forearm grasp, "Simon shes' such terrible injuries, it's a miracle there aren't more to her face."

Mike Winter continued, " the thing who did this, brutally cut her open down below, as if some kind of ritual."

Simon listened in disbelief as the head consultant continued, "she lost a hell of a lot of blood. If it hadn't been for the coolness in the old warehouse, where they'd found her, speeding up the clotting." With that he rubbed a tired hand over a drawn brow, "plus the maggots which actually staved off some of the infection. Not pretty though."

Visibly shocked by the detail Simon enquired, "will she live?"

Bowing his head rather than look into those green eyes, Doctor Winter said, "no, I don't think so, she's in a coma. If she comes out, then we have a chance, if not I fear we will loose her by the morning."

Simon sighed, he knew that Doctor Laurence had spoken with purpose and honesty. He asked, understanding Penny was in intensive care, when was the quietest time, during the night? Also, could he draw the curtains round for some privacy?

Dr Winter frowned, "sorry Simon not this time," the consultant had a superb memory, "but you can bring the curtains half way. You see the night nurse must be able to see the monitors at all times."

Simon checked his *mind.* Without time and space, moving forward then back, he knew Penny wouldn't die in the next twelve hours.

Looking at his old friend, "Mike, I will be back at ten tonight. Please try and do everything you can. I owe Mr Chang a hell of a lot and hate for them to be in such pain.

Simon left and drove deep in thought back to Summer View Cottage. He then explained to, a distraught, Lynda what had happened. She'd said, "thank God it hadn't been their daughter lying on the brink of death. Poor Lin and Danny."

With that Lynda got a few things together and left for Lin's, breaking the speed limit on the way.

Simon spent a period of time in the Hycienda Grande that afternoon, where he'd spoken to a number of his friends spending most of his time in The Treatment Room.

Later, for a long time, he sat mulling over the events as he watched some small birds mob a kestrel which had come too close to their fledglings for comfort.

Sitting there Simon knew he was almost at the peak of his power, seemingly overflowing with energy, *healing* energy.

Whilst there, he had met his newest guide. She was, unlike Doctor Klieman, fully qualified. Her messages were, however, confused by pain and anger. She'd managed though to give thoughts of troubling details, most of which were as yet clouded. Simon knew he would be able to clear the mist and get more information about the one who sat on the devils shoulder.

# CHAPTER 10

## *From the Brink*

Considering the catchment area, the intensive therapy unit was/is adequate with ten stations, as they were referred to with just under half occupied, patients with all manner of injuries and illnesses lying quietly. The major sound coming from heart rate monitors, hopefully beating rhythmically.

Entering the ward, as he did, sensing some of the occupants were close to *leaving.* A re-occurring near nightmare was that Simon couldn't help everyone, yet the rules were clear, patients somehow found him, not the other way round.

Mike Winter who accompanied him, palm open, directed Simon to the end *station.* Simon couldn't recognise Penny, the bandages all over her previously pretty face.

A canopy raising the blankets a foot above her legs and midriff. Seeing it Simon shivered as he recalled the detail Mike had gone into regarding the deep, callous razor slashes to the lower part of her breasts, as well as terrible deep gashes all over Penny's pubic area.

Penny resembled a broken puppet with so many tubes coming out of her right arm.

Mike explained that without them she'd be dead and although breathing independently her heart beat still remained dangerously weak.

"Thanks Mike I owe you."

"No you don't. We both know you gave me some special powers all those years ago."

"Get away with you Mike, I'm no superman, all I did was give you a friend to occasionally guide your knife."

Mike looked at him in disbelief knowing exactly what Simon meant as, sometimes during particularly dangerous and tricky surgery he'd feel a calming hand holding, guiding his.....

Blinking back into the dim lights of the unit Mike said, "I'm on night shift and we have a number of potential cardiac emergencies. See you later?"

"Thanks again Mike," Simon answer.

With that Doctor Winter hurried off. He had patients to save and all this mumbo jumbo was clearly unsettling to his clinical mind.

Simon went over and shook hands with the duty night nurse who stared at those gorgeous green eyes rather too longingly for comfort. Such kind eyes and a wonderfully warm handshake, although his voice was calm and somehow reassuring the nurse was certain behind the softly spoken words lurked a powerful man. Answering his question, of course he could sit with his *niece.*

Mike had lied.

---

I brought the curtain round as far as I dare. Nine deep breaths later I closed my eyes.

When I needed to, they came disregarding time and space.

The nurse shifted strangely uneasy, as if she was being watched, she was! Looking over, the night nurse could just see the patient, free hand under her uncles.

"Doctor Klieman, guides, helpers I ask you draw near. Work through me and give warmth and healing to this lady."

The nurse could have sworn she saw a small globe of light come down from the ceiling, moving down behind the curtain.

The globe, Doctor Klieman, sat on the edge of the bed. The heart rate monitor now inaudible, as if, like time, we were in some form of suspended animation.

Doctor Klieman spoke, "Simon I have seen similar injuries before during the great war. I can help but they are so terrible. You know we didn't have many female patients in the trenches."

"I have."

In timelessness you can be surprised, "hello who is here?" I asked almost rhetorically, knowing there'd be another. Looking over, instinctively I continued, "Lotte, meet Doctor Klieman."

Speaking I saw the shape of a lady focus. She was tall with a purposeful stance, sensible Birkenstock clogs on her feet. Her long honey hair combed back in a severe businesslike bun. Stethoscope round her neck. The woman's smile strong, handsome rather than pretty.

Approaching, Lotte sat on the other side of the bed to where Doctor Klieman and I were. Bending forward, she gently kissed Penny on the bridge of the nose, just below the bandages.

The smell of perfume reached the nurse deeply engrossed in the latest copy of Cosmopolitan.

I looked at both of them before closing my eyes, "helpers, guides, I need you to bring as many as you can to this lady. She is not ready to die."

My body warm now, sensing both doctors coming round behind. In doing so their souls merged with mine.

The power when *it* happens is incredibly. *I* was rushing around Penny's body, addressing every cell at once.

In doing so a healing force flowed with me, bombarding her very being with energy, healing energy.

The night nurse looked up from her article about botched cosmetic surgery in South Africa, rubbing her tired eyes. No she was not sure, did she not just see stars moving over the ceiling.

The night shifts were playing hell with her health. At this rate she'd have to get her eyes tested.

More and more energy flowed, time irrelevant.

By now *I* knew we were not alone, many spirits having joined us. Surging through me into, amongst Penny.

After a while, in actual fact about fifteen minutes, I opened my eyes. How I knew it was complete I don't know. I just knew.

Glancing around, "thank you for your love and energy, may your God go with you."

With that, turning to the two doctors still silently sitting next to me, " I know we will meet again. Until then go, be at peace."

With that Lotte and Doctor Klieman, started to fade away.

*I* looked over to the half drawn curtain, having sensed his presence, "you too *Mierti*." My Indian fighter having moved over to the curtain, as if on guard. Which was exactly what he was doing. Mierti had been my guardian for many years now. My other *protector*, Bill, felt so very uncomfortable in the caustic surroundings and had too many painful memories of hospitals, so had chosen to stay away. I understood.

Gazing upward watching as they dissolved, merging into visually warm translucent, glass marble sized, glowing orbs. They zipped about before slowing to a rhythmic dance, then just as quickly they were away, moving straight through the ceiling.

This time, the nurse probably saw too much. Witnessing what she later described as an Indian man, looking like he had just come out of the jungle. He'd been watching her. In disbelief she had gazed as small balls of light danced around the room before finally passing through the walls and ceiling. As for the little Indian man, he just seemed to turn into a mist before her very eyes...

Bolt upright in her chair nerves on edge. Magazine disregarded, irrelevant, dropping to the floor.

She was an experienced nurse and over the years had discussed with her colleagues what happened when people actually died. Did their spirits rise up from useless bodies? Some, even stating they'd seen transparent souls drifting from obsolete bodies.

Strangely calm, she moved across to comfort the, now obviously grieving, relative.

Stopping in her tracks she appeared, was, momentarily utterly speechless.

The woman who was on the critical list and would probably not make it through the night was quietly talking with her *uncle*.

Surely she had just witnessed her *passing away*?

Miracles do happen.

She rushed back to her station to phone the consultant as Mister Winter had insisted on being notified if there was the slightest change to her condition, there certainly had been.

Tears fell onto the bandages as Penny opened groggy, sticky eyes. What was Simon Boeck doing next to her bed?

Why was she in bed, obviously in hospital? The tubes in her arm hurt a lot and she couldn't feel down below. Worried now she turned towards Simon, "Simon," she mumbled, the taste of morphine on her tongue, "what's happened?" Childhood innocence returning to the twenty-two year old graduate as she said, "I want my Daddy."

"OK lie still, sssh," Simon replied, still holding her hand, "you don't remember anything?"

"Please, I need a drink," her simple reply. Obeying, holding the edge of the bendy straw sticking out of the plastic cup as Penny drank.

Finally, "no," she whispered. As she spoke, Penny moved her free hand down under the blankets, discovering the stitches and bandages all amongst her pubic hair. In terrible realisation, fear catching up with vague memories, she started to cry, her chest quivering. Through the haze, Penny now remembered fragments, something dreadful had been done to her.

Seeing her distress, Simon spoke again, "sssh now, Penny I want to tell you something. You will recover and the next time I see you crying." As he spoke he gently lifted a tear from her bandaged cheek, "this will be a tear of joy, on your wedding day."

Penny closed her eyes, the sobs subsiding. She did like Mr Boeck so very much, his words were so soothing. With these thoughts Penny wiped her closed eyes with her one free hand. Opening them, Penny smiled for the first time in over three days.

Mike Winter came rushing over, his eyes displaying utter disbelief, "it's unbelievable, completely impossible. The brain wave patterns were all messed up and I... well let's take a look at you Penny." Smiling at his patient, "my name is Mr Winter, I'll be looking after you for the next few days."

As he spoke Mike noted that her blood pressure had returned to near normal. She had fresh eyes and actually was very pretty when she tried to smile.

He knew the scars to Penny's head would heal. Thinking further ahead, apart from the scars below her breasts and the obvious ones down by her groin, she would totally recover. The plastic surgeon would certainly see to that.

Simon interrupted his thoughts, "Mike I will be going now, please take good care of her. Oh yes, would you phone mister and misses Chang and tell them, from me, their little girl is going to get better."

With that both men left. Penny was asleep in less than a minute.

Some way down the deserted corridor, "Simon how the hell....what did you do?"

Simon smiled at his friend, "I did nothing, others brought her back. You see, it wasn't her time." Changing tack, "I reckon she will be home in a week or so, what d'you think?"

Mike, still *gobsmacked*, "urrh yes I suppose so. The stitches will need to be removed. After that she'll have to have plastic surgery but that won't be for weeks or months." Staring at Simon he continued, "I wish I had you here full time."

Feeling his incredible abilities bare down heavily on medium shoulders, Simon would love to be able to be there all the time. Yet sadly life was never quite like that as some things he would never be able to explain.

As they parted, the warmth of Simon's handshake felt incredible. Mike was in no doubt that he held the hand of a miracle worker who had just saved his patients life, "God go with you Simon."

The faintest of grins darted across a now tired face as Simon replied, "sometimes, I think he does or rather *his staff* do."

With that they both laughed.

# CHAPTER 11

## *Ground Rules*

NEWCASTLE, 1997
TUESDAY LUNCH TIME, CHINESE DISTRICT

Sitting in Danny's number one restaurant Simon was enjoying divine plum duck. His friend, seemingly perched like a tiny finch, sat opposite looked so relieved now that Mike Winter had said that Penny was off the critical list and would be able to come home in a few days. She'd even been moved out of the Intensive Care Unit the day before.

Danny, sat studying his green tea, "Simon, you know that this is not the end." Frowning as he spoke, "I will forever be in your debt for saving Penny." His comments inducing a lame protest. "Don't keep saying it was the staff at the hospital. I went to thank them and had a long chat with the night nurse. She told me what she saw. You did it, you saved Penny. Lin and I will pray every day that you live long and be happy."

At last Simon got a word in, "I'm so relieved for you all. According to Mike Winter, it was a damn close run thing."

Danny smiled, "it was until you came on the scene."

"Danny, let's just say I'm glad I was there when she woke up," Simon's simple response.

After finishing a couple of beautiful fresh, sweet light pancakes, Simon gazed thoughtfully into a glass of dancing Winston Churchill, White Label. Looking up he said, "Danny, the person who did this to Penny moves with evil. You don't even have to ask, I must stop him before he does it again."

This was exactly what Danny wanted to hear as the bastard was going to pay with his life.

Almost reading his thoughts, Simon was, "listen Danny, as terrible as Penny's injuries are, she is going to recover. I can't just go around killing people, who have not killed themselves.

This wasn't what Danny wanted to hear, "damn it Simon, you heard what he did to her. She won't be able to comb her hair for six months. I can't even bring myself to think how long it will be before she will be able to make love again."

Danny shaken by the memories of the doctors diagnosis, scowled daggers at an approaching waitress.

Knowing better, the young Chinese waitress tactically withdrew, smiling, yet unable not to stare. She'd taken a second look at Simon, disbelieving that she had for a moment looked into those eyes. So the Green Eyed Dragon did exist!

Simon finished the last few bubbles of the rather good champagne, "Danny lets get things into perspective. We must try to find whoever did this. We can work out the ground rules later. D'you agree?"

Danny, for the first time, realising the enormity of trying to track down his daughter's attacker, sighed, "agreed."

Simon continued, " I am going to need your help and as usual, its not going to be particularly legal."

Danny was bloody sure it wasn't going to be legal. He wanted the bastard killed, preferably slowly, "anything, you know I have ways and means of obtaining whatever you need."

"For starters, I'll need to know who is conducting the investigation and I must visit the *crime scene*." Danny stiffened.

Realising how raw his friend still was Simon added, "sorry my old pal, I didn't mean to be callous. It's just that I must be totally ruthless about this. You do understand, don't you?"

He did.

"Give me two minutes', it was Danny. With that he punched numbers into a mobile. As he did Simon sat back enjoying a glass of, possibly not his favourite but still bloody good in his humble opinion, Louis Roedder.

Ten minutes later, Simon was seated in the back of Danny's Jag, the driver smoothly negotiating the busy Gateshead traffic on the way back to Summer View Cottage. He now knew who was heading the investigation. Danny didn't have informers for nothing.

Funny thought Simon, he an upright member of society mixing with an underworld king. Well, Danny wasn't really criminal, rather the squeaky clean tip of a very long powerful arm, stretching all the way from Hong Kong.

As the jag purred past Pelaw Grange Greyhound track Simon thought he'd like to take Lynda there before it, probably, all changed.

Twenty minutes further into the journey, as they left the motorway towards Gilesgate, Simon wondered how he should contact Detective Chief Inspector Neil Monk.

As Simon caught the first glimpse of the world famous cathedral, back in Newcastle Danny had decided upon his next move. If anyone could find Penny's attacker, Simon could. But he'd said murder wasn't possible. This, he would, could not accept. Such terrible things demanded his kind of justice. It was with these thoughts he picked up the phone.

Thousands of miles away, tentacles uncoiled and prepared to stretch across continents. The one they called The Giant Octupus, awoken in the middle of the night, listened intensely, incensed by such a deed. Putting the ivory phone back in place, Mr Bo pulled his dressing gown over his extended tentacles and went through to his office.

# CHAPTER 12

## *Meticulous Uncertainty*

### NEWCASTLE, 1997
### THE FOLLOWING MORNING,
### HEADQUARTERS REGIONAL SERIOUS CRIME SQUAD

Detective Chief Inspector Neil Monk could neither be described as old nor new school. That said he could and mostly was, described as a tough no nonsense detective, who got results. In his early forties, having risen rapidly through the ranks, a product of one of the first accelerated promotion schemes ran in the whole of England.

He asked for, nor gave, any leeway in attention to detail. The Chief Inspector knew this was what mattered, 'miss the little things, then you won't see the big picture,' he'd told his squad the day he'd assumed command.

Neil joined The Northumberland Police force straight from university. His superiors quickly identified his potential realising they must mould the bright, meticulous, tough copper.

Following various posts, he had made inspector after seven years. Chief Inspector then raced at the gallop. Many of his peers falling way behind his accelerated stride, a fair number remaining either sergeants or more often constables. This, occasionally caused problems, however Chief Inspector Monk's direct no nonsense approach, always resolved the issue.

The Regional Serious Crime Squad had been set up in the early 1990's. It's aim being to take on, head on, crimes of the most serious nature. Through evolution, by the mid 1990's, they tended to deal with murders mainly of a sexual nature.

In line with the bureaucrats appetite for statistics they had an eighty one percent success rate. Neil detested the objective nature of quantifying his results. The crimes he and the team solved invariably either ruined or sadly more frequently ended individual lives.

His team consisted of a deputy, another inspector, three sergeants and nine or ten, depending on manning, detective constables. It was a well known fact that two years with the squad led to promotion. Chief Inspector Monk though tough on his staff always ensured their hard work rewarded. They knew this and worked tirelessly for the 'Saint', Chief Inspector Monk's nickname. He had once been told it was due to the monastic nature of his name combined with his ability to solve the most unsolvable cases.

A happily married man with two young boys, it did not stop Neil from appreciating the good looking detective constable who brought several files into his large, cluttered office.

"Thanks Sue," seeing her frown, "yes don't fret I'll sign them before the morning." The

Chief Inspector frequently worked much later than the rest of his team. You lead from the front he was always telling them. Anyway, there was always so much damn paperwork to keep up with.

"Sir, one other thing, I've received a call from a gentleman who says he might be able to help on the *slasher*, sorry, Chang case," the young DC reverting to the cases slang name.

"What," Neil was already engrossed in some infernal internal audit about fuel consumption. Without looking up, he rubbed his sore neck. It hurt a lot, it always did. His doctor said he spent far to much time seated behind a computer screen. Sometimes Neil wished he was a bobby back on the beat. Looking up from the audit, "what, who? Which department is sticking their business in ours?"

"No one sir, it's a civilian actually."

Now annoyed, the Chief Inspector put down the thick file, "what, I said I didn't want the press release to go out just yet and anyway who has my personal work number?"

The DC checked her notes, "someone called Simon Boeck seems to have it sir."

The Chief Inspector glared at the woman, "what the hell's he doing calling me. I don't need to be bothered by an ex Army bod who's mixed up with the triads."

The penny dropped, he continued, "so some ex Army Officer gets away with murder, literally, five years ago. Now out of the blue he wants to talk to me about the fucking Chang case."

The DC noted his outburst, she'd only been on the squad for five months. Like every new DC she was doing the mandatory six months as the Chief Inspectors gopher. DC Sue Parish actually loved the job and was astute enough to know that the annual report she would get from The Saint would, in all probability, get her promotion having already passed her Sergeants exams the previous Christmas.

"Sir, what do you want me to do, he left his number. D'you want me to get him on the line now?"

With a very long heavy sigh, it was after six and he'd promised to get home in time to read the twins a story. Knowing his wife would go off in a huff if he was late again, it looked like another silent meal. It would be a lonely dinner in front of the telly watching Newsnight.

"Chief Inspector, it's been a long time. Please accept my apologies for contacting you like this. I know you are aware of my friendship with The Chang's. Having spoken with Mr Chang I was hoping that I could take five minutes of your time. I'm sure I can give you valuable assistance on this particularly unpleasant case."

Neil irritated, replied, "what the hell can you do? You don't know sod all about the case."

Simon, quick as a flash said, "I know the attack was vicious and sexual in nature. I also know that it was a frenzied attack with a very sharp blade. You are however unable to find any leads, even though the lab have given you excellent forensic and DNA information about the attacker."

That was it, the Saint had had enough. He opened his mouth to give Boeck a piece of his mind.

Then, as frequently the case, Chief Inspector Monk's brain raced. What the hell, this idiot might, just might be able to give him something. Wasn't he forever telling the team that they should follow a lead no matter how thin.

"Alright Lieutenant Colonel *retired*," labouring the employment status, "Boeck, I'll see you in my office tomorrow morning at nine sharp." Without pausing for breath he went on, "the headquarters is..."

Simon interrupted him. "I know it's in an unmarked building at the end of Northumberland Street, down from the fire station."

Annoyed, Chief Inspector Monk could not be bothered how he knew, he confirmed that the retired Colonel was correct.

"Good evening *mister* Boeck." *He* didn't deserve to be associated with the Officer Corps of The British Army.

"Thank you *Chief Inspector*, I look forward to seeing you tomorrow. Oh yes, a *nearby* cup of chamomile tea will get rid of your headache. Goodnight." With that, Simon hung up.

Neil stared at the very strong cheap coffee Sue'd just brought in.

Talking through the opened door, "Sue could you go along to the canteen? D'you think they have chamomile tea?"

Sue smiled, "no need, I have some in my drawer sir. I'll get it right away. Will there be anything else?"

Studying a performance chart stuck to the white board on the otherside of his conference desk, he said no that would be all.

That night Neil left early than he'd expected, his head now clear. He bathed the boys and far from his wife's using a headache as the oldest excuse, had made love for the first time that month.

The following morning, Chief Inspector Monk sat at his desk going over crime scene notes from the previous night's rape which had taken place on the outskirts of Byker, east of the city.

Outside, in his waiting room, Simon was having a very pleasant chat with a trim, tall, young, clearly bright DC, her dark hair in a glossy bob.

Having shaken hands with her on arrival at the outer office, Simon already knew a lot more about DC Parish than the detective did about him. Sue studied the smartly attired man sat opposite her. Sitting noticeably upright yet the man seemed somehow relaxed and totally at ease with his surroundings? After the few questions when they had spoken the previous evening Sue had already done her homework. Simon and his wife had been at dinner in Durham late into the night when the attack had taken place. Jolted out of her thoughts, "d'you not find working on such cases tires you?" asked the visitor.

DC Parish, knew better than to discuss her job. She had also looked up Colonel Boeck's file. Although he had no criminal charges against his name he was definitely a very close friend of the local criminal fraternity. Added to which he'd been photographed with one of the most notorious criminals in the whole of Asia.

"I'd rather not say," changing the subject, "did you have a pleasant drive here this morning? The traffic on the bridge can be a bugger at this time in the morning can't it?"

Simon smiled, realising her professional nature, "yes I did and no I went the back way across the Scotswood Bridge instead."

Regardless of the file, she instinctively liked the man and anyway he was damn good looking, if not a little old for her. The desk buzzer sounded indicating that he should go in, "excuse me, Colonel Boeck."

DC Parish opened the door for Simon as he went through.

The Chief Inspector didn't come round from behind his desk. A definite snub DC Parish thought as she closed the door on the way out. As she left, Sue had a tiny smile on her lips, he'd shaken her hand with both of his. Must be a foreign thing she'd thought? Moments later back at her desk Sue sipped Lapsung tea, thinking about the Chief Inspector's guests' eyes.

Simon, noting the slight, stepped forward to the side of the desk and shook Neil's hand in his usual manner.

Offering, actually, indifferently waving Simon to a seat the Chief Inspector spoke, "listen *mister* Boeck, we both know there is little love lost between us, so lets get on with this. I am extremely busy, as you can see." As he spoke Neil motioned his hand over piles of case files.

Simon looked straight into Neil's eyes, "nothing of the kind, I hardly know you Chief Inspector. Regardless, I think I can be of help in the Chang case. You were obviously a little surprised I knew as much as I did. Well it's because I'm psychic."

Not giving Neil time to speak, Simon continued, "I also know it was a frenzied attack and your psychologist has said that he, for you know it was a male, may be psychotic. The woman was also heavily drugged and had cuts to her head, lower breasts and extensively round the groin area.

Actually, Simon was only using about five percent physic ability. He knew the Chief Inspector wouldn't know Simon had been given a detailed brief by Doctor Winter the previous day.

Visibly shaken Neil stared, "now look here, I don't know how you know all that but I can tell you I'm not in the business of employing witch doctors on my cases." Immediately he had said it, Neil knew it was a stupid thing to say.

Simon noting his embarrassment, "Chief Inspector, yes I have been to Africa many times and yes I have met witch doctors as you call them. Actually some probably prefer shaman. Regardless, if I was to tell you that as yet you have no idea where to start to look for the weapon. I can definitely help you there. All I need to do is to visit the incident site and I am confident of results."

After a deep breath Neil said, "*mister* Boeck, surely you don't expect me to allow you to the scene of a serious crime just because you tell me your ouija board can help me!" He was far too busy for this.

Having discussed the visit in one of the special rooms in The Hacienda Grande early that morning, Simon had expected as much, "Chief Inspector if I have to *perform* then." With that Simon closed his eyes, ignoring Neil's sneer. Five seconds later, "your wife has a sore shoulder from when she fell off her horse last Tuesday. You are worried about your youngest boy. It looks like he may need glasses. I'd say yellow would be better in the kitchen don't you? Your neck hurts on the left. However your most pressing concern is your next medical. Will they find the rheumatism in your hand? It's your left by the way and they won't." It was Simon's turn to sigh, he didn't like putting on a show.

Chief Inspector Monk was rarely shocked. His analytical, precise mind failing to take on board that a man sat three feet away had just told him things which not even PC Parish, let alone his wife, knew.

"How in God's name, did you do that?"

Answering him, "Chief Inspector there is a lot which you don't know about me. Let's just say, I can and practice certainly helps and finally I do it in my own name." With a grin, "now do you think I could visit the site?"

The Chief Inspector knew he would be the laughing stock of the team allowing ex military weirdo's onto a crime scene. Yet there was something about the bloke. Immaculately dressed, he wore black Loake brogues, shiny but not military bulled.* Tie, smart and tight under his collar. Chief Inspector admired smartness. The man's smile was infectious and by God he could do *it*, whatever the hell that was.

"Listen *Colonel*."

Simon noted his being addressed formally, interrupted, "Simon, please."

"Mister or Colonel your choice?" The Chief Inspector couldn't bring himself to be that familiar.

" Mister Boeck will do just fine," replied Simon, he understood.

"Anyway, if you tell a living soul I'll have you stopped by every traffic cop from here to Berwick, d'you hear."

Simon heard and understood perfectly, "Chief Inspector, if you'd rather, I could go with one of your team. That way they won't connect you with me. I could go as some sort of government specialist checking up on procedures."

The Chief Inspector was more than a little unnerved now. How the hell did Boeck read his bloody mind. Trying to pretend he hadn't been thinking the very same thing ten seconds earlier, "yes that's not a bad idea. Actually you can take DC Parish with you. She needs to get out of the office and experience cases first hand. Now listen if..."

Simon interjected, "Chief Inspector, DC Parish will not hear a word of our conversation. I can assure you she won't even mention it to her fat cat."

As Colonel Boeck left DC Parish thought the departure was considerably more amicable than the two men's greeting. The Chief Inspector opened the door for mister Boeck before saying good morning and Simon replying, "until next time chief inspector." Apparently now all very civil.

As Mr Boeck left, DC Parish was called into The Saints office, "now listen Sue," he used her Christian name for only the second time that day, " I want you to do something for me but I really do need you to keep quiet about it."

A slight glow on his forehead, he wasn't used to doing things this unconventionally. Handing DC Parish a piece of paper, "that's Colonel Boeck's mobile number. I want you to call him and arrange to take him down to the Chang crime scene. Phone ahead and say he is a Metropolitan civie who is up here looking over our procedures. He is to be afforded every access. That said I want a full back brief when you return." Finally in a tone indicating the end of their one way conversation, "go, get on with it then."

As Sue started to leave with the piece paper in her long fingers. The Chief Inspector couldn't help himself, and asked if she had a cat and if so was it OK?

"Yes sir, I do actually and she's fine. Any reason?"

---

* Bulled refers to process of extremely highly polishing military footwear. Normally military boots or shoes are only bulled for parades.

"No, just wondered," replied a now thoroughly bewildered Chief Inspector.

Moments later back at her desk, PC Parish studied the number and wondered, did they bug squad members flats? No one from the team had ever been in her flat, let alone knew she had an overweight fluffy cat.

# CHAPTER 13

## Stone Tapes

It was only twenty minutes since he'd been buzzed out of the station that Simon settled down to a quality pint of OB bitter in the Market Tavern. Since officially retiring, he had been pretty busy with the agency, who part time employed him to do lectures. He'd also just started working in an advisory capacity for a new fitness company called *Fitness Breakthrough*. These two, combined with his Army pension and Lynda's part time job meant that they lived very well thank you.

His financial stability producing a broad handsome grin. If you added the fact that he'd never paid for a meal in any Newcastle restaurant for five years, plus both his and Lynda's cars were loan vehicles from a very grateful 'friend'. Add to the mix, the flat which they rented out, money was not really a concern. Actually it never had been, Sasha had told him years ago, 'remember Simon, you will never be rich in the Army but you will never be poor'.

Scanning the first edition of the Evening Chronicle, his mobile rang. Glaring, he hated the necessary things. Strange *his senses* were rarely able to determine who was on the other end of the line, "hello, Simon Boeck speaking."

"*Colonel Boeck*, it's Detective Constable Sue Parish. Chief Inspector Monk told me to phone you to arrange a meeting. He wants me to take you to the Chang crime scene." DC Parish continued, "*colonel*, may I call you colonel?"

Simon interrupted, "I'd far rather, Simon. It's my name and anyway I'm only a retired *Lieutenant* Colonel."

"*Simon*, could I meet you outside the police station, somewhere?" Having agreed a meeting place moments later, replacing the cheap receiver Sue studied her notes. *Simon's* alibi checked out as one of the other dinner guests, a very respected Professor Tower, had said he'd been with him all night. Also, the Head of Geography would be happy to make a formal statement to the effect that he and his wife had been with Simon until at least two in the morning. He'd added that Simon wouldn't have been in any fit state to even find his car keys, let along drive all the way to Newcastle. It had obviously been a very liquid dinner party!

With these thoughts a short while later Sue Parish was again shaking hands with Simon. This time, in the heart of city, seated on a bench overlooking the large grassy Fenwick Square. Nearby a few black headed gulls were noisily squabbling over a discarded sandwich.

"It is good to see you again Detective Constable Parish."

Sue immediately realising the inequality of the introduction waved a hand, "please call me Sue." Pausing, "that said when we are amongst the team if you wouldn't mind calling me DC....." Simon stopped her, he understood exactly what she meant, nodded.

During the momentary pause they watched as a sparrow stole away a crust from the fighting gulls. Sue continued, "Chief Inspector Monk has instructed me to assist you however I can. He told me that you are to visit the Chang crime scene. He did say that I was to be conservative with the truth about who you really are. So if anyone asks, just refer them directly to the Chief Inspector. That'll do the trick, trust me." Simon did.

They talked for a few more minutes before strolling in the hazy, smoggy sun, back towards the main police station.

Simon then waited whilst Sue fetched a squad car. Once she had picked him up, they set off down past the old castle towards the river. Under the bridge they then travelled past The Atlantic Pub. A few moments later up a steep road leading away from the river, where Sue parked next to one of the forensic teams vehicles.

Moving over and under the police tape, Sue went ahead.

DC Tom Flemming saw DC Parish come towards the entrance where the incident tent had been erected. Not recognising who she was talking to Tom, put his notes down and headed them off, "so the *saints'* let you out for good behaviour has he Sue?"

Simon stopping just behind the striking DC as she addressed her colleague,"Tom, from our conversation earlier, this gentleman is here at the request of The *Chief Inspector*." She'd never particularly liked her boss being belittled behind his back, "the Chief wants you to show him round. He said you're to answer any questions," looking over her shoulder, "Simon may have."

Tom immediately noted the absence of a surname. Something familiar about the chap though. Well if that was the way the Saint wanted it, then fine. Anything to relieve the boredom of holding the fort for the inspector, Neil's deputy, whilst he was forty miles away dealing with the latest domestic murder.

"Alright then *Simon*," Tom paused for what could have been mistaken as a theatrically deep breath, "in a nut shell. Girl gets drugged, dragged over here, through there and is brutally assaulted. If a passer by hadn't followed his dog into the warehouse and stumbled across her, she'd be dead for sure."

Simon, interrupted the prose, "how long do you think she was in there for, before being found?"

"From what we can tell, she was probably assaulted late Friday night. It's a bloody miracle she survived so long."

Stepping towards the rusty old fence, Tom told one of the DC's nearby to get some forensic suits, plus boots.

Once Simon, Sue and Tom were kitted out like babies in enormous jump suits they followed the taped off route into the warehouse. Sue's nose turned up at the disgusting, dank smell as they left the suns rays for the gloom within.

Inside it was still very busy as a number of uniformed officers were painstakingly going over every inch of the place. The small group moved over to the old office. As they did Tom gave the two visitors a detailed description of how the woman was found. Luckily, it was an ex copper called Olly Jones, who got to her first. His actions had made a big difference and probably saved the girl's life. They had photos and the chap had even showed them where the girls shoe was hidden, down in amongst the concrete.

Simon asked, "can I go in please and have a look around on my own for a while?"

"Be my guest," replied Tom. Finishing with, "but please don't move anything. They haven't finished the detailed search yet."

As Simon went forward, Tom and Sue started to talk shop.

I felt the anger and pain as soon as I walked into the room. The energy frequencies bouncing out of the walls. Feelings of anguish and pain, so much rage mixed with confusion.

I'd discussed the visit in the Hacienda Grande that morning, receiving confusing advice, a rare occurrence. My friends were a little vague and made the point over and over that I should move with care, dark shadows remaining.

It was very quiet in the room. No longer able to hear the police officers talking behind me. Breathing deeply as I moved round to the table instinctively touching the corner.

Tuning in, in an instant, I could feel pain and fear. It was Penny's pain. She was so very disorientated, yet not drunk? She had banged her head as she fell. He had picked her up, beer on his breath, only to drop her.

Eyes closed, I scanned the room. Yes, over there. I moved to the wall, placing my left palm on the cold, damp, clammy wall.

Like a tape replaying, I could see his dark almost black trousers, ankle boots, no not a denim but a lightweight, yet dark coat. Hair short, dark.

Sniffing, as if tasting a flat beer, I could smell him. His power. Yet there was something else, either he was not alone or somehow believed he worked with others?

He stood tall, vaguely talking to himself right next to me as if the stone bricks were projecting a fuzzy videotape of events from the previous Friday night.

It flashed in the light, a blade, no a retractable blade, a Stanley knife. That was the weapon.

My extrasensory fine tuning drawing me very close now. So close I felt the chill, heard the movement and sensed someone. Lotte somehow present. I understood, as it was her who'd made sure Penny was found and now wanted me to follow her scent.

The attacker wore a uniform to work. The images rapid, bombarding my mind. The man was not a local. No, he came from the hills or worked in the hills and was tough, yet afraid?

Bob, Rob, no Robert, I had his name.

He felt power when he attacked almost as if protected?

Focusing still further, could he see as I, sense as I, or even see things that normal people couldn't? He hadn't any natural psychic talent, no ability to tune into other realms, yet was being invaded by others. They were the evil, he, their tool.

"Sir, please you mustn't touch the walls."

In an instant I was back standing in gloom. Looking over, a young DC was frowning at me. Not his fault, I withdrew, the knowledge forever stored. I never forgot stuff like this and could, as if by some hypnotic memory trick, remember every detail whenever and in the blink of an eye.

By the entrance Tom and Sue stood trying to catch the clean air which was wafting into the building. They saw Simon walk towards them, as if like some human blood hound, sniffing the atmosphere.

Addressing DC Flemming, "thanks." Turning to Sue, "can we walk and talk?"

Sue thanked Tom, Simon shook his hand, frowned and then followed Sue.

Simon stopped by a big pile of concrete rubble. Kneeling, "you found her shoe here didn't you?"

"Sorry Simon don't know. It'll only take a minute to find out if you like. Is it important? "

Simon drifting off, "not sure, but yes please."

---

He had dragged her over the rubble. Seeing someone up the road, in the dark. His fist was not his own, yet was? My thoughts slightly clouded. He wanted sex but couldn't, so *they* had helped. Who the hell were *they*?

*They* somehow knew about me. What, was there a connection between the crime and me?

Breathing hard, I smelt Chanel perfume.

---

Sue wandered back, "how the hell did you know that? DC Flemming says that apart from the squad and the man who found her, no ones knows about that."

"It was blue wasn't it? Not waiting for an answer, Simon walked out back onto the road. He pointed towards the river, "can we walk down here for while?"

"Sure." Sue said frowning, yet followed almost dutifully. They reached the end of the road and turned right. Simon then went over to the rail and looked down into the murky, fast flowing river, debris drifting past.

"Have you checked in there?"

Sue leaning over, disgusted as a used sanitary towel crossed her vision, "the Inspector decided that it would be way too expensive and anyway where would we start? It's at least one hundred feet across and tidal. Anything thrown in there, won't be there now."

"It is," as he spoke Simon smelled Lotte's beautiful scent waft past.

"Get the diver to go straight down," he pointed, "about here, no exactly fifteen feet out, you will find the *blade*.

Sue looked down into the gurgling swirling river, the odd gull bobbing amongst the rubbish.

"Simon, that's not my call, but I will report back to The Chief Inspector." With that Sue produced a small black indelible pen from her bag and marked the thick four-foot high railing.

They headed back to the car. As they climbed in, Simon spoke, "Sue make notes, this may be useful." Perplexed, yet dutifully, Sue produced her police note book, pen poised.

As if stuck on *play*, Simon, eyes closed, blurted out, "his name is Bob or Steven, he's not local, I think but am not certain that he was alone. He had dark clothes on and attacked with a Stanley blade. He wears a uniform and is big, tough and vicious. He is cowardly yet dangerous and will attack again. He has also attacked before."

The outburst almost too fast for Sue to jot down.

Her hand almost aching, Sue looked up from her notebook, "Simon what's this all about. First you tell me to look in the river, now you tell me *his* name. It's as if your psychic or something?"

Inwardly smiling Simon replied, "well.....no, sort of. I can however tell you things which will help with your investigation."

"OK then, can we go now please?" Sue started the engine, "where can I drop you?"

Five minutes later, as the squad car swung off the central bypass, Sue was still asking questions, "but Simon, no one will believe you, least of all the Chief."

"He will, trust me, he will."

Simon pointed, "here will do fine. Thanks for your help Sue." As Simon climbed out of the car, shutting the Rover's door, he leant back in, "Sue, your cat needs to go on a diet."

The traffic was far too busy for Sue to linger. As a result she quickly pulled away back into the lunch time throng, her elegant face lined by a light frown.

# CHAPTER 14

## *Deadly Tentacles*

Simon sat relaxed in one of Danny's deep welcoming, dark red leather chairs, the office overlooking the River Tyne. Nestling just as comfortably, in amongst solicitors and accountants, the office blended in perfectly, anonymous.

Simon grinned, if Yates and Swithertons, Chartered Solicitors knew that the suite of offices next to theirs was occupied, not by Northern Oriental Importers Limited but rather, the headquarters for one of the countries biggest money laundering operations, they'd have filed a law suit of their own. As it was, everyone in the beautiful six storey Victorian building kept themselves to themselves; harmony prevailing.

Danny's private secretary smiled as she placed the green tea on the ornate occasional table next to Simon.

"Thank you Jenny. No phone calls for a while please," it was Danny.

"Of course Sir. Mr Boeck it's so good to see you again," his secretary addressing her bosses guest.

"The pleasures all mine," Simon smiled back at the middle aged lady who could, if she had wanted, put Danny and most of his 'associates' behind bars for many, many years. Danny knew that would never happen. Jenny was extremely well paid and deep down knew that no *safe house* on the planet would be able to live up to its name.

She closed the door on the way out.

"Well then?" Danny was understandably impatient for news about the investigation, "what have they found out? That Chief Inspector is meant to be the best." As he spoke a smile rippled over Danny's face as he winked at Simon, who laughed out loud.

Simon replied, " well he ain't that good, he never caught us!"

"No he didn't but it was close and anyway it was years ago and that case will be forever left under 'unsolved' murders."

Opening a leather folder on his lap, Danny continued, "I have found out that they don't have any leads and basically, although the forensic team and the DNA is providing excellent information, without anyone to attach it to, they're pissing in the wind." Danny's long time informant had left the clip of notes in a lunchtime Chinese takeaway on Benwell Road earlier that day.

Having listened carefully Simon replied, "actually your informant didn't have the results of my visit this afternoon did *she*?"

"I never said it was a *she*," replied a puzzled Danny.

"No you didn't."

"You and your *intuition*," shaking his head as he replied.

"The man who attacked your daughter is bloody evil. He's big and I think he may be either a guard or possibly military as he wears a uniform and has done it before. He meant for Penny to die."

Simon noticed Danny grimace but went on, "thank God some chap called Olly Jones found her when he did."

Danny jotted down the name. In time he'd reward his daughters saviour.

Simon went on, " I have given them one of my own leads which when they have it, so long as I can get to touch the weapon, I'm certain I'll be able to tell you, and them, a hell of a lot more."

Registering Danny's confusion. " I told the young DC where they should look. When they do, they will find the weapon used on Penny."

"How come you're so sure?" Danny realising the stupidity of his comment, "sorry, daft of me. If your sure then I'll wait until my informant contacts me."

"No need Danny, the police will call me. I will get to see the weapon in the next day or so."

"But Simon, even with all your powers, surely you can't track down an unknown person from the millions it could be."

"All I have to do it find this *thing* of a man, convince Monk to interview him and do some forensic checks and they and you will have your man."

"Hold on a second," the file dropping from Danny's knee as he leant forward towards Simon seated four feet away, "you saw what he did to Penny. Even if they convict him he won't get life. He'll be out walking the streets in less than five years. That my friend is not damn well good enough."

"*That my friend* is justice," Simon's repost.

"Not my kind of fucking justice. Simon if you won't kill him I will get others who will."

"Danny, you know that murder is murder and I can not, nor will not bring myself to kill. Penny is going to get better, so let justice take its course."

"Simon my dear friend, what if you find and identify him and he should be the casualty of a terrible," pausing, "fatal accident?"

Simon realised that no matter what he said Danny would not be satisfied with revenge ending in a court room. So knowing better than to fight an unwinable battle, he sighed, "I can not be any part of your business, you know that. I will tell you everything I tell Monk. After that I don't want to know."

Danny also realised he would never be able to change Simon into a cold killer. However with a name he had ways of getting to anyone.

Both men sat in silence. The only noise coming from Simon's delicate china cup setting down upon its equally elegant translucent saucer.

Simon studied the handsome room. It had wonderful oak panels. There were no pictures apart from, on his desk, Danny had one of his wife and daughter. It had a lovely old office mustiness about it. Simon normally enjoyed being there, this time however he had a resigned sad look to his normally handsome features.

"Danny I don't like what your planning on doing. That said I know there's no point trying to change your mind so I won't. Please be careful. Monk probably won't make the same mistakes twice." A rye smile returned to his face.

"I know don't worry. No one will find out. I will get outsiders in. No one will be able to connect you with any of this, I give you my promise on that." That was good enough for Simon.

"Danny, I'm going to head over to the hospital. Are you coming?"

"No I have a few things I need to do here. When you see Linn tell her I'll be over by seven tonight."

"OK my friend. I'm glad they can't bug your office otherwise we'd both be in Durham Gaol for a long stretch, with no chance of parole or a Chinese takeaway in sight."

Laughing, both men rose. Danny accustomed to the peck on both cheeks, embraced his friend, before opening the door for him.

Outside, Jenny who was finishing off a letter relating to the latest shipment of oriental artwork from Hong Kong, looked up, "Mr Boeck going so soon?"

Simon leant over and pecked two kisses on her blushing cheeks, "now Jenny I'm sure you have lots of work for Mr Chang to be getting on with."

"You take care Mr Boeck, see you soon?"

"You will I am certain, cheerio to you."

With that he stepped smartly out of the outer office door into the communal corridor. Simon was on route to the hospital in less than two minutes.

Back inside Danny's office, the adjoining door opened, "Jenny will you get my uncle on the phone." Jenny knew Mr Chang didn't have an uncle, but his wife did.

"Uncle, I promised I would keep you up to date. Yes, Penny is recovering much faster than the doctors could have hoped for."

A momentarily sleepy Mr Bo replied, "good, that is good. Your friend and mine helped no?"

"Uncle, without Simon, Penny would surely have died. He brought her back."

Again, the reply calm and concise, "good, good. Will she recover completely?" Mr Bo had listened appalled when Danny had detailed the injuries Penny had received to her groin area.

"Uncle, they say it is still too early to tell. They have said that she will be able to have children but not for at least two years. The great news is that the cuts to her breasts won't be noticeable once the plastic surgeon has finished. The gashes to her head will be hidden almost totally when her hair grows back. She only has a gash above her left eye, again the surgeon believes that this too will, in time, only be a very light line."

Pausing for breath and to allow his uncle to reply. Again the same response, "good, very good. You should thank those that have helped. I will reward Simon myself."

Danny interrupted his *relative*, "uncle you know Simon won't take anything by way of payment. He always says the greatest reward is seeing smiling faces."

Mr Bo's reply direct and commanding, "not good enough. The man who saved Penny will be rewarded. Otherwise I loose face."

Danny, understood but knew he was right. In a flash he came up with the solution, "uncle, he has never taken Lynda his wife, to Hong Kong. You could always give *her* a gift?"

The positive changed, "yes, yes, this is wise advice. In time I will remember your words. Now isn't the time though," Danny noted the arrival of anger in his uncle's voice, "we must speak of revenge."

"The devil who did this will pay with his blood as my beautiful Penny paid with hers.

I will not accept anything less."

Danny who'd known this would be his uncles response had thought of how to broach the subject.

For the next few minutes Mr Bo listened as Danny explained about Simon's silly high British morals about how he wouldn't budge and certainly would never commit cold blooded murder. Penny was alive and would recover, so the attacker would be found and justice would be done in court.

Mr Bo exploded, "no, no that will not do. He is a great man but understands so little about our ways. He is naive yet wise, a strange contradiction. You make him understand."

There had then been a unpleasant bout of words as Danny finally convinced his uncle that Simon would not change, not for money no matter how much. Reluctantly Mr Bo calmed down.

There was a long silence from across the continents. Finally Mr Bo took control, "you say Simon will find this thing of a man who attacked Penny?"

"Uncle if there is one man on the planet who could find him, it's Simon Boeck."

"Excellent." Danny could almost feel the invisible tentacles uncoiling as Mr Bo devised his plan, "Danny my boy, we both know that you are the legitimate end of my business. This way my beloved Lin lives well and safe from my enemies. I do not think it was one of them. They do not know of your lives in the round eyes world."

Pausing for what Danny thought was a drink, Mr Bo went on, "I will find those that can and will do this business. I will send *Force Lightening*. They are loyal and can speak perfect English. Yes, yes they will be the ones. I will tell them what I need. You should not tell Simon of these things as we mustn't cloud his vision of finding the thing. Once we know who and where, my anger will be unleashed.

"Uncle, I understand, Simon will know nothing of your plans, he will tell me the name, he gave his word. The creature who did this will never reach a court house. He will however wish he did because his death will be slow and so painful he will cry for the end to come quickly. It won't."

Returning to his opening words, "good, that is very good, stay safe my boy and give my darling girls kisses from their uncle." With that the phone went dead as Mr Bo had equally pressing matters of a more professional nature to deal with. Mr Patton had just handed power back to Beijing.

Danny, sat back in his creaking Victorian leather chair thinking. He'd heard of The lightening twins but only snatched words and rumours when he had visited Hong Kong. Then again he was so out of that sort of business. One thing certain, the two men his uncle sent would ensure justice done.

# CHAPTER 15

## *Beaming Opportunity*

"So you're telling me that all this detail about who attacked the poor woman just came out in a single blurt. Well that's crap and anyway no one will ever believe me if I put out a identikit of a man, suggested by a known *criminal*."

Chief Inspector Monk had listened intently as DC Parish debriefed him on her visit with Colonel Boeck to the crime scene.

Sue took mild offence, "sir he doesn't have a criminal record. Just because he knows Mr Chang doesn't make him a criminal, now does it?"

"So he doesn't have a criminal record and his alibi checks out. Well I don't care, I remember what happened a few years ago. Back then he was somehow involved in some murders I just couldn't fit him up with them. He and that hood Chang were both guilty as sin and as for that *lurch* of a creature from the coast. The whole lot of them were caught up in it"

DC Parish raised a defensive arm. In reply the Saint refocussing said, "alright you win. He's not a criminal, he's never been convicted. His day will come though, trust me."

Opening the case file on his desk, the Chief Inspector continued, "Sue, I've decided you need to get some operational experience and I think this is the perfect case. As you know Sergeant Ridge is away on his forensic course for five months."

Sue nodded.

"As such I'm a sergeant down. For the duration of this case, *your* case, I'm making you up to sergeant."

Noting *sergeant* Parish's instant beaming smile, "now listen, don't get ahead of yourself. At anytime you'll find yourself back a DC, so don't screw up."

"Sir, thank you. I promise I won't let you down."

"You'd better not otherwise your probationary report won't look to good now will it?"

Looking puzzled, the new sergeant remarked, "sir what about your desk officer. I can't do both jobs can I?"

"Now your thinking like a sergeant. Don't worry about that. I have a budget for emergency civilian cover. A Miss Palmer starts this afternoon. You'll need to brief her up on procedures before you can get on with the Chang case. You can take Sergeant Ridges' desk. You know the new DC who was meant to start in the New Year?" Receiving a positive nod, "well he is being posted in so you will have someone to do all the dirty jobs." Sue smiled, "what, make the Chamomile tea like I do?"

Neil Monk smiled for the first time that day, "yes make the tea like you *did*."

After studying the file for a few seconds the Chief Inspector continued, "how you run the case is now up to you. I want a verbal brief each day at nine sharp. I'll also need a formal report two times a week." Sergeant Parish knew the drill, she'd put together enough case briefs from the other sergeants to know exactly how to compile them.

Coming from behind his desk, Chief Inspector Monk shook Sergeant Parish's hand for only the second time, "congratulations Sue, do a good job on this and it won't be *probationary* for long. Now get on and catch the bastard before he does it again."

Still beaming, Sue nodded, "sir, I have a few ideas and intend to study everything on the case by tomorrow."

"Well then," with that the Chief Inspector opened the report on another rape from the previous night.

Withdrawing, still smiling Sue closed the door.

Sue had just sat down in her, soon to be, old chair when she recognised the usual bark from her boss. Reopening the connecting door, "yes sir, you *called*."

Neil looked up from the disturbing case, "one final thing, I have authorised a diving team to be on call for you at the site, eight tomorrow morning, use them."

"Sir?" Sue paused, then understood, "Oh sorry I see now what you mean. D'you think Colonel Boeck's right?"

"He's either right, stupid, crazy or committed the damn crime himself, now go."

The next morning at seven fifty, Detective Sergeant Parish was busy briefing the diving team leader.

"Yes I want you to go out, here." She and the dive team leader were standing next to her marked railing.

Pointing, "I want you to search in a ten feet span and go only twenty feet out. You're looking for a knife or blade of some description."

The experienced dive leader, Sergeant John Wagstaff, interrupted her, "listen Sue, you're telling me that you want me and the guys to do a detailed search in a tiny sector like that. Surely you know that the mud and filth combined with the powerful tide will have swept anything either deep into the mud or more likely upwards of fifty feet in any direction."

"Sue was ready for this, "John, you know this is my chance to impress the boss. He's the one who gave the order for you to be here in the first place right, so just get the guys out there, please."

Marginally irritated, yet resigned John nodded, "alright your call Sue but don't get upset when all we find is a tyre and sewage pipes."

Shortly the dive team were ready with two bulky search divers and a couple of safety officers bobbing about in the cramped inflatable tied to the vertical steps dropping down to the river. Each member wore a dry suit for warmth.

Diving like this was/is fraught with dangers. The visibility was, at best, terrible with a potentially lethal current. A diver could get snagged on almost anything down there in the murkiness. There was almost certainly any number of supermarket trolleys, bikes and other obstacles waiting, timelessly, to *foul* a diver and possibly endanger their lives.

John had briefed them as Sue requested. The two actual divers looked pissed off that they were going down to obviously find nothing of any interest. Also, although it was supposedly still summer the water was bloody freezing at the bottom, some twenty five odd feet down in the shadowy gloom. If you added the fact that they could catch numerous skin or chest infections from the filthy water, all in all they were two very unhappy bunnies.

Twelve minutes later there were plenty of happy bunnies in and out of the water.

The first of the divers had been tasked to lay out bright fluorescent markers so that they could commence the grid square search, normal in such poor visibility. Slowly as he had moved out on the marker cord, his powerful underwater lamp easily caught the glint at exactly fifteen feet. With difficulty, in the strong rip current, he marked the spot then placed the item in a plastic divers evidence bag. Flippering to the surface he resembled some medieval character, raising Excalibur. He was experienced enough to realise that the item had only been thrown in a day or two earlier, there was no rusting and anyway the thing was obviously brand new.

He passed it to the safety diver perched in the inflatable as it rocked about some ten feet below where Sue and John were standing. He in turn climbed onto the bottom step. Stretching a few rungs up he handed it to the team leader who drained the water and carefully with thin plastic gloves on, lifted out a dripping, brand new Stanley Knife. It's dull metal shone in the crisp early morning sun.

Sue's beam now almost a permanent fixture on her face, "see, I told you so. That's it, *he* even said it was a *blade*. You can't get more of a blade than a Stanley Knife now can you?"

Thoroughly impressed, John agreed, "no, I suppose not. How the hell do'you know it was at that exact spot."

Sue interrupted him as she noticing the safety cord being rewound. Almost rhetorically, "it was at exactly fifteen feet wasn't it?"

"Yes according to the measure," John said as he leant over the rail and looked down into the inflatable dinghy. "So we better get on with the rest of the search then."

Watching the swirling whirlpools drifting slowly down towards the sea, Sue vacantly said, "no don't bother, that's it. That's exactly where and what *he* said it would be."

"*Who* said?" interrupted a slightly bemused John.

"Oh never mind. Lets just say an informer impressed the hell out of the Chief, even if he doesn't care for this particular informer."

"Don't *care* for any of the worms myself," replied John. "Filthy stinking *things* the lot of them. Just like that down there" John nodded down toward the diver who was desperately trying to remove a used condom from his air valve.

Averting her eyes Sue replied, "not this informer. Trust me not this one."

The next morning Sergeant Parish sat in her glass cubicle. She had been very busy, since dropping off the Stanley Knife at the forensic lab, having visited Penny Chang in hospital. After nearly an hour with her taking notes, she'd' then gone over to Gosforth, on the other side of town where she'd interviewed both Miss Chang's friends. Each girl had been extremely upset having visited Penny and seen first hand the obvious injuries hidden behind the bandages. Both were still trying to come to terms with what had happened to themselves and more importantly their friend

That same morning, earlier in the hospital, "Penny there's a police women who would like to talk to you. Do you feel up to it? If you don't that's fine, she can come back later." The ward sister didn't really like so many visitors especially outside official visiting hours. Begrudgingly she knew this was different.

Penny looked up, her head still bandaged heavily, iodine yellow clearly visible where the surgeon had delicately stitched her. Her arms now free from drips, did however hurt a lot where the bruising had welled up. When she'd been admitted, the last thing they were worried about was if there would be any bruising to the woman's arms and wrists whilst hurriedly inserting drips.

She lay under a loose blanket. There was a noticeable bump lower down where the bandaging was covering her pubic area.

"That's OK thanks. I'd rather talk to anyone than listen to Terry Wogan on the radio."

"Fine, but if she tires you too much, just look over and I will get her out of here in a jiffy."

Penny attempted a light smile, her forehead pulling against the stiches.

"Miss Chang, my name's Detective Constable, sorry, Detective *Sergeant* Sue Parish." Sue still not used to her recent promotion, "I have been put in charge of the case and I'd like to ask you some questions, would that be alright?"

Penny studied the tall, slim woman who seemed just as unsettled. Without thinking she asked,

"Are you nervous?"

Sue went crimson around the neck and just behind her ear. The marks only appearing when either embarrassed or making love.

"Well not nervous, its just that I've recently been promoted and catching the man who did this to you is probably as important to you as it is to me." Penny weakly smiled, "well that's good isn't it? We both want the same thing."

Sue noticed the appearance of a watery glassiness swim over Penny's eyes, "don't worry, if at any time you want to stop, it's fine. I would however like to ask you about what happened. It's really important to ask such questions, no matter how hard they may be, as soon as possible before you forget."

Penny attempted a frown as she said, "trust me it will be a long time until I forget, if ever."

At that she started to sob quietly.

Sue immediately offered Penny her pretty little floral hanky which had been tactfully positioned up her blouse sleeve.

"Thanks. Sorry but it was all so horrid. What's worse is that I can't remember bits. Anyway it was probably my own fault. If I hadn't had so much to drink it may never..."

"Stop right there." Sue leant forward looking intensely into Penny rubbed red eyes, "now listen Penny, I can call you Penny?" without waiting for a response, "you did nothing wrong. Never ever think this was your fault because it wasn't. You were drugged and attacked by an evil person who I intend to catch. I do need your help though, so once and for all non of this is your fault."

Penny a little startled by the purposeful direct way Sue had spoken *at* her nodded slowly, the stitches pulling behind her left ear.

"Good, would you like some water." Sue sat back in her chair.

"No thanks and you're right, I know you're right but you understand don't you that it's hard for me to come to terms with," her voice almost a question, "he did some horrid things to me?"

Sue did. The nurse having outlined her injuries and also the case file had gone into probably information detail overload, with pictures showing paramedics swarming over the naked girl's body.

"Well Penny, could we go all the way back to early on Friday night when you met up with," studying her open, poised note book before adding, "Susie and Fay."

Breathing deeply in an attempt to extract the mental detail, Penny had then outlined the evening with her two best friends. They had had Italian. She recalled, her friends laughing as she'd insisted not to go to one of her dad's restaurants as she'd had enough Chinese for a life time.

Penny had no idea that *The Naples Mount*, was in fact one of a number of Italian, Indian and Mexican restaurants owned by her father.

They had then got a taxi down towards the river. As it wasn't late they'd decided to go into *The Atlantic* for some drinks before probably going onto a proper night club, possibly The Boat, to meet boys and dance.

"We were stood by one of the pillars in the pub when some bloke came over."

Sue interrupted, "this is important, try very hard to remember as much detail about him as you can, no matter how insignificant you may think it."

Sue's hand only getting a momentary rest from semi dictation.

"Well, he was tall with short dark almost black hair and said his name was *Roots*. It was dark in there with all the flashing lights and the smoke machine at full belt. He said he was from the coast and sounded kind of Scottish. He had a strange accent really, not sure but somehow it didn't seem *right*?"

"What do you mean exactly by '*right*'?" Sue's question.

Penny closed her eyes as if trying to gain clarity of thought from the darkness continued, "not sure, just that in amongst all the noise it was somehow as if he was putting it on, yes putting it on."

Without pausing, Penny went on, "he spoke to Susie first I think. We bought him a drink I do remember that, he had lager, a pint. Well after that he went and bought Fay and I a drink as Susie was already a bit squiffy. After that it all started to go blurry."

Seeing her obvious discomfort, Sue spoke, "Penny we can stop if you want and I'll come back later."

Penny looked at Sue, "no I want to get this over and anyway I probably need to get it out of my system."

Sue knew that was exactly what the psychologist would say, during the numerous forthcoming sessions in the weeks and months to follow. It was going to be a long road to recovery, the wounds as deep inside, as those requiring stitches.

"Well if you feel up to it. Can you remember anything else about what happened?"

Penny signed a sigh of resignation. She knew she would have to talk about it sooner or later,

"Oh it was so horrid. I remember walking along near the river. I wasn't walking really, as it seemed as if I was floating. He was holding me up and I can remember he stank of sweat and beer." With that, as if the memories were clearing her mind, Penny again started to sob.

"Listen Penny, I know it must be very difficult for you but no matter how horrid, if you can remember then please try."

"It's just that I remember nothing other than banging my head. It was pretty dark and smelled sort of musty, like an old damp house. I felt cold I do remember that, as if you don't have any covers on in bed. He was a shadow looking down on me. I seemed to be drifting, floating in and out. It was like a dream. I heard his buckle unclasp."

Penny's hand shaking as she drank the tepid mineral water through the straw, her voice weak, broken and faltering, "I said something and he hit me. He punched me. After that I don't remember much, I can't even remember if it hurt or not. I just felt a kind of warmth flow over me. I heard whispering as if people were all around me. It was dark and I could hear noises and somehow seemed to be drifting away and I do recall a strange dream. In it I was blind, yes blind and a doctor was talking to me. She was insisting that I keep trying to open my eyes. It was important that I open my eyes otherwise I would never see again. It hurt yet they wouldn't open. In my dream she brought her face next to my face, so close I could even smell her perfume. It seemed so real then the next thing I remember was a man's voice then shouting and pain, cold horrid pain. After that, only the ambulance and here."

Placing her pen in the clip, looking up, "wow I'm very proud of you Penny. Well done. I know that must have been hard for you."

Penny raised her free hand, "wait there's something else. Not sure why but he kept mentioning his mission. Yes, I distinctively remember him saying over and over again about his mission. He didn't have an accent when he said it either?"

Sue's hand hurt, "Penny you're a star, really you are. You don't know how significant this information will be."

Sue's brain was racing, So the man, for it was a *lone man*, wasn't Scottish? He spoke about *his mission*. What did that mean, was it significant?

Penny drove into Sue's train of thought, "excuse me, Sue, isn't it, I'm sorry but I need to go to the loo and its not.... well, very nice, so if you don't mind." Sue alert again, "Penny I'm sorry, forgive me. May I come and see you again soon, please?"

"Sure, anything to keep me away from either the hospital radio or Terry Wogan *blathering* away on radio two." Penny's momentary smile replaced by a painful frown, her eyes grimacing.

"I'll tell the nurse to come over and see you." Rising, almost instinctively Sue went forward and kissed Penny on the cheek. Smiling, she turned and went over to the nurse's station.

Addressing the pristine sister, "thank you for being so patient, I had to ask her some pretty tough questions." Almost by way of an afterthought, "can I ask who else has been to see her today?"

The ward nurse looked down at her papers. Her parents, a couple of girl friends and her *uncle's* been.

"Thanks, by the way she needs to go for a wee."

"Good day *Detective*," the nurses voice a one way command.

With that the ward sister went off to draw the curtains round Penny's bed knowing she would only have to dress the girl's wounds once more as she was being transferred into a private room, obviously she must have rich parents.

As Sue moved off she just happened to scan the cluttered ward Sisters desk, noticing the visitor's list. She half smiled half frowned, Uncle Simon Boeck ey?

# CHAPTER 16

## Force Lightening

Danny's uncle had summoned the two brothers immediately after speaking with his adopted nephew.

Mr Bo sat with his back to the office, high up in one of the commanding sky scrapers which dominate Hong Kong's bayside. It was a workmanlike room, large and plain with only a plant in the corner and the entrance patrolled by a three foot high terracotta dragon and a smaller three legged bronze frog. The only other distinguishing feature was the small step guarding the entrance. Mr Bo was a follower of Feng Shui combined with the ancient Chinese tradition of having a raised entrance to stop evil from crawling in.

With the early mist swirling many floors below, Mr Bo swivelled in his chair to face the prim, petite satin clad secretary who had just knocked gently on the ornate jade encrusted door.

"Sir, the gentlemen you wanted are here. Should I show them in?"

"Yes, yes and bring me some more warm honey water and anything that they may care for."

With that the secretary pivoted on stiletto heels, her tight purple dress swishing as she stepped over and out into her office. Moments later as she showed them in, "gentlemen if you would care for a drink?

"Thank you, " came a simultaneous reply. With that the two men stepping over the breached defences.

"Gentlemen, have a seat," Mr Bo smiled. He knew there was nothing *gentle* about the two assassins who had just entered his office.

Chu and Miki Ling were biological brothers. That said, anyone who saw them in the street would never have guessed. The two brothers were tall for Chinese, at nearly six foot. Apart from their height and short black hair there were few other similarities.

Chu Ling had taken up body building at fourteen and started using steroids two years later. Fourteen years later they had had a profound effect. He was a bull of a man with muscles seemingly bursting through his fitted suit. Chu's neck incredibly broad, his head disproportionably small, earning him the cruel nickname of Pinhead. Only his brother daring to call him this to his face. Due to the overuse of drugs Chu had acne scars on his neck and cheeks, which were full and puffy. The only other distinguishing feature, again a result of far too many powerful anabolic steroids, were his eyes, they were yellow.

His brother on the other hand was at the far end of the dichotomy of physical appearance. Miki was slender, the immaculate pin stripe suit he wore did however cloak a toned, tight body. If his brother's weapon was artificially, chemically forced by hours of pumping iron, Miki's were fine tuned by years of martial arts practice. Together, Pinhead and *Strike*, Miki's nickname, made a deadly duo. Seldom seen during the day as they were constantly training in their respective gym's. The brothers practiced their trade, pain, torture and death, by night.

As they had started as identical twins, inwardly they had retained a innate meeting of minds. Rarely did they not know what the other was thinking. Also possessing very similar tastes in most things; food, drink, relaxation, yet not necessarily women.

"Thank you, sir," the brothers responded half a second after each other.

Earlier Mr Bo had two large high backed chairs brought in which now faced the window with a small bamboo table between. The secretary brought in Mr Bo's warm honey, the brothers having the same tincture out of respect for their occasional employer. Once she had retired to her desk, closing the door on the way, Mr Bo stood facing away from the two men, seated four feet to his rear. He studied the ferries bobbing around in Victoria harbour, the mist having partially lifted.

"I need your skills to end the life of an evil worm stuck to my shoe. *It* is wriggling out of my sight, yet I have a friend digging him up as we speak. He insulted me to my core."

Mr Bo then explained what had happened to Penny, purposefully leaving no detail of her injuries out. Finally, turning, he studied the white and yellow pair of eyes fixed on him, "the slug is spending his last few days on this earth in England, you will see to it that my wishes are realised. *The Green Eyed Dragon* will locate him."

Mr Bo's noted their expression change when he mentioned Simon's Chinese nickname. Both men momentarily looking at each other. They knew about *The Green Eyed Dragon* and the formidable reputation. Seeing that they both wanted to say something, Mr Bo raised his grey wispy eyebrows toward Miki.

Again the brothers looked at each other, Mike spoke for the second time that morning, "sir, you talk of the legend locating this insult to your family. Why not get him to end his numbered days. Green Eyed Dragon needs no help from us?"

Mr Bo had expected this response. He too knew of Simon's reputation amongst the underworld, both on the Island and mainland China.

"Yes, The Green Eyed Dragon could easily squash out this revolting insult for life, yet he is clouded by his absurd colonial upbringing. He will not kill unless murder has taken place. My relative lives, so he will only relay the worm to the authorities. We all know that they will try the man and if, and it will be a big if, found guilty he will fester, comfortable, in a British gaol."

Mr Bo sat, sipped his health invigorating liquid and said, "the dragon has given his word that, one, he will find him and two that he will get the name and location to me before telling the police." Staring at the off putting yellow eyes, he swallowed some elixir before continuing, "you will have to act fast. It will take the police very little time to question and then arrest him. Once they do, we have little chance of getting to him."

Both brothers nodded in unison.

Leaving the silty, sweet sediment, Mr Bo put down his drink, "my secretary has two business class British Airways tickets, flying tomorrow evening. I know of your requirements. Please tell her and they will be transported to your destination. She will also give you a folder with the name of your contact. Do not remove it, memorise the name and number."

Once again both men nodded, only this time Chu spoke, "sir, it is our honour to work for you. We will be successful, the filthy white scum will die."

Interrupting them, Mr Bo bent forward, his eyes fixed, switching from one brother to the other, "not just die. He must feel pain before you send him to the underworld."

The brothers were simultaneously thinking the same thoughts. Chu replied for both of them, "sir, he will be in agony, such pain the dark heat of hell will be a blessing which he will beg for."

A tight lined smirk moved across Mr Bo's liver spotted face, "for this you will receive twice the normal fees."

Rising together, both men bowed slowly. They did not shake hands, that was a given. As they left Mr Bo turned and watched distant Star water taxis' plying their trade far below.

Chu thanked the secretary for the package containing the tickets, four thousand US dollars travelling money and a single sheet containing a name, a telephone number and a few words in English. Both men studied the paper before handing it back to the woman. After a short conversation they left. Moments later the women watched as the shredder cut through Danny's mobile number.

Back in his office Mr Bo went over and slowly stroked the head of his dragon. He liked using force lightening. He enjoyed the analogy that, like lightening, the certainty of the fact that if struck, death occurred. Also, similar to the natural phenomena, the brothers would not follow a straight path, striking without warning. In the flash of an eye, deadly, only to move on to an unseen future location.

Yes, force lightening was a very apt name for the most ruthless assassins working in Hong Kong.

---

Fifty hours later, *force lightening* had a smooth landing as the BA jumbo touched down at Heathrow international airport.

Two oriental men, like the mass of tourists moved through customs, British security tight.

"Good morning Mister Palmer." The customs officer said studying Miki's photo, "and what brings you to our lovely country, business or pleasure?"

Miki smiled, his immaculate white teeth exposed, "well actually a bit of both. I have relatives in the north who have a takeaway. Also, I would like to see some of your Roman history as it fascinates me."

"Does it indeed," the official glanced down at the concealed screen. Mr *Palmer* was clean and the passport checked out. And so it should, the pair had cost several thousand US to ensure the brothers passage through customs would be smooth.

"Actually not really my scene, far rather footy. Who do you support?"

"No one." Miki gleamed back, "I like martial arts actually and anyway I support myself."

Laughing the official handed back the suitably worn passport, "well you're sure to be safe then. Cheerio and thank you Mister Palmer."

Miki smiled, returned the passport to his pocket, picked up his holdall and moved off.

Two minutes later Chu went through an identical charade. He was also on business as he too had a relative with a takeaway. He was interested in visiting Stratford Upon Avon, being passionate about Shakspeare.

His customs officer had raised an eyebrow, doubting very much whether the man stood in front of him, who resembled a rugby prop forward, appreciated *The Bard.*

The official was new, so missed the opportunity to tactfully question Chu further. Had he done so he would have been convinced. Chu might not physically appear smart, yet he was wise enough to have spent hours on the plane studying a high school book on the Works of Shakespeare.

Nearly an hour later both men entered the British Midland business lounge, seemingly by coincidence.

Checking their tickets, the stewardess had shown them through the door and up the stairs. Having done so she then went back to the reception and phoned ahead so that the gold and silver card holder door opened as the two men reached the top step.

"Good morning, gentlemen can I get you a drink? The airline hostess enquired as they entered.

Chu smiled through crooked teeth, "yes please, a strong black coffee."

Looking at the more visually attractive brother, "and you sir?"

Miki's facial expression all together more appealing, "could I have a herbal tea?"

Of course Margaret replied. She had worked in the *special lounge* too long to pass judgement by guests appearances. Knowing that the ordinary business travellers were restricted to the very comfortable lounge downstairs. Upstairs reserved for the great, the very frequent and the rich. Margaret knew that looks were very deceptive. I mean who would have thought, Robbie Williams preferred The Telegraph to the Sun newspaper and no one would believe the singer Lulu always travelled with her dresser, sitting on the same sofa as far away as possible from the smokers and mobile phones.

"Gentlemen I will bring them over in a minute."

With that the brothers moved over and sat in deep comfortable leather chairs overlooking the plane parking lot, amusing themselves as they watched a lucky upgraded passenger pillage the free magazine shelf of everything from Hello to Cosmopolitan.

Sitting in silence until Margaret placed the drinks and a couple of sweets next to each of them, their host spoke first, "gentlemen, if you have not been in the lounge before." Simultaneously the assassins shook their heads.

"Well, past the magazine shelfs you'll find biscuits, cheese and a full bar, if you care to indulge."

Both men nodded. Margaret did a double take, the very solid Chinese man had yellow eyes, yet in line with her professionalism it was an imperceptible pause, even to Chu.

"If there is anything else just ask." Margaret smiled as she returned to refilling the sweet tray on the counter.

Chu spoke first, his English perfect.

"Well brother, again we work for the great Mr Bo. I respect him as he understands the ways of the assassin. Do you think he will get our tools to us as requested?"

Miki smiled at his younger, by ten minutes, brother, "yes, Mr Bo will have the very best weapons waiting for us. Grab a map from her," nodding towards Margaret.

Two minutes later, having moved the no mobile sign to the side they studied a basic flight map of The UK.

"So we are to go to Newcastle, they say it is full of heathens who speak with strange tongues. Do you know anything else about this place?"

Chu did, his appearance disguising the fact that he was truly a scholar of the arts and history,

"Well it is named after the replacement castle which was erected on the banks of the River Tyne to keep the Celtic hordes from Scotland out." Chu's level of knowledge probably better than most locals. "Most don't even realise that the 'new' castle is behind the telecom centre, hidden in amongst the high rise buildings." After a sip of his brew he finished with, "on the other bank of the river is a town called Gateshead. There is rivalry between the two, yet they are almost as one. Having gone through a slump the city is now regenerating into a thriving centre. It's reputed to be one of the best in the whole stinking, filthy country." The grin broad on Miki's face, his brother really was a dark horse as behind the scary yellow eyes and bulging muscles was a man of intellect and culture. Why he needed the damaging drugs was beyond him.

Changing tack slightly, "Chu, what d'you know of the one called The Green Eyed Dragon?"

"Well you know he saved Mr Bo's life. I've heard that years ago the great man sent relatives to live here safe in this country. A few years later triads and Russians came to take over *the business* in Britain. When they did the Dragon supposedly killed them all. It's said no one is meant to move as fast, some even believe he moves with spirits. He sees what we can not, he hears what we can't and is meant to have the dead protecting him. He's un-killable."

Miki smiled as Chu continued, "of course few back home have ever seen him. All they know is that his eyes are green, like a dragon. Mr Bo looks upon him as a silent saviour protecting his relatives, so far from his own embrace."

It was Miki's turn to smile, "well it's good he's on our side then."

With that the two men went through their plans, agreeing that they would have to move quickly as their plan was not without danger. Not danger from their target they both agreed, no the danger lay in their obvious lack of time for a rehearsal. Both brothers knew that preparation and planning meant success. Ambiguity spelt mistakes and mistakes could be trouble.

They knew this, yet they also knew that *ones* strength combined with the others speed would ensure that they captured and tortured the evil slug. They would do what he had done to the great mans darling. They would strip him naked, prop him up kneeling, before cutting off his cock and balls. They would place them in front so that he could see his worthlessness as a man before bleeding to death.

They had done it before. Not pretty, but the message it sent powerful!

Terror would scar their victims face whilst the brothers watched the mans life drain away. The sight of his castrated, soiled manhood, eating into the worthless man's pathetic brain. With this cheery thought the two men thanked the efficient stewardess, descended the stairs, moved out into the busy corridor before moving off to their gate. After a short wait they boarded taking the front row on the short shuttle BMi to Newcastle.

An hour and twenty minutes later they walked out of the provincial airport into the gloom of a chilly, compared to home, afternoon. Having collected their bags the assassins took a taxi into town, asking the almost incomprehensible driver which was the best hotel in the city centre. Not questioning him further, there being no point as they could hardly understand the man, apart from thanking and paying him, before entering The Windsor Hotel. Both men impressed by its grandeur as they had checked into, using their pseudonyms, separate rooms next to each other.

A short while later they wandered into the city centre and found a travel agent where they changed some money. After that they found the appropriate shop, each buying a pay as you go mobiles phone.

By about six, phones charged, sat in the elegant Princes' Bar, Chu punched memorised numbers into his phone. A man voice answered, "hello."

Chu replied, "yes, lightening does strike twice." These had been the only words on the sheet, back in Mr Bo's outer office.

There was a pause, "where are you?"

"We're at a hotel called The Windsor, in The Princes' Bar."

"I will be there in twenty minutes," with that, Danny hung up.

# CHAPTER 17

## *Battle Preparations*

Watching the swallows swoop across the parade ground was infinitely more interesting than listening to the Regimental Second in Command as Boots hated the fucking pre exercise briefs. The idiot rodney should just tell them to get on with it. Instead, he insisted on going into every bloody detail.

As the Sergeant was away at the dentists, Boots had been drafted and now sat next to his own platoon commander, who was busy making notes. The rodney would do all the work and anyway, he'd not take any notice of Boots even if he did suggest something.

They both knew it.

Boots failing to see the significance that his comments were always derogative and of little help and as a result his professional opinion was rarely sought.

"Gentlemen, you will need to ensure your dry drills are spot on. This will be live firing and we all know the SA80 is a dangerous weapon." The 2IC's comments brought a ripple of laughter from the audience of captains, lieutenants and sergeants, yet not from Boots.

The unit were going earlier than planned as The Green Howards had been delayed in Northern Ireland following the marching season.* As a result, The Welsh Boarders would swap slots at Workop.

The Regimental 2IC continued, "as you know all arrangements are in place and anyway the stores are already up there. So next Tuesday I want you," looking at Boots' boss, "to take an advance team to take over the accommodation and recce† the ranges. The main body will arrive on Thursday."

The ridiculously keen rodney scribbled like crazy as it was he who was going to command the advance party. Looking on disdainfully, what a twat the stupid idiot was thought Boots. Well, if they were all going, he'd make sure he was in the advance party. That way he could have a few drinks with the camp commandant.

The meeting broke up with the regimental 2IC empowering them that they had to adapt to change. They were in the Army and if it meant that leave would have to be cancelled then leave would have to be cancelled. The CO had taken on the local brigade commander's suggestion and as a result, they would, no mater what, be on battle camp in less than a week.

A short while later Boots left, his note book empty. Walking back to the platoon lines,

* The Marching Season is a period where Catholics (and Protestants) in Northern Ireland undertake a series of marches to celebrate historical events. In the past they had erupted into near uncontrollable riots.

† Army abbreviation for reconnaissance–old Army adage 'prior preparation and planning prevents piss poor performance'!

his platoon commander, Second Lieutenant Rory Browne seemed so God damn keen.

"Damn it, Corporal Wellington, I was meant to go up town this weekend with my girlfriend. Ah well I get to command the advance party. Its going to be great."

The fucking idiot was like an excited puppy. Boots wished he could pull his chain and give him a good slap. Even Boots knew he couldn't sadly do either, "yes sir, it will be such a *wheeze*."

Noting Boots sarcasm, 2Lt Browne carried on, "well, it will be such a *wheeze,* as you call it. For me, *acting* corporal Wellington *boots*, this is a big deal. If I'd wanted a job in the city on better money, I'd be wearing a suit, as it is I much prefer the challenge of command, the buzz I get from leading soldiers."

There, that should shut the ignorant JNCO up, thought the new subaltern. 2Lt Browne had only known Boots for seven weeks and already understood why, at twenty-eight, he was still only an *acting* corporal.

"Good afternoon corporal Wellington, I've got a squash match. See you tomorrow at parade."

"Yes *Sar*." Boots threw up a lazy salute. 2Lt Browne again recognising Boots' weakly cloaked sarcasm. Yes, he agreed with the sergeant, corporal Boots needed to be kept on a very tight rein.

Back in his bunk, Boots was having mixed thoughts about going back to Workop. Yes he'd had a great time with the jocks and the camp commandant, Tom. He had also completed his most successful *mission* todate.

As each day passed he had convinced himself that it had been so sexually exciting. Boots hadn't needed to penetrate the girl. She was a slag and probably had the clap and he didn't care if she was dead, anyway no one would mourn for such a filthy chinky bitch. Ultimately he wasn't to blame anyway, no one was. The creatures had cut her as it was they that wanted her. Maybe when Boots had left, they'd devoured her stinking body?

No evidence, dark sexual thoughts fuelled by the memory of her black pubes emitting a dark grin.

At the other end of his simple thought processes lay the nightmares. He had never had such terrible ones. Boots was now no longer able to differentiate between dreams and the reality of the terrible creatures which had invaded his world.

He had been awake and seen them, felt them, smelt them and they'd even spoken to him about completing the *mission.*

What was he to do? They would attack him if he didn't carry out their orders. What had *it* said, '*Fear us if you do not act for us.*'

What the hell, he didn't need to worry, this weekend there were having a special at The Ram, with back to back rave disco's. The Manager having promised two busses full of birds each night.

Eyes narrowing as the smirk returned to Boots pale thin lips. If necessary he would go on another mission, maybe two? He lay back on the bed, closed his dark eyes, hands interlocked behind his head.

The next thing Boots knew, the sun had descended down behind his thin ineffective curtains, the evening now still with only a few distant skylarks singing in the playing fields behind his accommodation block. Instinctively Boots rubbed his eyes.

In the twilight dusk he saw the creature drift from underneath his flimsy, issue bed. Boots was however for some strange reason this time not terrified, possibly because for once, he was sober. He watched almost with curiosity as the hideous four legged goblin crouched at the bottom of his bed. Its head clearly visible above his size eleven boots.

Almost friendly in tone he addressed it, "why do you want to watch me with those women?"

Sucking the air past its revolting fangs, most broken off, it replied, *"Boots, you are the tool for our pleasure. Through you we can get to the living, touch them. Enjoyment for us is the taste and warmth of human flesh."*

It then pulled its head back and let out a low groaning sound coming from deep down. Its tight, wolf life rib cage quivering. Again fixing its slit like tiny red eyes on Boots before continuing, *"you will feast again on another mission soon. You will not be alone as we will be there watching. Fear no one as we will protect you from those who would want to stop you."*

Scratching a filthy hideous claw across its hairy, scabby neck, it went on, "*taste blood and you will for ever be successful on missions. Then no one will ever be able to stop you."*

Boots blinked at the disgusting thought of drinking blood, tasting human flesh.

The creature then shuffled backwards, its shoulders lowered. Reaching the far wall, less than ten feet away it stopped. Slowly raising a hoof come claw before, in a flash, smashing it against the near empty bookcase. The sheer speed making Boots blink hard.

Opening his eyes again the creature was gone. Now drenched in cold sweat Boots slowly got up and went over to the bookcase. Bending down, there half stuck in the wood was a claw. He prodded it with his index finger. It was real. Touching again, instantly removing his finger, putting it instinctively in his mouth, tasting his own blood from the small cut. Boots then picked up one of his issue thick green socks which were as ever stuffed into his scuffed boots. Wrapping it round his hand for protection he gingerly grasped the blunt, jagged end. Pulling and twisting he carefully removed it from the cheap wood.

Returning to his infrequently used study desk, he opened out a copy of Soldier Magazine he'd taken from the corporal's mess. Why fucking buy the mag' when you could borrow it, semi permanently.

Studying the object, the talon was about four inches long, almost black and serrated with a golf ball sized knuckle. It was also incredibly sharp, having easily sliced through ten pages of the magazine. Carefully Boots took it over to the sink. With hot water he wiped it clean, exposing whitish yellow sinews where it had been ripped out. Staring at it Boots thought it was probably as big as a sharks tooth. Actually from what he knew, little, it looked remarkably like a sharks tooth. He wondered if the creatures were like sharks, in as much as teeth were regenerated when they broke or knocked out?

Carefully, he wrapped thick rocking horse shit* round the stubby end. Holding it between his middle fingers, gripping the thick tape in his fist, he waved it about. Actually it was an impressive weapon. Almost like a claw in his own large fist, his claw.

* Army slang for thick masking tape (basically an extremely rare commodity).

Boots then placed it in his sock drawer before washing his hands after which he wandered, deep in thought, over to the cook house and the corporals segregated area. He'd then sat eating slightly over cooked soggy pizza, listening but not contributing to the chatter about the new female documentation clerk who had inadvertently been posted into the regimental headquarters. Someone in The Adjutant General Corps had done them a favour. One of the lads had heard, supposedly, she fucked like a bunny. The discussion then deteriorating into bets about who could shag her first.

Boots didn't need to lay a bet...

# CHAPTER 18

## *Palmed Vision*

Detective Sergeant Sue Parish sat, her bright alert eyes transfixed on an irrelevant poster for Crime Stoppers. In her six years she had only received two concrete leads from the campaign. Yet Sue knew, even two were far better than none at all.

Breaking her gaze to the opened folder on the desk. The results from the forensic and DNA had been mixed with a few excellent fingerprints on the weapon and a couple taken from down by the crime scene. They had also found traces of blood inside the knife's simple mechanism which matched Penny's perfectly. As a result there was absolutely no question that the Stanley knife in an evidence bag, lying in the middle of her desk, was the attacker's weapon. Squinting Sue tried to drill her thoughts into the thing, as if by some magic maybe she could discover more about the man they now hunted.

Sue had briefed Chief Inspector Monk at nine sharp the day after finding the knife. Placing the written report in the in-tray as she left his office. The previous night Sue'd worked until eleven re-doing it over and over again as she was determined to retain her rank. He seemed to be impressed and had told her that, against his better judgement, maybe she should talk to Mister Boeck again. Sue thought better than to correct The Saint, she too having now adopted and resorted to using his nickname.

The evidence was certainly mounting up, yet without any more leads no matter how much evidence they had it was worthless unless they had suspects to attach it to.

They had none.

No one seemed to have got a good look at the attacker. Why had he been putting on an accent? What was all the talk of *missions*?

Questions without answers.

Why had all three girls said the same thing and anyway what kind of name was Roots?

How come Simon said he was wearing a uniform? This was possibly the only bit of information which she could work with as there were plenty of army units, regular and territorial around the area. If necessary they could get every single one of them tested.

Easily said, more difficult to action, the Chief had reminded her messing with the military always caused problems. They didn't like the police claiming that one of their own was a brutal sex attacker. Add the fact, they didn't want the local military police and the SIB sticking their noses into everything. All in all it was a recipe for a buggers muddle.

What the hell, the Colonel chap had been damn impressive and she had nothing to loose.

"Hello, could I speak to Simon Boeck please."

On the other end of the line, someone asked who was calling.

"Yes of course, sorry, my name is Detective Sergeant Parish and I was wondering if I could have a word with *Colonel* Boeck."

Sue listened as a, seemingly, unconcerned ladies voice call out, "it's the police for you. She said her name is detective Parish."

Hearing footsteps and the phone being passed from one to another, Sue held her breath expectantly.

"Good morning Sue, Simon here. How can I help?"

"Well I don't know how, but you were right. We found a Stanley knife exactly where you told me to look."

Picking up the item as if trying to send what it looked like down the line, Sue continued,

"Well, it is *the* weapon, it checks out," pausing monetarily, " I was wondering if you wouldn't mind coming in so that I could talk to you about it?"

Frowning, she went on, "I am sure you realise, it's a bit strange you knowing where it was."

Simon had not really thought of it like that. What, did she think he had something to do with Penny's attack?

"Now Detective Parish if you think I had anything to do with this then why the hell would I come foreword in the first place?"

Inturn, Sue hadn't meant it that way, "no it's not like that. I just thought." She paused, embarrassed.

Simon interjected, confusion dis-railing both their trains of thought, "Sue, don't worry I'm not in the habit of talking to the press, ever. If you want me to see if I can tell anything about the attacker then I'd be happy."

Their respective thought processes back on track.

The wheel of redness flushing just behind Sue's ear, "well, yes please if you don't mind?"

"Sue I would far rather not come to the police station again. Couldn't we meet somewhere else? If you like you could drive over to my house with the knife. Don't worry my wife, Lynda, will be in the garden so you'll be *safe*."

"No it's not *that*, you see I'm not really meant to take such vital piece of evidence out of the station without a bloody good reason."

"You now have one, please trust me on this."

Sue, against her better judgement, did.

Nearly an hour later, Sue stood, having knocked, outside a lovely large probably Victorian cottage. The solid maroon door opened and an extremely attractive, physically fit looking woman, who she wrongly assumed was in her mid thirties, smiled, "Sue?"

Sue nodded.

"Hello I'm Simon's wife Lynda, please come through. Simon's in the garden listening to the radio."

Sue then went through into the surprisingly large hall, festooned with pictures, objects everywhere.

"Wow you have so many lovely things Mrs Boeck."

"Please, call me Lynda."

"OK *Lynda.* You must have travelled all over the world to collect all these beautiful objects?"

"Well actually yes and no," as Lynda spoke, both women stepped through the kitchen out onto a pretty little patio surrounded by climbing plants. As she did, Sue smelt the wonderful fragrance as she past bye a large tub of lavender.

Simon rose, holding out his hand, "Sue it's delightful to see you again, please have a seat."

Sitting, Sue carefully placed the large brown zipper bag, she had been carrying, on her lap.

"Sue, can I get you a drink? Without waiting for a reply, Lynda asked, "are you allowed a glass of wine?"

"What the hell, its such a lovely day and I don't suppose I'll be driving for an hour or so, so yes please that would be very kind."

Lynda touched Simon's arm as she went passed into the kitchen. She understood, they had business to discuss and knew better than to linger and listen.

"Well then, it's in there isn't it?" As he spoke Simon knocked his head forward towards the evidence bag.

"Yes it is. Please, its very important I shouldn't have really brought it. I am taking a risk even being here."

Simon smiled "you should and the risk will be worth every second, trust me."

Again her intuition telling her she should do so.

As Simon spoke, Lynda returned with two glasses. Turning to Simon, "darling I thought you might like some of this." Seeing Sue look at the glass, "sorry its non vintage, but it's still rather good." Sue raised her eyebrows, not accustomed to house calls that obviously involved being offered a glass of champagne. More often than not, if she were offered anything at all, it would be cheap coffee or even worse, sweet warm and invariably stewed tea.

"Gosh this is very kind, thank you," as she took the elegant flute, bubbles dancing, cascading upwards.

With that Lynda retreated to the front garden to kill greenfly.

Driving over Sue had thought in for a penny in for a pound as she might as well tell the colonel nearly everything. Not least, because ninety percent of the information had come from Simon in the first place.

Sue explained what she had, by way of new information. When she'd finished, Simon sat toying with his glass of half drank Pommery. After a moment or twos silence, Simon turned his haunting green eyes full on Sue. As he did the redness deepened below her ear.

"Sue I need to ask you a favour. I need to actually touch the knife, also, I need to be alone.

Do you think you could go and have a chat with my wife. I'll only need about fifteen minutes. I promise I won't run off with it."

"Well I really can't let you touch it."

Simon finished his glass, "Sue this will be extremely useful for you, please trust me on this."

For the third time in a matter of hours, she did.

"Won't your wife mind talking to a complete stranger, especially a copper."

The grin returned to Simon's face. Sue rose, placing the half-finished glass on the wrought iron garden table, at the same time unzipping the package and placed the knife, contained in a plastic sheath, indelible marker pen scrawled along the documentation lines, on the table.

Simon went over to the opened kitchen door, "Lynda's in the front," pointing down the corridor, "just keep going."

Sue nodded and walked passed and through towards the far front door.

# CHAPTER 19

## Framed Sight

I knew that this was what I had been waiting for and also knew Lynda would keep Sue talking for as long as needed.

Carefully I picked the envelope up by the corner and entered the house moving through to the study, closing the door behind me I sat in my meditation chair. I pulled over the low, clear glass table which I'd prepared as soon as Sue had told me she was coming over.

It was covered with a white cloth, which I adjusted 'just so'. Very carefully unzipping the bag, letting the Stanley knife slide out with a dull clunk onto the table before putting the empty bag to one side, on the floor.

Then I pulled the table in front of me so that, without leaning, I could reach the knife – ready.

Getting comfortable I sat with my eyes open, studying the knife, the blade retracted.

Slowly I breathed in and out nine times. As I did closing my eyes, my tongue touching the roof of my mouth. The back of my hands on my lap, thumb and first two fingers touching.

Lifting my eyes behind my eyelids I looked, as if towards my eyebrows.

Warm breath, in and out, slowly now.

Drifting off, I was once again seated by the river, swallows performing like natures spitfires. Taking in the suns warmth on my back, the fragrance from the wild flowers all around, with hardly a cloud in the sky, I looked up, "hello Wagtail."

Pied Wagtail's, tail bobbing in its customary manner, "Simon, hello, wonderful to see you."

Flitting onto my knee, he looked up, "and where are we going today?"

Grinning at my guide, "my friend, I need to go on a journey, a distant journey, yet first I need to find someone."

Now over to the other knee, "well then Simon let's go for a walk."

Smiling down at my friend, who always gave me hope for a successful journey, I stood up, Wagtail swooping onto my shoulder. Walking up the same beautiful grassy bank, as we crested the hill I once again saw the purposeful Hacienda Grande.

Wagtail flew off ahead, this time perching on the barbecue lid.

Entering the garden I saw an old friend tending some marrows. We smiled but didn't speak as it wasn't him I had come to see.

"Enter, travel, be safe and return with knowledge and wisdom," with that Wagtail took off towards the roof.

Opening the door, as always, the headmaster came over, "Simon I know of your journey, remember beware of shadows who might seek you."

"Doctor Laurance I heed your wise words, move with those who would learn."

Almost in a salute he touched his mortarboard, turned and walked past the sweeping stairs. I followed him to the left.

Moving round to the far corner where there are a set of revolving doors spinning, always in motion.

Stepping through I entered The Journey Room.

The room is conservative in décor, roughly about the average living room in size. It has a sofa on either side and a comfortable arm chair in between. Although nearly empty the room somehow seemingly lived in. In front of the chairs was a table, low and also bare.

The only other thing in the room was a very large picture. Well hardly a picture as it was only the beautifully ornate frame, hanging opposite the table and chairs. It had no colour to it, it was just there.

Walking round I sat on the comfortable chair facing the picture, leaning forward closing my eyes.

The blade cold in my right palm, the left closed over the top.

Power, disgust, unfulfilled authority, arrogance. The feelings rushing at me all at once, bombarding my mind.

As if snorting air in a convulsion, I jerked back slightly. He hated them? He hated lots of things. Needing to drink and despised his sister? She was part of the reason why he used women. To get at her?

Then I saw, his hands where mine. They were big, powerful. His boots were meant to be shiny as was his uniform and only ironed on a Sunday night?

Rubbing my/his hands around in a circles over the blade.

He wanted to fuck but couldn't. They made, no helped him on his missions. The ram was his friend, his cover?

A flash of red as the dragon and ram came into focus. They were The Colours.* The stripes were falling, no, one was falling – he was a corporal!

Still in my hands the blade remained icy as I delved deeper, further.

Terror replaced by greed. There were others, slowly the feelings changed, darker more evil, coming closer. I opened my eyes ever so slowly, shaking. Could they sense me moving toward him?

Now glancing down at the knife in my hands as *I* looked at the picture on the wall before calmly once again shutting my eyes.

As if focusing with my eyes open, looking through water, the picture cleared as my vision adjusted. Travelling now in a town I recognised as Aldershot. Moving along the road to a bridge, down past some steps and along the banks of a canal. After a few minutes I walked up the side away from the water, through undergrowth. On a mound, in

* A regiment's Colours are their ultimate symbol of identify. Presented by The Queen, normally they take the form of a flag. Others, like Artillery regiments, have artillery pieces, or sometimes ceremonial drums as in the case of The Royal Logistic Corps.

amongst the trees lay a cleared out hollow the size of a large car. On the ground were some pine cones, the smell not unpleasant. Kneeling feeling the knife again, his knees scuffed by the cones as he pressed down on them.

I knew where this canal was.

Standing I returned to the bridge, walking along, it was quite dark and very still. As I did, looking to the right was a worn dirt track adjacent to the tarmac path. This was his route to the canal. Wandering on, the road was twenty feet off to the left, cutting across the short mowed grass. It was very dark now as I observed over the road a large quiet car park. I looked further, a neon sign.

I'd found him!

Turning, in an instant the picture loosing focus, blinking down at the knife still cold in my hands. Carefully placing it back on the table in front of me. Its temperature indicative of his character, cold and blank.

Leaving the room, the door already quietly revolving, with the banisters on my left, I walked over to the main double doors. There was no one else around. There didn't need to be.

Closing the open side of the double doors *I* stepped out into the blanket of enveloping warm air, before going down the steps towards the gate.

"You found what you seek?" It was my friend tending the vegetables.

"Yes, a troubling journey though."

The gardener replied, " not all trips can be as fulfilling and positive. I suggest you use the knowledge and act if that is what you must do. I bid you good day." He was always pretty abrupt, but very precise.

"May your crops grow tall and the fruit feed those in need," my standard response.

At last a smile and a wave as he knelt back down, next to some carrots.

Then through the gate I walked towards the river. Seeing wagtail swooping in his normal flight, towards me, "Simon your journey was worthwhile? Go and use your knowledge."

Again seated, legs out in front, arms behind resting on my hands. I looked over to the right and saw a steep bank rising through trees in a dense wood. Many times I'd raced up the challenging hill. Leaning back, closing my eyes listening to my own breath, in out, in out.

---

Opening them, I carefully used the cloth to put the knife back in the evidence folder and then returned to the garden, placing it from where I had picked it up.

---

Simon, didn't immediately go though to where Sue and his wife were enjoying discussing the new Karen Millen shop which had recently opened in town, instead he went through the new information.

A big uniformed man, a soldier, probably a corporal, his sister part of the reason he attacked? Maybe he had assaulted his sister? Something about him being able to *see* troubled Simon. He knew this was disturbing yet was convinced, no he was certain, especially as he had felt the very same back in the warehouse. His name was something like William Coats or Coots, yet Sue had said Roots, not certain there?

His regiment?

Sometimes, like an aftershock, Simon received additional information, bye way of a blast of fine tuned information like confetti, or *chaff* as he preferred to call it.[10]

He was in a regiment with a ram for a mascot, Welsh?

The Ram was more significant?

The regimental colours would be easy to check. Simon was almost certain it was the Ram and Dragon of the Welsh Boarders on a scarlet background.

No, he was certain.

Simon went through to the front garden where he found both ladies laughing, Lynda's raven hair sweeping across her high cheek boned face as her head rocked back. They were discussing where they should get together in town.

Sue saw no reason why she should not meet a wife of someone who, not only did not have a criminal record, on the contrary, was proving extremely helpful in a particularly horrid case. Anyway she really got on with Lynda , she was such great fun.

Sue saw Simon return first, "that was quick, we've only been out here about ten minutes."

Simon knew time was of little significance. knowing it was far more to do with his inherited ability, fine tuned by Section 9.*

"Hey darling do you think you could fill our glasses again."

Sue replied, before Simon's wife could respond, "not for me, thanks."

Simon, realising his manners. "I'm sorry, would you prefer a cup of tea? Turning to Sue, "is Earl Grey alright?"

Replying Sue said, "of course, actually I prefer it to Lady Grey,"

Once again, Lynda had far too much common sense than to take the request as a command, smiled and wandered towards the kitchen. It would take, easily five minutes for the kettle to boil. Anyway, she knew that Simon and Sue would have things to talk about and her husband would return to the large kitchen for their tea when he was ready.

Simon knew he would have to keep his promise to Danny, "Sue, you might like to sit over there." As he spoke Simon pointed towards a small two person well worn wooden chair in front of the bay windows. Now almost by habit, nodding Sue sat down and retrieved her ever present notebook and pen.

Deciding to give Danny a little time, standing Simon continued, "well he is called Stephen Roots or Coats. He's in a traditional *Scottish* Army regiment and is a corporal. He has a sister, or had a sister, sorry no name."

Seeing Sue scribbling like crazy he purposefully snapped into her train of thought, "Sue please remember that this is not a science and *I* sometimes get side tracked which affects the information. For example his name could well be Coots, *Boots* or even......."

Sue, pen poised, looked up at Simon as he'd stopped talking. "What is it?"

"Oh nothing I....., no nothing."

Simon inwardly knew, at last, he had his name.

* For more detail see Appendix A.

# CHAPTER 20

## *Informed Direction*

Surprise, surprisingly absent, missing from Danny's face as he entered the Prince's Bar.

It was not difficult to spot them. It wasn't that they were Chinese, far more, the fact that one of them was so bloody huge.

Going straight over, not giving his name, preferring only to acknowledge theirs, Danny had explained that their weapons had arrived the same day and they'd get them the following morning. He then went on to say that The Green Eyed Dragon would shortly be telling him exactly where the target was.

The brothers could contact him at anytime day or night by mobile. He would prefer however if they didn't call him, unless it was urgent. Also, unlike his landline to Hong Kong, they should be careful as their mobile phones weren't secure.

Finally adding that they should enjoy the town.

Answering their unspoken questions, yes the town did have any number of gyms, even the hotel had a perfectly good spa. Danny having no idea that the nearest they wanted to get to a spa would be *spar*'ing against some poor unsuspecting local fool.

The meeting brief, professional, almost as if discussing a new business venture, not bloody slaughter. Danny then left intrigued by the physical contrast. One a puffy scarred hulk, the other elegant, with an almost charming smile.

Danny knew that their appearance was deceptive, aware that they did not like to be seen during the day. Yet, force lightening had only agreed to take this job at the personal request of his uncle and anyway they had no idea, apart from the fact that he was some distant relative, who Danny's wife actually was.

Back in the bar, the two brothers had easily worked a lot of things out. Mister Bo would not have told such information to anyone other than a trusted friend or more likely close family. It was also very obvious that the man who had visited them knew little of the world in which they lived and moved, *theirs*, ruthless, cruel and often fatal.

Discussing the meeting they tried one of the revolting local beers, after which the brothers had sought out the restaurant which their visitor had recommended. Danny had even given them a card, on it written, honoured guests.

After a surprisingly excellent meal, no bill forthcoming, they walked back to the hotel. After a couple of, far better quality Scottish whiskies, recommended by the ancient barman, the brothers retired to their rooms.

Chu's, night far more restless, having phoned a hooker from one of the cards he found in the call box just outside the hotel. She'd almost been incomprehensible but not bad for a white round eye.

The next morning, both men dressed in the gym kit they had bought the previous afternoon, sauntered off to BodyZone, the highly recommended gym. Each carrying fully charged mobiles in their garish Puma tracksuits.

About the same time as the brothers were enjoying their spring rolls the previous night Simon sat in a, ever so slightly superior, restaurant less than three hundred feet along Stowell Street.

Seeing Danny enter, Simon moved round from the table. As always he had his back to the wall, ingrained training never leaving him, much to Lynda's irritation.

A hug and two kisses later, both men sat down at the eight-person table, set only for two. The waitress withdrawing discreetly having poured two glasses of Bollinger 89*.

"Danny, I hate to say it but there is further good news and there is bad news," grimacing at his own trite phrase.

Instinctively Danny said, "bad news first, always."

"Actually there is no *real* bad news. I know who and where and now only have to physically identify him." Seeing Danny's expression move toward negative and confusion, "I know his name but.."

Danny had had enough, "what's his fucking name Simon!"

Startled, yet not surprised by the outburst, Simon replied, "it's Robert Boots, he's a soldier, junior rank, He is based down south, near London. He's big and pretty screwed up."

Danny scowled as the only bit of *new* information he already knew was that the bastard was screwed up, "he's in the Army?"

"Yes I'm certain. I know where he goes. He has done this before and will do it again. Once I know what he looks like I think you might like to set your trap?"

"Trap, you talk of traps. I think I'll go down there and blow his fucking balls off myself."

They both knew Danny didn't have the nerve.

"Danny I will keep my promise. The police are currently on a tangent."
"What, you told them his name!" Danny's instant high pitched retort.

Simon sat back, ignoring his friends gesticulations and drank the remainder of his glass. Purposefully, slowly he placed it on the table knowing the attentive waitress would materialise to refill it. As she did Danny went silent, impatient smoke almost visible from his ears.

Alone again, the silence calming, Simon leant forward, "listen Danny, I gave my word. They have the wrong name, wrong regiment and even the wrong end of the country. Remember I was in the army. Trust me it will take them ages to get even inside a camp, even then the wrong one."

Danny calmed down, realising his friend was taking not inconsiderable risk on his behalf,

"Simon thank you, so what do *we*, sorry, *I* do now."

"Danny, remember your part of the deal, I said I would find him and I will give you more than that. That much I owe you. I know where he commits crimes against women and I'm prepared to show you and only you."

After a drink, Simon continued, "from then on you have two nights until I must give the real details to the police, I owe *them* that." Ignoring Danny's frown, Danny didn't

* 1989 was a magnificent champagne year.

think Simon owed the police anything.

Simon went on, "also, I may have to drip bits of information there way otherwise they might become suspicious, alright?"

Controlling himself Danny nodded, "what now *detective* Boeck?" Danny smiled, Simon didn't

"Well Danny, I will go down to Aldershot, you know West of London. I was stationed there years ago at Gun Hill Officers Mess so know it well. You could follow me down the next day, possibly? You could catch the mid morning flight? You'd probably only have to stay over night."

Standing his glass down, green eyed dragon said, "I will then identify him, trust me I will. Then you have two nights, Friday and Saturday, after that I tell the police his name and unit. They will pick him up the same day for sure.

Danny mulled over the 'offer'. It would work, he could get the brothers installed down south albeit that they would have to travel by car so as to be able to take their equipment. Maybe he needed some bait to ensure they trapped him. Yes, this evil bastard attacked young women, possibly he preferred oriental girls? He'd get his managers to get one of their call girls off the pay roll as they had any number on the unofficial books. He'd offer the girl so much money no pro would be able to resist.

Simon who'd had his glass refilled by the waitress sat back watching Danny scheming, so for the moment, kept quite.

Finally Danny came out of his mental, thought trance, "sorry Simon, I was just thinking things through."

I know you were," raising a hand, "listen I just don't want to know what your up to."

Simon then explained his flight details and where they would meet up in a couple of days time.

# CHAPTER 21

## *Hamona of the Trade*

The brothers met Danny at his office just over a minute before nine the next morning, having both received a call from Danny's secretary, Jenny, requesting they attend his office as soon as possible. By the time they had showered and descended to hotel reception, purring, the jaguar stood quietly waiting outside.

Similar to his uncle, Danny's staff had brought in another large comfortable chair into the office.

On arrival Jenny brought both men through as soon as they arrived.

Danny spoke first, "there's been rapid developments. A friend has provided me with excellent information. Your target is not here in the North of England, he's moved back down near London."

Neither of his 'guests' moved a muscle.

"He is a British military soldier. You should know he is big, tough and very dangerous."

Again neither brother moved.

"I don't know if he will be armed but I doubt it."

Still no movement.

"I have a car downstairs which you can use to drive down as soon as you like."

The brothers looked at each other, returning their gaze, they simultaneously frowned.

Noticing, Danny replied, "you would have flown but your *tools* can't go by air.

Using what Danny thought was their language went on, "the *round eyes* don't take kindly to those kind of objects on planes."

The brothers frown departed, they now understood, very good.

"I have rooms booked for you nearby, details in the car and anyway no one will notice two more *students* as there is a large foreign language school nearby."

Both men nodded in approval.

"You will however only have two nights to complete *your* business."

Again both men nodded. So be it, this meant little room for rehearsals, yet the payday balancing out the imposed risk.

"I am flying down at lunchtime. I should be able to physically identify him by tomorrow night so will be able to give you either photo's or a perfect description probably the following morning."

Chu spoke for the first time during the meeting, "how will we draw him to a place where we can conduct *our* business?"

With a satisfied, informed smile, Danny replied, " I have bait."

Neither brother quite understanding.

Seeing this Danny continued, "I've got a local *lady of the night* who will travel independently. Rest assured the slug will be attracted to her. I'm convinced he will try to take her away, somewhere quiet and it'll be then you strike."

"What about the bait?" It was Chu's brother this time.

"She is being extremely well paid. She is from across *your* water and will never talk. If she does, she knows it will be some of the last words she will ever utter."

This time he brothers understood. Chu again, "what does she look like?"

Danny pushed forward two colour photo passport pages, excellent copies which would have been sufficient to gain entry into any number of countries.

Allowing them time to study the photo, Danny enquired, "drinks?"

Two minutes later Jenny brought in one herbal tea and a strong coffee. Returning moments later, the secretary placed a beautiful leather, Edwardian, doctors holdall next to Danny's chair, then left.

As Jenny left Force Lightening studies the passport page.

| | |
|---|---|
| Japan | Type P |
| *Issuing Country:* | *Japan* |
| *Passport Number:* | *TZ0195258* |
| *Surname:* | *Yasuda* |
| *Given Name:* | *Aika* |
| *Nationality:* | *Japanese* |
| *Date of Birth:* | *1st March 1971* |
| *Sex:* | *female* |
| *Place of domicile:* | *Osako* |
| *Profession:* | *Ballet Dancer.* |

Even with the Japanese embossed mark partly covering her forehead, the photo was of a stunning young woman. Chu, who spoke excellent Japanese, thought it highly appropriate that the girls name translated in English to, Summer Love. Continuing to think in Japanese, so she was to be the esa.*

They placed the photo's in their respective pockets, Miki's seemingly lost in his great fist. The brothers then simultaneously took a drink from their delicate cups, before looking up.

As they did, Danny bent down picking up the holdall. Opening it on the desk he placed the two bundles it contained in front of his visitors.

Force Lightening were well known, along with many triad hit men, to favour knives.

Opening their respective packages revealing, protected by dark sheathes, two beautifully carved knives.

Danny motioned by opening his hands towards them, "if you would care to inspect them. They are yours to keep. I can and will have them shipped anywhere in the world after this is over."

The brothers smiled for the first time. Chu, "thank you, this is an unexpected gift."

Each weapon exactly fourteen and a half inches long. The Hamono† some eight inches long, the finest the best Japanese craftsman could fashion. Both were also over one hundred and twenty years old, each incredibly sharp. The front third being as sharp on both edges.

---

* Bait.

† Japanese description for blade.

In the right hands they could disembowel a grown man in one sweeping movement. Both brothers had performed this *procedure* a number of times.

Chu and Miki preferred Japanese blades. It was, with the exception of possibly Damascus craftsmen, the finest metal work to be found on the planet. Simultaneously taking them from their sheaths. Chu, the Japanese expert, held it towards the mornings light. The patination was beyond compare, with folds like sand at low tide, flowing down to the very tip. He knew that each was worth in excess of five thousand American dollars.

Seeing their obvious appreciation, Danny said, "you need not worry, they were bought by an anonymous buyer in Sotherby's four years ago. Even if they could be traced they could never get back to you or even myself." With a smile he finished with, "they are like a cold wind, piercing, yet invisible."

All three smiling in acknowledgment at the accurate analogy.

Danny moved the bag round the table. As he did each assassin wrapped their weapon in the soft cloth which had protected them in the bag. Placing the case on the floor, weapons secure, Chu closed the leather clasp.

"Mr Bo informs me that your initial payment has entered your respective accounts. The remainder will be paid when our business is complete. I will leave details of your return flight with my secretary. After it's over someone will collect your weapons as I take it you would enjoy using them in the future."

He received simultaneous nods.

Danny stood up by way of indication that their meeting was at an end, "I will be in touch later today as I may have to stay down south so we will meet again there."

The brothers pushed back their chairs, Chu with the bag in his hand. Danny came round from his desk. The men turned to leave.

"One final thing, *he* must feel pain that will last eternity."

"He will," their haunting reply.

# CHAPTER 22

## *Esa*

Aika Yashuda left school much to her parents displeasure when she was only eighteen. They had automatically expected, after Mino Koko* she would go to university.

Aika had had other ideas.

At one meter seventy eight or five foot ten in old money, she was tall for a Japanese woman. Her ballet training had been extensive and tough, Aika blessed with real talent. Her teacher said that with the right environment she *could* make it professionally. Aika translated this as, with further training in the West, she *would* make it as a dancer.

After secretly writing to every dance company in America and Britain she had finally received a positive reply from Manchester. They had said that, if her instructor's reference were accurate and she was capable of making her own way to Britain, then they would be prepared to take her on as a trainee. She should however be under no illusion, the training was tough, yet no way as fierce as the competition.

After six months they would decide to, either take her on with a one year contract, or release her from the *temporary* contract which they had enclosed in duplicate.

Aika had saved all her holiday work money for years for this very opportunity and was over eighteen, had her own passport and was determined, with youthfulness and skill on her side, that she'd make it.

When she announced she was leaving home her parents had obviously been mortified that their beautiful, innocent daughter was throwing everything away to follow her dream of becoming a professional ballet dancer.

Luckily the Manchester Dance Company had rules, so, two months after writing to her, they had ensured someone met Aika and took her to the shared flats where all the unaccompanied dancers lived.

Quickly settling in Aika trained incessantly, fearing for her livelihood, let alone her fathers certain wrath. Also, Aika knew she did not have the funds to get home. The dance trainee was determined not to have to call, begging for a wire transfer of money to get back to Japan.

Initially Aika did very well, her six week report, given by the dower Russian dance mistress, was promising if not quite glowing. After that Aika trained with new enthusiasm.

Just when things were going swimmingly it happened, a silly slip in the training dance studio. The resident physiotherapist said she had torn a ligament in her knee which needed at least six week rehab and at worst could require surgery. Aika had returned to her poky little bedsit in tears, where was she possibly going to find the seven

* High School

hundred pounds required to go private?

It was then she met one of the Dance company directors. Charlie Jones was a business man who really did not go in for ballet. Far rather, he particularly enjoyed watching the beautifully honed female bodies leaping about, all hot and sweaty. He even went to their training to enjoy the sights and smells of young woman stretching in front of his mesmerised eyes.

Charlie noticed Aika in her first week and had taken to smiling and saying hello whenever she went passed. The more mature girls understood he was after only one thing. Knowing he would shower her with gifts of flowers, presents, even money in an attempt to get her into bed. Once he had tired of one, the supposed 'supporter of the arts' would invariably move onto the next innocent newcomer.

No one warned Aika.

Before the grind of his daily business Charlie often liked a quick sensory fix. That particular morning he saw her limping, left leg ridged, towards the physio's room before morning practice. Although people respected his supporting the 'company', Charlie knew it was money well spent having slept with four trainee and junior dancers in the passed year.

Seeing his opportunity, he had paid for Aika to visit a specialist. Driving her back in his car she looked forlorn at the diagnosis. To comfort her he had said not to worry, something would come along to sort it out. Akia was not so sure, where was she going to get the one thousand pounds Charlie's specialist and friend, had said was required for the key hole operation.

Charlie said that if she liked he would pay the bill and anyway, he was one of the prime supporters of the troop, so was it not only natural to look after the dancers of the future? Aika failed to see through Charlie's plan. He had done it before, when a Spanish girl had twisted her ankle before paying him back in his private flat at least five times before her disgusted father had flown over, physically taking his bedraggled daughter back to Cordoba.

At first Aika thought nothing of the offer other than a kind middle aged man who was in the business, had offered to pay for her operation. She had no idea her father was right about Aika's naive childhood being her downfall, so far away from home. In her eighteen years she'd had boyfriends, yet it had never involved sex and anyway she was too strict on herself. Training never really allowing her to become sexually active.

Aika had few male friends and little money so had enjoyed the expensive meal they had and the beautiful flowers Charlie sent so brightened her drab room. He really treated her well and as he kept saying wasn't it in his interests to ensure the dancers were happy and any of them who had injuries must be given every opportunity to recover as quickly as possible. On their second night out, Charlie suggested that they go to his flat for a coffee before he took her back to her digs. Innocence prevailing, Aika had agreed.

After two large whiskies Charlie had apologised that he was unable to drive having *inadvertently* drunk too much. She was however more than welcome to have his room and he would sleep on the couch. Again innocence had the better of the girl from the busy industrial town of Osako.

Having drank rather too much at the restaurant, plus three glasses of wine back at the flat Aika guard was down. Charlie had sex with her twice that first night.

Early the next morning she'd awoken in total disgust with herself. He was clearly old enough to be her father, how could she loose her virginity to someone like this?

Later back in her room, after a long bath, Aika reconciled her situation and what had happened. She was an adult, she would loose her virginity to someone so why not a man who treated her really kindly? He was also generous and anyway he wasn't that bad looking.

They had sex a further two times that first week. Each time Aika convinced herself that she was an adult and so what if he was older than she was, Charile wasn't rough and always talked about how he was more than happy to front up the money for the operation.

Over the next few weeks Charlie took Aika out a lot, introducing his new special friend to some of his pals. They too had professed to be followers of dance. If only she'd known their appetite for dancing, more frequently involved poles.

Her operation, Charlie had promised, was scheduled for a couple of weeks time but as he was going away for a few days he had suggested, no offered, that one of his close friends take her out if she was bored, stuck in the bedsit whilst all the other girls were at dance practice.

Aika perceived this as a perfectly friendly gesture and happily accepted. Charlie's friends had been delighted as a string of them came and went. Most just taking her to expensive restaurants. One night Charlie's best friend, so he said, had the flat keys and had asked if she fancy staying in to watch a film. Aika thought this a splendid idea. After, again, far too much wine on a near empty stomach she had relented to the man kissing her. One thing had then led to another and before she knew what she was doing, the man was on top of her, sweating as he heaved against her. Just before midnight, after a quick shower he calmly announced he'd have to get home to 'the wife'. A short while later as he dropped her off back at the digs, he'd thrust an envelope into Aika's hand. Just wanting to get away, Aika had taken it before running back into the block of flats.

Later that night through sobs she opened the envelope to find five twenty pound notes. Physically shocked she stared at the money, tears landing on the bank notes.

The next morning Charlie had called and asked if she'd had a good time with his pal? Aika had been so embarrassed that she said nothing. Need and greed did however mean the notes were transferred to her previously semi barren purse.

Thus, like so many promising starts, Aika's life tumbled, spiralling downwards. The operation never materialised as Charlie always had an answer about his surgeon and friend being at a conference in America or just so busy. Anyway if she was short for cash here was fifty pounds and did she fancy going out that night?

Evolution took its course. Aika never really saw herself as a prostitute, the money she received was incredible. After six months, she knew that there was no road back to the dancing, Manchester having released her from her temporary contract. Charlie had found her a small efficient flat. It was *efficient* in Charlie's eyes as it had a large bed and plenty of booze and Aika's upbringing ensured she always kept it spotlessly clean.

Actually she rather enjoyed her new life. Not the sex as it invariably involved fat married businessmen fumbling about and lasting only a few minutes. After which they would shower, kiss her on the cheek, pay and leave.

The money was the thing.

In time, if she had one thing to thank Charile for it was that the circles he moved in were wealthy. She would never go out with more than one man a night and even started to discuss her fees before they reached the restaurant. Tall, slim and beautiful she had no problems being introduced to any number of wealthy men who would happily pay two, three even five hundred pounds for a night with a top quality oriental hooker.

In a kind of reconciliation process, after exactly one year she had called Charlie, who continued to bullshit her about the postponed operation. Aika didn't care and having saved a lot of money from her new found profession, told him that she was moving away.

Deep down Aika longed for a new start and had chosen Newcastle as it was supposedly an up and coming city with plenty of rich businessmen. Also, Aika knew she could never return home as her family, in time honoured Japanese tradition had disowned her. After a few nights in a hotel she had lied about her job and rented a pretty little flat in the Sandyford district, just outside the centre of town. It was quiet and everyone seemed to keep themselves to themselves. Not cheap, it did however ensure that, if she ever needed to bring a client back to the flat, discrete neighbours turned a blind eye.

Sad to see her go but already casting a longing eye over a young trainee from Falmouth, before she left Manchester, Charlie gave Aika a name of a business friend who worked in the North East.

Two days later Aika called him up and within a few weeks had a steady stream of clients eager to *sample* the new girl. She put her prices up but they didn't seem to mind. Now with a very healthy bank account Aika only worked three or four nights a week. Even if she had been the principle dancer for the whole troop she would never have earned up to two thousand pounds a week for only four *performances.*

Aika frequently went to the various Chinese restaurants in town. When she did it was invariably in the company of a client. After about nine months she was well known amongst those who knew about such things, that, the Japanese girl was without doubt one of the very best professional women in the whole city. Discreet, stunning, with style and such an elegance bourn from hours against the practice bar.

Danny had never had the inclination or need *to use* a prostitute, that said he knew that women like Aika came to his restaurants with clients. Anyway it was not against the law, well his law.

He had however, very discretely, got one of his managers to contact her with a business proposition.

Aika had heard the name Danny Chang a number of times. The thought that he might like to occasionally, very discreetly, introduce visiting business men to her certainly appealed not least as it was made very clear that she would be paid one thousand pounds per night regardless if she ended up in bed alone or not.

Normally she didn't, but the wealthy visitors were always delighted when they met the gorgeous twenty-year-old.

Thus the loose, very private agreement was taken up. Sometimes a restaurant manager would phone Aika on her mobile inquiring if she might be available for a dinner engagement in a night or two's time. Aika never refused, the money was just too good and anyway Aika invariably had a superb meal, was treated with respect and only one in three of her dinner partners actually wanted to have sex, the majority preferring, just someone to spend their otherwise lonely evening with.

She had taken the phone call from a manager Aika knew casually. Both knew each others profession, yet the conversation had been totally professional.

"Aika, hi it's Sam here. I was wondering if you might be available for a special business venture. A prominent person has asked me if you would be prepared to visit a town in the south. It should keep you away from the city for no more than three or four days."

Without waiting for a response Sam continued, "this venture has certain differences to the usual. That said, I am instructed to pay you twice the normal fee. Are you are interested?"

Without hesitation, greed getting the better of her, Aika, instantly replied, "yes, when?"

"Very soon. I would like to have a chat first to go over some of the details. I have further been informed that if successful you will receive a further payment of ten thousand pounds."

Eyes widening, Aika couldn't believe her ears as her normal fee was now in the region of one thousand pounds a night. She did the sums, four days work and she could be back in her flat by the middle of the next week with nigh on eighteen thousand pounds in her account.

Later that evening whilst enjoying the hospitality in The Great Wall restaurant, she met Sam. Earlier Danny had told Sam to confide in the woman, so Sam explained that this venture was extremely important to his associate as well as a little delicate. He knew the consequences if she subsequently opened her mouth about the venture, "look dear, the man whom I'm arranging this for told me to be up front about things." Aika sipped her Shanghai Sling as she studied the fat little Chinese man sat opposite her. Replying, "well we are all grown ups. So what's he want? I go down to some town, *look after* a *friend* of his for a few days then come home, right?"

"Yes, but, arr hell, basically he wants you to chat some bloke up so that he takes you off with him. After that some other associates will appear and you can then leave."

The penny didn't momentarily drop for Aika, "what d'you mean?

"It's like this Aika, my associate knows of a man who he wishes to *teach a lesson* to. He requires someone with your *skills* to lure him away from his friends. Throughout you will be watched and probably, as soon as he is about to become real friendly they'll turn up. As of that moment you should leave, quickly."

Hopefully having made the point Sam continued, seeing only the faintest frown on her light brown forehead, "you will have a flight leaving Newcastle Thursday lunchtime. With an executive motel room, near London, booked. Remember you may need to *use* it, if not, after that you are finished, you can return home our business complete."

Aika's penny finally reached its destination, "ah I get it now, you want me to be the bait so that you can catch someone with their pants down, so to speak. Then you intend to teach them a lesson."

"Exactly," Sam carefully leaving out some of the details. "One final thing," leaning his glowing face forward as Aika finished her cocktail, "if you ever breathe a single word of this to anyone, it will be the last breath you take. Do we completely understand each other?"

The glass ever so slightly rocking, imperceptibly, as Aika's now trembling hand replaced it on the quality, pristine, white table cloth, "I understand," she thought she did. Aika was liable to be *taught a lesson* herself, if she talked. Regaining her composure, "well that's fine by me. I take it you have all the bank details from last time," Sam nodded.

"Well then exactly where is it that I have to go?"

"You can get a taxi from Heathrow," as he spoke he slid across an ornate menu. Aika slipped the envelope it contained into her bag. Seeing her do so, Sam continued, "that's got the name of the motel you are to stay at, your executive room is booked for four nights. You'll find some travelling expenses in there as well. Your ticket will be waiting for you at the airport. You're on the eleven thirty down to Heathrow, British Midlands. I've got your mobile number so someone will be in touch"

Pushing back his carver chair Sam stood up, "Aika do a good job on this and my boss will be in your debt."

With that he left the elegant lady to enjoy her Lemon Chicken.

Aika watched him leave through the waitresses entrance, exit.

So she was working for Sam's boss now, Mr Chang certainly could introduce her to even wealthier clients. With that she picked at her complementary meal before taking a taxi home.

# CHAPTER 23

## Red Herring

If Danny's plans were steaming ahead, Sergeant Parish's were at best a damp *chug*.

She was giving the Saint his morning debrief. Chief Inspector Monk had arrived at work in a bad mood. His fingers hurt, they ached and were slightly swollen so God help him when the weather got shitty in a month or so.

He sat listening, clenching and unclenching his fist whilst Sue stood on the other side of his desk briefing him. Although he had been truly amazed by Boeck's information he was not prepared to let a detective loose, unguided. It would be like a cannon ball crashing into the military. If he found out, the Commissioner would have a fit, yet the Boeck man had been so accurate about the knife, studying his fingers as they grinded open and closed, let alone the stuff about his arthritic fingers.

Looking up as Sue spoke, "sir please, from what we know the bastard is roaming around, somewhere out there. We don't know where and I'm certain he will strike again, soon"

"Listen Sue, it's just not that easy. The military are very touchy about this sort of thing. They, quite rightly in my opinion, want to keep stuff like this *in house*. That's why they've got their own Special Investigation Branch."*

Standing her ground Sue replied, "please sir, I could just go in and have a chat with someone. I'm pretty sure it's the Scottish lot down at Catterick. They are always getting into strife in town. They come up here, get pissed and cause trouble."

Neil, sighed a heavy sigh, she was all said and done still a constable, "the best I'm prepared to do is to let you go and meet someone I know in the brigade headquarters. He may be prepared to talk to you unofficially," seeing Sue about to speak, "that's my final offer. Unless you can come up with solid *police* evidence, not mumbo jumbo from a friend to criminals." Remembering her previous outburst, "listen I'm not prepared to see the Commissioner to get formal authority to search any old army camps." In resignation Sue, stepped forward, placed the perfect interim report in her bosses intray. Nodding forward, "the report. If there's nothing more sir, I'd like to phone your contact, please."

Five minutes later, Sue sat at her desk, re-reading a copy of the report.

Had Simon told her all the truth, she thought so? Penny's *uncle* obviously seemed as desperate for the attacker to be caught as she did. She tried the number the Saint had given her, it was engaged.

After a trip to the loo and three more attempts, success. A controlled yet rapid voice answered, "G1, major Kell speaking."

"Major Kell, my name is Detective Sergeant Sue Parish. I was given your number by Chief Inspector Neil Monk. I was wondering if I could have a few moments of your time,

* Boeck's own note. In reality the Army tend not to react like this, preferring to afford the local police every assistance when dealing with such a serious crime.

please?"

"Sergeant Parish, can I call you Sue?"

Smiling, the military were so predictable. Simon had done exactly the same, "of course, please do."

Before she could continue, "please call me Tim."

Glancing at her notes, "Tim, I work on the Regional Serious Crimes Squad and currently I'm running a particularly distressing case. You see I've some information that there is a possibility that a local soldier may be involved."

Fucking hell, all Tim needed right now was another stupid idiot getting into serious trouble. He already had case files piled up, awaiting legal advice.

"Please, not more strife," his instinctive reply.

Sue continued, "Tim, a lady was brutally attacked in Newcastle last weekend. From the information we have gathered so far, we believe a soldier may have done it. We think it might be a Scotsman who could go by the name of Steven Coats or Roots.

Tim wrote down the name. God if the jocks had been up to their old tricks in Newcastle Lord knows they were capable of anything, "Sue, I will have a word with their adjutant and see if they have anyone by that name. Do you have any other details?" Not really knowing what an Adjutant was Sue thought better than expose her ignorance said, "only that he's big, tough and rough, to say the least."

Tim instantly recognised about fifty percent of the Black Watch, the remainder being rough, tough and *small.*

"Sue. I'll get back to you within the morning, is that OK?"

"Tim I'm really grateful and realise you really don't need the local fuzz sticking their noses in," as an afterthought, "what will the military police think?"

"They won't, because they won't know. Better that way," Tim's reply.

"I look forward to hearing from you soon, goodbye."

Sue sat and pondering the short conversation. Major Kell's voice sounded a bit upper class, yet soft, almost gentle. She wondered if he were married or not?

# CHAPTER 24

## *Safe Base Recce*

The flight down on Thursday morning was full. During which Simon had an enjoyable chat to a jolly, weather beaten turkey farmer from Texas who went by the name of Floyd Fletcher. Floyd was doing the ancestors trail and had no idea that, according to Simon, his ancestors would almost certainly have been arrow makers.

Having said goodbye to the Texan turkey farmer, leaving the terminal Simon jumped on the Hertz shuttle bus, picking up the Volvo up ten minutes later. Having joined the ring road, along the M3, he left at the Frimley junction and headed into Camberly. Turning off the main road he took the sharp left, before the railway bridge, onto Gordon's Avenue. Nestling in amongst the Vets and Physio's stood an elegant, tall late Victorian house. Simon had been here many times. Having parked on the road he approached a modest attractive semi. Out of courtesy he pulled the ornate brass bell.

As the inner porch door opened, a petite shriek rang out from a small person. The child scampered, opening the outer glass door. "Uncle Simon, Uncle Simon," the five year old leapt up, grabbing at his midriff.

"Well hello Claude, how's my favourite little soldier," Simon always used his pet name for the child he loved like his own.

Walking, legs stiff as the child clung like a leach, Simon tottered, actually struggled into the tastefully decorated long corridor.

"Mummy, mummy it's Uncle Simon."

At that moment another smaller person darted out from a side room, banged into her brother and promptly started to cry. Simon picked up three and a half year old Juliet in one sweep. Her tears instantly replaced by fits of giggles as Simon started to tickle her.

With even more difficulty Simon proceeded down the corridor into a large, well equipped kitchen. Anyone entering could certainly tell whoever owned the kitchen was an expert or dedicated amateur, glistening pans hung like ordered stalactites, two little mites randomly charging around below.

Big brown eyes smiling on her charming European face as, wiping flour from hands onto her apron, Louise came forward and embraced her dear friend and received the patter of kisses to her cheeks. Answering her question, Simon explained that it was really kind of her and Mark to allow him to stay. No, he was there on private business. Louise had far too much sense than to pry.

Yes he would probably be gone sometime over the weekend. Was that going to be a problem?

Simon knew that this was the perfect base from which to conduct business. If he lay his head down to sleep, he would do so soundly. There were few homes where an intruder would be met with such ferocious, protective, deadly venom. Mark, Louise's husband, was over six foot and muscular. As an ex marine, he was certainly more than capable of handling himself. Simon and Mark had on previous occasions discussed late at night, over too many whiskies, what would happen if anyone tried to burgle them when his family were in the house. They'd agreed any intruder would probably survive at the cost of permanent physical damage.

Handing over a Heathrow shoppers bag, "Louise, I will be out most of the time."

Studying the contents, "Simon this is very kind of you. Mark will be delighted, he'll be back just after six."

Seeing Simons frown, "well, whenever your back, we can sit down and have a glass of this."

Whilst speaking Louise lay the Bolinger 1996 in the fridge. Then after a brief chat Simon went upstairs, taking his bag to the prepared room.

Two minutes later, back downstairs, he'd sat, enjoying catching up with all the gossip about how the children were already completely fluent in both languages.

Louise had been a very high profile interpreter in the Army and worked in some of the most dangerous war zones in the eighties. Louise had only left, as a senior Captain, so that she could be with her new husband and as she pointed out, danger and trying to bring up two little ones was far from compatible.

Simon excused himself at one thirty and drove the short trip to Aldershot where he easily found the bridge from his previous *journey*. Parking the car about half a mile away in a sports complex carpark, putting on his sunglasses he casually walked towards the canal bridge. Turning off the road he went down the twenty or so steps onto the tow path. Moving along he noted that it was very quiet, even at that time of day.

Somehow Simon instinctively recognised the right point to leave the track. Checking round, not a soul. Then easily climbing the slight bank through light shrubs. Within twenty seconds Simon found what he was looking for. Almost totally circled by bushes and small trees was a shallow recess, about the size of a standard living room. Almost barren, only pinecones dotted about like natural confetti. It did seem however that most of the undergrowth had been trampled down.

Crouching as he moved around Simon knew that this was where the man he sought would come. Touching the earth sensing nothing other than confused distress mixed with cruel pleasure and a smell, *his* smell. Yes, this was exactly what he was looking for.

Squatting he went back to the canal path, still no one around before retracing his steps and up back onto the road path. Turning right Simon clearly saw the dirt track paralleling the main footpath.

Within two minute he came to a sweeping bend in the road by a major T-junction, on the far side Simon could see a very large car park. One end dominated by an enormous pub, the other taken up by a couple of shops. In front of the pub were about half a dozen wooden benches. Above the entrance the pub sign was swinging in the light breeze. Standing about beneath Simon could see a couple of bouncers. With a momentary frown, he wondered why this was, 'they were' somehow significant?

He turned to go now with a resigned look on his face before twisting his head round one last time to study the painting of a bulky ram, its massive curling horns swaying in the wind as it glared down at him.

---

On the way back to Camberly, Simon phoned Danny, detailing what he had found.

He explained that they would meet at The Locks Public House on the same canal but ten miles away, near Frimley.

Returning to Camberly, he'd enjoyed a very early single glass of the rather good Bollinger with Louise, as Mark wasn't back from work yet. Simon had then further surprised her with yet another bottle of the same vintage, this time insisting they keep it for themselves by way of a thank you for allowing him to stay at such short notice.

---

Danny and Simon met shortly after three that afternoon, the weather still golden. The gentle sun tinkling on the dark lock water, rippling, not more than twenty feet away. The Locks Pub stands by a working lock where many customers enjoyed a drink and pub grub as the canal barges negotiated the single old fashioned system. Deep in thought Simon watched as he had any number of times.

Seeing Danny park the Mercedes in the adjacent carpark, moments later Simon rose as he approached before they embraced in the customary manner, "Danny good to see you. We have much to talk about."

Simon then went inside and bought his friend a lime and soda and a rather too sweet ginger beer for himself.

No one took much notice as the two men were obviously discussing *business* over a drink.

Any casual observers were right, but owe how different the *business* was which they discussed.

"Danny I know exactly where he committed the crimes. After this," nodding at his untouched drink, "I'll show you the pub where I am convinced he spends time."

Seeing Danny's obvious approval he went on, "now listen I don't want to know what your planning." Pushing two palms towards Danny by way of stopping him before he had a chance to speak, "Danny I'm going to return there tonight to see what else I can find. I will try, if possible, to photograph *him* if he appears, then and I mean this, I go home, agreed."

Danny nodded, knowing far better than to tell Simon that he would visit the same location but with the brothers in the car, certain they would appreciate getting a look at the place. They may even get a look at the slug he sought. Danny knew the call girl was established in a executive motel, not ten minutes from where they were having their drink.

Later, once Danny knew what was going on, he would get the brothers to meet the girl and they'd all go over the plan of attack.

Not for the last time, seeing his friend deep in thought, Simon sat quietly working out his own plan. He would go to The Ram later that evening. At Newcastle airport he'd bought one of the new APS compact cameras. Sat outside, he could easily deceive by pretending to study his new purchase. Yet in reality, take photo's which he could quickly get developed at a one hour development place back in Camberly before handing over the photos to Danny. He'd then head back to Mark and in time for dinner.

Almost at the same time they both came out of their respective thought trances. Simon spoke, "well Danny I suppose we had better take a look."

Danny nodded.

Taking Simon's car, his passenger trying to memorise the route on the short trip to The Ram's car park. Having parked both men walked over the main junction and along the footpath towards the canal. Reaching the now familiar bridge Simon dropped down for the second time to the tow path. Moving along they came to the unmarked entrance to the secret hollow, not fifteen feet away. One after the other they went up through the undergrowth. Having had a quick look, they quietly moved back along the path to the bridge. Within five minutes they were sat in Simon's car on the far side of the car park.

Only a few passing customers sat outside enjoying a drink.

"Simon, are you certain this is where he goes?"

Simon nodded, "yes my friend this is where he is. He moves along the path that I showed you. Not the main one but the path set back amongst the trees. Where he goes then I'm not yet sure."

Frowning Danny answered, "I know this should make no sense but if you are telling me this is where he works and he takes poor victims along to the hollow then that's good enough for me."

"Don't forget I will have to come back later this evening as I have a plan and will be able to provide you with photo's."

With a satisfied grin, Danny nodded, the bastard would be no match for Force Lightening. They'd surprise him as he took the girl along the tow path and with any luck he would be sinking slowly into the murky canal.

"OK, so I'll go back to my hotel and wait for your call. You know where I'm staying so hopefully tonight I should finally get a look at the vile slime who did this to my little girl. Trust me he will be so very sorry."

With that Simon drove them back to The Locks Pub in near silence, finally broken when he had asked how Penny was doing.

"Oh Simon she looks so much better. They are going to let her out very soon. I chatted with Mr Winter last night as he said he'd spoken with the plastic surgeon who visited her two days ago. He said there should be hardly any visible scars. The doc' did mention that down below." As he spoke, gesturing toward his privates, "unfortunately she will have plenty of scars but hopefully only a few should show above her bikini line.

It was Simon's turn, "I am so relieved for you all. Please give Penny my love, tell her I will pop by as soon as I get back home."

As he spoke the car came to a stop, Danny tapped Simons knee by way of a goodbye, got out and back in his own car, waved as Simon drove past. Seeing him leave, Danny dialled the twins number.

After a brief conversation Danny dialled another number, again not giving his name. He told Aika that she should expect to be picked up by a Mercedes with three Chinese men in it as they were going to get a glimpse of the man he wanted her to chat up.

## CHAPTER 25

# *Preparations*

Friday afternoon parades were always a bit of a charade, most notably because they normally took place at eleven forty five. Ten minutes later, unless something was pressing, the troops were knocked off until the following Monday, ten sharp.*

This particular Friday being no exception.

Immediately it finished most squaddies bolted for the weekend. By twelve thirty Boots sat alone in the near deserted cookhouse,

After one, back in his room Boots did his dobie† and once his uniform was in the drier, went over to the NAAFI to watch a film with a few of the Tribe. Realising the time, he left Ms Weaver battling Aliens, to get a shower before getting ready for an evening *on the door* of the club. Putting a tie in his pocket, he would only wear it at the last moment and anyway it was a fake, no bouncer wanted some pissed squaddy pulling him down by a noose around his neck. Sitting on his unmade bed he paused staring upwards, the sun reflecting from the sink onto the ceiling. Watching the rays dance and flicker around the room Boots decided tonight he was going on a *mission.*

With all the girls being ferried in, he couldn't fail to get one of them either, pissed or easier, drugged.

Yes he would do it again tonight.

Having placed two phials of the tranquilliser in an inside pocket Boots moved over to his drawers and opened the top side one. Looking in he saw the crumpled army green sock. Carefully taking it out he unfolded the claw on the top.

For more than a minute Boots sat motionless, transfixed by the makeshift claw come weapon. Now completely dry it took on an even more sinister appearance. Almost black in colour, it contrasted only slightly with the dark green tape wrapped around its knuckle.

For the second time grasping it in his fist, the claw exposed through his middle fingers. Yes this was a mighty weapon.

God help anyone who caused trouble on the door tonight.

This time wrapping it in a brand new handkerchief Boot's sister had sent him for his birthday. Stupid bitch didn't even know he never used the things. Grinding his teeth as he placed the weapon into his jacket pocket.

Flopping a jacket over his shoulder before locking the flimsy door Boots strolled slowly, enjoying the pleasant afternoon sunshine, out through the camp gates, walking having lost his licence nearly two years earlier. As a result he decided not to get the

---

* Mostly, when not on exercise, units grant fairly generous weekend breaks, ie lunchtime Friday until ten the following Monday.

† Dobie is a military term referring to doing the washing. Originated from when the British Army were in India.

bus, preferring to walk the twenty minutes to The Ram, arriving close to five thirty. Not yet serving, the main double doors were however open as he stepped inside, instantly smelling the usual aroma of spilt beer, stale tobacco and cleaner's powerful fragrance masking spray.

Walking through to the small, sweat stinking changing room, he checked that there were a couple of spare jackets and trousers. The manager insisting each doorman looked smart and clean at all times, citing initial appearances were all important.

Boots placed a complete set into his own grubby locker. Moving back out into the empty expansive bar where there was still a lack of customers, opening time not being for a few minutes. After the chaotic previous night, the manager insisted they close between three and six. The fact that they had a weekend licence to serve alcohol until well passed two in the morning meant for a very long evening session.

Looking round a couple of the female bar staff had filtered in and started setting up behind the bar. Boots didn't fancy either of them, the real reason being that both having heard his reputation, had turned him down flat. Instead he wandered over and stood chatting with the other two bouncers who had taken up station just at the main entrance. At exactly six, nothing happened and it was not until fifteen minutes later when some of Boots own platoon turned up, that the bar got its first customers of the evening. At about the same time the travelling disco van arrived and two bearded, sweating, DJs started to unload their equipment.

Boots went outside and chatted with his four work *mates* at one of the wooden tables. They were drinking and discussing the up and coming field exercise. The only other people around were a couple of obviously, lost tourists, speaking what Boots vaguely recognised as Italian. Apart from them only some bloke sat on his own, fumbling with what looked like a new camera.

Ignoring all of them he went back and chatted to the DJs who agreed it was going to be a fantastic session, a heaving night, what with the expected influx of women combined with the fact that one of the Parachute companies had just returned from Ireland. Boots and his colleagues also knew it probably meant they would be called upon in a professional capacity.

Sauntering over to the entrance, Boots sat on a high stool. From here he could scan the bar, the dance floor, as well as patrol what was going on at the entrance and outside. He was just chatting with his mate about the possibility of picking up a bird, and would he cover for him for a hour or so whilst he had his wicked way when....

Boots heard the warning shout, by way of abuse, surely it was far too early for a fight, it was only twenty to seven? Stepping outside, he was wrong.

Looking over Boots saw two of his mates sprawled on the carpark. Another was frantically tugging at his shoe, which seemed trapped in the bench where he'd been sitting. The other, was fronting up to the bloke, who he'd noticed fiddling with a camera.

Running the last twenty feet, as he did, recognising Pte Graville as he went for the much smaller, older bloke.

Boots blinked.

A moment later, the bloke was still standing and Gareth Graville was sprawling on the ground. The other guy then seemed to leap straight up, stick his leg out and spin round with incredible speed, coming back down from exactly where he had started, balancing on the balls of his brogue shoes.

Almost at the same time, the one stuck by the bench had picked up a bottle to throw it, only to drop it smashing to the carpark floor?

"Oy what the fuck's going on here!" Boots came to an abrupt halt in between the, now, pile of soldiers and the other bloke. Directing his question at the man every so slightly swaying next to him, "what's your game then?"

"Well you see it's not my fault. They attacked me, they were being so damn rude to those people." The man gesticulated to the terrified Italian couple who had left their drinks and were now hell bent on getting back in their car and not stopping until they reached Winchester and hopefully quieter, safer surroundings.

The four young men had gathered themselves up and were approaching, menacingly.

"Boots, this fucker comes over lording it up telling us to mind our language."

Boots could easily weigh up what had happened. Some god damn do gooder had taken offence to their remarks about the Italians being greasy wops and the like.

"Well listen you lot," turning to face them with his back to the other bloke, "take yourselves inside and get Anne to give you each a free pint on the management." Boots didn't need a fight to break out, especially before seven.

His colleagues, though annoyed, accepted the *morsel* and swearing beneath their breath that 'he was really fucked if he was still there when they came out', moved off toward the other two bouncers who were coming over in case of real trouble.

Turning on the much smaller man, as he did noting the shiny brogue shoes and the smart Chino's. Bugger me if it's not a fucking rodney thought Boots, that's all needed.

Enjoying his words, "listen *mate*, I don't know what you said but you'd better get lost. I don't think they were too pleased about whatever was going on here."

Sensing not the least note of annoyance or fear in the mans posture Boots continued, "they will be back in a minute or two and probably won't like it if you're still around." Finishing with, what he meant as a command, "*OK*".

"You know it's just not right. No one should swear so loud in front of anyone especially guests in our country." As he spoke the man pointed to the disappearing Alpha Romeo, speeding down the road.

"I don't think you understand *pal*."

The response, immediate. "I do, trust me I do, anyway thank *you*."

With that the man held out his hand for Boots to shake. Slightly confused yet thoroughly convinced, fuck, he had to be a rodney, but what the hell, he took the outstretched hand in his. Three seconds later Boots physically pulled it away. "Alright mate, I think I get the picture, so *see ya*."

"I also get the picture, see ya.."

Across the car park Danny, Chu, Miki and a very worried Aika watched as Simon got back in his car and drove away.

# CHAPTER 26

## *Evil's Grasp*

Leaving Danny in the Locks Pub carpark I was in two minds. Should I go back to Louise and Marks' or just go straight to The Ram? As it was only four, I decided go back to Camberly.

Having spent an enjoyable half an hour playing with the children. Finally managing to extract myself, I told Louise I needed some time to think and could I be left alone in my room.

The children safely in the plastic paddling pool outside, I climbed the stairs. In the old house it was very quiet in my room overlooking the end of the street. Being the third floor I could hardly hear anything apart from a few birds on a nearby window ledge. With that I lay down to think.

The next thing I knew a wet little hand was tugging at my trouser leg. Claude had sneaked, dripping, upstairs as he wanted Uncle Simon to play in the paddling pool with him and his sister. Not wanting to get him into trouble I said I'd be down in a minute.

Changing into smart, fighting loose casual clothes, I went back downstairs, splashed the children before explaining to Louise that I had to go out and would probably be back by eight. Answering her question about a meal. Yes, dinner about nine would be great.

---

Parked on the edge of The Ram's carpark next to the front road, studying around I noticed a steady trickle of cars coming and going as they used the pubs carpark for the video shop which was just across the other side. I waited until a couple came out with drinks, the pub now obviously open, as I wandered over with my new camera still in its plastic bag.

Having bought a pint of shandy I moved back outside and took a table furthest away from the entrance but still in clear view. Shortly after I noticed, for the first time, four loud soldiers camped on the table, two away from mine. The only other people around were the two original customers, Italians, their accents clearly identifying them as coming from Naples. Although nowhere near fluent I worked out they were visiting Britain tracing roman history in the south of England, their next location being Winchester. Not quite lost but couldn't find  much about Aldershot in their Roman guidebook.

The four soldiers were however far more interesting, sensing something about them as there was a connection. Could one of them be the one I sought? Scanning them I breathed slowly studying each in turn. No, it was clear that they were only somehow linked.

Discussing a future event they were going to be on range three and would be conducting dry training before the live firing on Friday. Obviously all Welsh, the accents varying from Cardiff to the valleys.

The number three was somehow important? Logging it away for when I next visited the Hacienda Grande, they'd know. Also the date, obviously next Friday was important, vitally important?

It was at that moment the hairs stood up on the back of my neck. Smelling the air for a trail, I swung my attention like a radar around the area. The Italians were irrelevant, the lads important but not vital. Sensing they were somehow tools to be used. Interesting and confusing at the same time?

There was no one else around.

There it was again, a breath, a smell.

In an instant every nerve in my body reacted. Bill and Mierti around, danger closing in. Pretending to be studying the instructions, I loaded the camera. Again scanning the area, no change. As I looked at the camera's French translation I smelt the perfume. Looking up sensing Lotti's presence, over by the main entrance a big bloke had just gone in. Even the mans back seemingly significant as the air of anticipation heightened by the second.

Slowly, calmly I closed my eyes for clarity. Reopening them I knew what to do.

"Eyetals* couldn't get pissed in a brewery," one Welsh voice boomed.

"Yer your right, probably as much use as a fucking chocolate fireguard," another retorted.

The laughter loud, their words clear to all.

My Italian fellow drinkers understood only too well what the men were saying. Distain written across their faces. Ignorant, British football hooligans.

The early thirty year old Italian man restrained by the woman, who clearly wanted to finish her drink and get away as quickly as possible.

"Only good at retreating," the Italian's shifting uneasily at the barrage of insults, fuelling their antagonistic flames still further.

Standing, I saw the window of opportunity as to how to get a better look at the big bloke. He could possibly be a customer, yet from his attire was far more likely to be a bouncer.

Putting the camera down, drawing my legs back and over the fixed chair part of the very solid six seater wooden table. Ten paces later I stopped and leant on the soldiers table. Their conversation abruptly ceasing as they all turned to see who had interrupted their fun, "listen fella's I think you should lay off the Italian jokes. They," looking over to the Italians as they rose from their table, "and I don't think it's funny."

Without giving them time to close their gorping mouths I continued, snapping the words out, "if you don't," lowering my voice, "shut the fuck up, I'll shut you up myself."

They smouldered.

I knew I'd had the desired effect, "who the fuck do you think you are" one of them grunted spitting crisps out at me as he spoke.

Further fanning the embers, my retort instant, "you creatures are like a bunch of stupid baboons."

"Right fuckwit you asked for it," With that all four started to rise from behind the wooden table. One of them seemingly stuck. I saw the shadow seated next to him. Mierti

* Eyetals is Army slang for Italians.

was pinching the lad's jeans to the bench leg with an arrow.

The other three came forward. As they did I stepped back by way of a challenge.

"Alright then, so you reckon your tough?" my response lighting the touch paper before the flames erupted.

With experience you learn that white rage is dangerous. People make mistakes in battle if their rage and anger are left unchecked. These three brutes knew nothing of The Art of War by Sun Zi.

Almost without thinking, they allowed the supposedly toughest the opportunity to take me out by himself.

He rushed at me, very quick. In doing so I realised that if he managed to actually get me to the ground, they might over power us.

He attempted to grab me by the collar.

It wasn't his day. I smelt the cheroot smoke as I, we took action.

Easily twisting his outstretched arms into a single unit, the lad had no comprehension of balance. Rocking backwards and to my side hurling him past me twisting his hands under as I did. He cartwheeled off ten feet away.

The other two saw this and tried to regain the initiative, both attacking at once. Bill very close now as I swayed in the invisible wind, a swirl of smoke as the blows glanced by my head. My arms and hands flowed in slow motion, guided. The first one attempted to kick me in the balls. Half knocking half grabbing his heal, pulling at the same time, driving forward with my other outside shoe. Again he went headlong after his mate.

The third, now ever so slightly apprehensively, weakness exposed, moved forward, shouting at the struggling bench man to get a fucking move on and help. By way of answering the call to arms, he picked up a bottle of Becks, I knew he intended to throw it at me. As if time had become viscous, turning, rolling my fingers in his direction, as it slowly fell from his grasp.

Now too sticky, time stopped, the flight of the black bird over my left shoulder frozen, the cars stationary, silent. Even out of the corner of my eye I could sense real danger, dark approaching evil. In an instant I looked over, then regained focus on my attacker.

Someone else was joining in, someone more dangerous than these four put together.

In a boxer's stance, needing to go on the offence, I sprang forward, swaying away from the surprised youths instinctive fast punch. Smelling foul smoke over my shoulder I knew my back was covered.

Leaning forward grabbing the lads belt, I pushed my elbow up under his armpit. Sweeping my leg from behind, his momentum, my tug and the contact with the stiff leg, sent him tumbling over my two foot high outstretched scythe.

"Oy what the fuck's your game."

Time in an instant propelled to normal speed. Not quite enveloped in invisible smoke I sensed both of my fighters very close now, this man was real venom.

He went on, "what the fuck's your game?"

Looking deep, right behind his eyes, all I saw was darkness, cruel pleasure, pain, hate all intertwined. Staring the whole time as I waffled on about them being rude to the disappearing Italians.

The football yobs gathered themselves up, pride their only injury as they reluctantly headed toward compensation of free beer. One of them called out as they entered the darkness of the pub, "listen boyo, you'd better listen to Boots and piss off, otherwise we'll fuck you proper next time."

Again time stopped, time and space ceasing as the files inside my brain scanned; the wall in the warehouse, down by the river, the Stanley knife.

Chaff fluttering through my mind. Then, one piece stopped in mid air, spinning, glistening. Boots, Boots, Boots as I stared into the dark unwelcome eyes of the one we sought. Offering him my hand by way of thanks, not that he'd actually done anything apart from pulling the dogs from their supposed supper, not that their appetite would have been satisfied. Instantly my hand touched his I sensed the shadows racing towards my realm. They had found me, who and why now, why me?

Smelling his anger, distain for me this man thought I was an Officer. He was the one who had held Penny's hair tight in his enormous sweaty palm. He was right handed and it was this grasp which had held the knife. He was powerful with new fearlessness, a disregard which somehow brought him energy? Misguided lust, his weakness.

Scanning deeper I sensed shadows still racing toward this world.

Like a phone tap I knew I must break off to stop them. They were a real terrifying evil, Boots their portal, somehow toward me. In that moment the realisation that he must be stopped touched me.

Holding on, flickers of chaff like confetti, cascading through my mental filter. The number five hundred and fifty six, a dangerous hanky? Why was his sister so sad? A single shot of M four. He'd broken this wrist whilst playing rugby in a red and blue jumper in the mud?

Ignoring the seemingly irrelevant, confusing chaff, I let go, the entrance instantly slamming shut.

Cigar smoke blew in the wind as fragrant perfume lingered.

Letting go I could sense other eyes on me. Others were watching, observing me, yet they weren't a threat and as such irrelevant.

Glancing at him one last time before turning, walking over, picked my camera up I left.

# CHAPTER 27

## *Mixed Vision*

As Simon's car drew away from The Ram, silence reigned at the far end of the carpark.

Sitting in the back seat, behind his brother who had been driving, Miki gave a low, quiet whistle. Looking diagonally to the front passenger seat, where Danny sat silent transfixed, "so that's the great Green Eyed Dragon, sure as hell wouldn't want to annoy him in a dark alley. What d'you think Chu?"

Chu, who had been holding onto the driving wheel rather tightly, his knuckles stretched, pale, "yes he is very fast and moves with style and purpose. The idiot round eyes had no chance."

Swivelling round, he addressed Danny next to him, "at least we know who's on our side. Can I take it the big one talking with green eyes is our target?" With this, he cranked his head round still further to look at Aika.

Aika looked, indeed was worried. The money was fantastic, yet this was moving into a new realm where real danger existed. She had been slapped a few times by drunken clients, that said nothing which she couldn't handle yet this was altogether very different. She had just witnessed a fight where, by some miracle, no one seemed to have been hurt. A slender man had managed to disable four others without causing real damage? It was plainly obvious however that had the other men got hold of the smaller chap they would have beaten him up badly.

The slight man moved with such elegance, almost like a dancer. Gliding, swaying without even seemingly thinking about his actions. Yet there was something else about him?

Shivering, her scented long dark hair falling over her face. Somehow Aika just knew he was different, with a presence, almost as if he wasn't alone?

Her thoughts interrupted as Danny spoke without directing his words to any one in particular, "you have just seen one of the most incredible men I've ever meet. With respect," looking at Chu, "he really does move with *lightening* speed, almost in slow motion. He is our friend, yet his work here is done so you won't see him again." Not quite by way of a rhetorical question, he continued, "you all saw the big brute who came over and spoke with green eyes?"

Finally, turning to Chu and Miki, Aika directly behind him, "the one he shook hands with is your target." Almost sensing Aika's anxiety, he shuffled in his seat so as to be able to look at her, "don't worry these men will protect you. I want you to chat up the big bloke and hopefully he will try to take you away to some place quiet." Aika was now visibly worried, "but what happens if he takes me in a taxi and they can't follow."

"He won't and these men won't loose you, so just go along with him. Once he starts to get down to *business*," looking at each brother in turn, "they will appear. Once they do, just go. You have my mobile number and when it's all over call me just before nine in the morning."

Danny had it all sorted out, "then you can get a cab from your hotel room and be on your way. Now you know what I ask, your fees will be doubled and in your bank by the time you get back to Newcastle."

This time speaking to Force Lightening, "I need you to check out this place tonight, real quiet. Tomorrow you go into action."

Again addressing Aika, "don't worry, he won't harm a single hair on your head." Shaking his head this way and that, "these men are the very best of the best and will ensure your safety."

Chu, started the car and drove off, each occupant deep in thought. The driver contemplating how the man had moved with such agility when clearly he couldn't see the blow coming towards him. Certainly the myths about spirits surrounding him no longer seemed so unbelievable. Miki, knew his immense power would easily deal with their target. Aika was frightened, yet greed ensured she was going to go through with it. Anyway, if these two were anything like the small bloke then she had little to worry about.

When they reached the car park where Aika was staying, Danny spoke for the first time in the short journey, "you should know he is a very evil man who has cruelly attacked one of my family. Feel nothing for him, he is like the dirt on your shoe."

Nodding slowly before swishing her elegant long, toned, trousered legs out of the car, Aika lent forward close to Danny ear, "I don't want to know. He is nothing to me but I will make him want me, so I'll wait for your call about the exact details. Good evening." She nodded ever so slightly towards all three in turn, got out and closed the car door.

Three pairs of eyes watched her walk across the car park, each enjoying her cute bottom trapped in tight trousers, only the brothers entertaining real carnal thoughts. Both would love to get her into bed, obviously an absolute jewel to be coveted.

Jolting their lustful thoughts Danny spoke, "gentlemen, I will check to confirm your target but don't think I need to."

Miki this time, "he will be easy to get to as that," nodded towards Aika's disappearing behind, "will have his full attention."

Later that evening Danny called Simon and, after a brief conversation, had driven from the hotel to the same pub where they had met earlier. Simon turned up shortly before nine and gave him a folder containing the photo's he'd taken.

Danny studied the fairly good quality snaps. Boots sitting, menacingly, on a stool next to the entrance.

Danny was not the least surprised when Simon had said that he thought they'd been watching. Simon confirmed, yes Danny was right, the one he sought was the big brute of a man who he had shaken hands with. Five minutes later as they walked to their respective hire cars, Simon touched his friends arm, "Danny, I have an idea of what your planning on doing. Please be acutely aware that this is no normal man. He has real power and moves with dark spirits."

With that Simon kissed his friend, much to the amusement of the last few drinkers sat outside, enjoying the cool evening, and left hopefully not too late for Louise's Venison Ragu.

Danny drove back to his hotel, made a call to Miki, confirming they had the right man. He then phoned Aika, not really to reassure her, rather to make sure she had not bolted.

He had no such worries. Sitting in the motel bar Aika was enjoying herself, as two businessmen were trying to chat her up, such amateurs she thought, both were failing miserably. Add to the fact that, in about twenty four hours she would be back at the hotel certain in the knowledge that she would have more money than she'd earned in a year in her account, Mr Chang certainly good for his word. Maybe she could start afresh. With real money like that she could get her knee done and even start to dance again?

Knowingly flaunting her fabulous looks, Aika threw her long jet coloured hair back behind her ears. With that a perfect smile returned to her face as one of the men offered to buy her another glass of champagne.

# CHAPTER 28

## Clutching at Straws

Frustration, nearing irritation etched on her brow, Sue'd had words with her boss about the lack of developments.

"That will teach you to trust criminals," he'd snapped. Sue, knowing better than to goad her superior, especially when he was in such a foul temper.

Moments later, having calmed down a bit he conceded that it was particularly difficult when they had no witnesses. Those they did have had been drugged and even when sober had not had a good look at the attacker.

The Chief had however agreed that all they needed was a suspect and if he were the perpetrator of the disgusting assault, DNA would convict him.

Clenched, grinding her teeth, hell it was like looking for a needle in a haystack.

Having completed the brief she'd spent the whole of Thursday, yet again, going over every scrap of evidence, revisiting the crime scene, speaking to miss Chang, who she thought was doing remarkably well, all things considered.

At twenty to seven the following morning Sue stepped out of the shower having had no time for a run. Dressing in a formal dark Paisley knee length skirt and cream blouse, she had cereal and a glass of pineapple juice, washing down vitamins. Tablets her mum insisted she take, 'to keep your skin soft dear.' Then fed the cat, making sure to use the new *diet* stuff, watched the national news before switching the alarm on and headed out to the work's Rover she'd driven home the previous evening.

Hanging up her smart affordable Marks & Spencer jacket on a coat hanger behind the driver seat, she set off on the hour long drive down the motorway to Catterick Garrison as Sue had a meeting with major Tim Kell.

The journey only eventful in as much as she didn't realise that there were mumblings of a Maoist insurrection in Nepal. BBC Radio Four was always a great place to catch up on what was going on round the world. Leaving the duel carriageway, along passed the racecourse she travelled bye the drab married quarters, plainly visible, most behind *the wire.*[11] Arriving at the main gate, she was stopped by a soldier who Sue was convinced looked too young to have a water pistol let along a great big gun. "Mam, could I see some identification?"

Having expected this Sue opened her police pass, shoving it out of the car window.

Not being the customary military ID card flummoxed the young private soldier, "oh, I'm not sure..."

At that moment a beared civilian in a faded grey uniform came over, "hello, can I help?" Seeing the police identity card, "its all right Billy." With that the squaddie moved passed Sue's car to the next now impatiently waiting vehicle.

*Faded grey* continued, "is someone expecting you?

"Yes major Kell in brigade headquarters told me that you should ring this number and he'll meet me." At this DS Parish passed over a page from her note book.

Momentarily studying it, the secuirty chap explained, "that's OK I know Major Kell. Please could you drive over there," pointing, "to the waiting bay and come into the guard room to sign in and I'll give him a call."

All very efficient Sue thought. Having filled in her details and received a temporary visitor's card she then moved her car into the main visitors car park. Walking back as requested towards the guardroom, the civilian guard came over, "Sergeant Parish, Major Kell sends his apologies and asked if you could meet him in the Officers' Mess. He's sending over a driver to pick you up. Just go straight in the Mess and someone will look after you."

Noting her apprehension, "don't worry a soldier will take you there and the staff'll give you a drink in the mess. Major Kell said he would be no more than ten minutes."

Seconds later a beat up army landrover drew up, before a scruffy looking soldier leant over and opened the passenger door, "Sergeant Parish?"

"Err yes that's me." Sue thanked the guard and climbed in. Even with her long legs it was a little tight, army vehicles obviously not being constructed for knee length skirts. The driver, eyes not on the road, appreciated the design defect said, "it's only a minutes drive, Sergeant. One of the lads been naughty then?"

Surprised, Sue turned to the soldier who she reckoned would be about the same age as her although he looked a fair bit older, his short hair receding, "well I'd rather not say."

Noting her professionalism combined with embarrassment, "sorry, it's just that I normally drive the Deputy Commander and we talk about pretty much everything. He has to be able to trust his driver, don't you know?"

Sue didn't, but replied politely, "well I'd rather discuss it with major Kell as it's a bit sensitive," finishing with, "if you don't mind?"

"No sweat, here we are anyway. Major Kell said he'd phone ahead," looking into the near distance, "see one of the waitresses is coming out right now."

"Thanks for the lift," Sue said as, this time carefully easing herself out of the high seat. Her skirt once again rising up, much to the satisfaction of the driver. Seeing her gaze, he smiled, winked cheekily and drove off.

A waitress came down the steps and addressed Sue, "you must be Sergeant Parish, Major Kell said you'd be arriving. Please come this way."

With a nod Sue followed her, never before had she been on a military camp let alone in an Officers' Mess. With these thoughts she stepped up and into a different world.

---

Tim Kell's brigade had been raised in the Crimean War, serving with distinction in both world wars and had some special battle honours from the Korean War. Way back before any of that bloodshed, some of the regiments had been active during the Opium Wars in China.*

Following the waitress through the main entrance, Sue was under no illusion that the place was clearly swimming in exquisite silver. A massive two foot Chinese dragon stood guard on a perfect highly polished mahogany circular table. Walking into the main anteroom, she was confronted by yet more silver adorning nearly every table, each

* *Editor's note*–Simon has got his campaigns muddled here as The Opium Wars in actual fact took place some five years after Sevastopol.

piece oozing history. Gazing round with her mouth opened ever so slightly.

Seeing Sue's stare, "it is very impressive first time, but you try cleaning it." As she spoke the waitress, in her cheap smart uniform, pointed to a table, near the tall nineteen fifties windows.

"Oh thank you very much, This lot must be worth a fortune?"

Smiling the waitress looked around the large room, "suppose so. You kind of get used to it after a while. The Officers are very proud of it though, spoils of war and all that."

"Right," theft was nearer the mark Sue thought. With that she took a seat near the window. The waitress then left only to return placing a silver plated tray, carrying a cup and saucer, tea and hot water pot, silver milk jug and a small white plate with a few biscuits on it, onto the table.

"Major Kell said he'd be here as fast as possible. Would you like me to pour?" The waitress spoke as she nodded towards the army issue officers mess large Royal Doulton white tea cup.

"No that's fine thanks." Sue lent forward, put her bag down to one side and started to pour herself a cup of tea. As she did the waitress withdrew.

Letting it cool, she stood and took a turn round the room. Dotted about the substantial room were five or six circles of large deep comfy chairs with low tables in the middle. The walls were covered in paintings, pictures depicting the brigades and its composite regiments feats of gallantry. The sideboard had all manner of silver statues and trophies. Sue thought that any number of the criminals she had come across in her time, if they knew this lot were on show, would make mince meat of the non existent security. Christ they didn't even seem to have an alarm.

Moving back to her chair, shaking her head, the windows weren't even locked.

Picking up her cup, out of the corner of her eye she saw silent movement. Startled at first she quickly recognised the army uniform of a surprisingly small soldier as he walked slowly across her view outside. There was another, some ten feet behind slightly closer to the window. The figures stopped, disappeared only to reappear moments later talking quietly in a foreign language.

Glancing in, the rear man flashed white teeth, the Ghurkha smile famous the world over.

It instantly dawned on Sue that even the stupidest of thieves would think more than twice before stealing from a building, a mile behind a wire fence with these deadly warrior, terrier like soldiers crawling around. As the two men moved off, Sue noted the thick curved, sheathed Kukri visible on their belts.[12]

No the mess silver was going nowhere.

"Sue?" Tim received a nod, "I'm so sorry, we had an office call from some Australian Colonel so.... anyway please forgive me. Good, I see you have a cup of tea."

As if by magic, the same waitress walking in, "Major Kell, sir, would you like a cup? Would madam like a fresh pot?"

Tom said, "its fine Liz I'll grab a cup, there's bound to be enough for at least four cups in there." With that Liz silently retreated.

As they shook hands, Sue thought Tim was considerably taller than she'd somehow imagined.

Sue Parish was considerably prettier than Tim had expected. The silent subconscious *sexual chemistry* crackled.

Both were however thoroughly professional.

"Tim, it's good to meet you and I'm so grateful for you seeing me like this. As it is I really need all the help I can get." Seeing his frown by way of a negative sign, "I was hoping you might have something, anything that might help."

Tim sipped his slightly stewed tea before replying, "well Sue, I've been doing some homework for you but not sure I've anything of any use?"

"Anything," Sue noted his muscular arms tight against his rolled up sleeves.

Noting a slight reddening to Sue's neck behind her ear Tim asked, "is it too warm in here?" As he spoke the red *chemistry* on her neck deepened.

Sue inwardly checking herself, "no I'm fine thanks." Changing the tack a little, "you have such lovely things in here they must be worth a fair bit."

"Actually, as the Mess treasurer, I know exactly how much. Lets just say I could retire to The Costa Del Sol just on this room alone!"

Tim was a busy man so steered the conversation back, "the names you gave me don't, sadly, check out. I had my clerk check with all the local regiments. We have a *Coats* on the staff here. Yes he's big, but not at all Scottish and anyway *Colonel* Coats is in Northern Ireland and has been for two months. We have a couple of other *Coats*, but they also check out. Either they were on guard, so are accounted for, or are away on operations in Bosnia.

Seeing Sue's frustration, "sorry but we don't have anyone in the whole brigade who goes by the name of Steven or even Bob Roots or Coats."

Frowning Sue replied, "I realise I can't expect every single one of the troops to be tested just on the evidence we have."

With a rye smile on Tim's handsome face, "your right there. I spoke with the brigade commander. Trust me he'd be decidedly unhappy to allow every one of his five and half thousand soldiers tested." Tim went on, "he did say that if you had any firmer evidence then he might, I mean might, consider it for a select number."

Sue was decidedly fed up and now it showed.

"I'm sorry but we don't have any Scottish regiments in the brigade. We can dismiss the Ghurkha's as they definitely ain't big, nor Scottish."

A charming smile returned to Sue's face as they both laughed, certainly no one was going to mistake a five foot three Ghurkha for a tall, white, Scotsman.

She was a good copper clutching at any straws which might come her way, "alright then, you don't have anyone who vaguely fits the description we are looking for?" receiving a shake of the head, "well then what about other units closer to Newcastle? Tim was a good soldier, "I've also checked with the TA in Newcastle. They were all on exercise at Penhale camp."

Sue really was clutching at single straws, "so, could they not get back from there and visit Newcastle when the attack took place?"

"Sorry Sue, Penhale's in Cornwall," his reply.

Almost involuntarily Sue blurted out, "shit, oh sorry. You can understand my frustration as I must catch this bastard." Realising her outburst, her neck reddening again, "it's just that the person who did this crime will, I'm sure, do it again and I've hardly got anything to go on. Not even a photo fit."

A single strand was offered by Tim, "the only other place that I can think of is a training camp out towards Carlisle. They sometimes get regiments in for range work. They could, I suppose, get into Newcastle."

"What, who?" Sue asked.

"I have no idea who's been there, different department so to speak. I can get you the number for the commandant who runs the place. Maybe you could go and check with him?"

"Tim, thanks, anything is better than nothing."

Both were tired from their combined mental arithmetic, their *chemistry* as warm as the tea was cold so Tim fetched a fresh pot.

After that they briefly chatted about the mess. Sue was very impressed, "its like something out of an old film."

"Well at the moment it's home," Tim said.

"What, you actually live here?"

"A chaps got to live somewhere."

"But what about your family, don't you have your own house?"

"Not married," Tim waved a naked finger in Sue's direction.

The wheel behind her ear, really flushed this time, "oh Tim I'm sorry. I didn't mean to pry."

"You weren't and it's alright." Tim understood, "well I was, but it all went pear shaped* when I was in The Falklands two years ago. So here I am *living in*."

Military folk tending not to beat about the bush as, inaction sometimes life threatening.

"D'you fancy going out one night? Unless of course *your family* are waiting for you."

Sue smiled, then laughed, "not unless you consider my cat's jealousy dangerous."

"Great, I'll give you a ring," As Tim spoke Sue handed him her card. On the back she'd scribbled her home and mobile numbers.

They both were busy, so shortly afterwards Sue stood at the steps of the mess, having shaken Tim's strong rough hand, watching him walk purposefully back towards his office. As he rounded the corner with a final wave, Tim hoped Colonel Banister, the Ozzy brass, had gone as he was now behind the days work power curve.

The same landrover drew up almost instantly Tim turned the corner of the distant building.

Opening the door for herself, Sue carefully swivelled in, much to the disappointment of the driver.

"Good meeting? Good bloke that Major Kell. Tough but fair."

"So so, but yes you're right he is a good bloke."

The Deputies driver kept eyes on the road when he dropped her off, this sergeant was definitely out of his league, lucky bastard Major Kell.

Having signed back out of camp and moved over to her car. Climbing in Sue hitched her skirt up, settled down in her low comfy seat and drove away, handing in her temporary pass as she stopped at the main gate before setting off back to town.

Sue had her straw?

---

* 'Going Pear Shaped' is army slang for when something goes horribly wrong.

# CHAPTER 29

## *Dying Eyes*

### ALDERSHOT, THE RAM
### SATURDAY

Saturday's were always such a bore for Boots, well the daylight hours at least. Now standing in his room he thought Friday night had been a restless disappointment. Whilst dressing, having not shaved, his main regret was that he had failed to score the night before. His annoyance heightened by the large number of seemingly ideal girls who had swarmed like hungry bees all over the pub.

Slipping on scruffy trainers, his memory already fading, Boots having completely forgotten about the early events of the previous evening. Anyway, he had actually been called upon in his professional capacity to throttle some pissed Pioneer who had been ejected having spewed all over the toilets. Boots and another bouncer had managed, not without some difficulty to evict him. They might not be the sharpest tools in the chest but Chunkies, Pioneers nickname, were known to be tough strong soldiers, if not a little thick. Actually after sobering up, he'd let the lad, who contrary to the inaccurate stereotype probably had a couple of A levels, back in to fetch his bird.

Eating toast with a greasy fried egg sliding on top Boots recollected the events of the previous evening. Yes Chunks were his kind of soldier.

After breakfast, Boots went back to his bunk, vaguely tidying up which mainly consisted of picking up his dirty pants and chucking the lot; pants, socks, shirts, T shirts, jeans into the washer. He didn't give a bugger if the colours ran. What the hell, he had no white shirts and grey, pinkish pants didn't make any difference to him.

Twenty minutes later Boots went over to rugby practice. The regiment was still in training, their first match not until the Wednesday after they were due back from battle camp.

As most of the squad were recovering from the night before, the training had to be light. The regimental coach, the RQMS, swore at them for not running, tackling to the standard, "we'll get slaughtered by the Fusiliers if you act like a group of fannies. Now get a move on."

His verbal tirade failing to have the desired effect. Frustrated and in capitulation he'd allowed them to play touch rugby for half an hour.

By eleven thirty, Boots was back in the shower, after which he chucked the dobie in the drier, full on for two hours and went over to the corporals club. Slouching, legs dangling over a chair, he ate some crisps whilst watching a video.

After a lunch of two pints, more crisps and two further video's, the second of which Boots slept through, he went back to get ready for the evening at The Ram.

Although ready by four thirty, Boots decided to break with tradition and do some ironing. An hour later, annoyed with himself, now in a rush.

Dressing quickly, Boots shoved his jacket on, locked the door and set off to the pub. Having not even reached the front door to the block he turned and retraced his steps.

Back in his room reaching down behind the locker he found the package which was taped up under the back board of the cheap drawers. Opening it, he took out two phials. With only one left he'd have a word with the pusher, when, not if he showed up later that night.

Shoving back the drawers he leant on the top studying himself in the mirror for a full ten seconds, grinning. He then stood back and slid the second drawer open. Gingerly pushing odd socks apart, there it was, the folded thick green sock. Opening it, eyes expectant, eager. As he did so, carefully placing the clawed fist extension in his outer pocket.

This time achieving the front path, Boots went down passed the regimental headquarters. Only the adjutant and the commanding officer were working. What the fuck could the rodney's find to do on a Saturday? Mulling the question he booked out at the guard room and set off for the Ram. After last night's failure he would certainly score tonight and have a triumphant mission. Not caring what the target looked like, so long as it was the opposite sex and hopefully vaguely pretty.

The Ram was open all day on a Saturday, so as he approached, Boots could hear the loud banter from a fair way off. Mostly, actually over ninety percent coming from squaddies. The numbers made up by a smattering of locals. Boots knew most of the locals would be inside and only the younger ones would return later to seek out sex with the girls who would be bussed in, within a few hours.

Just before eight, the first of the buses arrived. Not quite luxury, the owner always keen to cut unnecessary expenses, it did however have the smell of used toilet. The manager alerted, came out of the pub and climbed aboard the giggling, raucous coach. Having read them the riot act, clearly explaining about the departure time, he stood or rather rapidly leapt aside as, forty females ranging from a few young, slim and pretty girls to sadly any number of thirty years olds who were trying to be young, slim and pretty, tumbled towards the darkness and music.

Almost on cue as the last of them were being engulfed by the pulsating beat, the second bus arrived. This one was not as full, but according to Boots' measured eyes, had far better prospects. The girls mostly clad in cheap clothes and even cheaper scent stampeded inside like pack animals, driving forward in tight hysterical groups. Most of the opposite sex already on hand, propping up the bar, watching eagerly. As they did no one noticed when a rather tall oriental girl melted in as the throng flowed and bounced, dancing towards the beating rhythms.

The bar staff were inundated. That said most drank bottled drinks so service was chaotic yet efficient.

By anyone's standards the night was busy. The manager was beaming, profits punctuating his smile as he did the rounds. All things considering, so long as they all stayed beyond twelve he would give all the staff a twenty pound bonus.

'Woopie do', how generous thought Boots sarcastically when he heard of the bosses generosity.

As most of the girls were not intent on violence, the only trouble which Boots and his four other bouncers would have to cope with was probably pissed squaddies. Young, testosterone fuelled military men invariably reduced minor confrontations, regarding two of them trying to score with the same semi pissed girl, into fights.

By ten thirty, the place was heaving. Boots had already dispatched two of his team to evict a couple of wrestling yobbo's. Apart from that, the night was plane sailing, profits crashing over the bows of the bar.

---

Boots noticed her first, not realising that the reality was altogether different.

Aika was stood chatting to a group of older girls laughing and drinking, the only one not smoking. Looking over through the smoke, they were about thirty feet away, he grinned as Aika flashed a smile. Reflective, pristine white teeth exposed.

She was smiling at him?

Telling the lads he was going for a turn round to check some of the darker corners for any possible trouble, Boots' motives ulterior, darker.

He went past smiling, her response by way of a reflection in a mirror, glistened back. As her eyes said 'hello' Boots' dick hardened, Christ she was stunning and seemed somehow keen.

He lingered at the bar before making another pass by, again under no illusion that her glance was more than coincidental. If he'd had any experience Boots would have recognised it as a subtle come on.

Starting to make a move back towards the front entrance, he noticed out the corner of his eye that the women had left the group and was heading towards the toilets. A collision course and on Boots' route.

As they closed in on each other, the girl swished her long jet black hair, in what Boots thought, a come on way and had no idea it was intended to be provocative.

Tall, slim and stunning, even Boots thought she looked way too good for the place. Qualifying the thoughts by the fact that she had fairly sluty clothes on. Aika's skirt, loose but short, above a crop top, which revealed, even in the semi darkness, a flat tight honed belly. Boots couldn't believe his luck as the girl again smiled. Boot's response was very predictable, "hi, fancy a drink?"

Almost shouting above the music, Aika replied, "yes that would be great."

Stepping in front of him, walking, seemingly gliding towards the far end of the bar where the barstools afforded some marginal rest bite from the heavy beat of the music. Boots couldn't keep his eyes off her arse, God he'd like to fuck this one.

After a few minutes Aika went to the loo, Boots was pissed off as she took her drink along.

Not dwelling on the missed opportunity he dashed over to the main door, "look lads I've scored some fantastic chink, you'll have to cope for an hour of so," finishing with a rhetorical question, "OK?"

Having received a mixture of grins, frowns and envy, he managed to get back to the bar just as the girl came out of the toilets. Aika smiled as she flowing toward him. Bloody *hell* the girl was *heavenly* thought Boots, failing to realise the contradiction. He'd have to have her at all costs as this surely would be the ultimate *mission*.

They chatted above the din for a few minutes before Boots, seeing his window of opportunity, asked if she would like another drink.

Receiving a positive reply, Boots said that he could go round the back and get the drinks much quicker without having to fight the four deep wave crowding forward at the bar, no more than ten feet away.

Crouching under the counter Boots went round the back of the bar to where he was out of line of sight, pulled two bottles of alcopops from the cooler, opening them he stepped through towards the office managers corridor. With skilled practice Boots broke the phials neck and poured the liquid in. Having first taken a small swig, the bottle didn't looked tampered with.

Moving back round, again ducking down, a man on a mission held out the bottle. The women didn't seem to have noticed anything untoward as a slender hand took the bottle, touching his fingers as she did before immediately taking a little drink, Boots smiled.

Ten minutes later her speech seemed slurred and Aika's eyes rolled in the flashing lights. Going round to test the water, standing close, he put his arm round her slim shoulders and whispered, shouted into her ear, "d'you fancy going somewhere quiet?"

Receiving an almost incomprehensible reply and a half nod, he stood up, Aika shakily mirrored his movements. *Sailing* his target over to the entrance, her *course* reduced to a normal walk now. The couple went straight past the bouncers who were far more interested in two big para's intent on shoving each other about. Although late summer bordering autumn the evening, even after eleven, wasn't cold. Boots looked down at the girl, who smiled back up to him, almost stumbling, he grabbed her roughly under the armpit. Aika imperceptivity, momentarily flinched, Boots didn't notice, before giggling distractively.

This was going to be too easy thought Boots, "lets go for a walk, what d'you think?"

Slightly surprised he received an answer, albeit slurred, "yes pleez big man, *wherewe goin*?"

"Owe I know somewhere near where we can be alone and have some fun."

"Grrrrate."

Boots' evil smile glistening in the last flashes of disco lights as they moved away into the car park, the night air seemingly having the desired effect on his target. Through the cars, past the two big buses, Boots steered her over the empty road and across to the darkly lit path.

As they did he studied the girl, she was incredibly beautiful and obviously oriental. He had really cracked it this time, knowing the drugs would ensure he could do anything he liked when Boots got her down by the canal.

About five minutes later Boots led Aika down the steps toward the canal. Halfway down, on the large middle step, he cruelly grabbed her face, squeezing it round toward his own. Callously, roughly he grabbed her thigh, riding his hand crudely up her flimsy skirt he felt her pants, what there was of them. Rubbing his sweaty palm against her, Boots eyes transfixed on hers. She stared at him, still smiling, eyes seemingly looking right through him. Boots couldn't make her out, no evident resistance yet the young women didn't seem totally drunk or drugged. Hell, maybe she actually fancied him?

Pulling back on her long dark hair, kissing her, Aika's mouth opening seemingly eagerly, her tongue meeting his.

Now thoroughly aroused, Boots grabbed her arm yet almost lost his balance as they tumbled down onto the tow path. Having regained his hold they pinballed along. As they did he felt her firm arm in his tight grip. Hearing something he turned, almost loosing hold of his meat. Peering in the semi dark he couldn't see a soul. Boots, not knowing, was in actual fact correct, he certainly couldn't see anyone with a soul.

Reaching the point where they needed to be off the path, Boots took stock. There was no one at all to be seen on the footpath. Although dark, the girls face was clearly visible, the nearby housing estate lights providing more than enough light to be able to read a non illuminous watch.

The slag almost stumbled ahead of Boots as they scrambled through the undergrowth. Reaching *his place*, Boots dropped her, as he did Aika gave a little gasp before sitting up, legs out front. Seemingly confused, "ees now we have some fun?"

He'd definitely not expected her to speak, "d'you feel OK?"

"The girls eyes rolled, "well I do feel very strange and things are spinning a lot. So I'm drunk, that's OK isn't it?"

A confused frown broke over Boots' face, the drugs were always effective, never before had one of his targets spoken to him. What the hell, she must want *it* and anyway he'd do whatever he liked, "I'm going to fuck you, get your skirt up."

Another response, "can't we lie down 'n kiss first pleeeze."

Fan *fucking* tastic thought Boots, the women was obviously under the influence now.

Pushing her down onto her back, kneeling by the side next to her waist, pulling his target's head back. Aika gasped quite loudly this time.

"Shut the fuck up bitch if you don't want a good slap. I'm going to shag you whether you like it or not so best enjoy it, right!"

He leant across groping her firm high breasts before stretching further, licking her neck, tasting, smelling her perfume. Moving round pushing his free hand up under her skirt before wedging her legs open, he flopped over her in between her legs.

As before, he sat back on his heels, studying her. This time with both hands Boots shoved her tiny skirt up. Seeing her dark red G string knickers, barely covering her nakedness, his erection stiffened.

Now motionless Aika starred at him, blinking fast.

Boots undid his belt and started to shove down his pants. As they reached his knees...lightening struck.

He hadn't heard a sound. The first Boots knew was incredible pain in the side of his ear. Someone, something had hit him with *force* and power as he fell over passed the prostrate girl. Hardly flinching, Aika just continuing to stare.

The next thing Boots knew, a man seemingly floated from nowhere, punching him full in the mouth, blood flowed freely. Regaining his senses monetarily, the women irrelevant, Boots lashed out in all directions.

It was no good, someone, unseen, behind, had him in a judo forearm chocker grip round the neck. Desperately fighting for air, a few seconds later his violence descended into tame thrashings.

Shoved hard into the ground face down, his legs pulled up behind him, yet it was at this painful moment Boots realised there were two of them. What the fuck was going on, where had they come from? How did they know he was there?

Refocussing through the pain, Boots saw the blade glisten in the dark light, fear not yet engulfing him. Just able to speak he said, "what the hell's going on, who are you, fuck off and leave us alone!"

One of them spoke, "you evil excuse of a man will now know the meaning of power."

Propped up against a small tree, Boots dick now lolling, one man knelt with a long knife not two inches from his face and the other incredibly large man stood almost blocking out any light which penetrated his previously secure bolt hole.

Boots finally noticed both were Chinese. One oriental sibling leant forward smirking at Boots vulnerable manhood, "listen, if you speak then my brother here will cut," his eyes looked down, "that out."

With his leg tied up, his heels under his arse, the pain in his knee intense, Boots was focused on the knife and their words, what the hell did they want with him? All he wanted was to use the girl and have another successful mission. Pathetically seeking some sanity, "what do you want?"

"You," came the alarmingly simultaneous response.

Boots sensed as one came round behind him, the others knife inches from his eye. "Move and you loose sight, understand."

Fear now wondering toward his consciousness, Boots hardly dare nod, so close was the razor point of the knife. If only he could get the fist out of his pocket he could strike back. There was no chance, his hands were roughly pulled behind a tree, tape binding them. He was now prostrate, exposed, his jeans still halfway down his thighs, erection gone.

Secure, both men came round in front of him, "so you would attack women, cut them and soil their bodies?"

What, he hadn't touched her. "NO , no look," Boots moaned.

Incredibly, throughout, the girl had hardly moved and was still lying transfixed, only a few feet away.

Eyes bugling Boots spoke out, "see I haven't touched her."

"You have before you filth for life."

Their reply confusing Boots, how did they know about his *missions*? Were they a new and more human form of devil come to haunt him. The one on the left looked almost inhuman, like some deformed minotaur, eyes not red but a dull orange. "What, no, see she's fine," Boots failing to make the connection, why, how could he?

Calculated, slowly Chu said, "remember up north?" Seeing realisation, "you attacked the daughter of the man we work for. You will never do this again."

In desperation, terror having sprinted the last few strides, "no, no never, I promise never." Boots sought a lifeline, how had he been so careless. Also, deep down lurking beneath his fear he was really mad, they had ruined his mission.

He watched the knife touch his stomach, incredibly it sliced though his shirt, his jacket open. The trail of blood starting just below his still bandaged cut from before. Not deep just superficial, it seemed to have only glanced across his skin, no pain whatsoever.

"Listen, please, what'ya want?"

Chu snarled menacingly, "you seek mercy, you pathetic excuse for a man. We will do to you what you did to her."

As an adequate soldier, training ingrained, Boots knew the best form of defence was often attack. He struggled violently against the tape, incredibly in an instant his arms came free so he lashed out at the slim one who had just spoken, catching him full in the face, pain and fear fuelling a powerful blow. Completely surprised, Miki spun away. At the same moment Boots' fear stopped in its tracks as rage and power surged to the fore.

At the same moment he saw the red eyes dart from the shadows.

What had they said, they would be there to protect him, to ensure he was successful on his mission.

The bull turned hearing a noise, Boots seized his opportunity. Reaching into his pocket drawing out his fist, slashing the ugly one right across the face, who fell sideways, silent, stunned in pain.

A wolf like creature leapt past Boots, descending on the bleeding man only a breath away, its claws gashing deep into Chu's prostrate body.

The other man having regained his senses, leapt with incredible speed at the goblin, wolf creature tearing at his brother.

As he did Boots went on the offence, having yanked his trousers up, catching Miki in mid flight, the claw's edge coming round, driving into his groin. Miki's momentum carrying him forward onto the creature. Continuing his attack, Boots jumped forward onto his back. He needn't have worried, Miki's femoral artery was severed and blood pulsed, almost spurted, through his fingers as he desperately tried to stem the loss of life force.

Crashing onto him, viciously punching with his free hand to the back of his neck. This time it was Boots who was knocked over by another creature as its jaw latched onto Miki's neck, now a bloody mess.

Thrashing, tearing the creature drank the last drops of life from one of the brothers.

Chu with sheer brute strength threw the creature against the nearest tree. Springing up with startling speed he smashed towards Boots, his eyes now turned from yellow to red, blood splattered all over his face. Mighty hands came round Boots neck, the pressure instant and all consuming, Boots kneed him, no effect. Starting to loose focus, in desperation Boots sank the claw into the back of his attackers neck. In an instant the vice loosened, Boots staring for the first time into dieing eyes. Chu twitched, tried to speak then, like a massive felled tree, went straight back still gyrating. Seemingly as he hit the ground unconsciousness accepted him, before cold empty death took him.

The howl sparked back Boots attention as the red eyes came forward, *"you have done well. Their blood is worth feasting on."*

Boots fell against the very tree he had been tied against. In doing so he noticed the tape remnants, where only moments earlier it had been silently sliced, releasing him to his revenge.

Looking down at the two dead men, "but what, how are they here? Why me?"

Spitting blood, its foul mouth overflowing, the one who was still at Miki's throat, swivelled a terrifying crimson matted hairy head, " we are close now, we will feast, you will feast. Together we are now able to roam your realm and soon we will get the one our master seeks."

Almost returning to the terror and nightmares of the old school building, Boots couldn't cope so ran, blindly crashed through the undergrowth. In doing so Boots could hear bone crunching, rustling's behind. Christ there were more than two of them. With renewed childhood fear he fell forward back onto the tow path.

In an instant all was silent. Boots panting hard, his heart, ear and lip thumping. Momentarily transfixed, he listened desperate to hear if hooves were following before leaning, almost falling over to the canal edge. Reaching the dark cold water, he splashed it onto a blood, not his, splattered face.

Regaining control Boots got up and ran as fast as he could back to the bridge, leaping the stairs three at a time, finally turning and looking, gasping, there was nothing in sight.

It only took him just over a minute to run to the back of the club. In through the work entrance to the staff wash room where Boots studied the dark eyes peering back out at him from the mirror as loud heavy music invaded the smelly room.

Shaking violently Boots washed his face before getting a large bandaid to cover the surprisingly shallow cut on his stomach. Moving through to the toilet, Boots sat for a long time, eyes sightless, his thoughts a numb mess. Like an aftershock through the clutter, the rumble in Boots mind grew to a crescendo, what about the girl?

# CHAPTER 30

# *Innocence Removed*

## MOTEL ROOM
## EARLY SUNDAY MORNING

"What, slow down, what d'you mean there what?"

Danny instantly bolt upright in bed, palms rapidly sweating. He had taken Aika's call, not checking, it must have been at least two in the morning.

Why was it Aika and not Chu as planned? He was meant to call him, only giving the code work, 'forked lightening has struck'.

"*Futari tomo shindern*"*

"Calm down take a deep breath, I don't understand what your saying, where are the men you met yesterday?"

All that Danny got by way of a reply was terrible gasping sobs. Deep soulful panting which only just managed to cloak real fear. Finally, "I did as you said then *Akuma*† came and I couldn't move for watching, then I ran."

Danny still not grasping any logic, meaning, "what, who came? Listen to me Aika, where are you?"

"Back in my room, please come I'm so very scared."

Right, get a drink and lock the doors and I'll be there in twenty minutes."

Hanging up, Danny twice tried both of the brother's mobiles. Each just rang and rang.

Down by the canal not a sound. In a hire car parked at The Ram, only the faintest of rings audible.

Nearly half an hour later, Danny knocked on Aika's door. The receptionist certainly didn't believe him but had agreed to let the visitor in so long as she phoned Aika's room for confirmation.

They didn't like guests at that time of night. On reflection, the receptionist thought the women in room 17 had seemed in a terrible state when she had returned to her room an hour earlier, only just coherent enough to get the taxi charge put on her room bill.

Opening the door, laying eyes on the terrified woman, Danny instantly realised his careful plan lay in ruins.

Having undressed, Aika had taken a hot shower, now only wearing the hotel robe. Standing there her hair damp and limp, complexion almost unnaturally pale, she looked, like his scheme, in tatters. Seeing him, she reeled back onto the bed crying hard. Having closed the door Danny moved and sat next to her instinctively cradling her shaking

* 'They're both dead'.

† 'Demons'.

head.

" Kami sama yurushite.* Mr Chang, it was so horrid, I did exactly as you said. The man chatted me up, bought me a drink just like you said he would." Tears getting the better of her, she again lapsed into convulsive gasps, eyes tight shut in an attempt to wash, squeeze out the ingrained memories.

Taking stock, Danny went over to the mini bar, got out a miniature, downing the contents into a glass tumbler, "here, Aika, drink this."

Innocence, long dormant, rekindled by fear engulfed Aika, "please I want to go home to my Oka-san."†

Being unsure what exactly to do next, Danny forced the glass into the woman's hand before going over and getting himself a large whisky. He needed it, "where are the men you were with in my car?"

"The *hentai*‡ managed to get free and then, *Akame no oni, akumano tsukai, chi, chi* everywhere. It, things got them. I couldn't move for fear."

Danny was finding it almost impossible to decipher what the woman was saying, what with the Japanese, faltered speech and the incessant sobbing. "Red, what did you say?"

Aika covered her face as she spoke, "Red eyed goblins, devils, Satan's helpers, blood everywhere."

Finally her tears subsided to a point where she drank the whole glass of brandy. Danny fetched another. Holding it out, this time she very weakly smiled by way of thanks.

Grasping the glass with both hands almost as if it were for protection, Aika looked Danny in the eyes for the first time.

In that moment he saw a terrified void, pain Danny hadn't witnessed since he had told his wife what had happened to Penny. Instantly realising the one he sought had somehow managed to overpower the brothers. Surely that was impossible and what was all the crazy talk about devils and goblins? Obviously the girl was in shock, babbling.

It took a further five minutes before Danny managed to calm her down enough for her to be able to speak again. Over the next twenty minutes he'd gained a partial understanding of the events. Clearly someone had attacked the brothers as they were just starting to get to work on their target. Danny was however completely confused what with all the talk of satanic wolves, demons and what the hell was she going on about red eyed goblins for?

Taking control, he had nigh on ordered Aika to get a taxi first thing in the morning to the airport. From there she was to fly back up north, as her return ticket an open one.

As an afterthought Danny had explained to the women that clearly she had witnessed a brutal attack which seemingly resulted in the death of two of his associates, as such he could not afford to be in anyway associated with such events. To ensure her silence Danny guaranteed her more than double her initial fee. Although clearly in shock, he sensed greed when it raised its eager head. Aika was going to be paid nearly

---

* 'God forgive me'.

† 'Mother.'

‡ Derogatory Japanese term to describe a yob or drunken bum

fifty thousand pounds to keep her terrified memories to herself. Danny had finished off by saying that it would be a good idea if she stayed at home for a while until things calmed down a bit.

Through the mist of fear Aika knew that this amount of money would alter things. Clearly her naivety not comprehending that exposure to such terrible acts had already robbed her of any remaining innocence. Earlier events ensuring Aika's life had been inextricably changed forever.

Danny left as dawn was in the throws of yawning. Aika didn't go to bed, preferring to dress in jeans and a sweater, pack her few things and immediately leave for the safety in numbers afforded her at the bustling airport.

Danny on the other hand went straight back to his hotel room. Not wanting to disturb Simon so early he had waited impatiently, checking his watch every ten minutes until eight before calling his mobile.

# CHAPTER 31

## *Mavis' Window*

### CAMBERLY, WEST OF LONDON, LOUISE AND MARKS'–6AM

Breathing slowly, calmly, tongue in its customary position behind the upper front teeth, just before six, Louise's children still blissfully in sleep, the house quiet. *I* didn't need to be in my own home to be able to visit the Hacienda Grande.

I'd woken after a disturbing dream. Hindus believe that dreams allow individuals to travel many thousands of miles and access, commune with others in their own dream state. *I* knew that my dream had been troubled, involving dark shadows lurking expectant, waiting to reek revenge. *I* even thought *I* recognised one of the figures from my past. The pain niggling just below my left clavicle clearly exposing the small star at the front and the much larger paint ball size splodge where the bullet had existed just behind my shoulder blade. *I* rubbed it hard, the itch never quite leaving me. The knick below the left ear was sore, still red, even after five years. *I'd* certainly had been through the wars so to speak.

There was somehow a connection between my old scars reminding me of their presence and recent events?

---

The bed covers seemingly vanishing as I drifted off, weightless. Opening my eyes I could feel the exquisite sun bathing my whole body. Sitting, legs out front on the grassy bank. The sights and smells familiar and as ever tranquil to my sensors.

Not quite in his customary manner, Pied Wagtail swooped down past my left shoulder, performing an elaborate turn, tumbled in mid air, only to swing back stopping in his tracks just before my feet, perching on my left sandal, "hello Simon, quite unexpected but a most welcome visit.".

"Yes I need to go to the Training Room as I seek guidance on a very troubling issue."

"Mavis knows of your visit and is expecting you."

Smiling down at my spirit animal guide who had been introduced to me years earlier in the remote jungles of Belize, "I'd hope she would be ready as things have changed and moved somehow in a disturbing direction."

Hopping from one foot to the other, excited, "she knows of your thoughts and cautions you in your movements."

I walked, he bobbed, as we chatted about how I should deal with the pain in my shoulder.

On reaching the top, as ever I gave an involuntary gasp at the sheer beauty and warmth of the vision caressing my sight.

Reaching the front door, I had not seen any of my friends, unusual for no one to be around?

Stepping forward out of the sun, Dr Laurance greeted me. He said that I should not linger with him as the Training Room was ready and Mavis sought my attention. Duly instructed I went straight forward climbing the stairs, not using the ornate baluster. At the top turning right and round back on myself towards the beautiful purple, crimson stain glass window, which dominated the front upstairs of both the interior and exterior of the building. Stopping ten feet from it, I knocked on a old solid door. A light airy voice called out, "Simon, please come in."

Duly instructed I entered. Before me Mavis sat on a Edwardian hard back, brass studded leather chair. The atmosphere subdued but not dark, curtains partially closed, giving the room an air of a circus fortune tellers booth.

This was no fortune tellers lightweight entertainment, it was one of the most demanding rooms in the whole house.

Moving across I could see my dear family friend, who, at five foot nine was tall for her era, that being the forties and fifties. Mavis' fine snow-white hair, draped over her craggy lined smile, teeth far from perfect, incredible warmth enveloping her. She was wearing black slacks and a deep brown llama Peruvian wool jumper. Smiling I recognised it as the very one which I'd given her many years earlier.

Walking straight over, she didn't rise, arthritis refusing to release her from her seated domain. Leaning up she gave me her normal tight hug, no kiss forthcoming.

Straight down to business, "Mavis I seek your guidance and wisdom. I need steering towards those I must face, yet I have limited experience in such matter."

Before I could continue Mavis stopped me, "you are misguided Simon, you have the knowledge, the ability and the experience. It's just that you don't want to face something which poses you real danger from beyond."

Shaking her head, hair curling round like a scarf, Mavis went on, "Simon, I know of those who seek you, together we can see them. Remember you should fear nothing here in the safety of the Training Room. So d'you feel up to it?"

I was no longer, never actually frightened, just apprehensive of what remained of the unknown, "you know I trust you as you trained me so well in the past. My skills are in no small way down to the path which you have guided me."

In line with her thin, worn, hardened features, Mavis barely tolerated dithering, her appearance cloaking a lady of immense power, especially when it came to the dark world lurking on the edge of this realm, "sit, and we'll get on with it."

Doing so not less than two feet from her, placing my open hand on her side table, she immediately placed hers on mine, holding on I could feel the knots, like barnacles, where her knuckles had suffered years of pain, instinctively my force flowed toward deformed joints.

From here, I knew we had to enter a different level. Like air travel in this world it was, is, totally natural, levels of consciousness transparent to those who care to look.

Closing my eyes we stood, and walked, hobbled in Mavis' case, towards the far wall where the old chalk black board stood. A duster and white chalk perched expectantly, ready for use. Without stopping we continued straight through the permeable darkness to the other side. Here only complete emptiness, black as night, as if coated by the board itself.

"Simon, you have been here before so walk with me, keep my hand in yours." Mavis need not have worried, having seen things in this level which had scared the hell out of me I was staying attached to my guardian.

Replying, "I feel the presence of eyes following me. Just the other day I sensed dark shadows rushing towards me in my world, intent on pain against me."

With my free hand I instinctively rubbed the scar on my shoulder, the ache stronger here?

Mavis, smelling the air like a bloodhound. Using the same technique as I employed in the living world. She was seeking to sense something physical, more dangerous.

I felt her hand jerk in mine. Eyes refocussing, in the void I saw a light rushing from a pin prick towards us, growing by the second. Turning to Mavis I could just see in the darkness that her body was motionless apart from the fact that she had raised her free hand clasping a small, pure, perfect quartz crystal. Hand open, almost pointing it like the weapon it was, she held it out in front of her. The approaching light seemed to slow to a crawl not less than ten feet away. At this moment I could see, as a TV screen in motion, similar to the journey picture I had gone through many times before, this however had dark black steel as its frame. As we looked a hideous form bulged forward as if pressing against thick black cling film. It was now my heart started to race, understanding here I did not have Bill or even Merti to protect me, all I had was a crippled lady with a tiny crystal in her outstretched, gnarled hand.

"Look at it Simon, see its intent, it is after you, why we may find out."

I was troubled not frightened, knowing I was far from a saint and had killed in the line of duty yet this was something else. Someone, something was intent on harming me from the void of darkness where evil lurks.

The faceless entity paced like the caged animal it was, constantly pressing against the thick malleable glass, seeking a way through to us. I quickly stole a glance toward Mavis, "Its from my past, yet it is not? It wants me, yet it works for another?"

"Your very smart Simon, also accurate, yes this thing and there are others have ventured into your realm and have killed and seek to feast again. You must beware of them as they draw with yet another."

Mavis looked over to meet my gaze, her kind watery pale eyes calming, "some time ago you faced the foreigner. His mission back then to destroy you and those you cherish. It is he who is causing unrest in this realm. You sent him beyond, now he wants to send others to face you. He uses another, a living man as the entry point. Close this portal and you will shut them all out.

"Boots?"

Squeezing my left hand firmly, Mavis continued, "yes, the one you touched with this hand, he is their window. You must smash it forever. Fail and they will flow through the open wound and hunt you. Know that when they have dealt with you they will turn their evil on the ones you love."

I hadn't thought of this, Lynda and my daughter in danger?

"Mavis they mustn't get to my family."

"They are driven towards you. It's their master who ultimately lurks in the murky foul water of the darkest recesses of all levels."

We silently watched as the thing pressed for all it was worth against the protective layer. It could never get through, in desperation it even disappeared into the void only to crash forward, this time making out lines on what seemed to be a face, the teeth barely held back, so clear was the outline against the malleable barrier.

"Mavis, I have learnt many thing with you but this is most disturbing. What way do you advise I move forward?"

"With care," her answer, succinct as ever. She continued, "The Commander has told me of warriors," pausing for breath Mavis continued, "who can and do protect you in your realm. Now you must trust and rely upon them more than ever. I see another, who is as yet unclear. They also move to your protection. Beware of their angry yet they seek the same as you, intent on justice. Take care as her anger may be misguided."

Opening her palm with the small crystal in it, Mavis blew over towards the framed devil creature. Seemingly, as if somehow it had inhaled poisonous gas, it recoiled, the howl audible even through the protection. With that the mirror slowly at first moved back, the creature still trying, desperately to get to us. As quickly as it arrived, the mirror was a dot before pitch-blackness once again engulfed us both.

Blinking I felt Mavis' hand tight in mine as we stood up close to the blackboard, light all around, the smell of dust chalky in my nostrils.

Letting go, Mavis returning slowly to her chair where I joined her in mine. Turning towards me, Mavis smiled a serious smile, "these are troubling visions you have seen Simon. You have though, learnt a lot about how to protect yourself. Know this, they will, if they can, kill you. Remember their portal is the key. Death surrounds them all, blood on their hands. They have no right to be in your world so you must send them back to theirs before it's too late."

I always knew instinctively what Mavis was inferring, that was the level of our bond of friendship. In life she had taught me much, now she was all wisdom. Her appearance totally deceptive, she was incredibly powerful. If required she could easily enter my world, having done so many times in both. In a rhetorical tone, "so I must act?"

"You know what you must do, you will receive confirmation from the one who set you on this path. His information useful to you, then you alone will know what to do, take care my boy."

Moving to her seat we again hugged. Releasing me from the embrace I smiled at the sun beaten face of a council member of the Hacienda Grande. "Goodbye and I hope you have some relief from the pain in your joints."

It was Mavis' turn, "thank you, your powers are in line but different to mine, your warmth payment indeed, my fingers feel better already." With that she closed her eyes.

Mutual support, admiration, respect as I watched Mavis' head gently loll down, now fast asleep.

Closing the door quietly I left the room.

Retracing my path all the way back to the grassy bank, no one around as they were obviously leaving me to my thoughts. Closing my eyes, breathing, enjoying the music of nature.

My mobile rang.

## CHAPTER 32

# *Refocussed*

NEAR CAMBERLY,
SUNDAY MORNING, 0805HRS

He'd forgotten that Simon had been in the dark regarding his clandestine operation to kill Boots. The phone slippy, sweaty in his hand, Danny spoke rapidly, "Simon, he got away."

"Calm down Danny, calm down, talk slowly." Simon knew that things were dark, yet was unclear as to the detail, "now what is it you're trying to tell me. I assume you mean the one in the photo's has got away. Escaped from what?"

Like the chilly mist clearing in the woods a few hundred meters from his hotel window, it finally dawned over Danny that Simon had no idea what his plans had been. "You knew I was going after him. Well, I sent two men to get the one called Boots. Aika kept going on about demons, she's in a terrible state." Without pausing he finished with, "he killed them and then somehow escaped."

Simon's mind peered through the swirling, confusing, mist which Danny had cast him, "first off, *where* and who the hell is *Eyker*?"

The trees now visible at the far end of the hotels gardens, Danny understood, "I got a hooker called Aika to act as bait so that we could get him down by the canal, where you showed me. I planned for him to be attacked by two hired men."

"Stop right there, who knows who's listening to this. I'll meet you at the canal pub, remember?" Without waiting for a reply, "in about twenty minutes."

"Yes you're right as always, see you there."

With that both mobiles switched off.

Thirty minutes later, Simon's Volvo crunched on the car park tarmac having taken slightly longer than planned, the school run ensuring he'd rarely reached fourth gear.

Danny stood with his suit collar turned up against the cold, breath like a visible trace, plumed out of his mouth as he spoke, "thank God you're here. Listen Simon its all gone wrong. I hired two assassins from Hong Kong to come over and kill him. They are the very best." Inwardly Simon had a cruel smile at, obviously, the inaccuracy of the tense.

Shaking from the cold Danny continued, "well the girl got away. She's explained that the men attacked and tied him up. Somehow just as they were getting to the serious business he managed to free his hands and attack them. The girl kept saying that he wasn't alone and that wolves came from nowhere, Japanese goblins?"

Simon ignored the confusion as Danny continued, "well these things came from nowhere and attacked my men. Aika said she only crawled away when the one we're after fled and the creatures were mauling my men. She did say that Boots had a knife of sorts and stabbed one of the assassins in the neck. She's sure they're both dead."

Clouds of smoke engulfing Danny as even the sweat on his brow steamed.

Simon understood now. It was in some strange way all making sense, so the one called Boots had opened the portal allowing shadows to enter his physical realm. They and seemingly Boots had killed the two men. The irony cruel, those sent to do the killing were in fact the prey. Either way, Boots had ensured the death of two men. This changed everything, "what about the girl called *Eyker*?"

Danny glanced at his Rolex, "Aika's flying back to Newcastle about now."

"Will she talk?"

"What to you or the police?"

"Both," Simon squirted back.

"The police won't believe her. No she won't talk. She knows that I will have her watched and it will be her who ends in hell if she does. To you, yes I suppose so. She is pretty screwed up though."

"Good," realising what he'd just said Simon went on, "no you know what I mean. I will need to see her probably tomorrow sometime. You know this now changes everything. It's more than revenge against Penny. This man is real danger to us all. Me, you, even our families. I will have to go after him myself."

The vapours surrounding Danny, only partially cloaking his smirk. At last he had Simon after the one called Boots. This meant certain death, probably not slowly but with The Green Eyed Dragon in flight after him, Boots had no chance.

"What are you going to do? Does this mean you will kill him for me?" "Damn it Danny, no not for you, not for Penny. He killed and has greater meaning, importance. Whilst he lives he will attack again, kill again and he doesn't realise it yet but he is releasing demons who seek me."

The grin replaced by a cold sweaty frown, Danny didn't understand but clung onto the essentials, Simon was after him, "what can I do to help?"

Like ice, the air from Danny's mouth froze, silent. Simon moved through his mind turning to a higher plain of thought. He must stop Boots and if that meant death then so be it. He had killed therefore this ensured legitimacy in his eyes. The files flashed, he assessed subconscious memories for information. Chaff thick and fast. Some recalled, some sent timelessly from friends in the Hacienda Grande and even beyond. A range, the number 3, information merging between known and sent, Friday at Workop? Distance the security, his red hand to use a weapon from afar, M4, five hundred and fifty six?

Jolted by Danny's words, "Simon, Simon, hello, what now?"

In a flash Simon filtered the information, "I need you to get me a weapon. A very specific type of weapon. The one called Boots is going to be in the North next week. I will track him down and he won't escape again. This time it is personal for you, me and those two dead men's families."

Danny deciding not to interrupt knowing neither Miki nor Chu would be in all probability missed. The only people who would do so were customers requiring their special kind of service.

"What kind of weapon, anything is obtainable?"

"A rifle."

"A what?" The thought had never crossed Danny's mind, Simon never carried a gun unless it was absolutely necessary, preferring, rightly to rely on his incredible fighting ability.

"A gun, actually a rifle to be precise. It must be accurate, with telescopic sights. Portable, easily assembled and must use five point five six millimetre rounds, that is critical. Something like the new American Commando M4 or a regular Carbine. You see although they are not a sniper rifle in the right hands they are extremely accurate."

Realising Danny had only taken in the fact he needed a rifle, Simon took stock, "Danny I'll write it all down. It mustn't be traceable."

As Simon went back to his car, like an obedient puppy, Danny followed. As it was still bloody cold they both got in quickly, the Scandinavian electronics rapidly heating the whole car, even Danny's numb behind.

Once Simon had finished jotting down notes, he turned to his friend.

"You know I wanted little to do with this, now I'm involved and I must go on the offensive. To do it I need you to get me this," he handed the note over. After Danny had a chance to read it, not understanding the detail, Simon continued, "it's really important about the round size. It must be 5.56.

Seeing a completely blank face, "Danny, it's the size of the bullets. They have to be the same size as those used in British Army rifles. This way it can't be traced. That way everything will seem like an accident. *Boots* as he is known, is going to be on some riffle ranges next week and it is there where I intend to strike. It will be quick, clean and certainly deadly."

"Simon thank you."

Irritated he replied, "no, don't thank me. I'm now not doing this for you or even for Penny. This man Boots is incredibly dangerous. I must stop him before he creates real terror."

Thinking about the shopping list Danny said, "I know someone who can help. He can get you this weapon of your choice," studying the notes Danny continued. "I'm sure he can get you one of these Colt M4's."

Simon smiled for the first time. Danny described it like some child's toy gun, not the stocky, lightweight, accurate and critically, reliable weapon it was.

"That would be great, thanks. I'll need it by Wednesday though, so you don't have much time."

"I'll phone my friend as soon as I get back. I don't trust these things." As he spoke he shook his mobile as he took it out of his pocket. Danny then made a couple of calls. One to Jenny, his secretary was always in the office early. The other to an unnamed person who seemed to do a lot of listening and not a lot of talking as Danny explained that he needed some equipment and it was urgent, top priority, the favour called.

Simon switched the heater off and opened his window, the steam roared out in waves. Simon then quizzed Danny about what the girl had said. Seemingly understanding more than Danny, even though it was second hand information.

Nothing about Simon now surprised Danny however, all he kept thinking was that Simon would kill Boots.

Simon left, going back, past the remnants of the school run, to Louise's. where he'd explained that things had changed and he had to get back north quickly and would she give everyone lots of hugs and kisses when they got back from play, normal school and work, respectively. Simon then drove quickly to Heathrow, met up with Danny and caught the lunchtime flight home.

As Simon left for Louise's, by the canal Danny sat motionless for a while before making a few more calls. The main one, again to his secretary. She was to anonymously call the hotel where the brothers were staying and explain they wouldn't be coming back. Jenny was also to get Sam his general manager to get in touch with the lady they had discussed previously, there were few secrets from his secretary. He was to ensure she was available and on call all day Tuesday as he had someone who had to meet her. The women was also to be told she would receive double her normal payment for just meeting this man and it wasn't a professional arrangement. Back in Newcastle Jenny grinned, she thought she knew what her boss meant.

Danny had then gone back to the hotel, changed into a casual suit and dashed to catch the lunchtime flight. Driving along he thought about the fact that somehow Simon could even mirror Aika's description of the creatures. Maybe they hadn't been the ranting's of a clearly terrified women after all?

# CHAPTER 33

# *Flicker of Hope*

## WORKOP TRAINING CAMP
## MONDAY MORNING

Just over twenty four hours after Simon's mobile rang, at Louise's, Sue Parish turned off the main road towards the small gate post. A bedraggled looking, yet remarkably sprightly elderly civilian guard emerged from a small glass sentry post, invisible heat following him.

As he approached the unmarked police car Sue stuck her head out into the Cumbrian wind, "I'm here to see major Tom Bride, he's expecting me."

"Oh good morning, you must be detective sergeant Parish," without waiting for a reply the guard started to return to the warmth of the hut. Over his shoulder, "I'll still need some ID please."

Having proved who she was, Sue followed the simple directions, driving round to the visitor car park where she parked in the vacant *Visitor* slot next to the bold white letters declaring,

'Reserved – Camp Commandant'.

Just as she was *blinking* the car shut, behind her she heard a creaky wooden door swing open.

"Hello, sergeant Parish?"

The Camp Commandant could have saved himself a question for, even in plain clothes, Sue looked the part. Smart dark blue trouser suit covering her customary neat blouse. All this housed in a thick, winter, knee length coat, it being definitely much colder out there in the hills. Sue was glad she had brought it along as hand outstretched she replied, "yes, hello Major Bride."

"Tom please."

Tom held the door open as Sue entered towards the welcome of tax payers electric heating. In doing so she said, "please call me Sue."

"Third on the left," Tom followed the directions with a simple choice, "Sue would you like coffee or tea?"

The answer as simple, "tea please, no sugar."

"Coming right up," as he spoke Tom disappeared off to the left, into a cluttered tiny room, come kitchen.

Sue entered a surprisingly busy looking office, the walls of the camp commandant's office evidently covered in charts. A large, quietly humming computer stood at its station over in the far corner, wires like discarded spaghetti spewing from the rear. Another laptop opened on a paper strewn commanding looking desk. Passing both machines Sue took a peak out of the back window. Smiling as she observed a covert, secluded dwindling vegetable plot.

"D'you garden? I like to. My old dad said it would keep the heart attack away. Anyway the veg' always tastes so much better when you dig it up yourself, don't you agree?"

Turning, Sue studied the smiling face in front of her.

Major Tom Bride wore a smart efficient non camouflaged plain green uniform. Shoes rather than customary boots and a dark green, clearly non-issue, baggy fleece over his army shirt. About her own height, he was filling out yet still looked in pretty good shape as he must have been about fifty years old.

"I'm in a flat, so it's pretty much impossible. I think the council would complain if I dug up the yard."

At that they both chuckled.

Moving past her Tom took Sue's coat and hung it up on the back of the door, then gestured towards a fatigued, red sofa chair.

At the same time as Sue sat down she received a mug of strong, piping hot tea.

Tom sat down next to her in an equally saggy chair, trying not to make it too obvious that he was casting a very approving eye over the good looking woman sat within perfume sensory distance.

Sue was impatient, "Tom, as I said on the phone I'm currently dealing with a serious assault case, actually in my mind it should be increased to attempted murder."

Tom's greying eyebrows twitched ever so slightly.

"We have reason to believe," Sue paused, shit that sounded so corny.

Both of them subconsciously agreeing, simultaneously smiling. She went on, "there is a possibility," leaning forward for impact, "I can go as far as to say a strong likelihood that the attacker was a soldier. As the attack took place in Newcastle, possibly someone from this camp may have been involved."

Sitting back to allow the camp commandant time to take it all in, Sue sipped her powerful brew.

"Arrh sounds like a nasty business. Well I'd need to know exactly what the date was then I'll see." Sue, notebook open, glancing down, told him.

Tom rose, moving over to a paper carpeted desk. How he could see or find anything was beyond the detective, what with papers resembling a pile of leaves blown all over by a bureaucratic autumn wind.

Digging in amongst the foliage, the commandant tossed her a bone.

"Here we are, bad news, we didn't have a camp on then. Only a few *jocks* clearing up after their main battle camp.

Sue nearly spilled pen, tea, note book, the lot on the floor. Seizing the morsel expectantly, "what did you say?"

"One of the regiments from up Edinburgh. I think they'd finished their live firing. The bulk then left, leaving only about fifteen tidying up. Messy lot them jocks," Tom's reply.

Sue stared at him, chewing, digesting every word, simultaneously trawling through her brain and note book, searching, at the same time drinking her brew.*

Tom on the other hand, in line with the gender stereotype, had knocked his tea over whilst rummaging through a pile of returns on the desk. "Yes, here we are. Twelve in block C, eight soldiers and three *corporals*," Tom said triumphantly.

* Editors own note–Women of course being able to do two things at once.

Shaking with excitement, her jaw tight in anticipation, neck red, Sue almost fired the words out, "there were three corporals here that night, Scottish accents?"

"Not that broad, most seemed from Edinburgh, but definitely Scottish. Why, is that important?"

Scribbling, Sue failing to reply. Noting her activity, Tom took the opportunity to fetch a cloth and two more, slightly more stewed mugs of hot tea.

Returning Tom noticed Sue had stopped writing, now clearly waiting, impatiently, for him to reappear. Placing the mugs down Tom mopped up the mess. As he did Sue pressed him further, "can you remember what they looked like, were any of them big blokes?"

"Who the corporals?"

Tom received a rapid nod before answering as he shook his head, "to be honest can't say I remember, maybe, sorry."

"This is important, did any of them go out that night?"

"Now that's easy. If any of them left the camp that night they'd have filled in the booking out register." Pre emptying her request, he picked up his tired grey phone, "Willie, Commandant. Could you check the booking out register for when the jocks were here. Did any of them book out on their last Friday on camp." As he spoke Tom received a very positive nod from the DS.

There was silence as both waited, activity in the sentry post. Tom was in no rush and anyway the last time he'd had such a good looking women in his office had been a female Staff Sergeant PTI with legs all the way to Newcastle.

Finally the answer, "I see, thanks Willie."

Seeing him frown, Sue's flicker of evidence evidently vanishing, "sorry Sue, the gate says no one left that night. The only ones who did went to Carlise and they weren't even jocks."

In that moment, inexperience exposed, Sue failing to exploit the lead presented, "shit, bugger, sorry but I thought I was really onto something. You see we suspect it's a Scottish soldier. To be precise a corporal."

She gulped back the cloudy tea by way of an acknowledgment of partial defeat, "I see, well I'm sorry to have taken your time up Tom but I'm sure you understand we have to follow every lead, no matter how trivial."

Tom, who had served in Northern Ireland too many times not to know the importance of intelligence and detective work, "well I must say I'm glad as I'd hate to think someone from this camp committed whatever it is they did."

"I understand, anyway Tom I'd better get going. Please, if there is anything at all that you can think of, no matter how small, please give me a call." As she spoke Sue handed him one of her cards, after which Tom helped her back into the thick coat.

They said there goodbyes, Tom promising to have a real good think back. Certainly, he had her card and would call the minute he thought of anything.

A disconsolate detective then left Workop camp on the forty-minute drive back to the station. Passing the bus stop Sue noticed the cows oblivious to events, swishing the remaining few summer flies from their backs.

Back in Camp, something was gnawing at Tom's brain, he always had a niggle in the back of his mind whenever there was a fact he needed to recall but couldn't. Normally it was trivial, usually no more important than remembering to fetch some extra milk on the way back to his quarter. Yet this was different and he knew it. There was something in the back of his mind which was significant, yet Tom was buggered if he could remember what.

Maybe it was time to take the pension and concentrate on the potatoes out the back?

# CHAPTER 34

## Smouldering Evidence

### ALDERSHOT CAMP, MONDAY MORNING 0935HRS

"*Stoppage.*"

The bark immediately followed by, "*apply safety catch, move the working parts to the rear. Tilt the weapon to the side. Seeing nothing, take aim, safety off, engage, weapon continues not to fire, reapply the safety catch. Looking in the chamber, seeing no rounds remove the magazine.*"

Boots continued, "*Check magazine, rounds in magazine, seeing no obstructions reapply the magazine, working parts forward, safety catch off, take aim, rounds fire.*"

It was one thing to conduct dry weapon training, it was another to treat soldiers, his section, like God damn school boy cadets.

Boots really thought doing stoppage drills in a classroom was like a worn out pencil, pointless. Continuing the analogy, in reality, sharp drills ensured both a useful writing tool and an effective fighting machine.

If the idiot rodney wanted to treat them like kids he could fuck off back to primary school.

"*STOP.*"

"*Apply the safety catch, remove magazines and stand up.*"

From the prone position six young men instantly jumped to their feet.

"*Magazines away and fasten pouches. For inspection port arms*" With that they held their rifles up and to the left. Boots and his LCpl went behind and past checking the working parts chamber of each weapon. As they did tapping each soldier on the shoulder. Again each Pavlov*ian* trained soldier in turn put the weapon up to their eye, took imaginary aim, flicked the safety catch and pulled the trigger.

Finally applying the safety catch the drill complete.

After six weapon firing pins clicked, Boots told them to take a rest but be back after NAAFI break. The six soldiers, weapons slung across their chests, left the platoon training room and trooped off.

Boots had had a terrible two days since the events of Saturday night. After closing time on the Sunday morning, he'd gone to the twenty four hour McDonalds and sat looking into space, drinking increasingly strong soupy coffee.

By the time he'd got back to camp at six in the morning Boots looked terrible. He was reminded of this by the duty NCO as he signed in. Snarling Boots took himself off to his bunk to take a long shower. In doing so, in an attempt to remove internal images,

Boots scrubbed himself until it stung.

By lunchtime Boots was starving so decided to go for a walk down town and after aimlessly wandering around had strolled into *The Pegasus* and ordered a pint. After two more and a steak and kidney pie with chips covered in brown sauce, he felt a million times better. In the dark comforting atmosphere Boots went, yet again, over the events of the previous night.

Everything had gone with military precision. The girl was more than perfect, she was better than any before. He'd got her down to the canal, still according to plan, then just as he was about to give her one, he'd been attacked.

What Boots couldn't work out was why, out of nowhere, two Chinese men wanted to, basically kill him? Why Chinese, did it have anything to do with the girl, she looked Chinese but darker in complexion, maybe Korean?

Nothing made any sense. They'd talked about some of the other girls. How did they know about them?

Eyes blank, Boots recalled the creatures coming to *his* rescue, obviously one of them had cut his hands free before attacking the bull of a man, slashing at his face and neck. Boots knew he had stabbed both of them with his claw. Yet it was the creatures who seemed to want to kill them. Surely they must be dead by now.

Maybe the girl was lying there as well, dead, eaten by them? Or *worse,* escaped and was right now in a police station explaining all the terrible details. Even more worrying was that Boots wasn't sure if she had been really that drunk and had even spoke to him, clearly witnessing everything that had happened.

The only glimmer of light was the fact that the police wouldn't believe her when she started to ramble on about the creatures.

If they did though and the cops went down to the canal they'd surely find the men's bodies. It would take them no time at all to trace back to The Ram and then to him. Sweating even though the pub wasn't warm, Boots tried to fathom out a plan to cover his arse.

Shit the claw was still in his bunk so he'd have to 'bin it' somewhere on the other side of town, better still he could easily chuck it in the incinerator round the back of regimental headquarters. They were always burning files, paper and stuff, yes, that was what he'd do when he got back to camp.

After two more pints, Boots calmed down. There hadn't been anyone at camp waiting for him. If the girl had survived and spoken to the police then surely they would have been on camp that morning looking for him. Cheering up he drank the remaining lager in one gulp.

By about three, Boots cautiously approached the camp gates, everything looked perfectly normal.

"Hi Corporal Wellington. *Yoo look rough now*," the young private from Neath observed as Boots stepped round the barrier.

"Urr, yeah rough night last night, anything up?"

"Quiet as my underpants were last night *corp,*" the guard laughing alone at the joke.

Ignoring him, Boots pushed still further and asked, "last night?"

"Ooow yes boyo," seeing Boots stern stare, "sorry Corporal, we have two lads in the clink, The civvy police brought them round after breakfast. They said all things considering a very quiet night."

"What nothing else?"

"Not as far as the Welsh Borderers go."

"Thanks," Boots replied before wandering with slightly more confidence toward his block and the comfort and solitude his room, he prayed, would afford him.

Boots again sweating, collected the now dried blood stained claw from its hiding place.

Shit why hadn't he just thrown it in the canal?

Too late now, Christ he must get rid of the evidence, so quickly and carefully he wrapped it up in toilet paper and placed it in a Woolies plastic bag. He tipped in half a bottle of cheap aftershave for good measure, certain it would burn now.

No one noticed as Boots strolled round the near deserted camp. Checking, he snuck back behind the RHQ where the incinerator was off to the side. A large metal contraption which smelled of a mixture between smouldering tar and cindered paper. Even though it hadn't been loaded since Friday, like a dormant volcano, it was gently smoking, a whisper of smoke silently rising from the chimney, some thirty feet up.

Quickly going over, opening the front shutter Boots looked in. From his vantage point at over six foot he could see in the darkness, red embers glowing down below. Looking round he found a wheelibin full of shredded paper waiting to be burnt and chucked a load in. After a few seconds, black clouds of smoke billowed out quickly followed by initial licks then flames erupted up towards the entrance.

Just to be safe he once again checked round noticing that the only window overlooking the yard was shuttered, so Boots took out the bundle from beneath his loose jacket and dropped it towards the bowels of the flames. He followed it by another heap of shredded paper. Within a few seconds the flames were pouring out of the opening, the chimney now clearing indicating it was active. Boots threw in a even bigger pile of paper before carefully shutting the now very hot hatch. In amongst the clouds of smoke the chimney now emitted black plumes of smoke. Smiling Boots ducked around the corner, smartly walking over to the far side next to the quartermasters building, stopping by way of a disguise to read the notice board he again checked before moving on. As he entered his own building, looking up Boots noted with a great deal of satisfaction and relief as a trail of smoke drifted up and across camp, little shards of blackened paper dancing in the breeze.

Back in his room Boots thought about what to do next now that the evidence having gone up in smoke, literally. All the clothes he'd been wearing would have, by now, gone off to the tip with all the other pub garbage. The local police had been but hadn't mentioned anything, clearly this meant two things to Boots, the women was dead and the three bodies were as yet undiscovered. However he wanted to get as far away, knowing someone would certainly find them sooner or later.

*Later* being only slightly accurate, Monday morning to be exact as someone jogging heard dogs barking aggressively. The sound seeming unusual, the runner had gone to investigate. He later admitted to his wife he wished he hadn't, as the sight and more importantly smell of two grotesquely mutilated bodies being eaten by a couple of stray dogs would leave scars which would probably never heal and certainly meant that he'd never run along the canal again.

The police quickly sealed off the whole section of the canal, initial evidence suggesting some form of ritual killing using two, now evidence, ornate oriental knives. The bodies had clearly been attacked by wild animals, probably urban foxes. As a result it was proving very challenging to identify *them* as they were so badly deformed. The police could however make out one of the bodies was of an enormous bulky oriental male of about thirty-five yet they were having great difficulty as neither corpse had any ID on it and any significant facial features were long gone. The level of violence so extreme, it clearly warranted national TV and radio news, in addition, on Tuesday morning, it made page two of most of the national papers.

Boots heard the news mid morning on Tuesday. It was like a bolt to the head, sat rigid in the army rover as the advance party rumbled north. Holding his Walkman in place with both hands, Boots listened intensely as the radio newsreader explained that the police were as yet baffled by a brutal vicious *double* murder which had probably taken place on Saturday or Sunday night on the banks of the central canal in Aldershot.

All the way up north Boots listened to every bulletin. Time and again wondering why they hadn't mentioned the girl?

# CHAPTER 35

## *Previous Acquaintance*

SUMMER VIEW COTTAGE
MONDAY AFTERNOON

Lynda had tactfully taken on a couple of cover classes, filling in for a friend at the gym so would be out until after five. She was so very understanding when Simon needed some time to work.

Hearing the Jag' purr to a halt, quickly followed by a smart polite rap on the inner glass door, Simon was already on route. Opening it, he allowed Danny and a tall elegant oriental lady to enter.

Smiling at his friend, Simon shook Aika's hand and in that instant knew what was going to be needed, "welcome, you must be Aika, my name's Simon please come in, you're most welcome."

With a timid voice, "hello, yes I am Aika."

As they moved down the corridor Danny spoke for the first time, "Simon, I've told Aika that she has nothing to worry about. Your definitely not the police," a rye smile trickled over the two friends mouths, "you're here to help."

With that they entered the front lounge room. It was purposefully a small room as Simon and Lynda preferring to entertain either in the large double dinning room or the even bigger back lounge overlooking the garden. Cosy and definitely lived it, the room seemed slightly cluttered. Books tight in the two large ebony wall size bookcases. Everything from Jane Austin to Tolstoy's *Anna Karininna*, via Hemmingway and HG Wells. Both parents enjoyed reading.

Although it was just autumn, residents of Shincliffe were still allowed under local law, just, to burn coal. As a result Simon had a ruby red coal fire quietly hissing and cracking. Above, on the mantle piece stood two exquisitely beautiful art deco greyhounds, each on patrol either side of an ornate Victorian mirror.

Gesturing his guests toward two seats on the far side of the fire, Simon sat on the near side on a single carver chair, "Aika, please, your safe here and have nothing to fear. Mr Chang has explained as best he can what happened. With your help I would like to find out as much as possible. This way we can ensure it doesn't happen ever again." With only a momentarily pause for breath Simon continued, "I'm sure you don't want anyone else hurt in this way."

Aika's reply a single nod.

"Aika, my friend Simon here can see things others can't. He reads tarot cards and can see into the future. He'd like to hypnotise you to help discover everything you can possibly remember?"

Frowning, Simon continued to talk directly at his guest, "firstly, I'm not a fortune teller and I don't want to hypnotise you."

"Sorry I obviously misunderstood," Danny interjected.

"That's OK," again turning to the trembling women in the chair opposite him, "Aika what I want to do is very simple. All I will do is hold your hand in mine, ask you to close your eyes and well, we'll just talk. Does that seem alright?"

Aika for only the second time replied, "yes that's fine. You must understand I'm still very scared but if it means that horrid *hentai* never does it again, I'll help."

Simon, who had some understanding of the derogatory Japanese term said, "good, Mr Chang will stay in this room and we'll go into the back study, don't worry it's very light and open and he'll be here all the time and I promise you're safe."

"I hope so."

Looking at his friend, "Danny you stay here. Please don't make any noise and don't disturb us, it shouldn't take more than half an hour, alright?" Simon's words clearly not a question.

"Sure, I've always wanted to read The Trouble with Lichen." As he spoke, Danny took out a slim paperback from the third shelve of the bookcase and started to leaf through the first pages of the classic science fiction novel, "ever since you leant me The Day of The Triffids I've been after a copy of this."

Almost ignoring him Simon addressed Aika, "come on Aika lets go through."

Opening the door for the women probably about the same height as he, Simon motioned to the left, "yes in there," Simon called out as Aika reached a closed door near the far end of the corridor.

Leading the way, Simon went through, the room arranged slightly differently this time, with two high back chairs seated next to each other, the same small table out in front towards the window.

Realising she should sit, Aika went and began to sit on the left chair. "Actually please could you sit on the other one," Simon said with a reassuring smile.

As they both took their places, not three feet apart, Simon turned and looked Aika full in the face. Without speaking he could tell she still had a terribly troubled mind, the frown on her, otherwise seemingly perfect face, clearly exposing her innermost feelings.

With a warm expression he said, "there is water in the glass there," pointing towards the crystal glasses full of mineral water on the table, "what I would like to do is for you to allow me to hold your hand in mine. Then all you have to do is close your eyes and listen to my voice."

Aika wasn't sure, "will it hurt."

"No, not a bit. If anything you may feel a tiny tingling in your hand at first, but no it won't hurt and never forget I'm here right next to you."

"Alright then lets go," came the timid response.

Aika didn't realise how accurate her words were, as they started on the journey.

I moved my open right palm onto the middle of our two chairs, Aika placing her left palm down onto it. Turning to my right slightly, I covered hers with my left.

"Close your eyes and breath slowly, slower, relax." Look as if you are looking through the top of your eyelids, only keep your eyes closed."

"Is it OK to talk?"

"Yes but you may find you don't need to." Trying to describe what I was going to do was always difficult. "You'll feel as if you're floating and then you will have a dream. In that dream we will be together and we will find out everything you know about what happened." Repeating for reassurance, "don't worry I will be there the whole time."

Aika, already calming didn't reply, she was obviously already feeling the power moving through my hand. Like a rhythmic lullaby her breathing clearly, now slowing, regular.

I spoke first, "hello Aika."

Aika replied her voice giving away obvious confusion, "what, where are we, am I dreaming?"

"Well yes and no, It's hard to explain," trying to reassure her I went on, "but it is such a lovely day isn't it?"

I watched as Aika turned gazing, eyes wide, all around, "where is this place, how can I be here? We haven't even left your room"

"Well we have as a matter of fact. Now we need to go for a little walk. Trust me it will be perfectly safe."

Looking across I recognised innocence on the face of the women less than half my age, "come on."

We then walked slowly up the hill. As an after thought saying, "here you may see and hear some unusual things but don't worry they are perfectly natural. If you want, just think of it as a dream."

As we reached the top Aika gasped at the sheer beauty of the building before us.

"Over there," pointing, "here comes one of my friends," Pied Wagtail hopped about on the front gate, "Aika how lovely to make your acquaintance. Simon hardly ever brings friends for us to meet."

Not looking at Aika's I knew she would be bewildered.

"Aika," it was Pied Wagtail, "just because I'm a bird doesn't mean I can't reason, have thoughts and communicate does it?"

"Well I suppose not, this is such a strange dream but I feel so secure and warm. It's so incredibly real."

I smiled, "yes you will feel warmth. Should we go inside and meet some of my other friends?"

It was Pied Wagtail again, "enjoy yourselves. May chat when you come out later?" With that he fluttered off back across the garden.

Opening the door for Aika, we both moved into the cool darkness.

"Arrh Aika I have been expecting you," the Headmaster, with a swish of his great flowing black masters cloak, stood welcoming us.

"This is my very dear friend Doctor Laurance, he often has a chat when I arrive." A now smiling Aika looked down toward the stocky man, "hello Doctor Laurance it's a pleasure to meet you."

"The pleasure my girl is all mine. I know you will complete your studies when the time is right. You understand," his words a statement not a question.

"How do you know that?" Aika's perplexed reply.

I answered for him, "the Headmaster knows many things pertaining to learning and often teaches, advises me."

It was the Headmasters turn, "Simon I would like to chat to Aika for a while and anyway Simon The Commander wishes some of your time."

Turning to Aika I said, "although we won't be together for a few minutes. The Headmaster will, I know, take great care of you. Is that alright?"

"Yes, I feel so safe here but don't be too long though."

"I won't," clearly Aika had no idea or comprehension, why, how could she, that time was relatively meaningless in this dimension.

Smiling I then moved forward. As I did, turning, only to see Aika and the Headmaster seated, her hand in his.

"Colonel, we must speak awhile," the Commander stood as ever up ahead, imposing, his words fired like a rifle straight at me. Instinctively bracing up as I raised my vision towards him, "General, I'm on my way."

Striding up the steps two by two I knew it was important that we discuss some issues relating to my up and coming campaign.

"Colonel, you are aware that those you fear are closing in." Seeing me nod, he continued, "you as yet are however unaware why and who is behind them, correct."

"Yes you are right. I've been trying to identify where these evil spirits originate."

Although I had intended to continue, The Commander, who had no time for small talk, interrupted me, "*Ransky*, it is he who would enter your world to destroy it."

The name hit me like a axe between the eyes as I recalled the formidable foe from my past, "Ransky, but he's d..."*

The cracked face grinned as the Commander looked down his hooked nose, teeth worn and stained, exposed, "yes, but you know it's possible to move within realms. You are here are you not?"

"Yes but I presumed....."

Once again I was interrupted, this time sternly "presume nothing, do you not know your philosophy? Making unfounded presumptions can be deadly."

I could almost taste the caution, mixed with care, power and concern when he spoke, "he comes after you. You know he uses the one called *Boots*. This *human portal* is his avenue towards you. How is unimportant, what is, is that *you*," said with meaning at the same time jabbing a hairy massive finger in my direction, "Colonel, must slam it

* *Simon own footnote*–Five years earlier, it was Ransky who shot me, leaving scars on my upper chest and neck.

*Editor's note*–Having scanned the next instalment of these memoirs I know that they cover, in great depth, the events which brought Simon and Markov Ransky on collision course. All I can say is that they are truly fantastic and although seemingly impossible, even more supernaturally haunting than anything contained in this batch.

shut once and for all." With this, he banged his palm down onto the solid staircase.

Taking this as my cue to reply, "yes, I see now this is my path."

Taping the wooden balustrade, "when you do act, take great care as it's at the moment of extinguish, as you pull the trigger, Ransky will sense your actions and will try everything to stop you. Never forget his soldier creatures are deadly."

As if by way of an after command, his words almost making a statement, "your warriors will cover you but they too are vulnerable from Ranky's dimension."

Our conversation drawing to a close, "one final thing, there is another who I sense has entered *their* world. She, however, means *you* no harm, yet it's unclear if they can enter *your* domaine."

With that as always, The General, smartly nodded his head by way of finality. I understood it was time to go, "lead those who would fight with valour and honour. Good day sir." With that, I descended the deep pile carpeted stairs. Near the bottom I looked over to the school bench.

Aika and Dr Laurance were sat deep in conversation, Aika nodding from time to time. As I reached the last step my old Headmaster rose, still holding her hand in his before saying,

"Here is Simon back. Now remember what we have spoken of. You can only learn if you study. Wisdom must be pursued, knowledge sought is never wasted."

"I understand now *headmaster*, you have taught me so much in such a short space of time. I only wish I could have met you years ago."

As Aika rose he looked into her eyes, "you only had to open your mind, I was there. That said, better late than never."

Aika turning saw me and smiled. By way of a reply my own smile reflected her charming perfect glisten, "headmaster thank you for looking after my friend, we must move on now."

Holding Aika's hand, we both nodded towards Dr Laurance as he walked back towards the stairs. We on the other hand moved over towards the side of the stairs. Again stepping round to the left. As we did I turned to Aika, "I will have to let go of your hand as we go through the door." Seeing the revolving door, she nodded understanding.

Once we were both through, I again held her gentle, long hand, "we must go over here." As I led the way towards the sofa. We sat down facing the large ornate picture frame. Looking at it before continuing, "what happens now might be a little unnerving. That said you are one hundred percent safe just think of it like this. What you will see is like a video tape and all we are doing is playing it again, remember it can't hurt you."

Sensing she didn't quite understand as I tried to explain something which had taken me many years to perfect, let alone comprehend, "Aika, its like a remote journey, we will move there, but we won't leave this chair. We will be looking through the picture at the events which you witnessed the other night."

Shuffling in her seat Aika was still nervous, "Simon, I'm frightened to do this. You can't know how terrible it was. I saw things, unspeakable beings not from this world."

"Listen, I know of such creatures as I have seen them also, many times. They can't reach you as long as we are in this room. They know that we see the past but are incapable of entering this realm, alright."

Sensing she was scared as, holding her hand, her emotion waves clearing readable yet knew she felt safe in my grasp, "what I want you to do is think back to the beginning of that night, don't' worry if it is a little confusing, it will make sense to me. You may even see yourself but don't be alarmed if you do."

Shifting in her seat as if preparing for the journey, uncertain Aika took a deep controlled breath, "well I was in the club, I could see the one Mr Chang was after. It was easy to get his attention, I'm not sure but I think he gave me a drink which was spiked. Anyway, I hardly had a drink from it before things got a little hazy. Trying to encourage him I pretended to be far more drunk than I actually was."

"Great, then what happened, you're doing really well."

"Well we left and he almost dragged me down to a river, We then went along the bank, it was extremely quiet and everything was going as planned."

Aika shivered as the thoughts came think and fast.

We both stood observing as events unfold. Aika lying face up, Boots over her. Then the first of the men approached quickly. As they did I noticed one had yellow eyes, things started to make sense.

We continued to watch as things develop until suddenly one of the evil creatures appeared from smoke, as if from nowhere. It resembled an enormous grotesque wolf, yet stood on its hind legs with a deformed black matted hairy head, skull. It tore at the bulky man.

Obviously Aika's memories were confused as, just as quickly Boots was crashing away, leaving the two creatures and the men. Clearly Aika wasn't trained at viewing things in the right order. Again just as suddenly, Boots was back, this time a blade clear in his fist as he lunged and stabbed deep into the mans neck, blood billowing out as the man gurgled inaudibly.

Quickly looking over at Aika, she was staring wildly, transfixed by terror.

Viewing again, the creatures now gave out a low haunting wail straight from the darkest grave before sniffing the air. Focusing on the, now clearly dead men, they seemingly didn't notice as Aika pushed with her shoes moving up the slight bank, continuing to stare, eyes swollen. Up and over, silently she was gone. They seemed uninterested.

In an instant the foul beings changed focus, turning dark soulless demonic eyes on us, had they finally worked it out?

Possibly able to comprehend time and space as I, they could sense we were playing the tape as they acted, watching from another realm.

Instantly both leapt with incredible speed, fangs and claws thrashing.

In a heart beat we were back in the Journey Room as the blank picture wobbled disturbingly.

Moving to reassure her, "Aika it's alright we are back here now, safe." She was crying, shaking, apprehension ingrained on her thin face, "they knew we were there didn't they?"

"Yes, but they can't enter via this world, here you are perfectly safe. You needn't worry they have no way of touching us." By way of confirming her safety, finishing with, "now that you have no contact with the Boots man, *they* are lost even if they wanted to find you."

In a more reflective mood she looked round towards me, "how did you do that? It was so real, they were the creatures I saw, exactly the same. Things were pretty much just as it was, like it only happened moments ago. How come I could see myself lying on the ground?"

"Aika, sorry, it would take a very long time to explain, let's just say it's a technique which I learnt a while ago. Here, in this room, I have developed strange powers and can travel pretty much anywhere I want from this very seat," I gestured to the sofa, "see and hear what I want."

Aika shook her head in disbelief before drying now dormant tears from her cheeks, "can we go now?" She was confused, clearly still frightened.

"Of course, but before we do I've two more friends I think you should meet."

"Oh please no more horrid stuff as I don't think I could cope."

"No this is quite the opposite," smiling I continued, "your leg troubles you and you are ashamed to return to your family."

In disbelief, "how can you possibly know that, I never mentioned….."

Interrupting her, "Aika, just by holding your hand I can tell a lot about a person. You want to dance but feel compelled to continue on the path you don't enjoy, trapped."

Without thinking Aika said, "well I am, I can't dance anymore and although it is a sinful thing which I do, it affords me more money than I could imagine."

"Money isn't everything," my instant frowning repost.

"I know your right but how'm I to return when there is no way back?"

Without speaking another word I led her towards the revolving doors. Stepping through first before holding her hand as we walked toward the stairs. They were now empty. We turned round under the magnificent baluster. The Treatment Room's door open, chatter flowing our way.

"Aika I want to introduce you to some of my friends. If you like I can see if we can help your knee."

"I never mentioned my knee?"

"I know but I'm sure we can help."

Standing in front Aika, uncertain, looked at me with questioningly eyes. Hers brown yet slightly red from the tears, "you promise nothing will happen."

"Well actually I can't say that, but I can promise that it won't hurt and you will enjoy the experience."

"After what I've been through recently it might make a pleasant change," replied Aika.

Releasing her hand allowing Aika to walk past me into the light airy room.

Following, talking past her, "Doctor Kleiman, Bobby a friend wants to meet you."

The response gently and warming, "hello Aika, we understand Simon wants us to take a look at your knee."

It was Bobby this time, "hi, I'm the *pet doctor*, so probably won't be that much help but you never know."

Her jaw slightly open, Aika turned to me, "who are these people, how can they be here and how come everyone seems to know my name yet I don't know anyone's?"

The doctor moved forward, "Aika, so many questions and not enough time. Hello my name is Doctor Kleiman, please take a seat and lets have a look."

Dutifully, Aika took the lead and sat in an upright hard backed chair. As she was wearing loose slacks, Dr Kleiman, who had knelt in front, his long white doctors jacket buttoned up in front, hitched her trouser leg up beyond the knee. As he did, as if seemingly perfectly normal, Aika didn't react.

I stood, looking over his shoulder, "what d'you reckon *doc*?"

"Well I think I can leave this to you Simon," he stood and moved to the side. Aika looked surprised, yet still remained silent, "Aika," *I* sat on a little stool in front of her exposed knee, "what I'm going to do takes no effort from you, so close your eyes and just relax, it won't take long."

Still mystified she enquired, 'what won't?"

"I'm going to have a look *round* your knee for you alright, now sit back and relax."

---

Some time later opening my eyes, patting Aika gently on the other knee, "you can push down your trousers now, job done."

Opening her eyes Aika smiled, "I feel fantastic," standing, the dancer stomped down her leg, " "I have no pain any more. It's gone? What have you done, it's a trick?"

Dr Kleiman took over, "no trick my dear, here those who are ill and injured can be helped.

All we do is sometimes lend a hand. In this place his," pointing at me, "hands and ours are as one," with that he gesticulated around the light airy room.

Bobby lightening the mood spoke towards her, "pity you don't have a pet cat or something."

We laughed, Aika frowning, not quite understanding.

"Well Aika we better get going now," with that both visitors stood and moved towards the door before Aika said, "thank you both for whatever you did, thank you."

"It is our pleasure," the doctor's reply, "dance, leap and be happy in your new life," Bobby's closing remark.

Aika through a smile, frowned, gave a tiny nod then followed me back out of the bright room. Once again we walked past the stairs, the Headmaster no longer around. Out of the opened doors into the fresh welcoming sunlight. As we did I said, "well time to go back down to the river."

Aika seemed almost at one with the place now. This was good as she needed to feel warmth, love, if she was to steer a new path.

"You should run," it was Pied Wagtail, as he swooped past our heads. Dually instructed Aika started to dash down the grassy, wild flower strewn meadow. Laughing she had a heads start so I had to chase after her. Pied Wagtail having no such difficulty.

As we neared the bottom, Aika slowed to a walk, giggling at something Pied Wagtail had said to her. In a flop, she sat down grinning. I caught up, sitting next to her. After a few moments silence as we watched Pied Wagtail curl off into the distance, I breathed long and deep, "OK Aika, take my hand," which she calmly did, "close your eyes and breath slowly and deeply."

Without a word she did as requested.

"Wake up Aika, wake up."

"What, where are we?"

"In my study of course, why where did you think we were, did you have a pleasant sleep?"

"Ey, was I dreaming. Did I imagine the doctor and that nice school teacher."

Almost in a school boy tone I replied, "not telling and anyway he doesn't like to be called a school teacher, don't forget he's The Headmaster."

For the first time in my home Aika, eyes dancing as she shook her head, hair flowing as she laughed out aloud.

Twenty minutes later, less than an hour since they had arrived, Danny and Aika left. As they did I said I'd give him a ring to discuss things later.

Once they'd gone, I sat in the garden silently going over our journey and the conversations I, we'd had.

I felt elated yet worried. Wonderful warmth knowing that Aika's knee would allow her to dance again, if she chose that path. I was however gravely troubled that, at last, things were beginning to make some sense. Boots was the portal, the receiver Ransky was using to transmit evil into this world. He was doing so in some bizarre attempt to find me, obviously intent on revenge.

Well he had found me and I wasn't happy. Attacking Penny had been a mistake, killing Lotti and then the two assassins was unacceptable. I couldn't allow Ransky to send those foul creatures towards my family. Needs must and all that rot...Boots would have to die.

# CHAPTER 36

## Special Delivery

Danny dropped Aika off at one of his better restaurants, with orders that his guest was to be treated like royalty and once she had dined, a driver would then take her home. He wasn't surprised that Aika seemed one hundred percent better, almost contented, he was however not going to let the thing, Boots, get away with it. Even before he reached the office Danny was taking action, if Simon wanted some special gun then he'd get it.

Opening the outer office door, Jenny was already waiting with a note book in hand, walking straight past her into his office; she had the good sense to have everything ready, including a clear access route. Jenny knew that Mr Chang might not be quite what you would clinically call part of any triad, that said she knew far too much not to know that he was more than capable of achieving whatever he wanted no matter how illegal.

"Sir, the man who you wanted to call you is, as we speak, on route. He said he would be here within the hour. I have also asked Sam to join you, he'll be here within minutes. Tea sir?"

"Hello to you as well Jenny," not letting her respond, "only teasing, you see it's been a bloody terrible trip but I intend to sort things out."

"Sorry to hear that. Will the two gentlemen be joining us?"

Danny had all but forgotten about the brothers, how bloody callous he thought, "Jenny, they won't be back ever. I need you to ensure that they never were in this office. That I don't know who they are, never did, d'you understand?"

Jenny replied, "I understand. I'll make an anonymous call to the hotel telling them they had to leave suddenly, their bills paid for the week anyway, cash." With a clinical grin, "well done, I can always rely on you."

By the time the tea arrived, so too had Sam, "come straight in Sam."

The portly, glowing from rushing, 'manager' came straight in and flopped down onto a chair. They had known each other long enough to relegate formalities, "what's up Mister Chang?" Some formalities, for respects sake, retained.

"You know of my plan to extinguish the thing who attacked my darling daughter."

"Of course, I hope he now rots in hell, pain forever bearing down on his worthless shoulders," as he spoke Sam smirked, he knew of Force Lightening and almost shivered at the thought of what they must have done to the deserving creature.

Flat and cold Danny said, "he's still alive and they're both dead."

Hardly able to believe his boss, "what, that's impossible, totally impossible. What, one stupid round eye has taken out both brothers. No you have to be wrong."

Leaning forward on his desk Danny, pushing the tea and saucer aside, "they are dead, its even made the news."

Without thinking Sam replied, "I've not watched the TV since Sunday and I don't like the radio."

Danny, who was impatient to get things moving, ignored Sam and continued, "listen to me, they're dead. Jenny is sorting out the hotel where they were staying. There is no way they can connect it with us and anyway we didn't do it."

"Sir what about the slug still clinging to your shoe?" Sam knew that, as gentle as his boss was, Mr Chang was capable of distant violence when the need required.

With a smash of his fist, the saucer shaking violently, tea spilled onto the polished table,"he will die, Green Eyed Dragon intends to see to it himself."

Eyes widened on his plump smallpox'd face, Sam was in reality a mister fixer for Mr Chang as well as acting as the direct link with Mr Bo.

Sam had met Simon many times. On each occasion it had been in some kind of awe. The second time they had shaken hands at a Christmas reception. Sam had fallen deep within those all-consuming emerald eyes sensing a kind of electricity almost jump up his arm. He hadn't been present when Danny's number one restaurant was attacked but heard from one of the waiters of how Simon had disarmed two sword wielding thugs whilst also taking care of three others intent on death. Yet throughout he hadn't had any weapons, only his body. Yes the legend of the one who moved with spirits was known amongst many in his circles.

"Sir whatever you need I will get."

"Not a lot actually. Look after the girl Aika. Watch her. She won't, but if she gets within thirty feet of a police station, pick her up. Be gentle. Simon Boeck has spoken to her so I'm confident she will be no trouble. Anyway she will be busy spending the fifty thousand Jenny is going to transfer this afternoon. Lets call it services above and beyond her call of duty."

Both men allowing the tiniest of smiles to creep unseen across their faces. Mr Chang continued, "any minute now Tiny Smallie should arrive."

Letting the fact that the other underworld king pin was about to arrive sink in. As he did Sam gave a whistle and a slight frown. "what can he get that I can't?"

"An M4 Commando, five point five six, with folding stock," Danny looked up from Simon's notes.

"You have me there sir. If it is a gun, I've never heard of anything like that. Why so specific?"

"Special delivery for Boeck."

"Oh I see, maybe it would be better if Mr Smallie helps on this one then."

At that moment Jenny quietly knocked on the door, "come in" Danny's instant response.

"Mr Smallie's here."

"Great, show him in, show him in." raising his voice past her, "don't keep the little runt waiting out there."

Sam said goodbye and squeezed past and out of the office. As he did, he received a powerful, yet friendly slap on the back.

# CHAPTER 37

## *Small Favour*

### NEWCASTLE, THE QUAYSIDE
### WEDNESDAY 9AM–DANNY'S OFFICE

Only an idiot couldn't grasp the simple humour. Tiny was anything but, if you added the surname, Smallie, then the joke was complete. Nearly six foot four and twenty-one stone, in old money, Tiny Smallie was by anyone's standards a big bloke. Big, ugly bloke to be precise. A long square, scared head perched on wide shoulders, gave Tiny a striking resemblance to Herman from The Adam's Family. Only the incredibly brave or mind numbingly stupid daring to point out the likeness.

Renowned, revered, feared throughout the north, he was a live wire known to have little patience. Equally well known that he was more than happy when required, to let his bulky fists do the talking. The giant of a man had ruled over a whole criminal fraternity since his early twenties, a quarter of a century ago.

Tiny knew of Danny's business and Danny of his. As a result for the past five years peace had reined. After previous events, there was certainly no chance of that position being altered. Respect and mutual, if not distant, support now given.

"Less of that you pint sized spring roll. How goes it? What can be so important that you drag me from my golf?"

"Sit down you oversized hippo," Danny's light hearted instant retort.

Laughter only subsiding as Jenny scurrying retreated. Springs creaked as the bulk of a man lowered his powerful frame into, the now well accustomed, sturdy chair.

"Tiny, I'm very grateful for you making this special effort for me cos' it's going to be me who now owes the favour."

"Well then? Time's money and all that."

With that Danny came round from his desk and took the seat adjacent to his sometime friend. He knew Tiny would not refuse and if anyone could get the weapon it would be him. Add the fact who it was for, he was certain Tiny would deliver the goods so to speak.

"You heard what happened to my daughter?"

Tiny nodding and replying at the same time, "yes I'd heard, sent her flowers and all that. I've been trying to find out who did it. Trust me when I do they won't last long when I've chopped their knackers off."

Raising an open hand, "thanks but castrations too good for them and anyway I already know who did it and intend to have him killed."

A broad worn smile stretched across his gritty face, "you just have to say the word and it will happen. All very quiet like, no fuss."

"Tiny, everything is always so simple to you."

"Well isn't it? Some git attacks your daughter so you have his balls shoved down his throat as he sinks slowly to the bottom of the river."

The response instant, "not this one, I promise, not this one. I hired two of the best hit men to come and take care of things."

Scratching the stub of what remained of his left index finger over his bald patch, Tiny didn't see what all the fuss was about, "well that's more like it my oriental chop stick."

Ignoring the fact that he was indeed extremely thin, "Tiny, those I sent were in turn attacked and he still lives. He killed them both."

"Tough fucker ey, so you want your old pal Tiny to set the dogs on him?"

Replying, Danny was in no mood for humour, "listen you giant Toon army supporter."

"I'm no Magpie and you know it," the words only just masked mild anger.

"Calm down, calm down, I know that temper of yours. No, when you mentioned guns you were closer to the target."

"I need you to get me a special weapon, for a mutual friend. You see he intends to take care of business."

"Now ya prawn cracka, we're getting somewhere. I know plenty of paddies who'd happily give your slug a double tap to the knees, then one through the skull for afters."

"For Christ's sake Tiny listen," Danny was getting annoyed, "I intend to do this my way but I do need your help, please."

Noting his friends impatient tone, Tiny replied, "anything, you know that. Who's the shooter? Didn't know you were into that kind of thing."

Having saved the ace up his sleave, Danny threw the words like the winning cards they were, "Simon Boeck."

Rarely was Tiny speechless, mouth ajar, words absent, his stare gave him a gruesome appearance as he pulled on what was left of his right ear.

"Yes Tiny, Simon has been helping me track the vile creature down. Now he wants, actually says, he needs to kill him."

"Fuck me, well no, on second thoughts you'd better not," continuing regardless of his own crude joke, "Simon Boeck is doing this for you, well, all I can say is, God certainly can't help the idiot who decided to attack your Penny and somehow get on the wrong side of Simon."

Sitting back satisfied, he now had Tiny's full attention, Leaning over Danny passed a piece of paper across the table. It was the same sheet Simon had given him.

Taking it, Tiny read the details, "new one on me, far happier with a sworn off shot gun myself, they tend to do the trick for my boys."

With a scowl Danny went on, "no he was very specific about the weapon. He also needs ammunition."

With a grin, "durr, well of course my wealthy pint sized friend, I didn't expect Simon to hit him over the head with it, now did I?" Almost reflectively continuing, "that said anything is possible when Simon's involved."

Realising he hadn't really spoken about the only man who Tiny actually deep down respected and in a weird way feared, "so how is he? I haven't had a beer with him for ages. Wouldn't be done for a Colonel to be seen with a man with three convictions now would it old chap." As he spoke Tiny tried to mimic, in his own way, what he imagined a lofty important colonel might talk like.

"He's very well but as usual confusing the hell out of me. I give up sometimes but know I 'd far rather have him as a dear friend than as an enemy."

"Amen to that."

Two sets of teeth, one punctuated by gold, smiled.

Sat there, discussing murder, they struck an incongruous juxtaposition. One small, almost frail Chinese man dressed in expensive designer suit and the other, an enormous beaten up bear of a man wearing faded cords, boots, a well-worn yet very expensive jumper and sprouting sporadic grey stubble.

"Back to business, Danny. If the great man wants a," Tiny checked the handwriting which he recognised, "Colt M4 then, my friend he will have one. When's he need it by anyway?"

"Tomorrow."

"Fucking hell that's pushing it a bit. In that case I don't suppose he gives a shit where it's from does he?"

"No he didn't specify," Danny said slightly confused by the question.

"Fuck off you know what I mean. Something like this ain't that easy to get hold of. I may even have to talk to some paddy friends of mine." With a childish giggle, "thatabe' ripe, me giving the great soldier a gun from the IRA."

Frowning disapproval, "I think we should leave that kind of detail out, alright, don't you?"

Almost ignoring him Tiny replied, "so, how many posh meals is this favour going to buy me, five, six?"

The man was intolerable, always making a joke out of everything, He never seemed to take things seriously, "don't worry, when this is all over you will have the finest tak-away...."

Gold teeth glistening, grinning, Tiny rode the gentle dig replying, "bugger off. Well mucker, best foot forward and all that."

"Exactly, no rest for the wicked."

Standing, the chair gave a creek of relief, Tiny said, "seriously, I will get it for you and for him. It's not going to be easy, but what the hell. I'll have it delivered to the usual place, alright?"

"Superb, give me a call. We'll call it the 'CM4', sounds like a good codeword?"

"You are such a careful suspicious bugger, yep alright I'll call you when CM4's on route." Always keen for mischief, "is there anything else you would like to order sir?"

"Shut up and stop taking the piss."

"Who me," the mighty palm slapping against the jumper, instantly serious, "oh yer, say hi for me. No amount of favours will ever repay him for what he did, you know that."

Danny did. He also knew that both Simon and Lynda's immaculate cars were on permanent free hire from a garage which went by the name of TS Ltd.

"I know old friend, I know," Danny replied trying not to look at the mess which was all that was left of Tiny's right ear.

Business concluded, the friends shook hands, one lost in the other before Tiny marched out, cheerfully saying 'tat tar old thing' to Danny's diminutive secretary. "I'm not old," Jenny retorted to the Goliath lookalike as he headed through the outer door. They both knew it was only a joke.

Only about five people were aware of the alternative exit Danny special associates used to get in and out of the building. No one suspected the sophisticated Indian restaurant two doors down on the other side of the building had a rear door that led to the alley, which in turn led to the back stairs of Danny's building.

On this occasion it didn't matter, the local serious crimes squad had all but given up following in the vain attempt that they may be able to nail a conviction on the well-known felon who went by the absurd name, Tiny.

# CHAPTER 38

## *Coincidence?*

### NEWCASTLE WEDNESDAY MORNING 10AM
### REGIONAL CRIME SQUAD CONFERENCE ROOM

The regional Serious Crime Squad was conducting its morning brief and Detective Chief Inspector Neil Monk wasn't in a good mood.

"Listen you lot," he cast a disapproving radar like gaze round the conference room, "last night I had the mayor and the local MP giving me real jip about the rise in serious attacks. I don't expect to go to a supposedly pleasant evening with my missus only to spend the entire evening getting an earache from busy bodies who don't understand the challenges I face." With that he sat back down behind the long fake wood table, surveying his team. Looking round most were either making notes or pretending to do so. No one daring to risk catching his glance for fear of becoming the sacrificial lamb for pent up slaughter.

All except Sergeant Parish, her naivety once again exposed.

The Saint seized upon his prey, "...and that's another thing, I've been waiting for some developments on that oriental slasher case and you," his eyes pointed towards Sue, "have achieved absolutely bugger all."

He was on a roll, "with all the forensic and DNA evidence the fucker who did it should already be residing at her majesties..." His voice trailed off, exhaustion merging as exasperation took control.

The thing was Sue wasn't experienced enough to realise this was the time to keep her gob tight shut. All the other Sergeants and one or two of the more experienced PCs desperately, subconsciously, tried to drive the message into her brain.

They failed,

"Sir, the fucker," Sue laboured the expletive, " I'm after continues to elude me, that said rest assured I'm trying everything possible to identify the attacker. With a little more time...."

"Time," barked her boss, "is not on your side Sergeant Parish." Emphasising the rank, the chief inspector was not singling her out however she offered him a vent through which to release the valve tightened by the ridiculous do gooder of a mayor he'd sat next to during the previous nights formal banquet for the Swedish tourism board.

"But sir," Sue was still on the defence of her first case, "I am doing everything possible to catch him but without any suspects it's proving very difficult."

"Don't but sir me," he took command, "right, you've until Monday to give me a name or you're off the case and you can go back to filing."

Finally her colleagues imaginary psychic powers prevailed, Sue realised it was time to shut up, so blurted out, "sir I'll have a name by Monday."

Ten minutes later after the gathered masses of the squad had endured the remnants of his tirade of abuse, mixed with supposed encouragement, the meeting broke up.

Back at her desk, Sue was pissed off. Surely the Saint understood what she was faced with. Shit she'd said Monday so had better come up with something fast. There must be a way of tracking down the attacker, the fucker as her boss had called him, 'think, think', she said in her mind.

After some mint tea and a Kitkat she thought it worth another try.

"I'm Sorry Sue," it was Lynda speaking, "he's not back from the shops. As soon as he is I'll have him call you."

"Oh that would be great. You know this case is getting to me. I must catch him."

"Hang on a mo' I think that's him now."

Thirty seconds later Simon had the phone. He hadn't expected this and was very busy himself but along a far darker route.

"Sue, hi, how can I help you? Have you got your man yet?"

"No and that's why I was wondering if we could have a chat just in case there was anything else you could give me to go on."

Simon had anticipated the call yet on the other hand could not let the detective close in on his target, as a result he was in somewhat of a quandary. He'd have to give her something else to go on.

"Well actually I've been thinking and did remember something but it might be of no use. You know I said he was Scottish, well I'm not sure now. Maybe he just had a distinct accent."

Sue seized upon the offering, "what like Welsh?"

This took Simon off guard, "well yes I suppose so, there again it could have been Scouse, Brummy or just even posh." As if seeming to mull over the question, "yes I suppose it could have been Welsh."

"That could be very useful indeed, thanks. Anything about his appearance?"

Simon now paused, checking his words carefully, "no, sorry only what I told you, he's big tough and deadly. I'm certain he either has or will strike again."

That was all he was prepared to offer. Sue stopped making notes and shifted the phone back from her chin cum shoulder to her left hand, "thank's Simon. This is so important to me."

"I know," replied Simon, "never give up and always remember in amongst the detail is the information you seek."

It was Sue's turn, "I know, well please if there is anything else give me a call."

Certain that he probably wouldn't call the detective until after he'd dealt with Boots, "I will I promise," the lie easy as he recalled what had happened to Penny.

A trip to the loo later, Sue sat mulling over the information. Simon had said that he would almost certainly attack again, maybe he had already done so. With renewed vigour Sue switched on the internal police website.

Knife attack, sexual motive, Stanley blades. Tap tap tap tu tap, her four finger typing quick as it was loud. Then slowly deliberately she pressed 'search'.

Frowning as if to speed up the machine, the tiny egg timer kept tumbling as it scanned the police files.

Finally, 658 hits.

Too many. She needed to narrow the field so typed in the dates from when the attack took place until that Wednesday.

Salt tumbled for a further thirty seconds.

24 hits.

Manageable. Quickly and precisely she read the synopsis of each attack.

At number 19 she stopped. No it hadn't been an attack on a women but there was something? Two men, oriental, clue number one, found mutilated in a military town, clue two, attacked with a pair of oriental assassins knives, clueish number three. Sue studied the details, noting the contact number she punched it into her phone.

"DC Cassidy, Aldershot police."

"Hello my name is DS Parish, I was wondering if you could give me a run down on that double murder case.

Identity confirmed, Sue had listened with a mix of revulsion, especially about the wild dogs or foxes, combined with a niggle.

She was a natural copper and knew she had something but what? Could there be a connection? There were plenty of links; blades, serious knife wounds, oriental victim (albeit two and male) and it took place in a military town.

"Thanks DC Cassidy." With that she sat mulling over what to do next.

The phone rang, "hello DS Parish speaking."

"Hello Sue, its Tom here from Workop camp, remember?"

Yes of course hello Tom, what's up?"

"Well you said I should give you a call if I thought of anything, well it might be insignificant but the night of the attack the Scottish soldiers weren't the only ones here. There were a few from The Welsh Borders on camp. They'd been here as part of an advance party and it just so happens that their main body will be arriving tonight for ranges over the next week."

Sue mind was racing. She'd asked Simon who hadn't said it wasn't someone with a Welsh accent.

"Thank you so much Tom, it might be nothing but it might just as equally be everything. When can I come and speak to someone from the regiment?"

Well I know their adjutant arrives tomorrow night, so let's say Friday morning just before nine in the morning."

Alright I'd prefer sooner but that'll do, what's an adjutant?"

At the camp, Tom surveyed his vegetable plot, "well he's basically the commanding officers right hand man. He is like a PA, legal adviser, a private confidante, boss of discipline all rolled into one. They tend to be quality officers, normally captains on the way up."

"Arrh I see, well I'll look forward to meeting him," by way of a throwaway question, "where they from?"

"Aldershot near London."

Silence.

"Sue are you there?"

"Yes its just that, no never mind probably just a weird coincidence."

"OK until Friday then," Tom stopped, "Sue you know I never did believe in coincidence, I'd follow that up if I were you."

"I intend to, when I meet this adjutant of there's."

Sue went over to the white board and started to add the new information. The new facts were so divorced, yet somehow linked. With a sense of urgency and renewed energy Sue decided to yet again go over the forensic evidence, visit the attack site and go see Penny. Then tomorrow she'd do the saints report before preparing for the meeting with the Officer from the Welsh Borders. In the mean time she'd call her new friend Tim down at Catterick. He'd be able to give her the low down on these Welsh Borders and what the hell an Adjutant was?

## CHAPTER 39

# *Fields of Fire*

### WORKOP,
### THURSDAY 0830AM

Way back in the 70's, Stargate had been the official name for covert psychic operations which the CIA had and, latterly, the highly secret Field Operations Group continue to, employ around the world.[13] These facts Simon already knew as he'd been on the program, having witnessed, first hand, what was incredible yet very possible. His own Remote Viewing training had lasted nearly a year. That said Section 9's, unlike Stargate, training had included far more military tactics and development.

It was however a tool cum skill which he had developed far beyond his military instructors. Simon could now travel pretty much anywhere he needed. When you added the assistance he received from friends in the Hacienda Grande, movement through time and space, many realms a distinct possibility. Rarely, anymore, did he try to explain the intricacies, as he knew through experience that in reality no one would believe him. Simon had even once years before, taken his wife Lynda on what he described as a journey.

The journey which now brought him to the front gates of Workop Camp, that Thursday morning, had been fairly normal by his standards. That said he knew he'd need to move with caution so as not to allow anyone to connect him with future events. He'd use a skill developed in America, thought control.

"Yes sir, can I help you?" It was the guard. As he stood waiting for a reply Tommie noted, with approval, the smart jacket accompanied by a regimental tie.

"Hello, I'm Simon Boeck, retired Colonel Boeck. I'm here to see the commandant, major Bride," Simon smiled as he added, "he said to arrive at eight thirty."

"Tommie's watch said eight twenty five as he checked the clipboard, "Yes sir," he knew an Officer when he saw one, "do you have any ID please, sir."

Having produced his driving licence, Simon preferring not to use his unofficial military ID card which he only produced on very special occasions. The barrier rose as Tommie physically braced himself up in a civilian attempt at respect. Nodding in reply, Simon drove round and parked in the identical space, DS Parish had used previously.

Simon locked his car and stepped towards the clearly marked Camp HQ. Realising the main door only led into a corridor he pushed it open. As he did, Simon called out, "hello, Major Bride, is anyone at home?"

Tom wiped his hands on the seat of his trousers as he came bustling out of the toilet, "Colonel, sorry I was...," as he spoke he nodded towards the Mens sign on the toilet door next to him, "well anyway good to meet you. Sir please come through."

With that Tom held out his now dry hand. He, as everyone did, received the two handed grasp from his guest, "Major Bride, please I'm retired, Simon's my name."

"Well hello Simon your most welcome," As he spoke the commandant acknowledged that, Colonel Boeck must have been promoted in his mid thrities to look so young and already be retired. Moving forward he finished with, " please, come this way," walking ahead towards his office.

Simon assessed the mans energy from their handshake. Decent man, he was no longer too bothered but happy with his lot, so to speak. So long as no one messed him around he was happy with green dirty hands? He needed to lower his cholesterol though. Simon mentally noting this fact. Maybe he'd mention it later?

Following, Simon sat in the chair offered to him. Having checked out the room, whilst Tom, as he'd been asked to be called, fetched two cups of tea, no sugar in Simon's case.

"So Simon, you said on the phone that you were doing some research for a book regarding training camps like this one."

"Yes that's right. I'm hoping to produce the definitive book on all training camps which are dotted around the north country, they do have such a fascinating history don't you think?"

Tom didn't, and actually couldn't think of anything more boring than reading the account of camps which, in the main, were located in god forsaken spots in the wilds of Northumberland and Cumbria. Well if that's what fired the chap rockets then fine and hell he didn't get many visitors.

"As I said on the phone you're more than welcome to see the journal from the war. Other than that what can I do to help?"

"Well, I'd like to have a look around and maybe take a few photo's if that's OK?"

"Sure, but please could I see them first. I'd hate to get into grief for allowing photo's of the camps security to get into the wrong hands."

Simon smiled, "no nothing like that and of course I'd let you vet them first."

Having lulled Tom into a false sense of security, Simon got down to business. In an almost off hand manner he enquired, "you control all the ranges round here as well don't you?" the necessary emphasis on the required word and without waiting for a reply continuing with, "is there any chance I could go out and have a look at a few on the way home this morning?"

Christ thought Tom, the guy was keen. Why anyone would want to go tramping over a range was beyond the commandant but heck they weren't being used until Friday, so fine, "sure I'll call the range managers and warn them you may pop by. Actually I might as well call all of them so you don't waste any time. They'd insist on calling me first."

Perfect, Tom had given Simon the green light he was after.

Word suggestion was such a powerful tool in the right hands and against unsuspecting minds it was incredible.

"Thanks thatabe great. I'm not interested that much in ranges but might just pop and have a look at a few on the road home." The subconscious seeds sown in Tom's mind.

"Well if you want to drink your tea, it'll only take a minute to phone all of them."

Simon nodded in approval as Tom dialled numbers from memory.

Workop Camp actually controlled five range complexes, each with at least three or four separate live firing ranges. Each complex was managed by a seemingly ancient soul who would trudge about checking the electronics on the targets, as well as putting the red flags up all round any range which was conducting life firing that day. A dull job, which paid poorly, yet afforded the incumbent plenty of time to keep warm at the tax payers expense, read books and wonder around the countryside. Most importantly, as the camp commandant mostly left them to their own devices, they were in effect masters of their own destiny, on regular pay with a surprisingly good non contributory pension.

Five minutes later all range wardens duly notified, Tom left his desk and rejoined Simon on the other comfy chair.

"Simon, they're all happy and ready for whenever you turn up. They did remind me to tell you that as of tomorrow range number three will be in use by The Welsh Borders so that's probably not a good option."

"Fine, I'll go to one of the others then."

"Simon, please you must excuse me but for once I'm actually quite busy. We've got over a hundred soldiers arriving today and there are things which have to be checked, you understand ?"

"Simon feigning surprise, "Oh I 'm sorry Tom, it's me who should be apologising. I'd better get going."

Both men walked along the corridor and out into the autumnal breeze. Turning, "Tom, once again thanks."

With that they shook hands before Simon started to move towards his car as Tom, with a final glance, opened the single storey building main door. Calling after him, "Tom one thing, I couldn't help but notice that cheese on your desk, you'd better watch it as that stuff can play havoc with your cholesterol."

Simon climbed into his car, started the engine and moved off.

As the car rounded the corner, Tom wandered back into his office. He enjoyed a chunk of cheese during the morning yet his wife was always going on about how he should cut down on the stuff. Maybe she had something and anyway it wouldn't be a bad idea to get his cholesterol checked. His Dad, shortly before he'd died, had shocked the doctors with a dangerously high cholesterol level of 10.9.

Yes that would be a good idea he'd get it done. Maybe the chap, what was his name? who'd just been had a point, he shouldn't be eating as much cheese as he did. With that he studied the range charts pinned to the board, already forgetting about his recent visitor.

Simon on the other hand was pretty pleased with the way his meeting with the commandant had gone. He knew Tom wouldn't dwell on the visitor who must be mad to even contemplate writing a book about range camps. Yes Tom would have moved onto other issues.

Driving due east from the camp he turned off the main road and headed north following the typical white and red small army signpost indicating ranges 1 to 3. Within fifteen minutes he drew to a halt on a deserted hilltop. The only distinguishing feature being a large empty flagpole. Climbing out into the bone chilling air he crossed over to the mounted telephone box, next to a closed fence.

"Hello?"

Simon hunched forward into the shoe box sized booth, "hello my names colonel

Si..."

Before he could finish the reply, "yes, the commandant said you might come over. Please close the gate behind you, I'm in the shed up the valley."

"Great thanks, see you in a minute then?"

The other end hung up.

Actually this was exactly what he wanted as the chap wouldn't even remember Simon's name by the afternoon so any tenable link would be severed.

The tarmaced single track road, weaved with the contours of the land down into a valley. At the road head stood a large gravel car park, a single battered old Cortina and a shed emitting smoke which blew at right angles the moment it hit the Irish Sea wind.

As Simon emerged from the warmth of his car a dishevelled, clearly underweight man opened the door and beckoned him forward. Reaching the partially open door, Simon smiled, speaking loudly above the now near gale, "hi the commandant said to check in with you first before having a look round."

"Yeah that's right, said something about writing a book."

"Yes that's right. I'm researching range camps."

Almost without thinking, ten years of almost daily solitude having robbed him of his remaining people skills, the gaunt range warden, who went by the name of Mr Card, looked Simon over, "Bugger of a subject, but hell if you're into ranges then be my guest."

Turning, leaving the door ajar, "but lets get out of this F'ing wind."

"Sorry yes," Simon almost having to yank the corrugated covered thick wooden door as it grated against the loose stones underfoot.

Ten minutes and one cup of revolting, thick over sugared coffee later Simon had left with what he came for. Mr Card happily giving his blessing for Simon to roam around the ranges. Making sure he mentioned at least four times that probably he'd stick to having a look at range number One.

Back inside his warm cocoon, Mr Card scratched his bony arse, there were certainly some queer folk around. With that the never married sixty year old picked up his knitting and continued doing the sleeves on the jumper for his nephew.

A short while later, Simon left his car in yet another carpark. This one large enough to accommodate at least four, 4 tonners. Surveying the surroundings, he saw the control shed perched up on the hill overlooking the range.

Live firing ranges actually look for all intensive purposes like any other bit of heath. That was the point, they were meant to simulate reality. The electronically activated targets carefully hidden behind knawels or dug in so as to obscure the equipment required to spring them up.

Moving up toward the building, he moved round to the front. Here there was an enormous window which ensured good visibility to every aspect of the range stretching off and up to the horizon, about a mile away. Standing looking out over the windswept hillside Simon was grateful for the restbite from the increasing wind.

It was fairly obvious where the range actually started, the clear bright red marker posts giving it away. The range simulated up to a platoon of soldiers moving up two sides of a sweeping valley, a small brook running down the centre. The clearly marked range stretched over two hundred metres up each side of the stream. Probably a further hundred metres further up the incline was where the first target would pop up. One section of eight would go to ground whilst the other dashed forward in sub groups shooting the targets until they flipped back down. The section commander would then call them to a halt whilst the other section did the same up the otherside, in a kind of leap frog motion. At all times the safety marshals would ensure that no one got in the line of sight of the forward section. If they did, individuals could conceivably be mistaken as targets. After about five or six leapfrogs, the senior marshal would scream, 'stop' and blow a whistle. At this point everyone concerned applied their safety catches, remained where they were regardless of whether they were lying in the stream or a pile of sheep shit. The only other time a whistle would sound was if any of the safety staff saw something dangerous happening, then they could stop the shoot immediately.

All in all a very realistic exercise so soldiers tended to take life firing seriously as, accidents although very rare, did happen.

Simon wandered down toward the start line and surveyed the surrounding land. It was mixed with heather, shrubs and occasional trees. The little banks of the stream weaved down from the skyline some thousand meters up ahead. He followed a sheep track up the right bank near the stream. Climbing still further he reached a natural rise. Looking over he could see a long way in both directions. Scrambling back down to the stream he gingerly leaped from stone to stone across. Having to use his hands he clambered up the other side, again to a rise. Looking back down he could clearly see where he had just stood a moment ago. Surveying to the left Simon could only see grass, heather and the odd large mound disappearing off into the distance. Turning round, about two hundred meters away up the slope, he could see a rocky outcrop jutting up on the near horizon.

Struggling through the rarely trampled heather he eventually reached the rocks. Panting, it was hard work through the thigh high foliage, Simon turned and looked back to the range. He could clearly see the two raised up mounds, the stream now obscured by the nearer rise. Anyone moving up the range would be visible as they crested the two features. Looking slightly to his left he could see the posts marking the finish of the range. In between the stream now fairly straight dissected the shooting gallery. Anyone who had moved up the beck out of view would be clearly in sight for the final one hundred and fifty metres.

Satisfied, Simon climbed the rocks until he had a commanding view all round. He could see the command hut, the car park and eighty percent of the range. Turning right round he noted with satisfaction that between him and the distance lay dead ground to the range and hut. This meant anyone could creep up to this point and more importantly sneak away completely unobserved. Next he clambered down and lay in different spots at the base of the rocks. Deep in amongst the rocks, bracken and heather he would be invisible. Shifting round to a spot out of the wind where an enormous rock, the size of a medium van, lay. Peering round he had perfect view of the second half of the range. Crouching down as if holding a rifle, he swung from left to right. In doing so noting with satisfaction that he had clear fields of fire. In reverse the marksman then crawled backwards. In a moment he was completely out of sight and stood up. Simon couldn't see anything of the range or buildings, both completely obscured by the substantial rocky outcrop. Walking away, every few strides, turning to check he remained unseen. After about a minute he entered a gully with a prominent animal, probably sheep track. Following it Simon wandered on, every so often just checking he remained invisible. The track then hit upon a walking path as,during a few months of the year, civilians were allowed to roam the ranges. After another ten minutes fast walk he came across a fence dissecting a small wood. Over a gate was a small single track road disappearing over the horizon.

Quickly retracing the route all the way back to his car Simon climbed in and checked the range map he'd been given in the hut by Mr Card. Seeing the road and the wood clearly marked he drove off, having completed his deadly recce.

# CHAPTER 40

## *Package Delivered*

JUST NORTH OF BLACKHALL TOWN, NORTH EAST COAST, THURSDAY 1.30PM

The package when it arrived didn't look anything unusual. Tiny had kept his word when he phoned Danny playing down the reality of the complexity of obtaining such a piece of hardware at short notice. "Hi pal," Tiny said once Jenny had transferred the call, " as we discussed our little bit of something is on route as we speak. Ow yer sorry, CM4 as agreed."

Even before Danny could speak Tiny went on, "it was a right bugger getting it all together. You can tell green eyes it wasn't without difficulty. Tell him though, he should be pleased as my source said he checked and actually used the piece of equipment and assures me it is as smooth as silk."

"Tiny that's great, I'll have it picked up shortly after lunch. Does it come with urr," struggling not to use the correct words, " you know small pointy things."

Tiny held the phone away from his sawn off ear and physically laughed at the mobile, replacing it he continued, "yes it's all there, I made sure no one will ever know where they come from, I had my bloke put twenty of them in for good measure."

It was Danny's turn, "excellent well done, I'll pass on your comments when I see Simon this afternoon. He said something about probably needing to have a go before he actually uses the CM4. Reckons he'll go up to a beach somewhere and... well have a go, d'you know what I mean?"

Both old pros were finding criminal telephone banter difficult especially trying to describe exactly what they were trying to say. Actually, each well aware that the fewer words said on the phone the better. It was Danny who wrapped things up, "Tiny, we'd better leave it at that, once again I'm really grateful for you doing this at such short notice, I won't forget this."

"Your damn fucking right you won't, I expect free meals for the next month OK."

Understanding his friend well Danny played along, "Indian Mondays, Tuesdays can be Italian, Wed...."

"Fuck off I want MacDonald's alright," mutual friendship warming their laughter.

After their goodbyes, Tiny hung up. Two minutes later Danny told his driver to take him up into the rough part of town where the package lay unobserved hidden in a back store room of a small, yet profitable takeaway. The owner forever in his debt, Danny having taken care of local thugs, who had tried to muscle in on the place, had been taught best to leave any friend of Mr Chang's well alone.

Even though Danny knew he was taking a major risk he told Tony to put the package in the boot. The gun was indistinguishable, wrapped in cloth and large plastic bags.

Actually it didn't look any more dangerous than a few large rolls of wall paper.

He told the driver not to speed as the three of them cruised south towards the coast.

---

Simon having concluded business inland had a bit of a rush to make the rendezvous at Blackhall. Danny had questioned why they had to go so far out of the way to deliver the package. Simon's simple reply was that the car park he had chosen was not only quiet and importantly wasn't overlooked, also anyone coming down the single tracked road would be seen half a mile away. Finally as the 'beauty spot' car park was new the chances of anyone being out there at that time of year were minimal. Those that did tended to be retired folk with little else to do. They'd sit in their cars watching the surf hit the shingle beach a hundred meters below and would definitely keep themselves to themselves. That Thursday, as the North Sea was rough, it wasn't a very welcoming spot. Deserted as, even the hardiest of pensioners having retreated probably to the warmth of Blackhall Rock's Working Men's Club.

Turning off the main road then down under the local railway line, moments later Simon's car drew up next to Danny's. Switching off the engine, as he did Danny told Tony to get the package from the boot, then he should get his coat on and take the driver for a stroll down along the coast path to catch the bracing air. As both men moved off the only thing they were certain they would catch, was a cold.

As they stepped away Simon nodded towards the two men before quickly climbing in the back next to Danny.

"Bugger it's shitty out there now," said Simon.

"Yes its crap, as soon as that sea wind blows this place is god forsaken, never understood why anyone would want to come up here to stare out to sea, can't see anything anyway."

"Well that's true but a blessing today wouldn't you say." Looking at the package on Danny's slim lap, Simon nodded towards it, "I'm hoping that's what I think it is?"

"Yes, Tiny Smalley sends his regards and says it's about time you and he had a beer together."

A little surprised, Simon had a lot on his mind and sort of forgotten that his specific requirements would have needed someone like Tiny to obtain the gun at such short notice.

"Yeah you're probably right, we'll drink later, let's have a look then." With that Simon picked up the package and quickly, yet carefully, undid the layers of protective wrapping.

Seeing the dark metallic weapon emerge, Danny's eyes expressed how impressed he was. That said he really had little idea at what he was looking at, other than it clearly was a gun of some description.

Simon on the other hand knew exactly what it was as he expertly flicked the catch releasing the magazine before instantly pulling the cocking handle back. Instinctively, years of training taking over, he looked into the breach checking it wasn't loaded. Then he let the working parts mechanism forward whilst pointing it to the floor, released the safety catch and engaging the firing pin delivering a metallic clunk.

As Danny watched on Simon released the compressed stock and held it to his shoulder for a moment. Then he undid the slimmer of the other two packages which the big bag contained. Taking it out and holding the telescopic sight up to his eye before quickly, with blindfold trained precession, attaching it to the weapon. Clipping the empty magazine on Simon flopped it up and down. Getting the feel for the weapon was critical.

Danny had no idea that Simon wasn't annoyed at been presented with the wrong rifle, "Simon, it's the right one isn't it?"

"Yes it sure is, it's perfect. See, holding the scope towards his friend, "it fits tight, no wobble. Also the rounds here," he'd opened the small box which held neat rows of bullets, "there exactly what I need. I think we both owe Tiny a beer."

Danny didn't mind but preferred not to be sitting exposed in a windswept car park with a, clearly powerful and illegal weapon two feet away. The only thing he wasn't afraid of was it would go off. Simon had seemed to become one with the thing as soon as he'd picked it up. Flipping it this way and that Simon dismantled it before reassembling it in less than two minutes. As he finished Danny asked, "Simon, what happens now?"

"Well, don't worry. I can see you'd rather not have a thing like this right next to you," as Simon tapped the weapon it clunked, knocking against the beautiful oak panelling of the jag, "I'll take it from here. I don't suppose you're hear from me until tomorrow afternoon. Trust me by then he'll be dead." With that Simon gave the weapon an almost loving gentle pat.

"Let the bastard rot in hell."

"Lets hope so," Simon's reply.

Looking out through the window Danny saw that Tony, Tony senior having been killed five years earlier, his bodyguard, now resembled a drowned rat. The driver stood next to him, shivering against the now strong wind and spray, looked in an even worse condition, "Simon I'd better let them back in. They look like crap."

"Yep you're right there," came the reply, as Simon deftly packed the M4 into the canvas wrapping, the box of rounds going into his deep jacket pocket and the unfastened scope sliding easily into his inner pocket. This he did carefully as a damaged scope could result in a missed kill.

Loaded up so to speak Simon said, "I'll get going then."

"Good luck."

Simon's green eyes as piercing as his reply, "luck has very little to do with what I intend to do."

"Well take care and break a leg or whatever you say to someone about to go into battle."

"Try, Gods speed and stay safe."

Danny looked serious as he held out his hand which Simon took with a little difficulty as the package lay on his lap.

"Don't worry Danny I certainly don't intend to come back with the same amount of rounds as I have in my pocket here." With that he patted the slight bulge in his dark green Gortex jacket.

As Simon opened the car door, the mist swirled in on the back of a blast of freezing air. Danny shivered as Simon nodded towards Tony junior as they swapped places. Driver re-positioned, the three men watched as Simon walked quickly over to his own car, opening the rear door he slid the package under the seat. With a wave he climbed in and promptly drove off.

"Where to sir?"

"Back to my office I suppose, one package delivered….." Danny's voice, like the mist, trailing off into his thoughts.

# CHAPTER 41

## *Startline*

WORKOP CAMP,
FRIDAY 7AM

"Thanks for nothing," it was the incoming guard commander.

"Well fuck you too and good morning," Boots hated guard duty. Even more so when they were away from Aldershot. Transit camps like Workop, at best had a little room somewhere with a crappy old television and uncomfortable bunks. Actually the usual lack of activity meant for a thoroughly boring night. Boots having taken over guard command at seven the previous night. He had a team of six crammed into the little building set off to one side, thirty meters from the sentry post at the front gate. Every two hours or so he'd send out a brick of two to patrol the perimeter fence. As well as this there was another guard on the main gate as Tommie, the civilian guard, who was always assisted by four other visiting soldiers during the day left, at four thirty sharp, only re-emerging at seven the next day. Boots only consolation was that his team wouldn't be on duty over the weekend, as that was even less fun. "Nothing to report, all quiet. I'll be off then," with that Boots yawned, stretched, farted and left the building, his presence lingering.

He and the other night guard then dashed across to the cookhouse, just managing to get very overcooked hard fried eggs and some soggy sausages. They ate in silence, each man left to his own daydreams.

Boots had spent a restless, sleepless night devoid of dreams, not least as he had to take his turn three times during the night stagging on. This amounted to listening to the local radio station just in case the phone rang or something untoward happened. Nothing did yet it had however afforded Boots the opportunity to go over the events of the previous few days.

Since getting back to camp after the failed mission the creatures hadn't been to see him. His sleep although restless was free of those terrifying red eyes, those fangs, and most horrid of all the sounds they made as they ripped and crunched, drooling all over the place whilst devouring lifeless victims.

Sat staring at the wall, ignoring the frayed poster suggesting that every soldier should check for testicular cancer at least once a month, eyes vacant as he'd shuddered at the recollection of what they had done to the two men who had attacked him.

They were dead but what about the girl? She must have fallen in the river or crawled away and died somewhere else. If she was still alive she'd obviously not gone to the police. Which ever way he looked at it Boots decided that he wouldn't go on another mission for a while. Yes he would stick to getting drunk then hopefully, finally, the devils who had invaded his world would leave him alone.

"Corp, we'd betta get a shift on."

It was one of his section. Snapping out of his own thoughts, "yer right, thanks." As he spoke Boots swilled down the last mouthful of greasy toast with luke warm sweet tea.

Thirty minutes later his platoon was on parade on the edge of the car park. The Platoon Commander was busy with the Adjutant for the moment so the sergeant was giving the brief,

"Morning," his greeting only receiving muted grumbled replies from a few, "I said good morning."

"Morning Sergeant," the instant loud reply.

"That's better. As you know were going to conduct live firing today. The CQMS has sent his team ahead with the ammo. We'll set off at zero eight forty five. It's the boss's intention that the first rounds down the range will take place at ten. That's pretty late so you'll have to cut about if we are going to get everyone through by three."

The sergeant then explained the safety drills, again. Boots wasn't listening as he vacantly studied the side of a truck. He'd hopefully do the first shoot as a safety officer. With any luck they'd run out of time before he had to take his section through. He knew live firing required excellent teamwork, strong command and a good level of fitness. Boots was pretty fit, other than that he lacked the required characteristics.

"Right, section commanders do your kit checks and I want everyone ready on the transport in ten minutes. Section commanders take over"

With that the sergeant smartly turned and wandered over to the make shift regimental headquarters building. Inside he found his boss, 2Lt Browne, in conversation with the Adjutant, "sir, all the platoons docs' are here," as he pointed to a large box on the table in front of the female clerk.

"Mister Browne they'd better be," said the adjutant, "I haven't come with the docs clerk here," she smiled, "all this way to waste our time doing the regimental one hundred percent platoon check only to find it's not all there."

It was 2Lt Browne again, "sir, I promise, my sergeant," looking over he saw his right hand man nodding supportively, "and I checked them before we left camp and again last night. They're all logged as you directed in your memo sir. The disk is stapled in the envelope on the top."

"Good, well done, now hadn't you better be moving as I seem to remember the 2IC said first rounds down the range by ten?"

"He did sir, so if there isn't anything else I'd better cut about." There wasn't, so the subaltern and his sergeant both saluted before stepping off together. Back outside, the men were busy loading themselves, webbing and weapons into the three trucks.

"Section commanders on me," boomed the sergeant. Four JNCO's came straight over, "everything ready then?" A hopefully rhetorical question before turning to Mr Browne," sir with your permission we'd better move out."

"Yes very good, thank you," 2Lt Brown was happy he had such an efficient sergeant. They worked well and as he'd told the experienced SNCO he wasn't under any illusions who was actually in charge whilst he learnt the ropes.

"You heard Mr Browne. I want section commanders to me as soon as we reach the range carpark."

Less than five minutes later over two dozen men bumped and bounced along as the three trucks and one Land Rover rolled out of camp.

Boots sat in the middle 4 tonner cab, the heater blasting his legs. The driver, a private from one of the other sections, was prattling on about the live firing and how great it would be and had the corporal been to that particular range before. Private Carter hadn't done live firing since he was in recruit training nearly a year earlier.

"Shut the fuck up and concentrate on getting us there." Boots was in no mood for small talk. The terror of previous days now seemed a long way away and he needed to get his mind into gear, live firing was serious and having wangled safety duty for the two shoots, needed to ensure everything went smoothly.

Opening his eyes, as they rumbled across the cattle grid, having dozed most of the way, Boots saw that the mist, as if possessed by a consciousness, had decided it was time to desert the range.

Leaving the cab he climbed down. In doing so the chilly air hit him as the sun, making fleeting appearances through the fast clouds, only gave momentary relief from the freezing air.

The range warden was all set up. Having even ventured out of his warm domain and down to the carpark. He wore an enormous military sandy coloured great coat, patrol gloves and a silly Peruvian hat, the tassels bashing into his eyes. Standing there Mr Card looked completely out of place.

Boots went round undid the trailplate, releasing it, the thing came crashing down as he shouted, "Convoy cocks' over time to get moving."[14] The section clambered out with little chatter as the men braced themselves against the cold and the prospect of careering around in the freezing autumn, early throws of winter, weather.

The men lined up, their kit checked, rifles ready, safety catches on. The CQMS's lads then came forward and distributed the ammo. Each of the soldiers undertaking the first shoot were given sixty rounds, twenty per magazine. Pouches done up, the men all marched off to the start line. Boot's and the other three safeties trudged along behind discussing the shoot.

Once they reached the clearly marked post, Mr Card having been out and raised the stiff, in the wind, red flag, they stopped. This time 2Lt Browne came round to the front to address his men "right listen, you don't need me to tell you lot that this is serious business. The range here is very demanding and you must watch out for the range safety distances. Once you cross the start line remember, if you hear a whistle, see a flag or the flair go up stop, engage your safety catch. Take out your ear defenders and listen out. Remember don't stand up, stay down."

The wind was easing, though the air still numbing their cheeks. They had better get on with it as there was going to be three runs. Luckily for Boots, his section were only going to go down once.

"One and three sections take up your positions," it was the sergeant. "Safeties carry out your checks."

"For inspection port arms," Boots and another corporal said almost in unison. Moving along they checked each breach to ensure no rounds had mistakenly already been loaded.

With that the platoon sergeant gave them their final brief before they moved towards the startline.

Checking on his radio with the control tower 2Lt Browne then called the two corporals forward and gave them the prepared snap orders. They were to advance up both sides of the gully and engage any enemy they came across.

# CHAPTER 42

## *Coiled Weapon*

MOTEL CARPARK TEN MILES FROM RANGE NO 3
JUST OFF THE CARLISLE NEWCASTLE ROAD.
FRIDAY, FIVE HOURS EARLIER

My car parked anonymously, amongst the travelling reps in the large hotel carpark I moved in on foot knowing I couldn't allow anyone to connect future events with me. In doing so I was fairly content knowing how things were to unfold, as– I'd been there already.

The previous evening having returned home, parking the car in the garage, explaining to Lynda that I would need the car in the morning, early as I had things to do. Knowing better, she just smiled only asking if I would be back in time for dinner the next evening?

After Chilli Con Carne we chatted and laughed whilst watching the telly. During our lap meal Lynda said she was going out to visit her friend Pippa and wouldn't be back until after ten as they were watching holiday video's of her recent trip to Portugal.

Half an hour later, silence reigned. After a glass of water and a turn round the semi dark garden, admiring the remnants of the season's tomato plants, I went through to the study.

Taking my place, relaxing, I sat enjoying the stillness which was only broken by the odd bird chirping in the garden. Closing my eyes I went through the ritual breathing exercise.

Opening them, looking around surveying the familiar surroundings. Wagtail wasn't about so I wandered with purpose up the grassy slope. Cresting the hill again smiling with enjoyment at the splendour of the building before me.

Moments later through the wrought iron gates I entered the walled garden, the flowers, as if perpetually blooming, afforded me pleasure to both senses.

Smartly going forward I climbed up the steps and, reaching the front double doors, turned the familiar worn brass door knob before leaving the warmth and sunshine behind.

Closing the door, I heard a familiar swish of cloth, so without even looking round said, "hello headmaster."

"Hello Simon, did you enjoy the flowers?"

"Yes they are truly beautiful," sighing before continuing, "you know I am here on a serious matter?"

"Yes I'm aware. Mavis has been expecting you and the Commander commands word with you."

"Thanks, hopefully we'll have time to talk later."

"Not certain, anyway if not move with caution and purpose."

With that I moved away and on towards Mavis' room. On reaching it a gently knock on the dark wooden closed door, as ever receiving the welcoming reply, "come in, come in Simon."

Doing as commanded I entered the familiar room. Immediately going over and embracing my dear friend, "Mavis I'm so glad to be with you again. You know that I seek information about events which have yet to unfold."

"Certainly I do, we should get going as I feel there is much to learn."

Dutifully sitting in my usual chair, her knotted hand warm in mine. I quickly glanced at the blackboard before closing my eyes.

After a timeless moment, opening them, we both stood up and walked seemingly, incredibly straight through the jet-black board. Blinking in the darkness, I could feel her hand in mine. After a couple of seconds our eyes became accustomed to the limited light as we moved forward towards the large screen in front of us.

Mavis opened her palm allowing the crystal to cast its magic.

In the subdued light, in an instant all my senses alert I tasted evil approach. Turning to Mavis as if for confirmation, she hadn't moved a muscle only continuing to stare straight ahead. Slowly the screen in front of us lightened, through it I could see the rocks where I recce'd on the ranges. Like looking through the lens of a camcorder we moved round to exactly where I had lain. As if a camera was taking a home movie the camera jolted as the view went down in amongst the bracken and heather.

A whistle blasted.

The camera quickly panned round to the right so that through the heather I could clearly see men running almost parallel across my view. The lens zoomed in on a fluorescent vest worn over a army camouflage. The man was running, bounding along through the rough terrain. As it zoomed back I just caught the fleeting glimpse of soldiers with bracken, heather and grass sticking out of their helmets and webbing, dashing about. They were darting from one firing position to another. Orders were being shouted out, "enemy fifty metres directly to your front, rapid fire."

With that a loud volley came from unseen men. Up ahead a wooden target which had momentary popped up, flipped back down as shards of plywood flew in all directions.

This time I clearly saw a man stand and dash forward. He was the one doing the shouting, obviously the section commander.

Another shout from the right, on the far bank past the stream. In amongst the trees I could clearly see another reflective jacket bobble forward with men in front rushing in amongst the trees and hillocks.

"Fucking get moving Flinders, enemy to your front," one in the fluorescent jacket screamed. Continuing to shout he turned to his left, toward my 'cineview', it was Boots. The man was sweating as he raced through the undergrowth behind the advancing soldiers. The lens now focussed in as he disappeared only to reappear momentarily. At that moment time stopped as the picture zoomed into where he was clearly visible through the trees. Withdrawing and moving back and to the left the screen picked out a clump of grass. The grass moved with a rifle visible for only a split second. Panning back further, all the way in amongst my clump of heather next to the rocks yet I could still see the soldier. Almost looking over him I could see he was in line of sight to the one called Boots.

As someone hit 'play', Boots stood there for a full three or four seconds before disappearing down the bank.

A whistle sounded at the same time as a distant voice commanded, "stop."

Another voice declared, "right that's the end of shoot number one, Section commanders commence safety checks."

In the distance a clump of heather stood up, "Get down idiot, wait for your section commander," it was a safety officer disciplining one of the rising soldiers.

With that the focus started to go as the camera panned back, loosing focus as it did until gloom engulfed us.

Looking over to Mavis who said, "Simon, you know when it is you must act. You see you will have little opportunity, so you mustn't miss."

"Yes Mavis you're right there. With this knowledge I can be ready and in exactly the right spot. I don't intend to, won't miss"

Mavis squeezed my hand as she closed her other hand over the crystal then slowly we retraced our steps backwards.

Blinking, we were again seated next to each other. "Mavis you're very special. I'm so grateful." She interrupted me, "don't thank me, this is a sad thing I have done but know without your actions, more could join me here."

Turning her snow white hair towards me, her eyes, seemingly transparent, serious, "Simon be on your guard. Remember the thing we saw last time when you were here? It won't be far away and will try to stop you."

"I know..."

"I fear you don't. This is different to other times we have been on journeys. Who is to know the outcome, only you can change that."

"I'll remember what you've said."

Releasing my hand, Mavis turned towards the blackboard, "move with your spirits as they might be your only protection against such evil lurking in some dark hellish realm."

"I will, I will, you should rest now, thank you Mavis."

"Go now and travel a straight path on your imminent journey."

"Goodbye."

With that I stood up, not looking back, moved over and out carefully closing the door silently.

By the stairs stood the Commander. He was waiting seemingly impatiently, "you colonel, here, I have little time to speak."

"Sir?" not sure what he meant as I moved over and stood next to the dominating figure. He looked me up and down before saying, "you might be strong and quick but your fighters will need to be faster. Others lurk close bye just as you squeeze the life out of your enemy."

With that he walked silently straight past me. Knowing when to and when not to speak I left it.

Looking around as nothing else seemed forthcoming, even the headmaster had moved away, I determined it was time to go.

It was with a troubled heart I stepped back out into the sunshine. Presently, seated on the bank by the river, never before being able to remember when I hadn't either spoken to Dr Laurance or Wagtail on my route back. Even looking around and back up the hill solitude. Closing my eyes I knew they were wrong as Bill would never desert me and Merti who hadn't spoken since the hospital would be silently watching my every move. His style being very different to the ex SAS troopers. He was quiet, unseen, able to use deadly weapons especially his favourite the blow pipe which could invisibly silence and eliminate an attacker.

It was with these thoughts my eyes opened, back in my study.

Things were moving towards a finale but what conclusion? Simon hadn't gained any foresight into the outcome of the event only knowing exactly when to shoot to kill. Realising he'd have to be up well before dawn to drive, then travel unseen to the technically named lying up recce position amongst the rocks and heather, Simon tiredly went upstairs to bed. Two hours later he hardly stirred as Lynda crept silently to slide into bed next him.

Five minutes before the alarm radio was due to go off, at three thirty to be precise, Simon woke. In all their years of marriage he'd never allowed the buzzer to wake his peacefully sleeping wife. He knew it was quite easy to train your subconscious to wake a person shortly before an alarm clock was due to go.

Having eaten two bananas' washed down by orange juice, the assassin set off. At four fifteen Simon quietly parked in the chosen car park. Not a soul stirred as he left the car, bland in amongst the others. Sticking to the shadows before leaving the deserted small road, Simon then marched, retracing his route.

An hour later, having silently approached and crawling round the rocks, Simon reached his cocoon hiding place, throughout the Colt M4 had been concealed in a large green ruck sac. The bag looked out of shape with the rifle point jutting up yet just managing to remain concealed. Simon removing it placing the bag behind him, amongst the rocks out of line of sight.

Simon remembered from his chat with the range manager that, when live firing was on, no one arrived until about seven twenty in the morning. As it was only twenty past six there was still time to check fire the weapon. This was going to be a risk but Simon hadn't had time to do it before so knew it would have to happen in situ'. He scanned the range for an obvious feature. About twenty metres to the left of the rise where Boots would momentarily appear a few hours later, was a prominent mossy stone, next to it was a large branch. It was about as thick as a man's wrist and had evidently fallen from one of the trees on the range. Obviously some bird's regular perch because there was a distinctive 'splodge' of droppings on the side of the branch.

Having made sure everything was connected and fastened, Simon expertly and quickly half filled the magazine with ten rounds. Ten would ensure that the pressure on the rounds would be ideal for them to be picked up as they sprang forward into place.

A stoppage would be unacceptable, so Simon gently released the pressure as the firing pin clunked forward. The working parts, having picked up the round, snapped home.

Breathing slowly Simon held the weapon up to his eye. Clearly, through the powerful sights, he saw the black and white mark on the branch. Selecting a particularly large distinctive white mark, he lay motionless. Not a sound, no cars, no pinking black birds and all other higher frequencies clear.

Safety off, Simon squeezed the trigger. The echo was shattering. Anyone else would be certain they'd be discovered, Simon wasn't. Carefully putting the rifle down to the side, Simon picked up his powerful lightweight bino's. Through them he studied the branch, seeing about an inch from his marked spot was a blunt mess where the branch was wildly swaying. The sights were almost perfect so he made the tiniest of corrections to the vertical scale.

With that he picked the weapon up and calmly, slowly squirmed back toward the began. Out of it he took a large dark green camouflaged poncho, a thick pair of black patrol gloves and a dark green fleece balaclava. Simon then slowly chewed on a Mars Bar retrieved from his deep jacket pocket before selecting a spot where he could just see the single track road to the range wardens hut. From there Simon would easily be able to notice when the army trucks rolled along. At over a mile away no one could possibly make him out. Wrapping everything around him under the poncho, Simon, like a resting viper, waited coiled, ready to strike.

# CHAPTER 43

## *Jigsaw*

### WORKOP CAMP,
### FRIDAY JUST BEFORE 9AM

Not many females arrived at camp that early in the morning, actually very few females ever visited the Godforsaken place. If they did it was usually female solders driving trucks or Land Rovers. That morning Tommie recognised DS Parish so having nonchalantly checked her ID, he'd told her to go straight to the Commandants office. With a silent thank you, Sue drove round, this time having to park carefully in her designated spot. The other spaces having been taken up by two Land Rovers and what was obviously the commandants battered Volvo estate.

Tom saw Sue arrive through the brew room window and went out to meet his guest. Smiling he'd held out his hand, the other keeping the main door open. "Sue its wonderful to see you again, please come in." With that he followed Sue who instinctively went straight through to the office and immediately sat down. Realising her potential rudeness, "Sorry Tom, I just thought.."

Understanding what she meant, "Sue no don't worry about it. Tea no sugar?"

Nodding Sue undid her small briefcase and took out her notebook.

Two minutes later Tom returned, this time carefully placing the brews on the side table before sitting next to his guest.

Having thanked him for the drink Sue was eager to get on with things, "Tom you said that I might be able to have a chat with someone from the Welsh regiment?"

"Yes that's right. I spoke with their adjutant last night, nice enough chap, not very Welsh though. From the home counties, you know the sort?"

Sue didn't.

Tom took a swig of his steaming tea, again being careful not to spill it over the next years training camp roster. Sue's frown declaring her lack of understanding, "you see some of these regiments tend to be littered with young Officers who are from anywhere but Wales or Scotland. What happens though is that they invariably end up commanding them. Daddy's influence, don't you know."

This time Sue got his drift yet was impatient to speak with the chap. "Tom, sorry to be rude but when can I meet him."

"As a matter of fact once you've finished your tea I'll take you over to their headquarters. He said he'd be there all day, something about doing a one hundred percent documentation check. They arrived with boxes and boxes of the stuff."

"Great," with that Sue almost winced as she gulped down the very hot drink before, with a certain amount of finality, placing the cup back down.

Noticing her obvious impatience, Tom understood, "well then, let's get going shall we?"

Rising Sue replied, "yes please." Clipping her bag shut and keeping her notebook out she put it into her winter suit pocket.

Within a matter of moments they had walked out into the cold, round the corner and into an identical building off to one side. Going ahead of his guest the commandant went straight in ignoring the temporary sign declaring, 'RHQ, Knock and Wait'.

"Hello anyone at home," Tom said in an almost theatrical voice. Immediately a trim uniformed female figure emerged from a room at the end of the corridor.

"Yes can I help you," noticing the majors rank slides, "oh, sir, sorry can I help you?"

"Hi there young lady and who might you be?"

"Corporal Capps sir, regimental headquarters clerk."

Before another word could be spoken a distant voice called out in pristine queens English, "ahoy there Corporal Capps we do have work to do you know."

Not knowing who to address first the young female corporal spoke almost over her shoulder, "sir a major," turning she saw Tom's name marker on his left chest, "Major Bride and," her cheeks started to redden.

Sue alleviated her embarrassment, "detective sergeant Parish."

Corporal Capps nodded a thank you Sue's way, "and a detective Sergeant Parish are here."

In the unseen near distance plum mouth called out, "well for goodness sake corporal Capps show them in."

Tom and Sue advanced as Corporal Capps turned round and walked back through the door she had originally appeared from. The rooms shape and size similar to Tom's yet this one was spartan with only a large table in the middle, covered in files with numerous boxes littered around.

The Adjutant saw the rank slides "oh sir," then seeing Sue enter his facial expression immediately changing as he took in her elegant features, "welcome, welcome, sir and...."

"DS Parish, Sue."

Coming round from the desk, Captain Stanton offered his hand. As Tom shook hands, Sue studied the young man. Her height, probably a year or two younger, with soft ebony hair flopping down over his face. Sue wondered if it wasn't too long for the army? He was handsome in a boyish kind of way with impressive, perfect white teeth.

Leaning around Tom towards Sue, "hello, Paul, Paul Stanton, adjutant first Welsh Borderers, delighted to make your acquaintance."

Tom inwardly smirked, this was an oily one and no mistake. He'd met them many, many times. The uniform, the voice, the patter. Yes he'd met this type before. That said a posh accent didn't make a bad Officer. Members of the Special Forces sometimes had serious plums in their mouths. Appearances meant little sometimes.

"Well Paul, please call me Sue. Tom, sorry, the commandant said I might be able to have a few words with you about a case I'm dealing with at the moment." With that she gave Tom an apologetic glance.

Gesturing over the boxes, "of course, of course anything to help the local constabulary. Corporal Capps would you make some teas please."

Sue noted the tiniest annoyed frown wisp across, actually beyond the drab uniform and fierce dark haired bob, Corporal Capps pretty face.

"Yes sir," turning instinctively to the commandant first, "how'd you like it sir?"

"Well, no sugar for the detective but I'll have NATO please.

Corporal Capps smiled at Sue by way of an apology and left the room.

Moving the boxes about Captain Stanton offered them a couple of unwelcoming steel rimmed chairs.

Once all three were seated, it was the Adjutant who spoke first, "Sue how can the first battalion be of service?"

"Well I have been dealing with an extremely serious case. A horrendous sexual attack which left a young lady terribly scarred, actually it's a wonder she's still alive."

Interrupting her train of thought, Captain Stanton said, "that's horrid but what has it got to do with my regiment?"

Sue recognising the protective inflection in his voice, "well you see Paul, it's like this." Sue paused to gather her thoughts into a concise chunk, "I have been given some information which leads us to think the person who carried out this attack may have been a soldier, possibly a corporal. Another piece of information we received told us it could be someone from a Scottish or Welsh regiment. Unfortunately we've drawn a blank there but, Tom," understanding enough about military etiquette she again corrected herself, "the Commandant told me that you had some men here a few weeks ago on your advance party."

"Well to be honest I'm not sure but Corporal Capps knows. She does daily standing orders and may even have a copy on the laptop."

Sue not realising how close she was getting agreed it might be helpful. Almost on queue Corporal Capps came back in, precariously holding three cups in her hands. Placing them down on the corner of the desk she immediately turned to go.

"Corporal Capps, just a mo', could you have a look on the laptop and see if you have any back copies of routine orders for," turning to Sue, who had anticipated the question had already checked her note book, giving the exact date.

"Of course sir it'll only take a minute. I keep them on disc and thought I'd better bring them along as I'll be able to do the silent hours gate roster on it."

It was Tom this time, "excellent, let's get it wound up then."

As Corporal Capps pulled out the correct disc and set everything up, Sue almost fired her questions at Captain Stanton.

"Do you have any particularly aggressive men in your regiment?" Sue pressed on, "have any been in trouble before with serious fighting or attacking women?"

"Now listen Sue, if we did they'd be courts martialled and kicked out. To my knowledge the only one who was kicked out was the Pay Sergeant last year for skimming money out of the corporals Club slot machines." Adding, irrelevant detail, "got three years in a civi jail and lost his pension."

Interrupting everyone, "sir here we are," it was Corporal Capps, "yes there were a few sent up that week." She then read out the names.

Sue listened intensely, non of them rang any bells. "Please, d'you know their Christian names?" Her question directed at the Adjutant.

"Well, I might not but Corporal Capps here probably does." With that he received a nod from the doc's clerk who had met most of them in the NAAFI. Actually most of them having probably tried to chat, the only female member of the regiment, up.

"Lets see," as she started to rattle their names off, "Oh yes, lance corporal Mark Miller couldn't go so Corporal Wellington went. He's called Robert," She finished the list.

Sue had written each name down.

The pieces of information not seemingly fitting together, "well what about the corporal could I ask if hes big and also is he aggressive?"

Without thinking Corporal Capps replied, "he's big alright."

One piece fitting perfectly.

The clerk continued, "actually he's well known for fighting, got a job as a bouncer in a club down town."

Another piece slotted into place.

"Does he have a Scottish accent by any chance?" It was Sue again.

"Actually quite stuck up really, his dads an officer in the RAF I think."

Feeling a little left out, Paul spoke, "actually for what its worth I have plenty of trouble with the tribe as they call themselves."

"The what?" it was Tom this time.

"They," Corporal Capps went on, "call themselves the Tribe. Corporal Boots is their supposed leader."

Finally after weeks of struggling, the final pieces fitted perfectly, "what, what did you just call him?"Sue's hand was shaking.

"Well Corporal Wellington's nickname is 'Boots', you know Wellington boots."

Now with authority, DS Parish demanded, "where is this Corporal Wellington right now?"

The Adjutant recognised trouble in her voice, "what, do you think Corporal Wellington might be involved? Come to think about it he's a thing so I certainly wouldn't put it past the jumped up lance jack."

"Lance what?' asked Sue.

Tom then explained that it was army slang for lance corporal. As he did Sue's brain crashed through her memory cells. What had Simon said 'has stripes, one but possibly two'. Christ he'd even said the name 'Boots.' Anyone who could pinpoint the weapon to within twenty feet could have given her the name.

"He's on the ranges," said Corporal Capps. Actually the clerk certainly didn't like the rough foul-mouthed yob of a man. Boots had tried it on with her but she'd sent him packing. 'Yer he could attack someone no fear', thinking better than to verbalise her thoughts.

Sue was sweating under her dark trouser suit, her hand slipping on the pen.

What should she do next?

Taking control, "I must see this man as soon as possible, can we go out to the..... wherever they're shooting?"

"My range," it was the commandant, "we can go in the Land Rover, its only about thirty minutes away."

The others startled by the speed with which Sue got up, "lets go then." The words far from a request, everyone understood.

"Christ I hope he's nothing to do with your attacker, that's all we need, The CO'l go mad," exclaimed a now thoroughly worried Captain Stanton.

"Can we contact them from here and make sure they don't leave until I've spoken with Corporal, " checking her notes, "Wellington 'Boots'."

Tom and Sue rushed back to his office so that he could call Mr Card. Putting the phone down Tom explained that the range warden said they would not be going anywhere for hours yet as they'd just started the first shoot.

Five minutes later Sue sat in the front of Tom's Land Rover as they quickly left camp.

## CHAPTER 44

# *Colliding Forces*

"With a magazine of twenty rounds, load," the range officer shouted, as sixteen soldiers snapped magazines home. "Remember section commanders you must keep close command of your men. Weapons must face down the range at all times."

All the men wore camouflage kit with webbing belts holding their two spare magazines of a further forty rounds. Standing like bushes, each had sticking out of their large helmets; firns, grass, heather and the odd twig. Similar foliage littered their webbing and jackets. Boots and the other two safety officers went along behind the line checking each one had fastened the magazines correctly.

The whole party then moved forward to a small hollow, all the time the wind stiffening from right to left. In doing so every man felt the cold, yet each knew that they would be sweating in less than five minutes. Each section of eight men huddled together as the officer in charge came over equally camouflaged, "section commanders, 'on me, orders'. Enemy have been sighted at grid two, seven, five….." Lieutenant Browne then went on to give the general scenario and the fact that the sections were to advance with their objective being to take the hill, dealing with any enemy on the way. With that the sections commanders sat quietly, frantically scribbling notes in their battle note pads. Each in turn returning to their respective huddle, giving their own 'snap' orders. Three minutes later the men duly briefed, stood up and moved to the start line which was indicated by the large red tipped post. "Ready?" shouted Lieutenant Browne.

The reply from the command post some two hundred meters behind came over the radio, 'go now'. With that they spread out in a long line before moving forward, safety officers just behind. The left section dashed ahead twenty metres, taking up firing positions in amongst the shrubs to cover the other sections advances.

Standing on the start line Private Carter was ready. Live firing was to him a combination of adrenalin, excitement and fear as he had only completed two other live firing ranges since basic training some twenty months earlier. He waited impatiently as the other section took up their positions.

"Forward and keep your distances," his section commander shouted just off to the left. With that his section moved forward about fifteen feet apart, each half section of four men pausing and going down on one knee as the other moved someway in front. Once they'd in effect leap frogged some fifty metres in front of the other section his commander shouted to take up covering positions. Carter dashed slightly to the left to what looked like an excellent position in amongst some heather and bushes. Crashing to the ground he crawled quickly forward. Taking aim he scanned the horizon as Carter knew that during this bound forward there would be targets going up to his front which he should engage. Gingerly he carefully flicked the safety catch off. In doing so, out of the corner of his eye, he could clearly make out the edge of the other section moving forward. Concentrating intensely the sweat dripped from his brow so with his trigger hand he wiped his eyes. As he regained the trigger a target popped up straight in front. Instinctively he fired two rounds in rapid succession. A couple of his mates also saw the target spring up resulting in a barrage of rounds smacking into the thin target, shattering it as wood flew all over. A second later the splintered target flipped back down. As it did another target swung up further ahead and to his right. As Carter adjusted his position to get a shot at it he blinked feeling the wind blow directly into his eyes. It was an unusual kind of wind making his eyes smart, almost as if someone had sprayed him with something. Struggling to peer through welled up eyes, he smelt the sweet perfume of what he instinctively thought was the late autumn flowers. 'Shit' he said to himself as the target disappeared. Regaining his composure he scanned the grass and bushes to his front. Once again out of the corner of his eye, off to the left, Carter thought he saw the edge of a targets spring up. Not waiting for orders he swung his rifle round and started to take aim. As he did the wind again seemingly blasted into his eyes. Through now watery eyes, peering, glimpsing the targets outline he fired.....

An hour earlier, just as the first lorry crested the distant hill, the coiled dragon stirred as Simon slowly glanced round the side. The lorries had stopped and men were tumbling out. Having watched this he moved back round to prepare. Firstly, after a moments quiet he checked his 'senses' only to be relieved as nothing unnatural was present. Next he carefully checked the weapon, quietly moving the working parts backwards and forwards, instinctively checking the chamber for rounds before releasing the safety catch and squeezing off the trigger. Then he fastened the magazine holding ten rounds. Safety catch on, he then put it under the poncho and had another quick peek round the edge of the rocks. The men were obviously receiving the safety brief as he watched them go into their little section huddles. Being careful to move slowly, remaining vigilant whilst they moved almost out of view at the start line. Noticing that his target was wearing a fluorescent safety jacket, Simon could clearly make out on the left stood Boots. The command to advance clear to Simon as the wind was blowing strongly into his face. He thought this might affect the flight of the rounds but by no more than a fraction, it did however give him the distinct advantage that, when he fired, the rifle's loud crack would be blown away from the troops.

Around in his safe well-hidden den he stuffed the balaclava and poncho into the ruck sac before expertly leopard crawling to his selected firing point. Calmly adjusting his position, even taking a peak towards the troops. In doing so he heard the shouts of commands, then the first blast of rounds. They were obviously engaging the targets which were popping up all over. Prepared, he slowed down his breathing, relaxing the weapon in his arms so as not to fatigue them. He saw a wooden target go up almost directly to the front before moments later shattering in a hail of bullets. They were getting close now. Taking aim through the sights he clearly saw the tree stump from his previous target practice. He then lifted his view above the weapon waiting to refocus and take aim, safety catch off.

"Enemy to your front,' the shout clear in the wind. It was at that moment Simon caught the first glimpse as Boots' bright green and yellow jacket came into view. After all the time and effort preparing for the moment, Simon focussed, concentrating solely on his target. He held the rifle scope up to his eye, yet maintained watching with both. A moment later he focussed with his right eye. Boots clear in his sights, cross hairs aiming six inches below his neck, Simon intended to fire two rounds rapid. Boots momentarily paused, as he did Simon began to squeeze the trigger.

I held my breath as the target came into view and started to squeeze the trigger. As soon as I realised, it was already too late. Out of nowhere came a claw sweeping round into my trigger hand, straight into the fleshy part between my thumb and trigger finger. I felt as a vice grabbed at my boots, pulling me back with incredible force, the rifle lying prone on the ground out of reach. With inhuman power something spun me round onto my back and with it all thoughts of my target lost as a wave of pain engulfed my hand and ankles.

Blinking at my attacker, the one who had struck my hand and obviously dragged me back round next to my ruck sac, stepped back. Not so much a step as a shuffle.

It was only then I realised that he, or it, that being a far better description, was not alone. In total three things were before me less than five feet from my prone outstretched legs. I recognised the central one as the creature witnessed from within the Hacienda Grande. On his left and right stood two other creatures, both no more than four feet tall and only resembling humans in as much as they had two legs, two arms and something resembling a head. My initial attacker had the appearance of a grotesque matt black haired hyena, come goblin.

It snarled as it spoke through menacingly jagged fangs, "Boeck at last we have you. Your actions brought us here to this realm." With this it sucked spit and phlegm back into its mouth as the other two bobbed and rocked from side to side, "Boots is our window through which we were sent for you. Our master has been waiting for revenge as he it is who will enjoy slashing you in our realm. Your days of breathing this fowl air are at an end."

Speechless as I digested the words, so all this time it had been a plan, a scheme to position me into lowering my guard far enough so that these creatures could drag me to their dark world.

Spitting the words out, "I can't let you do this."

Squinting its eyes, "against mortal humans you are indeed without equal, yet we are from a realm where you hold no such advantage. You see Boeck you can't kill us." With that the other two quivered with excitement, the central demon also shaking as if it were laughing at me. Hissing the words out, the dwarf creature on the left spoke, " one of us you might hold down, but three together and you are an easy feast." With that I watched as each in turn licked the central ones claws where it had ripped into my hand and legs. As they did I could feel the blood welling from my fist. Also, warm blood oozed from both ankles into my boots from the other cuts. Watching and listening I slowly brought my left leg up and under into a crouching position. Seemingly together all three of the creatures pushed a foul mixture of spit and blood between their fangs, letting it drool down their hairy grotesque faces.

"It is time," hissed the middle one, with that it leaped straight for my throat.

My reflexes not letting me down as at the last moment I lifted my thick boot straight into its face. The howl was lost in the wind. Leaping up on the offensive, smashing my fist into its neck, blood gurgled up from its throat as it fell back to the others which hadn't even attempted to make their numbers their advantage. I snapped a look over my shoulder, the rifle was out of sight round the corner.

The two on the sides moved out slightly as the central ghoul clawed its neck, pain insignificant, "eventually you will tire, we will feast on your blood then you will leave this realm to enter ours."

They started to move forward, as they did the other goblin, as it scratched a jagged claw over its matted, hairy chest said, "lets get it over." Taking its lead all three moved a step closer, so near I could smell their foul stench. This time they all came at once, something I had anticipated. Moving onto the balls of my feet, slashing out at the one on the left at the same time as I leant over to kick out to the neck of the other two. My first blow successful as the globin to the left crashed into the rocks next to my head. The one in the middle again not managing to evade my brutal kick to its neck. As I connected it crumpled down in a ball. The blow from the third, which I knew was inevitable, when it came stung my senses. There was no initial pain only the shock of being struck to the head, something that had rarely happened. Fortunately the creature on the right had punched me on the head just above my ear. Had it slashed, it would have opened up my face viciously. I fell back, blood warm in my ear.

Regaining control the middle devil leaped at my chest with startling unworldly speed, head down. It was like being hit by a cannon ball, physically lifting me off my feet, hurtling backwards catching my head on the rocks about five feet up on the outcrop. Not panicking, I knew that the end was near. They too knew it. As I slumped down near to unconscious, they fanned out around me watching, waiting to see my next move. Shaking my head, the blood spun from my head wound stinging in my eyes.

"Creature from the upper world you are no match for us. You are weak now and our time has come. You could fight for hours yet we would return time and again until it is done."

The hyena who I had struck twice now snarled the words out like a mantra, "human pain is joy, your terror our pleasure. You're near the beginning of suffering."

Trying to stand, my legs were giddy, the blow to the head stealing both speed and focus. Blearily making fists with both hands, I had no intention of making it easy and would fight until there was no life left in my body.

"Prepare to meet our master," with that they came forward slowly, death almost visible on their ghoulish minds.

The wind stealing cigar smoke away from his mouth as he spoke, "oy, beasties he canit kill ya in this realm but fuck me I can." Bill's punch to the back of the central beasts head incredibly powerful, so strong I heard its neck snap such was the force before crumpling motionless. Disbelief on their jaws the other two turned to see who or what had intruded their feast. Instantly the one nearest Bill leapt at him slashing with its claws. With trained precision Bill squatted down and shot out a curved edge of his boot catching it on the upper leg sending it spining past him. Bill then leapt onto its back ready to snap the neck. Realising he was the intruder and real danger to their plan, the final fiend leapt towards me. Not having fully regained my senses it was all I could do to grab its throat not more than six inches from my own face. Luckily catching one of its flaying fists by what resembled its wrist. With its other claw the creature slashed deep into my shoulder, the pain instant. Seeing me flinch it dug crooked talons even further as I frantically struggled against its inhuman power. The grotesque face slowly inching towards mine, teeth ready to rip me apart and as Bill was still struggling to deal with the other creature, again my life was on a precipice towards hell.

Large red eyes bulged as it came within an inch of my nose ready to bite, then in an instant all power seemed to desert its sinewy muscles. As its grip loosened I pushed back with all my strength, flinging it away from my blooded face. In doing so the reason for its sudden loss of power plainly visible as the dart had gone straight through the neck and was now sticking out both sides. Frantically, increasingly lamely it clawed at the protruding feathers sticking out its wire like hairy neck. Trying to stand, blood gurgling up, Bill caught it full on the temple with a flying kick hurling it against the rocks. It flopped down quivering.

Unseen Merti was deadly accurate. The poison on the darts tip was now causing the creature to froth at the jaw. Unseen, he had realised that Bill could not deal with them all and I was weakened by the blows to my head so had decided to even the odds a little.

Bill came crashing to the ground next to me, "Simon are yareet, ya bleedin somat orful."

"Once again, you and Merti were the only way I was going to rid the world of ..." my voice trailed off as my head begun to spin, spin, spin, then only darkness.

---

When Simon awoke, the grey pain numbing his thoughts, blinking through mattered eyes he was incredibly cold and could hardly move, yet with determination he sat up and surveyed the surroundings. The creatures had vanished, as had Bill and the unseen Merti. Gaining more control he went carefully round to the firing position where Simon couldn't hear a thing above the blasting wind which ripping into his face. The weapon lay exactly where he had dropped it. With difficulty Simon focused on his watch, it was three o'clock. There was no one to be seen on the range, it was deserted.

Collecting the weapon, he struggled back out of the wind behind the rocks before clearing it of bullets, placing the magazine, its contents and the rifle into the ruck sac. Having pulled the balaclava over his cold sticky hair Simon put the poncho on. Then, lifting his tired arms up so as to put the sac over his shoulders, real pain shot through his wounds where the deep cuts went in either side of his clavicle.

Checking round so that he left no trace, slowly crawling then half stumbling, trudging, Simon limped back along the sheep track, his failure as painful as the physical wounds. Clearly he'd only remained with the living with the help from the dead, yet what would he tell Danny? He couldn't fail. The thing, Boots, lived and Danny would never forgive him for not delivering justice. God knows what his friend would do now.

Finally reaching the car, dropping the ruck sac in the boot he climbed in and started it up, the blast of hot air making him drowsy. Checking in the rear view mirror Simon could tell he was in a bad way. Blood covered the left side of his face, short hair sticking up coated with red goo. Carefully and with difficulty he removed the poncho and jacket, the shirt was dark underneath, steaming from sweat mixed with blood. His ankle throbbed and his hand was now a swollen purple ball of pain.

"Danny its Simon."

Answering his mobile, "well, where are you?" Danny was totally impatient as always, I'll be at the back of the Chinese on Westgate Road in an hour and I need your help, you see I've been injured."

"What shot?" Danny was confused.

"No, knife wounds. I'll need someone to stitch me up," the shock still confusing, "better go to hospital."

With that Simon hung up as he didn't want to tell Danny over the phone that, for the first time in his life he had failed his friend.

Simon was mistaken?

# CHAPTER 45

## *Maroon Stream*

Boots was knackered. It was bloody hard work in the bracken, thick tussocks of grass and heather. When you added that he was constantly shouting at the stupid dicks that they must keep their weapons pointing down the range, he was sweating hard after only a minute or so. On the left of the range, the section he was looking after were moving forward into their positions as the other section engaged targets. Boots dashed along the line screaming at the stupid squaddies to get a move on and take up proper positions and he didn't give a flying fuck if that meant falling down into rabbit shit.

As they rushed forward Boots crashed after them. Just as he went between the trees behind the forward facing squaddies, someone or something hit him hard. 'What the fuck' thought Boots as the force physically flung him sideways into the gully, out of sight of the soldiers up ahead. He tried to shout out but couldn't. Strange, he was sweating so hard, his shirt soaked. Lying there in a heap next to the small stream pulsing down the valley, Boots tried to get up but suddenly felt dizzy. In doing so he looked down at the stream, the water was turning crimson. He followed the stain up towards where he lay. The trail was coming from him and it was blood, his blood.

Realisation wafted over him like a thick dark cloak as first touching his chest Boots stared at his palm. The fluorescent vest was clearly covered in blood. As he involuntarily coughed, the agony freezing him in an instant. Clutching where Boot's throat used to be his hands completely soaked in dark red goo. It was only then that it dawned on Boots that he'd obviously been shot. Trying to shout again, only to realise his voice, a frothy gurgle, had deserted him. Lying on the thick heather Boots felt so very cold, his eyes fixated by the maroon water dancing away down the valley. Surely someone would have realised and was now rushing over to help him?

Seemingly in answer to his thoughts, at last someone was coming down the bank to help him. As he looked up Boots' head was incredibly heavy and painful and he didn't understand, why were they wearing a white coat? His voice a bubbling mess, so he pathetically tried to raise a desperate arm.

The person came closer, stopping right next to him, looking down. Obviously the loss of blood was affecting him, hallucinating, smell the first thing Boots recognised. Christ it was the boxhead German bitch from Spain, the perfume now clear in his nostrils, he frantically tried to struggle to his feet, yet now as weak as a kitten all he could do was flop back down.

"You feel pain?" Lotte's, almost calm, question.

Boots was desperate to call one of the squaddies but his throat was full of phlegm and blood.

"Struggle? Yes, I see in your eyes, you recognise me. It was you who robbed me from my life, forcing me to another place. You abused me." Lotte's voice nearly a hiss.

His mind trying to make sense of what was going on, Boots focused on the white clad figure now kneeling only inches from his blooded steaming face.

"It was unacceptable to allow you to go on attacking others. It has been I who manipulated your destiny to bring you to this moment...." her voice trailed off. Then with a smile, the white spectre of death finished with, "to die."

Boots eyes stared wildly, he was going mad, how could the girl he'd killed in Spain be talking to him. Slowly through the mist of pain and cerebral arithmetic Boots realised. Only now when it was too late did he understand what had been happening. He'd done such terrible unspeakable things, wicked evil acts, which had been at his own hand. How he ever thought he could keep getting away with it? His mind with uncharacteristic clarity understood, he should have sought help as he was truly alone now. It was all so impossible, the devils, his claw, sex with drugged girls, the chinky bitch who he'd slashed, it was all so very wrong. Only now did Boots understand that he would have to pay for his warped, selfish, deprived mind. Yet, even now at the end, he remained resentful.

In the biting wind Lotte's words were icy, "revenge is a bitter pill, yet this medicine is my cure which will ensure you won't attack again." Boots' transfixed stare meeting Lotte's calm gaze as she spoke, "where you're going a man's soul is Satan's currency."

Boots lay watching as the white spectre stood, turned and calmly glided away, vanishing with the wind.

The loss of blood appalling, Boots watched transixed as it danced, merging with the brackish water of the stream.

"Fucking Jesus Christ, stop." Boots now only vaguely aware of the shrill whistle blast right next to him. One of the other safety officers having noticed Boots absence had come to find out what the lazy bugger was playing at but seeing the blood stained stream brought him splashing up the beck. One look at Boots grey face, then the bloody mess where his neck had been told the young man that this was a desperate situation.

The voice even louder now, "Boots, Boots some fucker's shot you. Boots can you hear me? I'm going to get help, lie still."

With that he desperately, frantically scrambled up the bank screaming at the top of his voice, "stop stop, corporal Wellington's been shot."

These were the last living words Boots every heard.

As he lay, Boots watched the stream tumble by. He felt numb, strangely no longer scared, defiantly angry yet incredibly cold.

Just cloaking his rage, only now at the end, finally Boots understood what he saw in the eyes of his victims, it was terror. As the darkness and his own closed in on him, the only words wrapping round his ebbing consciousness were, "Boots, welcome to my realm."

# CHAPTER 46

## *Bagged*

As they raced along the main road, Sue and Tom travelled in silence, finally she said, "Tom I've a hunch about this. This man Boots fits every scrap of evidence I have and I'm certain he is somehow involved."

Keeping his eyes on the busy road Tom replied, "well from the look on your face I'd say you were certainly onto something. What exactly did this bloke supposedly do?"

Sue didn't care any more, "well a few weeks ago a young women was found down by the old warehouse area of Newcastle...."

Five minutes later, Tom scratched a sweaty palm over his clean shaven chin, "bloody hell that's absolutely appalling. I hope the bastard rots in hell."

Sue noticed Tom was slowing down hard, "what's the matter why are we stopping?"

"Sorry I've just seen in my rear view mirror an ambulance coming, lights flashing."

Sue apologised, "of course you're right, sorry. Maybe try to get in behind it?"

"No point, army LandRovers can't keep up with this," as he spoke the lights flashed, a siren wailed as the ambulance zoomed past.

Rejoining the road, "Sue it's only about another ten or fifteen minutes, then we can get this Boots fellow off the range for you to have a word with."

Nearly twenty minutes later, the road having been busier than normal, it was a very impatient DS Parish who almost willed the LandRover on as it bumped up the side road towards the range.

As they crested the hill Sue spotted it straight away, "that ambulance was coming here?"

"Bloody hell," Tom replied as they bounced along with renewed vigour. Skidding to a halt, Tom leapt out as he saw Mr Card standing talking with a couple of camouflaged soldiers. "What's happened?" Tom's simple question.

Mr Card looked pale and worried, his silly hat blowing in the wind, "sir I've been trying to call you ever since you phoned. Some squaddies been shot. It's bad sir, real bad. This young lad here says someone's dead."

"Oh fuck, no not on one of my ranges!" Tom's instinctive reply.

The feeling mutual with Mr Card, "sir I've just called the military police in Catterick who are already on their way. They said they wouldn't be here for at least an hour though. Said we were not to touch anything and you should call them when you arrived."

"I'll use your office," turning to go inside Tom had all but forgotten about the purpose of the trip out to the range. Sue had been listening right next to him, "sorry Sue your questions are going to have to wait." With that he dashed inside to use the phone.

Alone now with a group of soldiers for company, Sue decided she should make herself useful, "who's in charge? My name's Detective Sergeant Parish."

Two minutes later Sue and Lieutenant Browne had things organised. Those who had been nearest the accident were in the back of the lorries, silently writing statements. She had also phoned the station who were sending out a car.

Sue finally stopped herself and remembered why she was there in the first place. Excuse me, "you found him didn't you?"

"Yes ma'm," said a grey, pale stocky corporal, "God it was terrible, poor old Boots."

Snapping her attention to the soldier, "what did you say?"

"Corporal Wellington, his names is urrh fuck," realising he was talking to a female copper, "sorry its just that he's dead. He was called Boots you see. Christ I'll never forget the fear in his eyes."

Even in the blasting wind, sweat dripped beneath her top. Leaving the forlorn soldier Sue quickly set off across the path towards the starting line.

Behind her no one cared to question what the police were up to. Even though many didn't really like Boots the whole platoon was in shock, especially as another safety had gone into far too much detail relating to the fleshy mess where Boots throat had been. Two squaddies had already puked up the remains of their breakfasts. They all knew now, live firing was serious and no mistake.

Seeing a group of soldiers on a rise, Sue weaved her way through the bracken toward them. Approaching she held up her badge, "DS Parish where is he."

The three men standing huddled against the wind were smoking. Their thoughts revolving around how it could have been them down by the stream. One of them gave a bleak smile and pointed, "over there."

Following his direction she moved down. As she did, initially the back of the paramedics jacket obscured the view as a result Sue couldn't see the casualty. Getting closer she announced who she was, and was there anything she could do?

Standing, a tall paramedic faced her, lines tight on his forehead, "oh hello there, not much anyone could do for this poor sod. He's very dead, massive haemorrhaging from the carotid artery. Plus his lungs are probably full of blood. Can't really tell if he drowned or not."

Approaching, Sue gulped back as she finally saw corporal Wellington Boots. His eyes had been shut but his face was a complete bloody mess with a pale blue look to what was left of his complexion.

The paramedics had cut off his bright jacket and had sliced open his uniform in a vain attempt to resuscitate him. Bits of clothes and a discarded bandage lay all around.

Sue's mind was a melting pot of emotions, what if this was the one she sought. Just deserts, or if not, what a terrible loss of innocent life.

Without asking she reached into her ever present bag and took out a plastic forensic bag. As the two paramedics were busying themselves packing up, she quietly and quickly knelt down and picked up a piece of what must have been his blooded shirt. Unfolding the plastic envelope over the cloth Sue turned as she stood, placing it carefully in her bag.

Having told the paramedics they should hang around until the local police arrive Sue retraced her steps.

Getting back to the car park, Tom was stood talking with some of the soldiers. Seeing Sue walking down the path, he went over, "Sue sorry about this. Everything's different now so you're going to have to wait before you can interview that chap."

Obviously no one had told Tom who had actually been shot, "Tom it was Corporal Wellington. It was Boots who was shot. He's dead."

"Jesus Christ, sorry Sue but a range death is terribly serious. Now you will never know if he had anything to do with it."

As he spoke a police car came flying over the hill, lights on but sirens unnecessary.

Twenty minutes later a young PC was driving Sue past Hexham on the way back to Newcastle. There was nothing she could do at the range anyway.

As they raced towards town DS Parish sat in stony silence deciding what to do next. Concentration as firm as her grip on the evidence she'd been so desperately seeking.

## CHAPTER 47

# *Stitched Up*

When Simon entered the small cluttered back office at the rear of the takeaway Danny almost shouted out, "Fucking hell Simon, what happened?"

Without speaking Simon sank into a chair next to a large pile of packed takeaway cartons.

"Danny, it was me they were after all this time. They wanted to kill me."

Danny's confusion was mixed with fear. His friend was in a hell of a state. Concern taking control, "sit still and I'll have the car out the back in a jiffy."

As Danny dashed through the shop to tell Tony to get the jag round the back like yesterday, Simon weakly called, "phone Lynda and tell her some bullshit about me staying over at your house tonight. I don't want her to see me like this."

Without answering as he returned, agreeing, Danny took out his phone.

Five minutes later, Danny sat as Simon lolled in the back of the jag, Tony driving as they raced towards the hospital. Simon's body ached and the pain deep within his muscles was energy sapping. The bleeding had stopped but each time he moved one or more of his gashes belched dark redness.

Finally, "Simon what happened?"

"Danny he's not dead. Just as I was about to kill him I was attacked by some creatures and I only just managed to survive."

Still confused, "what Boots' still alive? But you gave me your word Simon." Simon was too exhausted to try to explain to his friend and decided on deception, "Danny, oh my shoulder." With that he slowly moved his swollen bloody hand to his shoulder and squeezed. As the pain hit him Simon moaned as the blood oozed through his jacket, droplets landing on the cream leather of the arm rest.

In a failed attempt at reassurance, seeing his friend's eyes roll, "don't worry Simon. Tony get a fucking move on."

"Simon is there anything I can do? I've called Lynda, she was fine and sends her love as usual. I told her nothing."

Closing his eyes the words washed over him as Simon felt incredibly tired and even though the heater was on, very cold. As he sat quietly Simon knew this wasn't a good sign and was clearly ruining the upholstery.

He tried to breath slowly, yet his pulse was racing, thumping in his head. Another serious symptom which Simon recognised.

Twenty minutes later Simon blearily opened his eyes to be confronted by the bright overpowering hospital lights, as they flashed above his head.

Then darkness.

"Simon, Simon can you hear me?" a distant familiar voice asked.

Opening sore eyes Simon recognised the smile and the youthful looks. His mouth incredibly dry as he croaked, "Mike it's good to see you."

"Simon you're all patched up now and I've given you a pint of blood. Apart from a few meaty scars you're going to be fine. What the hell happened?"

Having regained some semblance of consciousness Simon reached out with a bandaged hand and sloppily took a drink of water, "you're right, it was like hell. I was attacked by wild dogs." Simon thought this the best line of explanation.

"Pretty fierce dogs if you ask me. Damn good job I recognised your friend Mr Chang sitting in the emergency when I walked through. I took over and stitched you up myself. Actually I think someone else had a hand in there as well, don't you know?" With that he grinned and winked

Lying there Simon weakly smiled up at his friend, "thanks Mike, this time I owe you."

Over an hour later Mike finally, reluctantly, allowed Danny to come in to see how Simon was getting on.

Danny spoke first, "Simon, shit you scared me. I was really worried for a while back there in the car. Tony broke the land speed record getting you here. Good job that the consultant Mister Winter was around. How you feeling?"

Simon now fully cognisant scanned his friend. He seemed somehow elated and it had nothing to do with Simon's condition. "Danny what's up? You haven't forgotten what I said in the car have you? I didn't get Boots."

Placing a comforting hand on Simon's unbandage arm, "I think it must have been the loss of blood or something. All that talk about being attacked. What the hell Simon, you got the bastard, so I have my justice."

It was Simon who now experienced a wave of confusion. He definitely hadn't fired the rifle as he'd counted the rounds very carefully. "But Danny I...."

Patting gently, Danny interrupted him, "Simon my informant has got a message to me that the detective in charge of the case told him that her number one suspect was dead. As she only had one, Boots, then I'm pretty sure you took care of business." Without allowing Simon's frown to interrupt, "you paid dearly to keep your word. This is something my uncle and I will never forget."

Finally getting a word out, "what your telling me Boots is dead?" Then Simon realised there was no point in challenging Danny, if the one he sought was dead then he was dead. He'd find out for certain soon enough.

Having apologised to Mike when Danny had insisted on paying for a private room and the consultant's time on a private patient basis. Simon would want for nothing. Lying back, the pain now only a numb thud, Simon tried to make sense of things. A minute later he was in a deep sleep.

Twelve hours after arriving, the next day, Simon sat in, the now stained jag as it quietly purred along towards Danny's house.

Simon had bluffed Lynda that he was staying in town on business and would be back possibly that night. The stitches would take some explaining but he'd think of something. Anyway it wasn't the first time he pulled up to the front door with stitches or some other wound to explain away. Actually all Lynda really cared about was that

Simon came home alive and well.

That afternoon Simon sat in Danny's kitchen reading the Evening Chronicle. The second headline declaring. 'Corporal killed in shooting accident on local range'. He had read on in disbelief that Corporal Wellington of the ......' The words took a while to sink in. Well if he didn't kill him who did? He certainly didn't believe all the bullshit about a terrible accident and would find out from someone in the Hacienda Grande.

It was a refreshed and patched up sore Simon who drove himself home that night. He knew Lynda would be fine.

Sergeant Parish knocked smartly on the opened door of her boss's office, "yes, Sue what is it?" Chief Inspector Neil Monk hadn't read the local papers for days so knew nothing of events out in the countryside. Thinking, yes he had been in a terrible temper the previous week yet knew he couldn't be seen to back down. With no closure to the case DS Parish would leave his office a DC.

Sue stepped into the office carrying a thick blue case folder, "sir, you said I'd better solve the slasher case by Monday or else." She let the words hang in the air.

"Yes, I've decided to hand the case over to one of the other teams. Sorry Sue, you had your chance."

Sue placed the folder on the table and opened the front so that the Saint could read it, "what, you know who did it? Impossible you only had forensics and no one to pin it on."

"Wrong I'm afraid sir. A soldier was killed out on the ranges and I've had forensic do a match and the blood on the blade and the stuff found at the crime scene match perfectly with that of a corporal William Boots Wellington, late of the British Army."

Not allowing her boss to interrupt, "there won't be a trial, no point. I've already explained to the Chang's who were amazingly non plussed about not bringing the culprit to court. Mr Chang even said he knew justice had been done. I suppose in a way it has."

The Saint finally stopped her, "yes that's as maybe but we don't usually put them up against a firing squad though."

As far as Sue was concerned, the Chang's had their justice, "sir the file is complete and with a one hundred percent positive forensic match to a deceased male I reckon this case is closed."

The inspector's fingers felt a lot better today. As he flexed them the saint smiled and said, "good work Sergeant Parish, well done."

# CHAPTER 48

## *The End Begins*

### NEWCASTLE, EARLY JANUARY, 5 MONTHS LATER

Olly Jones' wife opened the card whilst her husband sat in his study sniffing an extremely rare, signed first edition of The Day of The Triffids by John Wydham. "Christ Olly it's reet layt tabee inviting us ta a new yars eve party, now isn't it?"

Olly looked up and replied from his study, "what dear, bring it here and lets have a look."

Having handed it to Olly, sure enough it was an invitation to a New Years Eve Party. Studying the expensive embossed card carefully, "no your wrong pet, see this is an invitation to a Chinese New Year party.

The table was full. Mrs Jones was very impressed by the interesting man, with beautiful, kind smiling eyes, sat next to her, as he described shopping in Hong Kong. Mike Winter was joking with Lynda about how he should be going to one of her keep fit classes. Mike's wife also laughing at Lynda's ribbing of her husband. Sue Parish sat with her boyfriend deep in conversation. Olly silent, he was far too busy savouring the magnificent food.

With everyone chatting and enjoying themselves, no one noticed Danny quietly surveying everyone gathered. He saw his daughter sat opposite, giggling with Simon and Olly Jones wife. Penny looked so beautiful with hardly any scars visible above the table. Smiling he knew she was going to be fine.

Danny Chang was a man of his word. Lynda who sat across from him, wearing a beautiful jade antique necklace, looked radiant. Only he and Simon actually appreciating that it was probably worth many thousands. In addition their first class all expenses paid trip to Hong Kong had been a great success.

Mike Winter, having flatly refused any form of personal gift, had happily conceded to a brand new clever piece of equipment in the emergency department. Olly Jones, still engrossed in the teriyaki chicken, would keep receiving a signed first edition on his birthday as long as he lived. Danny's friends in very murky high places would ensure that DS Parish would never get into any physical harm and anyway seemed far too much in love to worry about crime. As Danny watched he breathed hard and deep, it had been a terrible time last autumn, yet his friend had sorted things out. He never believed Simon when he later told Danny that he honestly had not done the actual shooting. Anyway, Uncle Bo didn't care and had ensured Lynda and Simon had the most amazing time when they'd been in Hong Kong over Christmas.

Drifting from his thoughts Danny looked up straight into those great green eyes.

Simon, reading them, staring back at him, respect mutual.

## NEWCASTLE, SAINT NICHOLAS' CHURCH
## 5 YEARS LATER

The sun shone as, with military precision, the guests filed into the church, the chief steward ensuring things went smoothly. A small crowd had gathered and stood respectively thirty feet away, behind the low wall surrounding the two hundred year old church. The spectators included passes by, mixed with employees and lesser associates, plus a smattering of minders ensuring security was complete. Discreetly, two uniform police officers who had just happened to be passing on foot patrol, watched on. Their nod of respect only just visible as Detective Inspector Parish smiled, accompanied by her husband and walked under the entrance wooden canopy.

Reaching the churches grand entrance door Simon kissed Sue on both cheeks before giving Tim the same treatment and shaking both their hands in the usual manner. Smiling to himself as they walked off, Simon wondered if Sue knew she was six weeks pregnant?

A few minutes later as the wedding car drew up, Simon checked inside to ensure everyone was in his or her seat. Content, he gave a distinct nod to the nervous looking best man, that the bride had arrived.

Back outside, when Penny stepped into the sunshine there was audible gasp from those present, her beauty was beyond words.

Slowly Danny and Penny walked towards Simon. Moments later Danny received the double tap of kisses first and moved in. Simon embraced Penny on the steps, holding her in both arms as he gazed at the beautiful young woman in front of him. Looking into her eyes he noticed a single drop of joy fall from her cheek. Kissing her on both cheeks he whispered in her ear, "I told you the next time I saw you cry would be on your wedding day."

Carefully wiping away the second tear with his hanky Simon said, "right, I think its time you got married, don't you?"

The music started and Danny and his daughter moved to take up their places ready to walk down the isle.

Simon stood in the entrance closing the doors. Looking outside all he saw were happy smiling faces. It was times like this that he had real joy in his heart.

In a flash joy turned from fear to rage. Scanning the low wall all that he could sense were happy faces looking back to him. He shook his head.

"Simon, your time draws near." Sweat now dripping down Simon's back as he frantically looked round to see who had spoken. He noticed a gap had opened along the fence where no onlookers were standing. Only visible to Simon, leaning on the wall, stood Boots. Next to him another recognisable figure, that of his nemesis, Ransky. The words drifting silently through the warm air, "Boeck of the living, from behind these walls your safe but in time we will come again for you. Against us two and another you won't escape our realm, there to be forever our play thing." Boots' grin, grey, empty, utterly evil.

Simon closed the doors, safe in God's house. With that he briskly paced down the side isle to join his wife in the second row.

"Where've you been everyone's waiting?" Mild irritation in Lynda's voice.

Simon Boeck replied, "sorry darling. Just seen a ghost from my past, so to speak."

Here the 1st package of Simon Boeck's memoirs ends.

The 2nd, which I am currently editing, Simon has provisionally called, Pyramid Wars.

APPENDIX A

# Section 9

Section 9 was/is the unofficial name given to a small, highly elite unit within the British Army, few even knowing of its existence. Those that did/do cast aspersions as to the units employability, let alone validity. Supposedly it was formally disbanded in the late 1990's.

As a result of Lord Mountbatton's murder at the hands of the IRA, outraged royalty became involved, forcing the issue, demanding every possibility avenue be pursued in attempting to track down the perpetrators. After a chance meeting with the head of The Stargate, remote viewing program run by the American CIA, The Chief of The Army manufactured a new unit be bolted onto 14 Intelligence Company. 14 Int' or 'The Det' as it is sometimes referred to, was/is the mainstay of highly secret undercover military operations conducted around the world. This unhappy marriage caused tremendous problems for those selected for the unpopular association.

Simon Boeck was selected, trained and along with only 9 others, successfully completed the one off training program. Cast out, dispersed throughout the Army, rarely were they given the opportunity to employ their incredible skills. Simon and only a handful of others ever actively engaged to use their powers to fight terrorism around the world.

Simon's own note – I have written in a different batch of these memoirs the period in my life, which details my selection, training and subsequent employment surrounding the aftermath of The Maze prison break out in 1983. The embarrassment the break out caused forced the government of the day to try absolutely anything to track down the fugitives. This included reforming Section 9, led by a certain – Captain Boeck.

# APPENDIX B

## Psychic Understanding

### EDITOR'S NOTE

When compiling these memoirs Simon was adamant that I should repeat verbatim these appendixes. He explained this in his covering letter to me that it was important for the reader to gain a better understanding regarding the whole area of the supernatural, Extra Sensory Perception (ESP) and the psychic mind.

As a result what follows is, I can only describe, part education, part explanation and above all a tremendously intriguing insight.

Understanding how the psychic mind works can be confusing even to those of us who profess to have one. I would however like to attempt to explain my own perspective. Well here goes and hopefully deep down every one of you will see the logic and possibly recognise a certain amount of themselves in what follows.

Psychologists will have you believe the physical brain is split in two halves. One half dealing with rational, logical thought, the other with artistic and creative behaviour. It is also common knowledge that only a surprisingly small amount of the brain's capacity is actually ever utilised.

I along with a large number of like minded people believe that the mind is actually split into three conceptual areas. Firstly there is the logical mathematical portion. On the other side is artistic creative area. Then I believe there is a third, which every living soul has the ability to expose themselves to, this being the area allowing access to the greater elements of the universe.

Before you all fall asleep or have a seizure from laughing, let me try to explain.

Possibly the best way to do this is to think of two solid side to each and everyone's brain. These in turn relate physically to the opposite side's of the body – fact. One side dealing with creativity and other rational stuff. Somewhere in between lies a third – theory. This area may consist of two thirds creative and one third rationale. Alternatively it might be a completely separate area of the brain, I just don't know. As I've explained, human beings utilise a fraction of the brain in their daily functions.

This extra third is the domain of intuition, foresight, and hunches. Very importantly this portion is also connected to the whole area of psychic ability and it is here all individual's 'psychic radio receiver' exits. The good news is that every one of us has this third as well as a fully functional radio receiver. Why some are born with the ability to switch it on or even tune it in, is still an enigma. Some are just born with the ability, others can train, yet more have the batteries connected, so to speak, by a traumatic event such as a near death experience. An excellent example is the Russian man who was pronounced dead, only to wake up three days later in the morgue! The experience affected him so greatly that he is now a clergyman in America.

How often have you heard people say; well my mother or grandmother was psychic and I think I've inherited it? How often have small children spoken about their invisible friend, or that their grandfather, who died before they were even born, spoke with them during the night.

Upon reaching adolescence this ability usually withdraws as the daily exposure to the logical physical world we are brought up in drives this capability further into the subconscious. For a small number however it remains. Why I have no idea. The other bit of excellent news is that all living beings have some level of psychic ability. Let's say someone is born with ten percent psychic ability. This can never be reduced but can get lost, clouded in the modern world we are exposed to. This ten percent can, with minimal practice, be reawakened, even enhanced.

Each of us is born with a certain starting psychic ability, like a baseline or starting percentage. Some individuals can with practice improve this to say fifty percent. Others may intrinsically be born with fifty percent but for some unknown reason are only able to improve it by ten percent.

In my own case I do not feel extraordinarily gifted. My mother was psychic but suppressed her ability strongly, until it was almost too late. She did however pass on the ability to my sister Alexandra and myself.

I have, through design and choice, over the past twenty years expanded my gift greatly. I feel particularly blessed that my, expandable capacity, for want of a better description is now in the region of seventy percent. Not knowing where I started from, I now feel comfortable that I am utilising this aspect of my mind to its capacity.

There is yet further good news. Everyone of you can develop and train their ability, expanding it close to, if not, their preordained capacity.

It is not my intent to expand further on how to develop ones ability. In a subsequent edition of these memoirs it is my certain intention to cover my time with Section 9. Here I will expose you to the military way of psychic development. That innate ability combined with my own development has brought me to where I am now.

I would also like to explain my theory pertaining to wholespace. Those individuals who inherit, develop or have it given have the ability to access wholespace. Prominent American physicists have recently called this area of the frontiers of science, hyperspace. I prefer wholespace as it encompasses absolutely everything out there.

**Wholespace:** *"Wholespace encompasses the superhigh frequencies of the mind which are above normal perception. They include other levels of consciousness, dimensions, even space and time itself."*

It is here that, those able, can tune into these borderlands where superhigh frequencies exist. Individuals can improve, extend and increase their frequency range/number. In addition a person can fine tune different wavebands within wholespace. The analogy is fine tuning a FM radio. Further, as with physical radios, different wavebands can gain access to various levels of clarity as well as greater distance of signal. An example would be an individual who is fine tuned into what is known as 'remote viewing' can experience, see, sense even smell somewhere thousands of miles away. Similarly objects and physical things such as a wall or wedding ring can broadcast at a high quality, yet very localised level. Examples of this are psychometry or a room which feels somehow occupied although it is physically empty!

As a result those switched on and fine tuned to one or more of these superhigh frequencies can even venture to as yet totally unbelievable, supposedly absurd levels or dimensions. Examples of this could be out of body experiences or the ability to become invisible. Fantastic, unbelievable? Yet there are people who have had their superhigh frequency radio switched on without their knowledge only to roam around unseen yet present within this world – fact. What appears to have happened here is that they have momentarily been shifted to an alternate frequency, invisible to those without perception. This is only the very tip of what is possible. Remember what was unbelievable two centuries ago is the norm today. Space travel and the humble mobile phone, which can connect people (with pictures) almost anywhere on the globe, seemed the domain of witchcraft in the 18th Century. Yet unlike the computer or the Internet, the superhighway of wholespace has been around since the dawn of rational thought. It is just that only a few have been able or inclined to access it via their own unbuilt radio receivers. In time it may be possible to train even the most closed of minds to switch on their receivers and experience what is without doubt out there. Never forget the mind is physically a small object, yet its power is, frankly, unimaginable.

So with this new understanding you can start to see it is possible to become psychic, sense things others can't, even experience other frequencies within wholespace. There are however challenges, dangers associated with such development. I hate not being able to heal everyone I come into contact with. Far more worrying however is the fact that you can act as a funnel through which others can gain freedom in the conscious world we live in. Seemingly this is ridiculous, the stuff of horror fantasy. I would only point out that the dark side does exist; spontaneous human combustion for example. Some would have you believe it is related to body fat content or some other physiological rationale. True or not I would support the theory that others from parallel realms, can from time to time, gain a portal and cause much fear, danger and real pain, to those they come into contact with in this world...Simon Boeck

# ENDNOTES

1 *Editor's note* – Simon has made a slight error here. Ordinary 'O' level academic qualifications, taken at 16 years of age, had, in 1962, yet to be introduced into Scotland.

2 The Junior Leaders was where the British Army sent the best and brightest recruits. It was designed to provide them with every possible advantage to accelerated promotion. It was closed down in the 1980's only to be reopened under the new guise of Army Foundation College, Harrogate in the mid 1990's.

3 Milling is a short boxing bout which mainly airborne and special forces recruits are subjected to. In the 1960's it was practiced widely throughout all initial training establishments.

4 British Army business is typically split into various areas. G1 tends to deal with Personnel, disciple, G2 Intelligence, G3 Training and G4 logistic matters and so on.

5 The Falls Road is a notorious road in Belfast. Many consider it still to be the domain, stronghold of Catholic terrorist organisations.

6 Doctor Who is a famous UK science fiction program. The TARDIS was the Time Lords 'ship' . The TARDIS interior had no concept of size. Outside, a police box, yet inside housing a maze of rooms.

7 Although not art deco, such a picture does exist. Merchandise is a sexually explicit painting by the famous Australian artist which depicts a travelling Arabian harem. Lilli had copy no 19 of 500.

8 Clamidia was only properly recognised in the 1980's, only now reaching epidemic proportions amongst teenagers in the UK.

9 Chi Gong is an ancient form of medicine and martial art. *Peeping Monkey* is a slow meditation, defensive movement meant to encourage good health and longevity. Amazingly this exercise stops the onset of grey hair!

10 *Chaff* is used by military planes. It is a confetti of small flat aluminium squares designed to put off, or deflect attack missiles from their intended target. Simon's *Chaff* are fragments of information sometimes useful, at times at a tangent, seemingly irrelevant sent through the superhighway of *Wholespace*, see appendix B.

11 *The Wire*, indicated the outer perimeter fence surrounding all Army camps. Very frequently army housing is located, for security reasons, within and behind *the wire*.

12 A Ghurkha's Kukri is their personal weapon ( foot long, curved, razer sharp knife). Once taken from its scabbard it must draw blood. Fact not fiction!

13 Field Operations Group (FOG) was previously and more commonly called the Intelligence Support Activity. The Activity was set up after the debacle of an attempt to rescue American hostages from Iran in 1980.
Simon's note – I worked with 'the Activity' on a number of occasions, most notably immediately after the 2nd Gulf War during the hunt for Black List One – aka The Lion of Babylon.

14 Soldier joke that, the vibrations from sitting on the hard lorry bench induce an erection.
Editor's note – Don't believe me? Ask any squaddie who's spent time in the back of a 4 Tonner.

ISBN 141209518-2

9 781412 095181